A DECENT DECEIT

Nicholas King

February 2010

A Decent Deceit

by

Nicholas King

SilverWood

Published by SilverWood Books 2008
www.silverwoodbooks.co.uk

All characters in this book are fictitious and any resemblance to real persons, living or
dead, is purely coincidental. For the most part, places mentioned in the narrative are also
invented. In those cases where actual locations are used, licence has been taken with their
geography, appearance and function.
The liberal rendering of Fyodor Tyutchev's quatrain is the author's own.

ISBN 978-1-906236-09-0

British Library Cataloguing in Publication Data
A CIP catalogue record for this book is available from the British Library

Printed in the United Kingdom by Biddles Ltd

© **Mixed Sources**
**Product group from well-managed
forests, controlled sources and
recycled wood or fiber**
www.fsc.org Cert no. TT-COC-002303
© 1996 Forest Stewardship Council
FSC

For Helen,
who shared Russia with me

ACKNOWLEDGEMENTS

First and foremost I wish to pay tribute to my wife Helen and our children Charles and Eloise for their belief in this book. Their enduring love sustained me in times of doubt and their firm resolve contributed to its eventual completion.

Many others have supported me in this endeavour and I take this opportunity to thank them collectively. But I extend special thanks to Sandra and David Hopkins for their wise suggestions and apposite comments and to Neil Pattenden for his advice on matters Russian. I have also greatly appreciated the encouragement offered by my fellow writers and I thank them for their companionship and shared commitment.

I am indebted to Helen Hart of SilverWood Books for steering me through the publishing process with such diligence and consideration. The finished product stands as evidence of her professionalism and of the skill of Adrian Hart as the designer. My thanks also go to my wife Helen, whose artistic hand produced the original painting for the cover.

I reserve my deepest gratitude for Louise Green, who has guided me patiently along the narrative path over a number of years. I am the beneficiary of her use and love of language and continue to appreciate her intelligent criticism, invariably delivered with sensitivity and good humour. I contend that, without her inspiration and direction, the writing of this novel may have remained an unfulfilled ambition.

Умом Россию не понять,
Аршином общим не измерить:
У ней особенная стать —
В Россию можно только верить.

Russia cannot be sensibly understood
Nor measured in an accepted way
She has a particular character –
Thus in Russia, one can only believe.

Fyodor Tyutchev 1866

CHAPTER 1

Peter Standridge lounged on his couchette as the Eastern Express shuffled to a halt in a stretch of open country. He accepted this latest delay with his usual equanimity, even appreciating the brief respite from the constant clamour of the train. A still silence filtered into his compartment, interrupted by occasional murmurs from the corridor. He stared idly through the dirtied window at the batch of low wooden houses and the cattle scattered on the meadows. Not a soul was in sight.

Peter had a rough idea where he was. The rudimentary map was vague, perhaps deliberately misleading, but it showed the sinuous line of the railway running towards a river. It seemed his stationary train was perched on a curved embankment with a bridge a short distance ahead. He imagined the proud express would be lost in the immensity of its surroundings like a mere discarded thread on a cloth of mottled green.

The locomotive finally gave a defiant hoot and snatched at its trail of carriages. The long train looped onto the lattice bridge, its wheels echoing on the hollow track-bed as the steel struts flicked rhythmically by. Peter ran his eyes routinely over the bridge structure, assessing its condition. Tilting his head closer to the window, he counted the distance markers and scanned the smooth surface of the river to the opposite bank.

"Standard box girder, 200 metres across, water level low," he murmured and entered the coded data in his notebook. He waited for the train to clear the bridge abut-

11

ment with its disused guardhouse before sitting back and sipping his glass of sweetened tea.

Such journeys were not unpleasant, even if some were measured in days and nights rather than hours. The 'soft class' compartments were adequate and they gave him privacy and room to work. He liked to be self-sufficient, carrying enough food and drink to see him through, although the platform traders at remote stations usually had something edible to buy. The hot meat pies, dumplings and soups were the safest, but if caught out, a small ration of distilled spirit remained the remedy of choice.

Peter confirmed the details of the crossing before zipping his notebook into the inner pocket of his coat. He admired these rivers, respecting the major ones for their strength and spirituality. The passengers often performed a solemn ritual, gathering in the corridors and watching reverently as another broad river passed beneath. They were the natural lifelines and travel routes before the railways came and they broke up the monotony of the endless landscape. There seemed only two choices: wide plains to the horizon or dense forests up to the rails. Such dullness doped the brain, exposing the unwary traveller to one of those surprises this mysterious country liked to spring.

The bridge and river were left behind and the forest advanced towards the railway track, hemming it in on either side. The train accelerated down the narrow avenue of trees, shaking and spiralling as its speed increased. Peter had become used to these 'fast trains', which frequently bucked and twisted as if trying to unseat their passengers. But this felt worse than normal. One violent jolt lifted him clear of his couchette, scattering his books and maps across the floor. Securing everything as best he could, he wedged himself in a corner ready to ride out the turbulence.

Despite the noise of the train, Peter heard the lock turn in his compartment door. He had a strict routine when travelling and securing the door was his first priority. In an emergency the carriage attendant could always gain entry, but otherwise she would knock first if bringing tea or wanting to make up the couchette. Such courtesy gave him a few vital seconds to tidy things away. Fortunately on this occasion everything was already discreetly stowed.

Peter did not move as he watched the compartment door slide open. A plump, balding man stood in the doorway in his stockinged feet. He wore a close fitting tracksuit and grasped a bottle in one hand. With the other he steadied himself against the door, absorbing the pitching motion of the carriage like a seasoned sailor.

"Good evening sir," he slurred in passable English. "Welcome to Siberia."

For a moment neither spoke. Peter sculpted into his corner sat rigid, whilst the stranger smirked and swayed. A sudden lurch of the carriage broke the stand off, propelling the man into the compartment and throwing him sideways onto the opposite seat. Behind him the freed compartment door closed with a click.

The man elbowed himself up and held his unbroken bottle aloft in triumph. He grinned stupidly at Peter, his eyes rolling as the carriage bounced along the uneven track.

"Ah, my friend, going to say hello to Kolya? No? Such silence... that's big pity, very big pity. Kolya very, very sad." He lowered his eyes, trying to get the bottle in focus. "So old Kolya must drink alone. That's bad for you and bad for me," he mumbled, jabbing a finger at the label. He glanced sideways at Peter. "Vodka for hunters. Too strong for feeble foreigners. No good for you."

"Please leave my compartment at once. I don't want you in here," Peter said petulantly. The man shook his head, but made no attempt to move.

"I full of sorrow for you. Perhaps you unhappy man, you no like to talk, you have no pleasure for company. Maybe you not love my country, Englishman... our ways different, they make you, how you say, not comfortable."

He grunted and flicked the cap off his bottle. It bounced across the floor, settling close to Peter's feet. With a flourish the stranger aimed the bottle at his mouth, suctioning his thick lips onto the open top. He gulped the dark liquid, belched and slobbered on his sleeve. He stared round the compartment.

"Why you have two-bed compartment for only one? What you afraid of? Perhaps you make private things here, not for others to see."

"If you do not get out this minute, I shall call the attendant," Peter said, his voice quavering.

The stranger guffawed. "Call her if you want. She's silly old bear. She won't do nothing."

Peter knew he was going to need some assistance to get rid of the intruder. He reckoned he could probably reach the compartment door before the man realised what was happening. But he could become aggressive and Peter shuddered at the thought of grappling with him if it came to that. Nevertheless he felt he had no option but to make a dash for it.

The drunk, bemused by the absence of the bottle cap, patted the seat around him. Peter tensed and was just about to launch himself at the door, when it slid open and a man with a huge head of white hair stepped into the compartment.

"You must excuse me and my good friend here," he said to Peter. "I have come to take him back to our compartment. Come Kolya, this kind gentleman would like us to leave now."

At the sound of his voice, the stranger looked up and wobbled to his feet. As he did so, he spied the bottle cap on the floor and bent down to retrieve it. To Peter's amazement he grasped it without toppling over.

"So my little one, thought you could run away from old Kolya, did you?" he said looking at his prize with affection. "Now you must go back where you belong." After much cursing, he wedged the cap on the bottle and was shepherded out of the compartment, calling behind him, "Goodbye sir. Farewell, my friend."

Peter listened as the two comrades made their way down the carriage, bickering like children. Their voices faded. Peter looked at his watch, surprised to find the episode had lasted less than ten minutes. He unwound himself from his corner, embarrassed by the way he had reacted.

The smell of the stranger lingered in the compartment and Peter reluctantly left the door wide open. How he had come to detest that pervasive mixture of stale sweat, pickled garlic and old vodka. He craved some fresh air and scowled at the sealed window. Despite the heat in the carriage, he shivered. Delayed shock, he reassured himself, or perhaps Kolya's words did disturb him more than he was prepared to admit. Was he as glum and unsociable as Kolya had indicated in his drunken state? Shy and reserved perhaps, but that was all. And why did Kolya suggest he might be doing something no one should see? What did he suspect?

A soft cough interrupted his thoughts. He looked away from the window to see the white-haired man standing in the doorway.

"May I come in?" he asked politely.

"If you wish, but please leave the door open as it is."

"I have come to say sorry for the unacceptable behaviour of my colleague," the man said sitting down opposite Peter. "I left him in our compartment for just a few minutes and when I returned, he had gone. It took me a while to find him in here. I had already disturbed other passengers with my searching. He is a naughty fellow."

"I'm grateful for the apology, but I can't say I found the company of your friend very pleasant. Drunks are always fickle, sometimes threatening." The man shook his head.

"Old Kolya is an amiable man, even when he has

finished off half a bottle of vodka. You need not have worried, he would not have harmed you. But he may have fallen asleep on this couchette given the chance," he added with a laugh. "And now it is me who is the rude one. I have failed to introduce myself. Dimitri Krotkin, it's a pleasure to meet you."

"Peter Standridge," Peter said, shaking Krotkin's outstretched hand.

"So you are visiting Russia as a tourist?"

"No, I'm here on business. It's a six-month contract. I've done almost two months, four to go. Sorry, I've made it sound like a prison sentence."

Krotkin did not smile. "Yes, that is an unfortunate comment to make. We find it hard to talk about prisons in this bleak region," he said, staring at the passing forest before returning his attention to Peter. "No, I don't suppose you would understand. How could you?"

Peter had no wish to get into this kind of conversation and quickly changed the subject. "Where did you learn to speak such excellent English?" he asked.

Krotkin recovered himself. "Forgive me for speaking about bad times. You are right to ask more simple questions. My English? Well, I studied languages at university and then I became a professor of English. I used to prepare our diplomats before they went abroad, but now I am the Director of our Institute for Foreign Languages in Nizhny Novgorod." He paused. "And what about you, Mr Standridge?"

"I'm a consultant, advising on communications, urban renewal and infrastructure," Peter said importantly. "I'm here as part of a British Government programme to assist Russia and other East European countries. I expect you may have heard of the Handsome Fund. It was set up just under a year ago in December 1991."

"Handsome Fund? That is an interesting title. No, I'm afraid I have not heard of it, but then I'm neither a government official nor a businessman." Krotkin studied Peter for a moment. "You are so young. Must you not have much experience before you can come and advise a Superpower what it should be doing?"

Peter shifted on his seat. "I've been with my firm for five years and received special training," he said, before adding naively, "perhaps in a small way I can help our two countries to work together after so much hostility and suspicion."

"You speak like a politician and I don't trust politicians. But let's not disagree. I come often to Moscow with my work. When I come next, I would like to give you some hospitality to make amends for your experience with Kolya. I shall contact you. Where are you living?"

Before Peter could answer, the shrill voice of the attendant was heard in the corridor shouting for Krotkin. She appeared in the doorway and hurled a stream of angry Russian at him. He answered her briefly and stood up.

"I am sorry, Mr Standridge, I must go now. Kolya has been causing some more problems. I shall see you in Moscow then?"

"I'll look forward to that. I'm staying at Hotel Leskov."

"I will find you there. Goodbye for now."

Peter watched the attendant bustle down the corridor grumbling at Krotkin, who trailed obediently behind her. As they disappeared into the next carriage, Peter turned back into his compartment. Dusk was approaching and he lowered the blind on the window and drew the curtains. He rummaged in his bag for a tin of rabbit pâté, glad the train would reach Irkutsk the following morning. It had been a more bothersome journey than usual and he had three days ahead of him dealing with a succession of sullen officials.

"No more interruptions I hope," he muttered, as he stuck his fork into the pâté and pressed the meat onto his hardened bread. But while he ate his meagre supper, he began to wonder who had opened his compartment door to let old Kolya in. Might someone other than the attendant have assisted him, someone with pernicious motives? He tried to dismiss such suspicions, but as he thought about the various possibilities, the more aware he became of his vulnerability. For the first time since arriving in this unpredictable land, he started to feel anxious for his safety.

CHAPTER 2

There was a fine panorama of the city from the terrace. Peter occasionally took the bus up to the Lenin Hills and would walk down past the university to this popular viewing point. But this Saturday was a cheerless day, the greyness of the sky blending with the dull concrete buildings stretching to the horizon. Despite the gloom it was possible to pick out the golden domes of monasteries and churches, the red ochre of the Kremlin walls and the green tints of Moscow's celebrated parks. At the base of the hills the wide river curved serenely, its banks dotted with fishermen unruffled by the passing barges. On the far side, a huge heating plant, belching smoke and steam, limbered up for the coming winter.

As Peter solemnly leant on the balustrade and absorbed the familiar scene, the autumn chill and early snow flurries did nothing to lift his mood. The incident on the train to Irkutsk the previous month still disturbed him. He accepted he had handled it badly, his awkward behaviour revealing a side to his character he would rather have kept hidden. Since then his sense of insecurity had increased, rupturing the safe cocoon of routine work and simple relaxation.

Yet it was his fault he had got himself into this position. He could have said no at the time and nothing would have come of it. "How could I have been so stupid," he said out loud, immediately turning to see who might have overheard. The others were all preoccupied, the soldier with his girlfriend, the old *babushka* with her grandchildren and the two men with their earnest conversation. They had of course noticed him. They could not miss these foreigners with their different clothes and funny ways of walking. Other than that he was of no importance, unless he had some dollars to sell, but frankly, he didn't look the type.

Peter was relieved no one appeared to take much interest in him. He always preferred to be ignored and left to go about his business without attracting attention. Even so he remained unsettled and underlying his general anxiety was a nervousness about his unofficial duties. Not for the first time did he find his mind returning to that day back in the summer.

It had been near the end of Peter's preparation programme in London. He had called into the office to collect his final list of visits and perused the schedule quickly.

"It all seems fine, except isn't there a mistake on 29 June, serial 13?" he said to the clerk. "It's got *Ministry of Defence, Metropole Building, Room 67A*. Surely that's wrong. I don't need or want to see anyone from the military."

The clerk was unabashed. "I only draw up the programme. I don't decide who you see and who you don't. If the MOD liaison boys say they want to see you, you see them. End of story as far as I'm concerned."

"But whatever for? And look, there's no name down here, just a room number."

"You do have a lot to learn, don't you. You are very new to Whitehall and its quirky ways. The MOD doesn't like to release names to outsiders. Too sensitive, you must realise that. Anyway, your appointment is probably only for an additional security briefing. And someone will be there, I assure you."

Peter dutifully found his way to the entrance of the Metropole Building. It had been due for refurbishment for several years and Peter was surprised by its shabby appearance. It was almost as if it wanted to remain camouflaged behind its grey exterior, unworthy of a second glance. Inside the uniform colours did little to lighten the drabness. The dusty lift which took Peter to the fifth floor was in no hurry, weighed down as it was by a messenger and his trolley carrying the buff envelopes and blue folders of the Ministry at work.

It was with some trepidation that he emerged and turned down the corridor signed for rooms 59 to 71. He found 67A, which displayed a large notice: *Strictly No Admission. Enter Through Room 67C*. Peter moved further down the deserted passage, wondering in passing what they had done with 67B. The door of Room 67C had an equally large sign with the warning: *Do Not Enter. Knock And Wait*. Peter obeyed the order.

After a while the door was opened by a middle aged woman, who looked at him enquiringly. "Yes?"

"I'm Peter Standridge. I have an appointment at 11 o'clock, but not sure with whom."

The woman sniffed, checked his pass and ushered him into a small stuffy office, indicating that he could sit down if he could find a seat. "I'm Miss Teller, by the way," she said over her shoulder as she disappeared through an interconnecting door.

Glancing round, Peter made out a typist in the corner hidden behind a heap of folders. He nodded to her, she scowled back.

"You can come through now," Miss Teller called out. Peter followed her into a larger office where a middle aged man was writing at a government desk. He sat straight backed in an expensive pin-striped suit and wore a maroon tie emblazoned with silver swords. His face reflected the colour of the tie and was topped by black lacquered hair and adorned with a neat moustache. Peter heard the door close behind him.

The man continued with his work, his fountain pen scraping across the paper. After a few moments he looked

21

up and seemed surprised to see Peter. Without warning he barked, "Pomfrey... Major... Retired," and returned to his writing, whilst Peter lamely muttered, "Peter Standridge, pleased to meet you."

Without being invited, Peter decided to sit down. He looked round the sparsely furnished room. A tall filing cabinet stood against the far wall with an immense map of the former Soviet Union peppered with different coloured pins adjacent to it. In one corner a new computer stood unused accumulating dust.

A rustle of pages indicated the Major had finished what he was doing. Tossing the file into a tray marked *Armageddon*, he leaned back and glowered at Peter.

"So you're the chappie setting off for Russia. Going to give them some help I hear. Very sporting of you. Quite a few changes over there since my day." He got up and walked to the window. He stood there for a moment before teasing the slats of the Venetian blind apart and peering down at the street below.

"Can't trust the Russkies, you know," he said gruffly. "Never could and, in my book, never should. Devious lot they are, very cunning, very sly. You'll find that out for yourself when you get there, Standfast."

"Its Standridge actually," Peter said, but the Major didn't respond and continued to scan the street below. "Look," Peter added in exasperation, "I really don't know why I'm here. I'm wasting your time and my time. If it's all the same to you, I'll be on my way."

The Major, apparently satisfied that all was well outside, released the blind and commenced marching up and down the office. "The truth is, Standfast, we want you to give us a little assistance, too. Surprisingly there's a lot we still need to know. Some of it we get almost routinely. The little Eye in the sky is amazing, really super technology, but the Eye can't see A and M."

"A and M? What on earth are you talking about?"

"Attitude and Morale. The Eye can't do it," the Major growled. "The Eye can read the number plate of a taxi in Smolensk or Krasnoyarsk, but it can't tell us what the bloody driver thinks about the government or the price of pickled garlic. And that, Standfast, is where you come in."

The Major returned to his desk and took a large gulp from a mug decorated with a hammer and sickle. "You're a geographer by trade, aren't you?" he asked. "We'll also want you to keep your eyes open on your trips around the country. Bit of O and R."

"And what exactly is that?" Peter asked wearily, aware he would have to go through with the charade if he wanted to escape from this lunatic before lunch.

"Observation and Reporting of course, what else? Just look and tell us what you see. Anything and everything is important to us from the field. We judge its value here. That's not for you to do."

The Major opened one of the desk drawers and found a half eaten biscuit which he crunched, scattering crumbs over his files. He looked up at the map on the wall. "Bloody vast country and you're going to have the privilege of going all over it. Marvellous opportunity." He turned back to Peter. "By the way, Burroughs in Commercial. He's your man. They've got a building separate from the main embassy. Very useful that. You just tell him where you're going and he'll brief you up. No kit needed, except on some trips he'll give you one of these little beauties."

The Major rummaged in the drawer again. This time he produced a leather case from which he extracted a metal box the size of a mini camera. "This, Standfast, is the ultimate in the art of miniaturisation. You are probably thinking it's a camera. Well, it isn't. In any case cameras are a real no-no where you're going." He paused. "It's a tiny Geiger counter. Really wizard, don't you think?"

Peter felt himself perspiring. The room was unbearably hot and airless, but it wasn't just that which was making him sweat. He was now seriously worried he was entering unmarked territory. He simply did not understand what was going on. Why on earth had his firm allowed the MOD to set up this appointment in the first place? Worse still, perhaps they hadn't, perhaps they didn't know anything about it.

"I'm sorry," Peter said, "I'm not interested in any of this. It's not my line. I do a straight job of work. I shall have to report this whole meeting to my director. I'm sure he will take a very dim view of one of his consultants being asked to act as a third rate spy on behalf of the MOD."

The Major stared at Peter as if he was the one who had completely lost his head. "Now you listen here, my lad. Do you think you'd be sitting in this office if your boss didn't know? Your firm is one of the most helpful. We've had excellent results from them in the past. Now surely, Standfast, you're not going to be the one to bugger it up for everyone, yourself included?"

Peter was dumbfounded, yet did his best to stay calm. Major Pomfrey had already selected another file from his in-tray and was flicking through the pages oblivious to Peter's presence. In the end Peter reckoned he had no alternative but to get up and leave. Collecting his briefcase, he opened the door and, without another word, walked through to the secretary's office. Miss Teller rose from behind her desk of papers.

"Your pass, Mr Standridge, your pass. I need to sign you out." Peter watched as she wrote in the time and carefully added her signature. He wanted to say something to her about the Major: was he all right, was he a bit stupid, was he completely mad? But he couldn't bring himself to do so. He needed to leave this surreal world as quickly as he could.

Miss Teller returned Peter's pass. He said goodbye and heard her lock and bolt the door behind him as he hurried down the corridor to summon the antiquated lift.

* * *

The memory of that day in London and the sharp wind blowing across the Lenin Hills made Peter shiver. Pulling his coat more closely round him, he decided to walk back to the bus stop through the woods which offered more protection. He made his way to the end of the terrace, passing a team of women leaf sweepers relaxing on their brooms. They chatted and shared a cigarette, unconcerned that the wind was scattering their gathered leaves back across the pavement. Peter took care to step round the diminishing heaps and passed the waiting refuse truck. The driver sat gloved and well padded in his cab, idling the engine. The smell of the exhaust made Peter choke. He held his hands close to his face as he turned onto the track leading through the silver birches.

Peter was still angry with himself for getting involved in Major Pomfrey's scheme. He deeply regretted not being more resolute, but events seemed to overtake him. It was unfortunate his director, Derek Carbonnel, happened to be abroad on business just when Peter most needed to talk to him. It certainly wasn't something he wanted to discuss by phone or fax: it had to be face to face or not at all.

Without managing to meet Derek, Peter decided to put Major Pomfrey out of his mind. He was not going to do anything other than his proper job and there would be no gathering of information. For the first few weeks in Russia his tactics seemed to work. He established a good working relationship with Ruth Rumbelow in the Embassy's Commercial Section, whose main responsibility was to manage the Handsome Fund operations. At no point did she mention or even allude to any additional government requirements. Peter believed he was in the clear until the day the Moscow heat-wave ended and he met Burroughs in Commercial.

A tall man had knocked and put his head round the door of Ruth Rumbelow's office saying, "Do excuse me,

Ruth, but could I just have a quick word with your Mr Standridge when you've finished." He didn't wait for her to reply, but turned to Peter and smiled. "Christopher Burroughs, nice to meet you. Pop in when you're through here. My office is at the end of the corridor. Its got James Fortune, Commercial Liaison Officer, on the door, but don't worry about that. " He laughed and left as suddenly as he had appeared. Ruth Rumbelow continued her discussion with Peter as if nothing unusual had happened.

Peter was again at a crossroads. He could have ignored the invitation, but knew he really had no option but to go and see Burroughs. He walked down the corridor and tapped on his door just as the first crack of thunder hit the city.

Christopher Burroughs seemed unusually casual and light hearted, concluding most statements with a laugh or chuckle. He also fussed round Peter in an unctuous way, making sure he was comfortable in his chair, asking him how he liked his coffee and insisting on being called Chris. Peter felt himself relaxing in his company, beguiled by his over-friendly manner. They talked at some length about his job, his trips to different parts of the country and how he was enjoying the whole experience. Peter believed the meeting was going far better than expected.

There was a short pause in the conversation. Chris Burroughs went to his safe, removed a small pad of paper and tossed it across to Peter. "You will find this handy on your travels. Let me show you how it works." He opened his desk drawer and took out an eraser board, incongruously decorated round the edge with smiling jungle animals. "Borrowed it from my daughter," he said, roaring with laughter. He wrote quickly, holding it up for Peter to read: *Where are you going on your next trip? Write the answer on your pad using a pencil.*

Peter complied, spelling out *Ryazan*. Chris took the pad from Peter, tore off the sheet and dropped it into a glass

26

of water. The paper instantly dissolved. Chris giggled with delight. He returned to his eraser board, removed what he had written and scribbled some more. He held it up again: *Don't forget your A and M and O and R. Let me have your report as soon as you get back.*

For reasons he now found difficult to explain, Peter had gone off and done what he was asked to do without argument or protest. He managed to gather one or two snippets of information in Ryazan and Chris had given him a desk in his office to write up the details. What really took Peter by surprise was how complimentary he had been about this report and indeed about all his subsequent efforts. "They just keep getting better and better," he had said, and on his eraser board had written: *London is mighty pleased with your product. You are becoming quite a professional.*

Peter began to take more interest in this side of his work and perversely began to enjoy it. He convinced himself that he was not doing anything improper or illegal, but at the same time he was always conscious of his security. He even started to fancy himself in this undercover role, encouraged by the appreciation he received. At least that was the case until the trip to Irkutsk.

He remained lost in thought as he emerged from the wood. Hearing a bus approaching, he quickened his pace. He jumped on board, punched his ticket and found a seat near the back. He wiped the misted window and watched the snowflakes linger briefly on the pane before sliding down the glass and disappearing.

The bus trundled on towards the centre in the fading autumn light. Peering through the murk, Peter watched the busy crowds heaving along the pavements with carrier bags of provisions. He enjoyed the small cameos he witnessed, his impassive face belying the fascination this city held for him. Despite his current apprehension, Moscow remained constantly intriguing.

Returning to his hotel, he was handed his key at reception together with an envelope with his name neatly written on the front. Peter opened the note inside.

Dear Mr Standridge,

You will remember our meeting on the Eastern Express. I find myself unexpectedly in Moscow today. The hotel said you would be here this evening. I shall return and will be in the foyer at 19.30. We shall have some suppers.

Best wishes.

Dimitri Krotkin.

CHAPTER 3

To reach his room on the eighth floor, Peter often used the backstairs in preference to the hotel lift. But as he got to the foot of the staircase, he found a rusty chain looped through the handles of the double doors and secured with a padlock. A metal chair wedged under the handles bore a lopsided notice in Russian. The stairs, it seemed, were closed.

Peter squashed into the lift. Russians, talking and grumbling, left and entered, many being caught, compressed and then released by the automatic doors. He recognised another foreigner. They nodded, but didn't speak.

His room was much as he had left it earlier, except the cover had been pulled over the bed and the dust redistributed. The hotel's heating was on maximum and the room stifling. Peter opened the only unsealed window, inhaling the fresh air. Despite his status as a semi-permanent resident and his firm paying good money for the accommodation, his room was not large. Nevertheless, the hotel manager had assured him in his rudimentary English that it was *best one body room in hotel with most upraising outlook*.

Peter understood what he meant. There set out before him was the Kremlin in all its glory: the golden cupolas of the churches, the majestic palaces and the high, crenellated walls with their towers and gateways. He could also glimpse part of Red Square and the extraordinary coloured spiral domes of St Basil's Cathedral. Peter was not in any way an artistic or sensitive man, but he knew he was privileged to have such a view. He doubted he would ever tire of it.

He sat down in the armchair which faced into the room. There was not much to see. The bed, a desk, a built-in light-wood cupboard and on the walls, two prints of rural scenes. One was the all too familiar subject of forests and fir trees, but the other depicted a village festival with peasants drinking and dancing. It was a simple, idealised picture, a rural version of their nights out in Moscow.

Saturday evening was the most social occasion for foreigners living in the hotel. Those who had not flown off for the weekend with their wives, girlfriends or mistresses, teamed up for a night on the town. Gathering in the hotel's bar was the custom and after several drinks, someone decided on the evening's entertainment.

Sometimes the outings were a disappointment, but normally the *Hooligany*, as they nicknamed themselves, had a wild time. Peter usually went along with whatever the rest wished to do. He was never the one to suggest where they went: that was not in his nature. His colleagues noticed how comfortable he was with his role as a follower and how, although he came along happily enough, he never got drunk, never lost control, never let his hair down. But he was generous with the drinks he bought, so was always welcome.

Picking up the note from Dimitri Krotkin, Peter thought it would be a shame to let the *Hooligany* down. He could always leave a message for Krotkin saying he had another engagement. But he didn't want to lose the chance of seeing him again. More than anything else he needed Krotkin's help in resolving the incident on the Irkutsk train. It was important to find out if Kolya was simply a drunken buffoon or whether there was something more sinister behind his antics.

Shortly before 7.30pm, Peter stood in front of the mirror and looked himself over. He had shaved and showered, and dressed well but informally. He couldn't decide on the tie, but in the end he kept it on. It was quite difficult knowing what would be appropriate. He had endured many lunches and dinners with officials on his travels, but attending such functions was all part of his work. Socialising off-duty with the Russians was something different. He had never done that before and he doubted his colleagues had either. So when he rang to say he wouldn't be joining the *Hooligany* for the evening, he was brief with his excuses.

Peter slipped his coat over his shoulders and took the lift. The foyer, lit by its huge glass chandeliers, was packed, and he worried he might not find Krotkin. It was unbearably hot, yet everyone kept their hats and coats on, making identification doubly difficult. There was a heady smell of damp serge and sweet perfume. At one end of the foyer an aggressive group, physically restrained by the doormen, besieged the entrance to the restaurant. Inside the band for the evening tuned up, its amplified chords sending a frisson of excitement through the pressing crowd.

In desperation Peter searched people's faces and many returned his stare. He was to them an anxious-looking foreigner, a vulnerable species, especially on his own.

"Mr Standridge, how very pleasant to see you again. I presume rightly you received my message?" Peter turned to see Krotkin standing immediately behind him, grasping his hat in one hand and extending the other in greeting.

"And very nice to see you," Peter said, shaking his hand. "Thank you for the note. I'm glad I got back to the hotel in time." Krotkin nodded and looked round the foyer.

"It is very mad in here. It is better if we set off now." Peter followed Krotkin towards the hotel exit. There was no time for politeness and it was very much a matter of forcing a way through the dense mass of people. Krotkin seemed adept at using his elbows, and by keeping close behind him, Peter was able to squeeze through the narrow gap he made. Once out on the street, Krotkin brushed his broad brimmed hat and pushed it firmly onto his head.

"From here it is a short walk or a faster ride by taxi. I

believe we should walk."

"Whatever you wish," Peter replied, not wanting in any way to offend his host, assuming of course he was his host. Krotkin's note had not been entirely clear: was he inviting Peter to supper or would they divide the bill or might Krotkin expect Peter, a wealthy foreigner in his eyes, to pay for them both? Whatever transpired, Peter with his wallet of roubles and dollars would not be embarrassed.

The two walked side by side, moving as a pair to avoid other pedestrians on the busy street. Peter glanced across at Krotkin. He was shorter than he remembered and his face seemed more lined. His cascades of white hair were still there, but they were now groomed and less wayward. Peter saw his coat was a good one, undoubtedly foreign, and he glimpsed a smart suit and tie beneath. One thing he hadn't noticed before was his pronounced limp. It seemed to be his right leg which he dragged, causing his whole body to tilt as he walked. Despite this disability, he kept up a steady pace.

"How well do you know Moscow, Mr Standridge?" Krotkin asked.

"Not as well as I should. As you know, I do a lot of travelling, so have less time to explore your capital. I'm not sure where we are at the moment."

Krotkin did not reply but, grasping Peter by the arm, steered him into a small cobbled side street. They walked for another fifty metres before Krotkin, still holding Peter by the arm, turned into a narrow entrance and descended a flight of steps. At the bottom there was a half open door.

The restaurant occupied a converted cellar or store-house with brick walls and a low vaulted ceiling. They did not need to adjust their eyes as the interior was lit solely by candles, some held in stout iron brackets on the walls, others placed in small candelabra on each table. Even the waiter who took their coats and showed them to a corner table carried a candle lantern.

"What an incredible place," Peter remarked as he looked round the restaurant. The atmosphere appealed to him but he also found it ominous. It reminded him of some of the Russian paintings of Ivan The Terrible's time, pictures full of long shadows and menace set in dark, low-roofed rooms. The candlelight too threw a similar glow onto the diners' faces as it had onto the scheming figures in the paintings. But unlike them, here there was constant movement, strident voices and wild laughter. Hanging above it all was a thick stratum of cigarette smoke.

Krotkin had said nothing to Peter since entering the restaurant. He was also looking around, but more intently, half turning his chair to get a better view. He seemed agitated. Peter was on the point of breaking the silence when Krotkin stood up. A smartly dressed man came up to their table and embraced him. They talked excitedly for a minute before the man abruptly left, merging into the shadows at the far end of the restaurant.

"He is the owner," Krotkin said with some pride. "He is the cousin of a friend of mine. Soon I think this cousin will become a good friend for me as well." Krotkin lit a cigarette and let the smoke drift across the table. Peter waved his hand to disperse it. Krotkin stared at him, his face ugly in the candlelight.

"So you like this place, Mr Standridge?"

"Yes, very much. I've obviously not come across it before. Has it been open long?" Peter asked quickly to avoid another silence.

"This restaurant is new but, even if it was old, I don't think you would find it by accident. There are many restaurants opening recently, some good, some not so good and some very bad. This one in my opinion is good. I expect you will soon agree."

"But does it have a name?"

"Yes of course. It is easy, yet difficult to translate. It is called New Confidence. It conveys the idea of a new sense of trust. But it also has a more subtle interpretation. It means a place where people come to exchange their confidences, their latest secrets." Krotkin drew heavily on his cigarette and watched the smoke float over the table and eddy into the arches above.

Their waiter arrived with a decanter of vodka, a basket of rye bread and a selection of hors d'oeuvre. He placed two bottles of mineral water in the centre of the table and arranged the dishes round them. Peter was longing for a beer but felt it impolite to ask.

"You are familiar with our *zakuski* I expect," Krotkin said.

Peter saw the usual bowls of potato salad, chopped tomatoes, pickled cucumbers and sour cream, along with the plates of cheese and sliced sausage. But there were some dishes he was not familiar with. He looked at them more closely.

"Yes, we are having some specialities," Krotkin said. "Smoked sturgeon, marinated herring and a pâté made from sardines. The owner chose these things for us." He leaned forward and, picking up the decanter, poured the vodka into the small glasses in front of them.

"So I will propose the first toast. It is to our reunion." Krotkin held his glass up, clinking it against Peter's. He drank his vodka in one, tore off a piece of rye bread and ate it quickly. Peter, taking only a small sip from his glass, detected a look of disappointment on Krotkin's face. He watched as Krotkin recharged his glass and helped himself to the *zakuski*.

"Come, you must also eat," Krotkin said and started to spoon a selection from the different dishes onto Peter's plate. Peter protested at the portions Krotkin gave him, but he just shook his head. "Winter will soon be upon us. It's important to eat and also to drink," adding as an afterthought, "a very great amount."

Peter had never been particularly interested in food.

His attitude to Russian food was much the same and he usually ate his meals without enthusiasm. He noticed too how the Russians themselves went to the larger restaurants mainly to have a good time. They danced, smoked and got drunk and the food was picked at and pushed around their plates. But as Peter started on the *zakuski* in this new restaurant, it tasted very different and very good. To his surprise, he began to enjoy it.

"You must drink your vodka and then eat something straightaway," Krotkin said. "It stops you getting drunk too quickly."

Peter followed his advice but due to nervousness, he drank more than he intended. Although he sensed the colour rising in his face and the mist obscuring his mind, the vodka worked its special magic. He relaxed, lost his apprehension, found a new courage. He felt benevolent and generous, already regarding Krotkin as an old and trustworthy friend.

Although the *zakuski* on their own could have provided an ample meal for both of them, the waiter later returned with plates of grilled steaks, fried potatoes and beans. He also removed their empty decanter and placed another half decanter of vodka on the table. Krotkin, as he had done throughout the evening, recharged their glasses.

"So, Mr Standridge, how do you like being a guest in my country?"

"I'm enjoying it very much thank you. It's quite an experience for me. I must say it's a privilege to travel around and see so much." Peter immediately regretted his words but Krotkin showed no adverse reaction.

"Yes, travelling is interesting, as is meeting new peoples. You may not admit it, but I expect you find my country-men a little suspicious of you as a foreigner. Our history has made our nature, invaders have come from all directions, east, north, west, and also from the south as you British will remember. So Russians don't like foreigners, they think they come to steal from them, to harm them, to make slaves of them." Krotkin coughed and stubbed out his cigarette. He started on his steak. "It's good. You must eat yours." He chewed as he spoke. "Do you know what the Russians called the first foreigners? No, I don't suppose you do. They called them *nemtsy*, which means the mute ones. You know why? Because when they first came to Russia the peasants couldn't understand them so they assumed they must be dumb!" Krotkin laughed out loud, his gold teeth gleaming in the candlelight. "Now we reserve the word only for the Germans, but we remain the most xenophobic people in Europe, if we are in Europe, but that is another story." Krotkin fell silent.

Peter hoped the history lesson was at an end but soon realised his optimism was premature.

"It is wise to be untrusting at the beginning," Krotkin continued. "It makes it more difficult for the bad foreigner to rob us. If he tries, we hate him and throw him out. Sometimes if he is very bad, we kill him. But on the other hand we are very warm hosts. So when we like a foreigner, a visitor to our country, we take him to our hearts, we embrace him, we love him." Krotkin drained his vodka glass and put another large piece of steak in his mouth. "Do you understand what I say, Mr Standridge?"

"Yes, of course, you put it very well," Peter said, absorbing Krotkin's words through the numbing effect of the vodka. It was as if he heard everything he said perfectly clearly but found his comprehension delayed. Was Krotkin just talking in a very general way or was he astutely aiming his remarks at him? Perhaps he was trying to warn him off, either because he knew something specific or because he didn't want him to get into difficulties through ignorance. Peter simply didn't know, but with new found bravura, he decided he should try and find out.

"May I propose a toast?" Peter asked. Krotkin nodded and filled up their glasses from the decanter. "I would like to drink to the health of your friend Kolya. May he have a long life."

Krotkin hesitated momentarily, then raised his glass.

"That was a generous toast to make," he said narrowing his eyes. "I believed you would not want to remember my colleague after the difficult time he made for you on the train."

"I bear no hard feelings. He was drunk at the time and not responsible for what he did. Anyhow, is he well?"

"As far as I know he is well. But I have not spoken to him for over a week and he may have been up to his old tricks." Krotkin looked thoughtful. "You know he only came to your compartment on the train as part of a practical game."

"You mean a practical joke?"

"Ah yes, that is the right expression. You must excuse me, sometimes my English is a failure to me. Yes, I only discovered after some conversations with the carriage attendant what had happened. It seems that Kolya in his wanderings had entered the compartment of some young men. They had some fun with him. People get very bored on these long train journeys. But soon they grew tired of him too. For a joke they said there was an Englishman all by himself in a compartment further along the corridor. They said he must go and see this Englishman and make some company for him. And that, as you know, is what Kolya did."

"But how did he get in? My door was locked."

Krotkin considered the question for a moment. "I know it is not good but these things happen sometimes. The young men bribed the carriage attendant with perhaps some money or maybe some perfume and she unlocked the door. It is not right, so I must apologise to you."

"So that's what happened. Thank you for telling me. When you see Kolya you must say I am sorry for not being more hospitable! I was just so shocked to see him." Peter felt quite liberated by Krotkin's explanation. He finished his steak, relishing the tenderness of the meat and without protest allowed Krotkin to empty the last of the vodka into his glass. He drank it, chasing it down with a glass of mineral water and a slice of garlic cheese.

Krotkin beckoned to the waiter. "Some coffee, Mr Standridge? The waiter will bring some coffee." Looking relaxed, Krotkin lit another cigarette and returned his attention to Peter. "You know we Russians and you foreigners do some things very differently. Russian travellers on the trains may lock their compartment doors in the evening when they get undressed or in the morning when they want to put on their clothes. But you had your door locked in the afternoon, in fact the carriage attendant said you had it locked most of the time. Now why do you do this Mr Standridge?"

Peter sensed his unease returning as Krotkin waited for his answer. "I like to travel alone and undisturbed," he said without conviction. "It's just the way I am."

Krotkin gave no hint as to whether he was satisfied with Peter's answer or not. He let the waiter serve the coffee and place the glasses of cognac in front of them.

"Look," Krotkin said, "I want you to be a friend of my country. Don't be an enemy. Don't be one of those foreigners who comes to take things from us. And I don't just mean the things you can touch, you can lift and take away. The greater crime is to take the things that you see, the things that you hear." Krotkin poured some sugar into his coffee and stirred it. He took a small sip and tried the cognac. "If you become one of those, I cannot be a friend to you. I cannot help you."

Peter did not know what he could sensibly say. Each time he spoke he seemed to give Krotkin another opening to probe, another opportunity to find out something more about him. Just when he felt himself in the clear, Krotkin would come back at him from a different angle.

Krotkin leaned back and took pleasure in his cognac and cigarette. He did not seem to expect a response from Peter. It was almost as if he had no further interest in him or his opinions. But the silence unnerved Peter. He felt it was almost an affront to this lively restaurant that the two of them should sit and not converse. Krotkin, though, seemed unaware of any tension. He appeared content with his thoughts.

"Now we must go," Krotkin said, taking Peter by surprise. He stood up and placed a ten dollar note on the table. He exchanged a few words with the waiter. Peter did not know whether he should offer to contribute, but there was no bill, and other than the tip, Krotkin had paid nothing. Peter decided it was best for the moment to be a grateful guest. They made their way towards the exit, gathering their coats and Krotkin his hat. They climbed the stone steps back to the street.

The cold air refreshed Peter after the atmosphere of the restaurant, but he felt unsteady on his feet. He realised he had drunk far more than was wise. Krotkin too seemed less stable and Peter suspected his swaying walk was not due solely to his limp. After a short distance, Krotkin grasped Peter by the arm and the two of them meandered slowly along the broad pavement like a devoted father and son.

At the hotel entrance Krotkin signalled to a taxi. "I shall ride to my friend's apartment in comfort. From here it is too far to walk, even during the day."

"Well, thank you very much for the dinner," Peter said. "It was a pleasure to see you again. And please don't forget to give my regards to Kolya."

Krotkin nodded and shook Peter's hand. "I think we shall meet again soon. Good night and sleep well."

Peter entered the hotel, making his way through the foyer. It was less crowded than earlier, but more full of drunks and partygoers who jostled him as he passed. He reached his room and, without undressing, lay straight down on the bed. He felt his head swell and contract, as if his brain was about to explode.

He rolled over on his side and closed his eyes tighter than before. Yet when sleep came, it brought no rest. Krotkin's face appeared and faded, only to reappear as dream raced after dream. One moment the face was open and smiling, the next dark and threatening. He heard Krotkin's voice, mild and pleasant, then mocking and angry. It was a night full of distorted images and muddled words.

CHAPTER 4

Yuri Poliakov did not enjoy his job, but was fortunate to have it. Certainly there were those who were surprised that someone of his limited ability was sitting in such an enviable position. They had to admit he was pleasant enough, but he was obviously not up to the intellectual standard demanded by the Ministry. Under normal procedures he would never have been selected for the post and they hoped no amount of bribery would secure his further advancement.

The Internal Section of the External Department of the Interior Ministry in which Yuri Poliakov worked was situated off a poorly lit corridor on the first level of the basement. It was not the most agreeable location and Yuri resented his subterranean existence. He found the lack of natural light depressing, the air quality poor. With no floor coverings, the sound of footsteps and the scraping of trolley wheels reverberated off the whitewashed walls while whirring machinery constantly swished the lifts up and down their shafts. Long tubes of pipework ran through the labyrinth of passageways, entering Yuri's office through a back wall and exiting through the ceiling. They gave off a smell of warm metal and the occasional loud report as they expanded and contracted. The one compensation was that the temperature was stable throughout the year.

In contrast to his workplace and to increase the evident importance of his job, Yuri told Olga he occupied an office suite. He was safe to do so, since she would never get past the guarded front doors of the building, even if she were brazen enough to try. Thus Yuri had the freedom to describe his fantasy office to her in the most extravagant terms and she would never know the extent of his deception. But as an intelligent woman she could not balance in her mind the miserly government salary her husband received with the obvious elegance of his surroundings. It simply did not add up.

The reality of Yuri's work was not something he was permitted to discuss and he appreciated this restriction. Other than the Section Head, there were only two of them in the Internal Section. Both Yuri and Ivan had a very small office each, not much larger than a storeroom, with cream coloured walls and a grey concrete floor. They both did the same job, except Ivan looked after all the foreigners whose surnames began A to L with Yuri taking care of the rest. As the Deputy Director pointed out, it was unnecessary for them to communicate with each other given such a division of responsibility.

Yuri always had a desire to meet some of the foreigners whose photographs he perused and whose personal details and activities he so sedulously recorded. But he knew such a wish was unlikely to be fulfilled due to the sensitivity of the information he handled. Instead, in his less busy moments, of which if he were honest he had many, Yuri would stare at the tall filing cabinets with their neatly indexed files and try to imagine the daily lives of these curious foreigners. He wondered, too, what so many of them were actually doing in his country in the first place.

The full title of Yuri's job was Collator Third Class. It was, he discovered, the lowest official rank in the Ministry beneath which toiled a large support staff of typists, messengers, porters and others. Yuri was proud of his status and the nuance of privilege that went with it. Rightly he was very short with anyone who addressed him incorrectly, particularly if they referred to him as a clerk. But in truth, what Yuri did on a daily basis differed very little from that of more junior staff in the building, except he was probably less efficient than they were.

42

Yuri had held his present appointment for almost two years. Although he found the work boring and the atmosphere demoralising, even in his most despairing moments he knew he might have been much worse off. With his qualifications or lack of them, he could have finished up in a factory or driving a tram. As it was he was secure in his routine and undemanding job and, although the pay was a limiting factor, he really had no alternative but to continue in the Ministry's employ. In any case he had convinced himself that promotion was but a step away.

He struggled, though, to discover the best way to advance himself and bring the quality of his work to the notice of his superiors. Initially he submitted what he regarded as carefully crafted reports to his Section Head, indicating patterns in the conduct of certain foreigners and highlighting the strange diversions of others. He believed he had exposed the most flamboyant and spirited individuals, who through their activities were a danger to the security and moral integrity of the State. But the only response was a brief note with the words *situation normal* written in red.

Undeterred by such insouciance, Yuri persevered. He turned next to practical matters, suggesting better ways of collating information and even proposing the replacement of his old typewriter and bulging files with a computer database. This too was rebuffed with another terse memo *forget it, idiot*. Yuri felt doubly insulted, since he had borrowed the idea from a friend in another Ministry, where, to his annoyance, it had been accepted and the young man promoted.

In the end Yuri decided that what he needed was a scoop of such profound importance that neither his Section Head nor the Deputy Director could deny his brilliance. But how could this be achieved? Although a succession of ideas floated through his woolly brain, each had its flaws, some serious enough to bring him to the attention of the

Security Service. The prospect of them paying him a visit quickly returned him to reality.

After many more testing days of thought, the idea he eventually settled on was the safest and to his mind the most subtle. In contrast to his earlier scheme, he would now choose two or three foreigners who seemed particularly dull and uninteresting. He would hint in his reports that there were things which the watchers and followers hadn't picked up about their activities and contacts. After all, Yuri surmised, even passive foreigners must be up to something. It would be a gradual process, but after a while all the signs would be there. He had of course to rely on his superiors reading these reports and having the acuity to spot the vital clues. Judging from the response he had received to date, this was also going to be a challenge.

As soon as Yuri had decided this was what he was going to do, he set about the long and tedious task of selecting the foreigners he wanted to use for his scheme. It meant sifting through all the files and re-reading the many reports from different agencies. Although he did not deal with diplomats or tourists, the list still ran into several hundreds and was growing by the day. Most of them were businessmen, company representatives and those working on inter-governmental projects as well as a number on the cultural and sporting side. Most foreigners only stayed in the country for a few weeks with others making shorter but more frequent visits. A small minority came for six months or more and it was on this group that Yuri decided to concentrate.

After about three weeks of work, Yuri made his final selection. He wrote down their names and nationalities on a separate sheet of paper:

Herr Rudolf Metzinger – Federal Republic of Germany

Mr Peter Standridge – United Kingdom of Great Britain and Northern Ireland

Dr Wang Ho – People's Republic of China

Yuri looked at the list with satisfaction. "There you are, my little collaborators. I trust at least one of you will be destined for my gratitude."

There was ample time during Yuri's working day to absorb the extra work he had set himself. He applied his mind in his slow but methodical way and started to include more innuendo in his weekly reports. Using the official information he received, he added a hint of something not being quite right in the behaviour of the three foreigners. Yuri did not dare to invent anything too fanciful: his ruse was to suggest and sow the seeds of doubt and suspicion.

By early October, Yuri was becoming disillusioned. He had been working on his scheme for a little over six weeks and neither his Section Head nor the Deputy Director had paid the slightest attention. He had feared that this might happen, but he was at least encouraged by knowing his reports contained the vital signs going back to late August. When his superiors did at last sit up and take notice, they would have to admit to missing all the clues he had so assiduously provided.

His other problem was that the three characters he had chosen did turn out to be as dull if not duller than expected. Since starting his little scheme, the information he received showed their routines had hardly changed at all. He had to use every gram of intelligence to squeeze something suggestive out of their daily lives.

At first he thought Herr Rudolf Metzinger was going to prove the most productive of the three. He was a musician on a sabbatical in Stambov. Yuri himself was not into classical music but was nevertheless surprised that music making of any sort went on in the town, a pertinent observation as far as Herr Metzinger was concerned. He also learnt from the incoming reports that he spent almost all his time in the Advanced Institute's library, which, while apparently having a good section on music, had much larger sections devoted to geophysics and rocket science. That became another area for suspicion.

What really convinced Yuri that he had chosen well was that Herr Rudolf Metzinger never went for a walk. In fact he rarely ventured outside at all, except to cross the road from his apartment to the Institute each morning and to re-cross the same road on his return in the evening. Yuri knew his memory was far from perfect, but he did definitely recall one presenter on a course he attended, titled *The Characteristics of Foreigners*, stating that the Germans spent a lot of time walking. Apparently they walked everywhere, on roads, on tracks, through forests and over mountains. Was it not most curious then that this German hardly walked at all?

The second of the collaborators, Mr Peter Standridge, was a disappointment. Yuri knew all about the good work General Philby had done for the Soviet Union together with Mr Maclean and Mr Burgess. He really hoped that Mr Standridge would be a man of similar stature, but of course working solely for the British. Unfortunately when each new report arrived on him, it stated tersely there was nothing new to report.

Mr Standridge did indeed seem unadventurous. He did very little during his free time with the exception of his Saturday outings with a group of foreigners from his hotel. They were indeed *Hooligany* judging from the reports, but there was nothing sinister nor suspicious about their nights on the town. The only point of note was that Mr Standridge tended to watch the action from the sidelines. He always kept control of himself, drank very modestly and avoided the girls in the bars. There had to be a reason for that. Maybe he liked his own company too much.

This Mr Standridge also travelled a lot in his role as an adviser. But wherever he went, whether to Irkutsk, Murmansk or Novocherkassk, he followed the same set and predictable routine. Yuri did give a little chuckle when he read in one report about an interpreter declaring he had never had to translate for such a boring man in all his life. It was also noted that he always reserved a whole compartment for himself when travelling by train, pre-booked at a considerable premium. As it was much quicker and cheaper to fly, why on earth did this Englishman prefer to travel around the Motherland in a railway carriage?

There seemed little doubt that of the three foreigners, Doctor Wang Ho was going to be the most difficult to fathom. For a start he was from the Chinese Government's Ministry of Animal Husbandry and located on a remote State farm south of the Ural Mountains. Although Yuri deduced that the farm was less than five kilometres from a military test centre for new armaments, Doctor Wang did nothing to arouse suspicion. He worked until six each evening, ate a small supper in the guest house by himself and then retired to his room. He seemed indifferent to the gunfire and explosions coming from the test centre. Yuri reckoned the informers could be missing something.

But just when Yuri began to think his little scheme was not going to work, he received three reports in quick succession which cheered him greatly. On the Wednesday he read with particular interest that Doctor Wang had started some research into the auditory responses of pigs and chickens and particularly how they reacted to loud and sudden noises. The report gave no further details, but Yuri immediately saw the connection to the military test centre. He was sure his Section Head would be as excited as he was about this latest piece of information.

The following day in a very full in-tray, Yuri found a new report concerning Herr Rudolf Metzinger. It stated in its normal factual way that for the last week Herr Metzinger had spent each evening in the rehearsal rooms with the violinist Lydia Kuznetzova. Instead of returning to his apartment at about 6pm as usual, he had not emerged from the Institute before 11pm and on one occasion he did not appear until 2am. The report made no comment, but Yuri knew that Lydia Kuznetzova had suspicious contacts with Westerners during the Soviet period. Although she was now rehabilitated, Yuri was able to insinuate in his report that, even in the climate of the new Russia, she could not be trusted with a foreign percussionist.

By the time Friday arrived, Yuri's morale was greatly improved. But there was even better news to come. At first he could not believe the report and had to go over it again. But there it was: Mr Peter Standridge had been seen in one of the new and expensive Moscow restaurants with none other than Professor Dimitri Krotkin. Unable to conceal his excitement, Yuri gave a whoop of triumph. It was a double success. Not only had he established sufficient suspicion in his earlier reports about Mr Peter Standridge, but now here was evidence of him consorting with a man who had done time in Siberia. And from Yuri's personal point of view, there was even more in this report to give him cause for satisfaction.

The only subject Yuri had shown any aptitude for at school was English. His father, as a senior official in the Ministry of External Affairs, had a good command of the language and encouraged his otherwise slow and disappointing son to work hard at the subject. When he left school, Yuri applied for a place at the Institute for Foreign Languages in Nizhny Novgorod. It had a very good reputation and Yuri's father also knew the Assistant Director who handled all the applications. It was an ideal solution for Yuri himself, and he was particularly keen to go.

In retrospect it did seem that the Institute had taken longer than normal to consider his application, but no one appeared too concerned. Even so, it was a huge shock for the Poliakov family when the Institute finally wrote to say that Yuri had not been awarded a place.

Yuri was bitterly disappointed and his father extraordinarily angry. He made a series of loud and lengthy telephone calls to the Assistant Director, but he was unable to persuade him to alter his decision. The Institute took the line that Yuri was not acceptable because his English was not of a high enough standard. Yuri's father was familiar both with the Institute and its standards, particularly from his experience as an external examiner for both their oral and written exams. He knew his son's English was more than adequate for the course. The Institute must have had an ulterior motive for rejecting him.

Before the end of the year his father received an unexpected visit from the Assistant Director of the Language Institute, though Yuri was not told about their meeting until much later. Apparently his father had thought long and hard about divulging the details, but in the end decided it was important his son knew the facts.

It was assumed quite naturally that the Assistant Director had come to their apartment to at least apologise for not taking Yuri. He did indeed do that, but after a drink or two, he told his father about the involvement in the selection process of the newly appointed Director, one Professor Dimitri Krotkin. He was adamant that what he said was to be treated in the strictest confidence. Were Professor Krotkin to discover his disloyalty, he would certainly lose his job. There was an unpleasant side to the Professor and he did not wish to cross him.

It transpired that Yuri's father had met Professor Krotkin about three years earlier. They were at a Canadian Embassy reception and were introduced through the Cultural Attaché, whom they both knew. Pleasantries were exchanged and an easy conversation followed. The subject then changed to language teaching and they had a difference of opinion over English pronunciation. Professor Krotkin, who seemed to have done well on the Canadian whisky, became very heated over the issue and made some derogatory remarks about North American English.

The Cultural Attaché challenged Krotkin diplomatically. Yuri's father did likewise and suggested it would be polite if he apologised to their Canadian host. Krotkin lost his temper and, raising his voice, became very abusive towards Yuri's father. Those around them witnessed his outburst and wondered why he was making such a fool of himself. Krotkin's rage only increased as he realised how badly he was behaving. Spluttering with anger, he drained his whisky and staggered rudely out of the reception. The Cultural Attaché was naturally shocked, but treated the incident lightly. Yuri's father apologised for Krotkin and quickly forgot about the whole affair.

Professor Krotkin apparently had not. When Yuri's application for the Institute for Foreign Languages came to his attention, Krotkin asked to see Yuri's file. Through a number of telephone calls, he established that this Yuri Poliakov was indeed the son of the Poliakov who had humiliated him in public three years earlier. All the other candidates put forward were accepted by Professor Krotkin with the exception of Yuri, against whose name he had written: *Not up to the required standard for entry. Under no circumstances to be reconsidered.*

Yuri now looked at Krotkin's name lying exposed in the agency's report on his desk. Revenge was not a sentiment he cared for. It was important not to lose face, but there were ways of dealing with situations when this might arise. Professor Krotkin had disgraced himself in front of others and could not bear the shame of it. His vindictiveness required retribution. Putting his scruples to one side, Yuri decided he should settle the score with this Professor. It would be nice justice were Krotkin to become the catalyst for the advancement of Poliakov the younger.

CHAPTER 5

It was normal for Yuri Poliakov to emerge from the Interior Ministry building in a buoyant mood at the end of the working week. This Friday was no exception and he said a particularly cheery goodbye to Ivan as they went their separate ways. Even the crowded metro, which he railed against from Monday to Thursday, did not deflate his spirits. In the packed carriage his constant smile persuaded those closest to him to inch away as best they could, for fear he might be one of those unfortunates who ought to be detained.

Yuri enjoyed the fresh air as he left the metro station and walked the few hundred metres to his apartment block. As usual Olga was home before him. He found her in their minute kitchen chopping cucumbers and tomatoes and drinking lemon tea.

"You seem to be very excited this evening," she said, as Yuri curled his arms around her waist in anticipation of a kiss. "I know it's the start of the weekend, but are ministry officials allowed to be this lively?" She turned to enjoy a close embrace.

"It's simply been an interesting week," he said, running his hands down her back. "Can't tell you about it of course, but it does happen occasionally. You never know, they may even recognise my efforts and consider me for promotion. Now that would be worth celebrating, wouldn't it?"

Olga smiled at him, knowing in her heart that her adorable husband, despite his other talents, would not be in line for promotion yet. She had heard from friends, who knew about such things, that it was not unusual for some lower ranking officials to spend their whole careers in the same job, at the same grade and even in the same office. She was determined, however, that this would not be Yuri's fate. She would do everything she could to ensure his progress to a higher rank, but patience was required.

Yuri left Olga preparing supper and went into their bedroom to change out of his office suit. Once he was more comfortable in his casual clothes, he stood on a chair and pulled a box off the top of the clothes cupboard. He removed the lid and sorted through the stacked papers until he came across a particular envelope. It was tucked in a folder on which he had written *Language Institute Application*.

Taking the envelope, Yuri sat on the side of the bed and leafed through the bundle of papers inside. He felt a long subdued anger as he re-read his application and the subsequent letter of rejection. But this was not what he was looking for. He delved deeper into the envelope and removed a well-thumbed copy of the Institute prospectus. He turned to the first page and found what he wanted.

The introduction was written by the new Director, Professor Dimitri Krotkin. His glowing account of what the Institute had accomplished and was going to achieve in the future sounded impressive. Alongside the introduction there was a dignified photograph of him in his academic dress. Yuri studied the face for pointers to his character. Was that downturn at the corners of his mouth the sign of a vengeful nature, were the slightly closed eyes a hint of slyness, did the high forehead and mass of white hair indicate a scheming mind beneath? The photograph, though, revealed no answers.

What interested Yuri more was the brief summary of the Professor's career. He had read it before but now he went through it forensically, looking for clues and snippets which might be useful to him. Professor Krotkin had graduated with a top degree in English, served as a tank officer during his military service and then spent most of his career teaching in a number of prestigious institutes and academies. Yuri smiled when he saw that he had spent three years at an unidentified *school* in Eastern Siberia. Was this a convenient way of describing his time in some detention camp? But what Yuri didn't know, and couldn't find out from the papers he had in front of him, was why Krotkin had been sent there in the first place. At some point he would like to get hold of that particular piece of information.

Yuri removed the prospectus and put it in a separate envelope. He would take it into the office on Monday and photocopy the parts he needed. He packed the remaining papers into the box and returned it to its place on top of the cupboard. Satisfied with his efforts, he went into the main room, turned on the television and sat down to watch an ice hockey match.

It had been a deliberate decision on Yuri's part not to tell Olga why the Language Institute had rejected him. His father had forbidden him to mention it to anyone and he believed this extended to his wife. Olga obviously knew he had not gained a place on the course and did think it curious. His English after all was quite good, but more mystifying was why his father had not assisted him. She knew first-hand how the system could be manipulated and someone of the standing of Yuri's father would normally have had no problem in ensuring a course place for his son. She never raised the subject, though, aware that Yuri was still smarting from his rejection. She also believed it would be prudent not to enquire too closely into the part his father may or may not have played in his original application.

Olga had met Yuri's father through her academic work. Moscow State University was her *alma mater* and after graduating with a distinction in History, she had accepted a research post there. Her subject was a comparative study on the rise of the maritime empire of Great Britain and the land-based Russian Empire. As part of her research, she was put in touch with Yuri's father and visited him in the Ministry of External Affairs. He had been very helpful and congratulated her on the quality of her work. He was a man she immediately liked and respected. Most important of all, he had introduced her to his son.

Since her marriage to Yuri just over a year ago, Olga's life had become very pleasurable. She was relaxed, content and optimistic about the future. But there was a minor matter which irked her: their apartment, although a good one by Moscow standards, faced the concrete walls of a neighbouring block. Olga felt deprived. She needed a view, but not just any view. She needed the view of the Moscow River, which only the apartments on the opposite side of their building enjoyed. In her quiet way she was determined to get one of those apartments.

Quite early in their marriage, Olga learned it was counter-productive to push Yuri too hard or too fast on any matter. She knew she was in the ascendancy when it came to intelligence, but he was way ahead of her in obstinacy. She had to gently flatter and coerce to get what she wanted and had become an expert in wily persuasion.

"Can't wait for next weekend," she called out as Yuri settled comfortably in front of the television. "Your Ministry's *dacha*s are so much nicer than the others. How clever of you to get that late booking, such cancellations are so rare. But then, I am married to someone who can make the ground move." She heard Yuri chuckle, hoping it was for her and not the hockey game. She glanced through the doorway. "I know it's short notice, my love, but do you think there's someone we ought to invite to join us?"

Yuri was intent on the match, but always paid attention to Olga when she spoke. "Haven't thought about it. I don't mind if you want someone to come, but I'd rather they didn't stay the night. I'd envisaged a quiet country weekend with just the two of us. Perhaps they could arrive for Saturday lunch and have a short walk in the forest after." Yuri went back to the television, satisfied he had made his point but none the wiser who his wife had in mind as a guest.

Olga continued to do things in the kitchen and left Yuri to enjoy his favourite sport. She laid out the supper things, found him a beer and some mineral water for herself. She served up and they sat down at the cramped kitchen table.

"I came up in the lift with Ludmilla this evening," Olga said. "Oh, and Fat Alex squeezed in too." Yuri smiled at the image of bulky Alex wedging himself into the lift with the two trim girls.

"I bet he enjoyed that. He probably doesn't normally get so close to such beauties. I haven't bumped into him either for a while." Yuri laughed at his own joke and Olga laughed with him. She let him eat a little more before laying a hand on his arm.

"Yuri, you know you haven't got that book of poetry back from Alex. He's had it for ages and your father did give it to you as a New Year present. If you don't retrieve it soon, knowing Alex, he'll probably sell it or trade it in for box of cigarettes."

They both smiled, but Yuri less so as he wasn't keen on Fat Alex. He didn't dislike him, yet Alex managed to make Yuri feel inferior. Though lazy and chaotic, Alex was both intelligent and quick-witted and Yuri was no match for him. He had suffered humiliation at his hands once too often.

"Why don't you go and ask him for that book after we've finished eating," Olga suggested gently. "It would be over and done with, especially as your father's coming round for supper next Tuesday. It could be awkward if you didn't have it by then."

As usual, Olga was right. His father would undoubtedly find some way of establishing whether the book was around and whether his son was making progress with it. Not that Yuri was particularly interested in the bound volume of *The Oxford Book of English Verse*, but he felt obliged to make an effort to satisfy his father.

After he had finished his stewed plums, Yuri finally agreed to go and see Fat Alex, but indicated without much subtlety that Olga should make it worth his while when he returned. He found some shoes, combed his hair and headed for the door.

Olga followed him and putting her arms round his neck, kissed him long and lovingly. "You know Yuri, I think you should invite fatty Alex to come to the *dacha* next Saturday. We do owe him a meal after he took us out to that restaurant. Why don't you just ask him whilst you're up there?" She kissed Yuri again fully on the lips, stifling any reply. With one hand she skilfully eased the door open and guided him to the lift. She drew her head back provocatively.

"You will, won't you?" she simpered. The lift arrived before Yuri could think of a good reason to say no. With Olga's help the metal gates were clanged shut and whether he liked it or not, Yuri found himself encaged and ascending to see Fat Alex in his lair.

On the top floor Yuri let himself out and followed the corridor round to the entrance to Apartment 82. An embossed card on the door confirmed it was the home of one Alexander Petrovich Stroynov. Yuri rang the doorbell briefly, half-hoping Fat Alex would not hear. He could then tell Olga he'd tried to raise him but he hadn't answered. It would be credible to suggest he was either out, asleep or dead drunk.

Yuri was disappointed when he heard sounds in the apartment. There was the shunting of furniture, a crash of something heavy falling to the floor and then shuffling footsteps, gradually more audible, the other side of the door. Yuri was aware of being observed through the spy hole before a key turned in the main lock and a chain rattled. The door was edged open and a large head appeared round the side. Satisfied the spy hole had not deceived him, Fat Alex moved the rest of his body into view, filling the doorway.

"Ah, Yuri Pavlevich, a sighting of two Poliakovs in one day. What a privilege. Some might say a coincidence, but surely not. If I travel in a lift with a wife in the afternoon, the husband comes to pay me a visit in the evening. Your appearance is therefore not entirely unexpected. Have you arrived to deal with me for making suggestions to your pretty wife?" he asked grinning like an ape.

"No, no, not at all."

"Oh, come now. I am all prepared. See here how I steel myself. Use your fists on my generous belly or punch me on the nose and honour will be restored." Fat Alex posed mockingly, screwing up his eyes ready to receive a blow to the face and pushing his protruding stomach even further forward as an unmissable target.

Yuri knew he was being taunted, but as usual he felt inadequate and unable to respond with suitable repartee. "No, honestly, it's nothing like that," he replied weakly.

"What a relief," Fat Alex sighed, allowing his body to slump into its normal shape. "One day I know I shall go too far and have my ears boxed for daring to flirt with someone I shouldn't. But this time you have let me off the hook, for which I am deeply grateful." He studied Yuri for a moment, his dark intelligent eyes scanning his face. "We mustn't stand here, my good friend. It's bad luck to do business in a doorway. Come in."

Yuri had hoped he would not have to enter Fat Alex's apartment. On the way up in the lift he planned to collect the book, invite him to the *dacha* and leave. He believed he could accomplish all this on the neutral ground of the corridor. But as the door was held open for him, he knew he had to cross the threshold into Fat Alex's territory.

The layout of the apartment was similar to Yuri's, though the rooms were reversed. For a moment it was disorientating to see the narrow kitchen where he'd expected the bedroom to be, the small alcove instead of the bathroom. But the major difference between the two apartments was the outlook from the window in the main room. Unlike Yuri and Olga, Fat Alex had a sweeping view of the river across to the distant hills. In the darkness, with the city lights reflected in the water, Yuri had to admit it was an enchanting scene. He now understood why Olga wanted to move to this side of the building and why she chided him for his indifference.

It was unusual for a single person to occupy such a spacious apartment. Yuri wondered how Fat Alex had managed to acquire it, especially as he was not sure what he did to support himself. Whenever Yuri had inquired, he received evasive and noncommittal answers. The closest he ever came to explaining his source of income was 'a bit of trading in this and that', which left Yuri convinced he was operating on the edge of legality. He also seemed well known in the city's ritzy new restaurants. When he'd taken them out to supper a few weeks previously, they were interrupted by friends and acquaintances coming over to their table to greet him. Olga remarked later that they all looked like the American gangsters she'd seen in the films.

However fine a view Fat Alex may have had from his window, his apartment was a mess. Yuri had to thread his way through discarded clothes, piles of books, magazines and tapes to get to the nearest chair. This too was heaped with papers and old socks which Fat Alex turfed onto the floor. Yuri sat down, making himself as comfortable as he could. He saw Fat Alex disappear into the kitchen and return a moment later with a couple of beers. Yuri was offered a hastily wiped glass, but he indicated he would rather drink straight from the can.

"So, Yuri, my good friend, I drink to your health, to your long life and to your beautiful wife." Fat Alex raised his can in an exaggerated salute and drank greedily. He ran the back of his hand across his lips and balancing the can between his ample thighs, lit a cigarette. He coughed, his whole body quaking in response.

"How very remiss of me, Yuri Pavlevich, not to also toast your visit to my apartment. Such a rare event to find you ringing on my door early on a Friday evening when you should be out enjoying yourself. Something important on your mind is it? Something so vital that you need to come and talk and drink my beer when you could just pick up the phone and say whatever it is you want to say?" He took another gulp from his can and smirked at Yuri. "So may I inquire, dear sir, as to the purpose of your visit?"

"It's very simple really. I came to collect the book I lent you."

Fat Alex appeared perplexed. "A book, you say. Well, that is interesting in itself, but the more so since I can't remember borrowing one from you. Are you sure you lent it to me and not to somebody who looks like me?" Fat Alex laughed heartily, fully aware that there were perhaps no more than two others in the whole of Moscow who resembled him in any way. Far from being ashamed of his size and appearance, he rather relished his notoriety.

"No, I definitely lent it to you. You specifically asked to see it. It was an English book, *The Oxford Book of English Verse* to be precise. It was a present from my father. A bound volume."

"An expensive present from your father? That is a very grave matter. Now as you can see the arrangement of my books does not compare well with a properly ordered library. I am a little haphazard in the way I keep them. But if you say I have your book, it has to be here somewhere."

Putting his beer can on the floor, Fat Alex stuck his

cigarette resolutely behind his left ear. He worked his way out of the chair and with surprising agility got down on all fours. He crawled around the stacks of books on the floor mumbling the titles out loud and occasionally grunting. Yuri watched him with disbelief and not a little concern as the search continued into the kitchen.

Yuri heard Fat Alex collide with the cooking pots and then shout, "Got you, my little beauty." This was followed by a series of curses as he realized he was unable to turn round in the narrow space and would have to reverse out. He did this without elegance, clutching a book between his teeth. He emerged perspiring, took the book out of his mouth and exclaimed, "This has been missing for ages. It's on mushroom hunting." He looked shamefaced. "Sadly it's not in English verse." He placed the book on a chair and crawled off into the bedroom, his bottom bobbing like a baboon's.

Yuri could no longer see him and wondered whether he had lost his book for ever. He began to think of some of the excuses he could make in front of his father when Fat Alex reappeared.

"Yuri Pavlevich, I have your esteemed volume of verse. It's in pristine condition, not a page has been turned," he said pushing himself up with the aid of a broom handle. "It was always my desire to read some of these beautiful poems if my English were up to it. But I have not succeeded and in literary circles I shall be judged a failure, a philistine of the first rank. That will be suitable condemnation for one so indolent." He bowed in front of Yuri as far as his stomach would allow and handed him the book with a flourish.

"Thank you," Yuri said. "If you would seriously like to borrow it again, I would be happy to lend it to you."

"That would be temptation indeed. I could not have that precious book in my house for a second time. If I did, it would surely disappear for good. You keep good hold of it, Yuri Pavlevich, guard it with your heart and soul and never permit my eyes to alight on it again."

Yuri finished the rest of his beer. He had his book and had survived this brief meeting without rancour. Fat Alex was now bending over the stereo system in the corner and Yuri saw the silver flash of a disk as he inserted it into the player. He stood up to go.

"You are leaving so soon?" Fat Alex queried. "Unexpected in arrival and departure... what's got into you? Do you not wish to hear my music and have some entertaining conversation?"

"I have to go. Olga is waiting for me." Yuri blushed and started to pick his way carefully across the room. "By the way," he said as he reached the door, "if you are free next Saturday, would you like to come out to our Ministry *dacha* for the day?" Fat Alex moved to join him, stumbling over a pile of books on the way.

"A day at one of your official *dacha*s," he said, his eyes twinkling mischievously. "That sounds captivating, Yuri Pavlevich. I accept with pleasure and with the normal apprehension of one receiving an invitation from the Interior Ministry. I shall come prepared to resist interrogation, unless of course it is carried out by your lovely wife – in which case I shall submit immediately and confess to everything."

Yuri smiled feebly. "We'll be pleased to have you as our guest. I'll let you have the details next week. Good night."

Fat Alex opened the door. Yuri quickly shook his hand and set off for the lift.

"Don't forget to bring the handcuffs with you," Fat Alex shouted after him. "I just love them."

CHAPTER 6

Peter Standridge relaxed in the back of the taxi as it lumbered along like a lolloping tramp ship. It veered from side to side, buffeting through the swell of traffic in a reckless duel for road space. But despite the constant change of course, Peter no longer gripped his seat in terror. He was now quite accustomed to Moscow drivers demonstrating their skills to foreign passengers.

Peter expected the journey from the city centre to Scheremetyevo Airport would take about forty minutes during the evening rush hour. He had allowed plenty of time and hoped Derek Carbonnel's flight would be on time. If there were any delay, he would treat himself to a beer and put it down to expenses.

It was a cold, dry evening, raw in the easterly wind. An early October snowfall had thawed though more snow was forecast for the weekend. Peter thought it would be a shame if Derek didn't see Moscow in the snow, but he seemed determined to restrict his visit to three days. *I'll come in on Monday evening and get out of your hair late Thursday. Make sure I meet all the people I need to. Quite happy to work late if necessary.*

Peter was gratified his director was at last coming to see what he was doing in Russia. Although there had been communication between them, it had been over three months since they had met face to face. His visit also provided the chance for Peter to talk about his unofficial duties. This issue mattered more to him than having any of the difficulties with his normal work resolved.

The taxi thundered on and the rows of apartment blocks lining the Moscow road gave way to open fields and patches of woodland. The driver turned off the congested highway to take a short cut, the bright street lights terminating abruptly. Darkness enclosed them with the vehicle lights cutting through the blackness and illuminating the pot-holed surface. Set back from the verge was an occasional lamp lashed to a wooden pole, its feeble light casting a yellow ellipse on the rough and hardened ground. Pale squares of light in shadowy houses appeared briefly and then were gone.

This rural interlude reminded Peter of that other Russia he frequently encountered: the reluctant, obstinate Russia which suspected progress and innovation and held to the old, sure ways. It sat side by side with the brash, new, go-ahead Russia of fresh ideas and different values. The old Russia, with its centuries of wisdom and mistrust, watched and waited, scornful of encroaching change.

The taxi turned sharply onto the airport road and the lighting along the dual carriageway was restored. In the distance the night sky reflected the bright aura of the airport and the flashing silver lights of circling aircraft. The quiet countryside remained hidden, still, patient.

Peter consulted the board in the Arrivals area, seeing the BA flight had landed on time. There could be long delays before passengers appeared, but Derek Carbonnel was soon barging through the waiting crowds and greeting Peter.

"Good to see you," he said. "Car nearby?"

"Not far." They followed the signs to the exit and, with bags stowed, the taxi was soon rolling back to Moscow. They chatted about Peter's work and the London office, who was doing what, who was new, who had moved on. As they got closer to Moscow, the conversation stalled. Derek seemed distracted and stared out of the window, taking in the unfamiliar sights.

Peter had booked him into Hotel Leskov. It would be easier for them both to be under the same roof, given the busy programme for the next three days. Derek's room was on a different floor, but still had a good view across to the Kremlin.

"I won't bother with supper," Derek said as Peter escorted him to his room. "Feeling a bit weary... think I'll have an early night if you don't mind. I've got the programme so I know what I'm doing. We'll meet up for breakfast at 7.30 and you can brief me then. By the way, I suppose all the telephones are still insecure?"

"I have always assumed they are. It's denied officially of course. Is there something I can help with?"

"No, that won't be necessary. I'll sort it in Commercial tomorrow. Thanks for dragging out to the airport to meet me. It's always nice to see a friendly face when you touch down in a new country. See you in the morning, then."

Peter said goodnight and made his way down to the hotel restaurant. The menu was sparse but he ordered a beer and stew with dumplings and cabbage rolls. As he waited, he mulled over in his mind how strange it was to see Derek out of context. Previously they had only been together in the offices of Duggan Meade or on project sites around the UK. It was already difficult to adjust to him being here in Moscow, a place Peter regarded as his own. He was pleased he had been allowed to work without closer supervision and, in a way, he almost resented Derek's intrusion.

Peter slept badly, a problem which had obviously not afflicted Derek Carbonnel. He was ebullient when Peter came down for breakfast and found him hacking into a boiled egg.

"Morning, Peter. I woke early, wrapped up, went out for a walk, got an appetite, started without you. Sorry."

"I thought my watch must have stopped. A relief to find I'm on time and you were early." Peter sat down. "I see you've solved the riddle of the Russian breakfast"

"Didn't know there was one. Anyhow you order what

you want and we'll get down to business."

As Peter was used to starting the day slowly, he had little appetite for work and food. Their cramped table was inadequate for the expansive Derek Carbonnel and soon papers and documents competed for space with pastries, jam and tea. Peter had to do most of the talking, explaining why he had arranged each meeting, who would be present and what he wanted to achieve. It was all clear in his mind, or at least it was until Derek interrupted with well-directed questions. Peter became flustered, spilling yoghurt on his crib sheet and performing far from his best. He could only hope the meetings would run more smoothly than the breakfast.

Derek Carbonnel remained on top form throughout the day. He was dominant and impressive, never seeming to flag nor lose the initiative. Peter felt himself caught up in Derek's enthusiasm and acquitted himself well whenever he needed to contribute to the discussions. He also discovered another side to Derek: he had a very hard head. Two of the day's meetings were held at the Russian Ministry of Communications and Transport where vodka was served along with canapés and coffee. Derek managed to drink a couple of glasses of vodka at each session and remain perfectly coherent. It was as if the clear liquid in his glass were water.

By the end of the day Peter was beginning to tire, but knew they must attend a small reception organised by Ruth Rumbelow in Derek's honour. She had hired a room in the Praga and the guest list ran to about sixty, Russians outnumbering the British two to one.

"Ok, Peter, so who are the key players?" Derek asked as they made their way through the traffic.

"Deputy Minister Kondrashin will be the most senior Russian present, assuming he turns up. In addition there should be the Director from the Central Urban Planning Committee. He works for Kondrashin, his name's Lokutin.

I have met him on a couple of occasions. He's cooperative but a bit stuffy."

From the moment they entered the reception, Derek was again in his element. He worked the room like a professional, keeping Peter in tow. Wherever he was, the conversation picked up and he managed to blend productive discussions with amusing banter. He was also careful to ensure Peter's work was mentioned and missed few opportunities to talk up the value of his current projects.

"Derek, the Deputy Minister has just arrived," Ruth Rumbelow said, grasping him by the elbow and steering him towards a clump of suited Russians near the bar. "I don't think he's staying long, so you'd better come and meet him straightaway."

The appropriate introductions were made and the Deputy Minister nodded as Lokutin whispered briefly in his ear. The interpreter moved in alongside.

"So you are in Russia for the first time I understand," the Deputy Minister said. "I hope you are finding your visit beneficial."

"Very much so," Derek replied. "I am impressed by the speed with which changes are being made. I hope my firm can continue to help in the restructuring."

"Yes, sometimes it is important to take advice. It helps to avoid mistakes. But your methods in Great Britain will not always fit our methods in Russia. We must in the end do things which suit us, not you. Many things from the West are not appropriate for us. We will always listen, but we may not always act."

"Of course, Minister, you are absolutely right. We would not be so presumptuous as to expect you to do everything we suggest. Our role must remain purely advisory."

"That is the purpose of the Handsome Fund, Minister," Ruth Rumbelow interjected. "You will recall we had some discussions on how you could best use the money the British Government has allocated for the assistance programme.

The Minister nodded and sipped his drink. "And is this Handsome Fund very wealthy?" he enquired, raising his eyebrows. "Is it well enough endowed to provide advice on the reconstruction of Russia, a country a hundred times bigger than Great Britain?"

"We would like it to be," Derek laughed, "but our Treasury officials would not agree. But as I am sure you appreciate, Minister, size is not the issue. It's the quality of the advice that's important."

"That is of course true. At the moment we are interested in what you have to tell us, but in a few years time when we have the necessary resources, we will return the compliment. But, please, now you must excuse me." He bowed slightly, turned and accompanied by Lokutin, who had remained mute throughout the short exchange, left the reception as quickly as he had arrived.

"Not perhaps the most grateful of ministers," Derek remarked as he considered who next to engage in conversation.

"Oh, he's fine," Ruth said. "He was just making sure that you know Russia remains a great and powerful country. It's something we forget at our peril."

With the departure of the Deputy Minister, the other Russians at the reception took their cue and began to leave in rapid succession. Derek seemed disappointed, particularly as none of the British representatives were anxious to stay either. Once the last guest had left, they took Ruth out for a light supper. At the end of the meal, Derek uncharacteristically declared that he was too exhausted to explore the Moscow nightlife and was going to bed.

The second day of the visit was very much like the first, except that Peter had a better working breakfast. On returning to their hotel after the day's meetings, Derek announced that Peter deserved a break from him and he would make his own arrangements for the evening. Peter protested but was overruled.

"One thing I do need to do tomorrow," Derek added on the way up to their rooms, "is buy something for my wife and daughter. Any suggestions?"

"There is a very good gift shop opposite one of the old monasteries. I'm sure you would find something suitable there. If we have time and the weather is half decent we could go for a short walk in the monastery grounds. I, for one, feel like some fresh air after all these stuffy meetings."

"Excellent. I don't think I need to spend much more than a couple of hours in Commercial in the morning. We can set off directly from there."

Derek had provided Peter with the ideal solution to his problem of where and when to raise the issue of his unofficial duties. It would not be wise to discuss such a sensitive matter in any room, building or vehicle for fear of listening devices. He had thought about using the eraser boards but they had their limitations when it came to lengthy conversations. The only option was to talk outside in the open air. Even that was not without risk but Peter felt the likelihood of their conversation being overheard was small. The monastery grounds would provide excellent cover and fewer people would be there on a weekday. He hoped the promised snowstorm would be delayed.

Novodevichy Monastery lay on the west side of the city and still provided a peaceful sanctuary for Moscow's weary inhabitants. Its fine churches with their glistening domes sat confidently within the turreted walls and looked magnificent at any time of the year. Swans moved with grace and speed on a small lake between the monastery and the river. A circular walk wove through the trees offering a changing view of this ancient religious fortress.

The cold air and sharp wind ensured the two Englishmen set off at a brisk pace once they had inspected the imposing gate-church. Derek Carbonnel marched ahead with Peter struggling to keep up. Both men wore new fur hats, but as it was not yet November, they drew strange looks from the Russians they passed.

"We're a bit early to be wearing these," Peter gasped. "Apparently the earflaps aren't lowered until it's very cold."

"I don't give a bugger. Mine is staying firmly on my head," Derek said robustly.

They walked on quickly and found the wind less incisive on the far side of the lake. Here Derek slowed his pace and motioned to Peter to the shelter of a clump of birches. They were as well screened as they could be with no other walkers in sight.

"This Russia venture seems to be going well, Peter," Derek said. "Yes, very well indeed. You're generating a lot of business for the firm. The place suits you, doesn't it?"

"I think I can say I'm enjoying it, despite the frustrations. Breaking into a fresh market is a new experience and of course there is this huge cultural difference. It's everywhere, how they relate to you as a foreigner, how they conduct their business, how they are wedded to this giant bureaucracy and how they are afraid to make decisions. But having said all that, there is immense potential here. It's actually quite exciting."

Derek nodded and watched the swans gliding across the lake against the backdrop of the monastery. He seemed mesmerised by the timeless tranquillity of the scene. "You know, I didn't really come on this trip to get a closer view of your projects, nor to meet all those people you're working with. I came here specifically to put some proposals to you." He didn't turn to face Peter, but continued to gaze over the water as if wishing to deliver a slow soliloquy to the swans.

"You may not like the idea," he went on, "but I – that is the firm – want you to stay in Russia until next summer. A six month extension in effect. It may not be that long, but we do need you here," he added emphatically. "We will of course see you right, an increase in your salary, higher allowances and plenty of free flights back to the UK to see your girlfriend. Does it appeal?"

Peter was wrong footed. He hadn't counted on Derek coming up with a major surprise and certainly not during a walk in the park a couple of hours before his departure. Peter had intended to make the running on this occasion and wanted to work to his own agenda. Even so he had to respond. "I reckon I could survive here, but I'd like time to consider what you've proposed. When do you need an answer?"

"Must know by the end of next week," Derek said, still not addressing Peter directly. He adjusted his hat and pulled at his gloves as the cold moved into him. "I think it's also only fair to tell you that the firm has been having discussions about our involvement in the old Soviet Bloc. We have decided to open an office in Eastern Europe to look after the business development in the region. It's in its infancy at the moment but we feel a foot on the ground will send the right message to the new governments and allow us to get ahead of our competitors. Not sure where we might locate the office. Budapest and Prague are the favourites, but we're not ruling out Warsaw or even Moscow at this stage."

"It all sounds very logical, but how does this effect my extension in Russia?"

"You need to get as much experience as you can of their way of working," Derek said, at last turning to look at Peter. "My fellow directors and I have you in mind to both set up and run this new office. We have confidence in you, Peter. You have earned this promotion through your work here."

Peter said nothing. He felt flattered yet uneasy. There had been absolutely no sign during the previous three days that Derek was going to make such a dramatic proposal.

He had kept his cards very close, giving every indication that his trip was indeed a routine visit to assess the current state of business. Peter was offended by the way Derek had acted. "Why didn't you mention all this before? You had plenty of opportunities to talk to me about it much earlier."

"Sorry. Wasn't possible. I only got the go ahead from the others late yesterday. One director, who must obviously remain anonymous, felt you were too young and inexperienced to be the senior consultant for such a vast region, but he was talked round. Anyhow," Derek stamped his feet from the cold, "we ought to get moving before our balls fall off."

Peter still resented his treatment but knew in his heart of hearts that the offer was just too good to decline. He also had a suspicion that Derek knew this too. But he could not comprehend why it was necessary for him to be so devious. The explanation about the anonymous director sounded mendacious. Peter was sure Derek Carbonnel had the authority to put the proposals to him long before he'd left London for Moscow earlier in the week.

They again set off along the path at a good pace and the wind caught them in the open. In the distance a bank of white-grey cloud signalled the approaching storm and the first snowflakes began to circle round them. They had to raise their voices against the wind.

"I don't want to get snowed in," Derek said walking faster.

"No chance of that. The Russians are very efficient when it comes to snow clearing. They'll make sure you get away." Derek's unexpected proposal made Peter almost forget that he had some important questions of his own to ask. He felt that he, too, should show a little cunning. "One area where I have made some preliminary enquiries about future consultancy is with the new Russian military. It seems that they are not interested. But, just in case they change their minds, have we anyone in the firm who has worked with our own MOD?"

"No, I don't think so. They tend to look after themselves when it comes to the kind of consultancy service we offer."

"Wasn't it a bit strange then that I had a meeting in the MOD as part of my preparation for coming over here? In fact, did you even know they asked to see me?"

Derek Carbonnel kept moving steadfastly forward with the light snow gathering on his fur hat. "No, I didn't. But then I don't really need to approve every detail of my consultants' briefing programmes. Gave you a bit of security advice, did they?"

"Well, no they didn't, as it happens. I saw a retired major called Pomfrey. Is he someone you know?"

"Never heard of him. Are we still going the right way? The snow's getting a bit thicker. Can't see the path too well."

"But Pomfrey said our firm had assisted the MOD before," Peter puffed, "several times in fact, and we were one of the best in terms of cooperation." He waited for some response, but Derek continued to trudge on in silence. "Pomfrey wanted me to do a bit of A and M and O and R. Do you know what they are?"

"Not a clue, enlighten me."

"Attitude and Morale and Observing and Reporting."

"And have you been doing what they asked?"

"I didn't want to, but was persuaded to get involved by Chris Burroughs. You met him in Commercial, remember? He briefs me before each trip and I produce a report which he then sends to London through the diplomatic bag."

Derek Carbonnel stopped and turned to face Peter. "And you've been involved in this for the last three months?"

"Yes I have. I was assured the firm knew all about it. I would obviously have walked away otherwise. I wanted to raise it with you before I left London, but you were abroad at the time. It wasn't something I could mention over the phone. I needed to talk to you one to one."

"It sounds as if you have been rather foolish, Peter. I shall have to do some investigating when I get back to London. Come on, let's keep going."

They set off again, their minds more concentrated on their conversation than the swirling snow.

"My advice for the moment is to continue as normal," Derek said. "Don't vary your routine, don't do anything differently. Keep gathering your bits and pieces of whatever they are. It sounds pretty small beer, so if they do catch you at it, you're not going to finish up in the *gulag*. I assume you've not been rumbled so far?"

"No, not exactly. I had an unpleasant experience on a train in Siberia a few weeks ago and have felt a bit vulnerable ever since. Recently I've just been working on local projects so I've done less collecting."

"Well, keep your head down until I get back to you on this one. And don't mention this conversation to Burroughs."

By the time they reached the monastery, the snow was falling heavily. They stood like white sentinels under the arch of the gate-church waiting for their taxi. It arrived on time, slewing across the road and skidding to a stop. Brushing themselves down, they eased into the back seat. The suffocating heat silenced them as they sped to the hotel and then on to the airport.

They arrived with time to spare but Derek seemed anxious to check in as soon as possible. He grabbed his bag from the boot. "Goodbye, Peter, and thanks. I'll be in touch shortly. Take care."

"Safe journey," Peter replied. "I'll let you know about your offer very soon."

Derek Carbonnel looked as if he intended to say something, but merely nodded his head. He turned and entered the terminal building, striding purposefully towards the check-in desks. Peter watched him disappear into the crowd of passengers, wondering whether the job offer would still be on the table after his confession at the monastery. He hoped very much it would be.

CHAPTER 7

They lay in each other's arms under the blankets and the furs, awry and yet warm from the energies of the night. The cold dawn advanced across the room, its pale lemon light evading the thin curtains and casting faint shadows in the retreating darkness. It picked out the furniture piece by piece; first the wardrobe, next the chair and finally the wooden bed standing on a broad, tasselled rug. The silence of the night snow was broken by the rasping of the ravens as they scrabbled on the rooftops and scavenged the frozen ground.

"Yuri, my love, my beautiful bear, don't you think it's time to bring your wife some tea?"

There was a grunt, a brief movement, a long kiss. An arm appeared from beneath the blankets like some arctic animal sensing the morning air.

"It's too cold, too freezing for a prince and his fair princess. Let the serfs stoke up the fire and bring the tea and pastries. And meanwhile we will..." Yuri could not complete his sentence as a knee intended to push him from the bed caught him between the legs. He howled like a wolf.

"No, no, please don't be angry," Olga pleaded. "It was an accident, I promise. Look, if you're badly injured, I will attend to the stove and you can stay and recover in our cosy bed. Does it hurt a lot?"

Yuri's groans turned to laughter. "Not too much damage to report. Seems the affected part is ready for immediate action."

"Oh no you don't. First you light the fire, make the tea nice and hot and then maybe, just maybe, I'll welcome you again." This time Olga connected more accurately and shoved Yuri out from under the blankets and onto the floor. He gathered his fur coat round his naked body and stomped out to do battle with the *dacha*'s stove.

Olga felt the bed chill from the absent Yuri and longed for the warmth of his return. She wrapped the bedclothes more tightly round her. What a pleasurable night it had been. The rough *dacha* felt more natural, more in touch with the rhythm of her body. The sensuality of her surroundings both relaxed and invigorated her as she lay contented and complete. She regretted she seldom had such a feeling in the artificiality of their Moscow apartment. Out here, the primeval spirit of the land had aroused her in a way the city never could.

She listened as Yuri vigorously raked the stove and then threw in some kindling followed by a few hefty logs. The sound of the fire and the smell of the burning wood worked their way into the bedroom. There was a clattering from the kitchen as the old kettle was filled, followed by a noisy search in the cupboard. She heard Yuri pad into the main room and poke the ashes in the grate. He crumpled pages of *Rossiyskaya Gazeta*, snapped some wood and struck the matches. The fire took with hisses and crackles and then calmed as the larger logs were added. The screeching of the kettle summoned him back to the kitchen.

They cradled each other in the closeness of the bed, alternately kissing and sipping their glasses of steaming tea. Olga snuggled up to Yuri.

"I'm really sorry I got you to invite Fat Alex to join us. We could have had such a good time without him. I just hope he doesn't arrive too early."

"I told him to come to the gate at midday. I expect as usual he'll be late. But whatever time he arrives, we've got to make sure he leaves before supper or he's here for the night."

As befitted the *dacha* for the most junior officials, theirs

76

was the smallest and the closest to the main entrance. They could see the gates and guardhouse and part of the perimeter fence which paralleled the country road. Occasionally a bored soldier from the Interior Ministry Troops would wander out and patrol a short section of fence. His comrade would emerge to open the gates, inspect papers and passes and to salute smartly when senior officials arrived or departed. On a cold, still day such as this, the smoke from the guardhouse stove rose vertically into the air and the Ministry's banner lay limp against the flagpole.

There were several *dacha*s dotted about the estate varying in size and grandeur depending on the seniority of those entitled to use them. The most imposing were partly hidden in an inner compound with their own high fence and guarded gate. A single rough track served all the *dacha*s and linking paths criss-crossed through the trees. Patches of grass acted as makeshift volleyball courts in summer and sites for snow sculptures during the long winter months.

The smallness of the *dacha* did not bother Yuri and Olga. They had managed to book it twice a year and with each visit their fondness for the little house had grown. It had only a small bedroom, kitchen, bathroom and main room and the furniture was sparse and tatty. Inevitably Ministry principles applied. When considered too worn and old, furniture from the senior officials *dacha*s was moved down to the middle officials *dacha*s and then to those for the junior officials. It was accepted that this was the system and there was no sense in complaining. Most of the furniture was serviceable, although the bed and mattress were so well used that they sagged badly in the middle. For the young lovers this was merely another of the *dacha*'s attractions, but for some of the very long serving junior officials, the unaccustomed proximity to their wives was disturbing. Repeat bookings were a rarity for them.

Yuri and Olga were dressed and finished with breakfast

when a fist hammered hard on the door.

"Oh God, not Alex," Olga said with alarm. "It's not even ten thirty!"

Yuri made his way to the window and peered out to see who was there. An old man stood patiently in the cold.

"No, it's only Volodya," he said and went to throw back the bolts. The door fitted poorly and he had to tug hard to get it open.

"Logs. You need logs," Volodya said without greeting.

"Do we? Well… yes, perhaps we do, if you say so. Anyhow good morning to you, Volodya."

Volodya did not answer but pulled his sledge closer to him. There was not much of Volodya to see. He wore a long scruffy coat to his ankles, thick gloves and a pair of army boots. His fur hat was pulled down almost over his eyes with its earflaps sticking out horizontally like the wings of a bird. The only visible part of Volodya was the lower part of his mottled face, ravaged by the vodka and the frost. His stubby greyish brown beard made him difficult to date, but most agreed he must be somewhere between 45 and 70.

No one knew for sure, least of all Volodya himself, just how long he had worked on the Ministry's estate. He had no family and nowhere else to go. After his military service in the estate's guardhouse, he had stayed on as the yard-man and paid a few roubles a month. They had allowed him to build a small log cabin in the forest well away from the *dacha*s and there he lived his life. Twice a year they deloused him and fumigated the cabin but otherwise he was left alone. He had no formal duties, but generally kept the estate tidy. He was usually seen sawing or chopping wood near his cabin or wielding a birch broom or snow shovel on the paths between the *dacha*s.

"I'll fill the log basket so there's more room," Yuri said putting on his coat.

Volodya grunted and bending over his sledge, started to

undo the twine securing the load. He removed the pieces of old sacking over the wood and began to stack the fresh logs in the shed. As he worked, Olga watched from the window. Whilst she knew it was wise not to get too close to Volodya, her heart went out to him. She put the kettle back on the stove.

There were not many logs to unload, but the old man took about fifteen minutes to fill the woodshed. Olga saw him finish and pile the twine and sacking back on the sledge. She found her coat and hat and, grasping the tea, made her way carefully down the steps.

"Here you are, Volodya. A nice glass of tea with plenty of honey." Volodya straightened up from his sledge and stared at Olga in confusion. He turned to see who else might be around, not thinking this offer of hot, sweet tea could be for him. He looked back, bent his head in thanks and quickly took the glass. He drank thirstily, swallowing the welcome liquid before it cooled. Yuri scowled at Olga but made no comment.

"It's a very cold day for early November," Olga said. "I hope the tea has warmed you just a little."

"I thank you, my lady. May God bless you for your kindness."

"Is this early cold a sign it will be a harsh winter, do you think?"

Volodya raised his eyes and looked at the trees and the sky. "Perhaps it will be so. The animals are already busy and making ready. I watch them every day. But only God knows what will come." He shuffled his feet as if embarrassed to be talking to such important people. "I must go. There is much work to do. Many generals are coming to the great *dacha* tomorrow. There will be a big feast and much drinking." His battered face crinkled into a smile. "Maybe there will be some for Volodya if he does his work well."

He stood shakily to attention and saluted Yuri with

79

his gloved hand. "Goodbye sir," he said and then turned and bowed low in front of Olga, "Goodbye my lady, may the Blessed Saints protect you." Picking up his tow rope, Volodya trudged back down the path, his empty sledge zigzagging behind him over the frozen ground.

"Don't be cross, Yuri. He's a poor old man. The least I could do was give him a glass of tea."

"Of course my love. He earned it. Did you hear what he said about all those generals coming here tomorrow? What an opportunity for me, I mean for us, to be noticed. Perhaps we could even get ourselves invited to the party!"

Olga shook her head in disbelief and shivered slightly. "Come on. We need to tidy the place before Fat Alex arrives and I've lunch to prepare."

"Food and drink are important, but tidying is not. Fat Alex simply wouldn't notice whether the place was neat and clean or a complete shambles. Don't waste your time."

They fell silent as they went about their tasks. Olga stayed in the kitchen to make the cabbage soup. Yuri took the beer and vodka outside and buried them deep in the snow to chill. He sorted out the fires and when Olga wasn't looking, he straightened the main room. By noon things were as organised as they could be. Yuri went into the kitchen and kissed Olga passionately. She sighed, whispering how boring it was to have to entertain Fat Alex for the afternoon rather than each other. She went into the bedroom and applied some make-up. They wrapped up in their furs and set off arm in arm to meet their corpulent guest.

The sentry was summoned to unlock the gate and they went out to see if there was any sign of Fat Alex. The road was deserted: no cars, no trucks, no one on foot, only a horse drawn cart moving slowly in the distance. They scanned the snow covered fields towards the village; it was improbable, but Fat Alex might have decided to come cross country. But there was no evidence of human life, just the black shapes of birds circling above the trees. They could hear the distant sound of trains moving in the station.

"Let's go and wait in the guardhouse," Yuri said. "He could be ages. If he's not here by half past, we'll go home. The soldiers can bring him up."

"I think I'll just stay out here in the fresh air," Olga replied.

Yuri didn't demur. The guardhouse was a masculine sort of place and none too fragrant. He was already irritated by the way the soldiers leered at his wife. Olga wandered a little way off and screened herself behind the trees. The sentry escorted him in to see the guard commander.

The small duty room had an old army table and two upright wooden chairs for furniture. A black stove with its long metal chimney filled the room with a suffocating heat and the acrid smell of burning. Standing against the stove, two off-duty soldiers smoked their cheap cigarettes and further choked the air. Yuri took off his hat and undid his coat.

Spread out on the table were passes for visitors and permits for workers on the estate. There was also a sheet of paper headed *Reception* with a long list of names. The sergeant saw Yuri trying to read it upside down.

"You invited, then? Want to see who else is going to be there?"

"No, I'm not going. Not senior enough. But one of my bosses might be."

"Well, no harm in having a look I don't suppose," the sergeant said pushing the paper towards him.

Yuri ran his eyes down the list which, as far as he could determine, was in order of seniority. He saw a number of names he recognised, but the one he was looking for was near the bottom: A.T. Popov, Deputy Director External Department.

"My Deputy Director's on the list. It seems he's going to be the most junior person present."

"Doesn't surprise me. We've been cleaning all our kit and this place for the last three days. Our Colonel General's coming and the regiment's in a real flap. We've got a full inspection at 0900 and we're all on duty all bloody day. Anyone would think the Tsar was turning up…"

The sergeant would no doubt have continued his diatribe had he not glanced out of the guardhouse window and seen a farmer's cart stop outside the main entrance. "Stupid old idiot. They know they're forbidden to block the gates. Sasha, tell him to move it fast or he'll get my bayonet up his arse!"

Yuri sniggered but, looking out of the window himself, was horrified to see a figure emerge from the pile of sacks in the back of the cart. Yuri stuffed his hat back on his head and without doing up his coat, ran out of the guardhouse after the sentry.

"Olga! Olga!" he shouted, "I think he's arrived."

Olga appeared from her hiding place and joined Yuri by the gate. "My God, it is him. Where's he been? He's all covered in straw and sawdust."

Fat Alex resembled a baby elephant as he clambered down from the cart rump first. Once on the ground his unmistakable outline became clear. He started to brush himself off, but gave up. He adjusted his hat and pushed a bundle of notes into the waiting glove of the farmer. Picking up a carrier bag in each hand, he advanced towards the gate.

"My dears, how good of you to come and meet me. The lateness of my arrival is of course something you always manage to anticipate so well. But today the travails of travel kept me from you most inconsiderately. Were it not for this true son of our dear soil, who so generously permitted me to climb aboard his lovely cart, even now I would still be standing at the station at Zavidovo. But here

82

I am. Let me embrace you both."

Fat Alex put his carrier bags down in the road. He wrapped his arms first round Yuri and then for longer round Olga, kissing them both with passion. Perspiring from the effort, he stood back and admired his hosts.

"What a beautiful, handsome pair you are. You should go in for one of these new competitions they're having on television. The best-looking married couple. You would get my vote." Fat Alex laughed, holding up his large, gloved hands like scorecards. He gathered his bags once more and going through the main gate, gave the guardhouse a quizzical inspection.

"So Yuri Pavlevich," he said taking him to one side, "you had better show me the way down to the interrogation cell. I am so looking forward to the strip search and having those electrodes attached to my balls. Quite stimulating, eh?"

Yuri led Alex into the guardhouse to collect his pass. It only took a few minutes, but even in this short time Fat Alex was laughing and joking with the soldiers. They seemed instinctively to warm to him. By the time they left, he had won them over. Yuri was envious, wishing he too had such an engaging personality.

Settling Fat Alex into the *dacha* was no problem since he sat down at the table in the kitchen and stayed there. He made quite a ceremony out of the gifts he had brought, removing them one by one from the carrier bags: caviar, garlic sausage, special vodka and French perfume. In one bag he kept some items concealed, his silk nightshirt, bed socks and toothbrush all bundled in a towel. Yuri and Olga were so delighted with their gifts, it never crossed their minds he would come so well prepared to spend the night.

Fat Alex enjoyed his lunch, especially the cabbage soup of which he had three helpings. He also devoured most of Olga's little meat pies and half a loaf of bread. Yuri topped up his vodka glass continuously and went outside to cool another bottle in the snow.

"Excellent. Quite, quite excellent," Fat Alex exclaimed as the long lunch drew to a close. "Yuri, you are married, you lucky devil, to the finest cook in Muscovy." He rubbed his stomach with satisfaction and turned to Olga. "Will you have pity on a poor soul and teach me how to make all these heavenly dishes? Perhaps I shall come to your apartment one day when your hard working husband is chained to his office desk. We can practise some cooking together and perhaps some other things too."

"You will not," Yuri burst out, his face red from alcohol and anger.

"Calm, calm. Such tempestuous words. Yuri, my good fellow, my good, upright and honest friend... I made a joke, a simple joke. If I offended, I apologise. Never let it be said I was a boorish guest in your house. Were it to be so, throw me out into the snow until I come to my senses."

Olga put her arms round her husband and kissed him. "You boys need to clear your heads. Let's go for a nice relaxing walk in the forest. We should go now before the evening frost."

They left the remnants of lunch on the table and finding their coats and hats set off into the trees. Olga walked in the centre like a referee. She grasped each of them by the arm, providing a physical link to assuage their bad feeling. For a while they walked in silence. Olga and Yuri were exhilarated by the cold, but Fat Alex could only gasp, lighting a cigarette to help his lungs repel the freshness of the air.

"I feel very uncomfortable out of town," Fat Alex coughed. "It's a fear of all this nature which just happens without any human interference. Unnerving it is. My greatest terror is for these forests to get up and invade the cities, planting themselves everywhere and anywhere

84

and making human beings climb up and down their high branches all day and night."

"You should write a short story about it, Alex," Yuri said. "You can use words so well. The publishers would love it."

Olga squeezed Yuri's arm in appreciation. "Yes you should, but you would have to come out into the forest more to do your research."

"That would be impossible," Fat Alex said. "Without the two of you to guide me and protect me – oh God I sound like a priest – I'd be completely lost. Even now these silver birches, these huge firs are eyeing me up and saying, *There's a tasty dish, plenty of flesh on him. Let's try and make him run, he'd roll around all right.*" The three of them roared loudly in the silence of the forest and held each other more tightly for fear Fat Alex's prediction might come true.

"A wonderful fantasy, Alex," Olga said. "But for me this is reality. You may dislike the countryside, but why do you like the city so much?"

"The women of course," Fat Alex said, "they really excite me. And the men, they're delicious too. You just don't see the same kind of beautiful faces and curvy bodies out here in the woods. These peasants are all bound up in their scarves, coats and footcloths. Even if they were attractive, you couldn't see them through all that padding."

"I suppose you've got a very powerful telescope in your apartment to focus on all those city beauties," Olga said.

"Most certainly. I spend hours with my right eye stuck to the lens. Amazing what you get to see, especially in the summer. The only trouble is I've only got the outdoors to spy on. Can I come down to your apartment and try my luck on some of your neighbours?"

"Definitely not, at least not whilst we're living there. If you're so keen, why don't we agree to swap apartments… permanently?"

Fat Alex tensed at the slight change in Olga's voice. The conversation had ceased to be flippant and was now to do with business. He was sharp and alert. "An exchange of apartments, you say. That's an interesting proposal and one you have been contemplating for some time I think, Olga. You chose your moment with care. An Alex who would like to spy on his neighbours when they take their clothes off and suddenly an opportunity to do so. And you have me terrified here in this forest where you are quite ready to abandon me to the trees if I don't consent. Very clever."

"You are perceptive," Olga laughed, anxious not to spoil her chances by appearing too keen. "It's just a suggestion. You need time to consider it. Let's not ruin our walk by discussing it now."

Yuri had remained silent. He knew his wife wanted an apartment with a decent view, but had never dreamt it was Fat Alex's she had her eye on. He had his reservations, since it would need a thorough clean and a week's ventilation. But what worried him more were the demands Alex might make to seal an agreement. One thing he did not want was to owe his portly acquaintance a favour of any sort.

They decided to retrace their steps through the forest. Conversation cooled and for once Fat Alex was silent. With arms still linked, they walked faster, anxious to be back in the *dacha* before the evening darkness fell.

Olga made tea whilst Yuri attended to the fires. Fat Alex lay spread along the sofa like a pasha. Now she had raised the subject of the apartment exchange, Olga was keen to see the back of him. The invitation had served its purpose. She took the glasses of tea into the main room.

"How are you planning to get back to the station, Alex?" she asked. "Yuri has the phone number of a villager with a car. He'll take you down for your train. He doesn't charge much."

They could hear Yuri outside by the woodshed stacking logs in the basket. Fat Alex smirked at Olga.

"My intention was to spend the night in your bed in place of your husband. We could send him out on a wolf hunt. He could borrow a rifle off the soldiers and sit up a tree in an all night ambush. And we, my dearest Olga, could enjoy each other's bodies until the first glimmer of dawn."

Olga was embarrassed, but it troubled her more that the very thought of Fat Alex in the flesh did not revolt her. She shook her head, dismissing his words as a joke.

"No chance. The bed would collapse under your weight. Anyhow, here's Yuri. If he hears any more of your lewd suggestions he might just get that rifle and use it on you instead!" She smiled lovingly at her husband as he struggled through the door with the log basket.

"Yuri, Alex has to get his train. Would you telephone Andrei from the guardhouse and get him to come to the gate in fifteen minutes?"

Yuri, still dressed for the cold, left before Fat Alex could protest. He now seemed content to sprawl on the sofa, slurp his tea and smoke a cigarette. Olga sat on a small peasant stool a safe distance away, relieved he was going. She didn't want worrying thoughts of him to ruin the rest of her weekend.

They could see the lights of the car from the *dacha* and the three of them went down to the gate, Fat Alex clasping his carrier bag with its undisclosed contents.

"It was good to see you, Alex," Yuri said, "and thank you for the gifts. Very generous."

"Yes it certainly was," Olga added as they embraced.

"Well, my dear ones, my charming, generous hosts, it seems I must depart from you with the utmost reluctance. To stay or not to stay is always the question. Tonight it is not to stay, but as far as my beautiful apartment with its magnificent view is concerned, that is a question yet to be answered. About it we will talk further and at length and over a good many bottles of vodka. I love you both from the bottom of my heart. Farewell!"

Listing heavily, Andrei's battered *Zhiguli* careered off down the snow covered road with Fat Alex's arm flapping from the window. They waved back until the car disappeared. Hugging each other, they hurried back to the *dacha*.

Her struggling legs and thrashing arms woke him. He turned to calm her, but she screamed as if the Devil had possessed her soul. She began to weep, gripping Yuri like a she bear.

"Oh darling, it was horrible, horrible. So real, I could see and feel it all. I tried to run but couldn't get away."

"It's all right, it's over, it won't come back. Try and relax." They lay still for some minutes after the frenzy of the dream. Slowly Olga began to breathe more regularly but complained her head ached. Yuri fetched some tablets and a glass of water. Soon she fell into a deep sleep. He lay wondering what had so terrified his precious wife. She hadn't said and he hadn't asked. Maybe in the morning, with the darkness gone, she would remember.

The sound of shouting woke Yuri a second time. He looked at his watch: 8.30 and still dark. He peered more closely at the window. He could just make out a trace of first light. How unusual the morning should be so dark, when only the day before their room had filled with sunlight: all that strange shouting, too, rending the peace of the estate.

Yuri hoped the noise would not wake Olga. She seemed to be undisturbed, breathing deeply and lying very still. He eased himself out of bed.

It was foolish of him not to have remembered the parade. From the window he could make out the dark figures of the soldiers moving by the main entrance. They shovelled and brushed as the sergeant barked his orders, clearing the ground and sweeping out the guardhouse. Low grey clouds moved swiftly on the wind. The smoke from the guardhouse stove and the Ministry's banner were now stretched against the sky. The *dacha* creaked and the windows shuddered. The temperature was rising, the thaw would soon begin.

Keeping as quiet as he could, Yuri lit the fire in the main room and made up the stove. He brewed some tea for himself and settled on the sofa to watch the inspection. The military still interested him, though naturally he avoided conscription. After his reserve officer training, he even considered going for a commission in the Interior Ministry Troops. Perhaps if his present job showed little promise of promotion, he would take another look at a career in uniform.

A junior officer arrived in a jeep and marched briskly about trailed by the sergeant. Not everything was in order or up to standard. More shouting, more soldiers running, more wielding of brooms and shovels. Frantic last minute cleaning and sprucing, worried glances at watches.

The soldiers were shooed into the guardhouse. Ten minutes later they reappeared smartly dressed and carrying rifles. They lined up in their ranks, harried by the sergeant. They stamped their feet on his commands, moving their heads and arms in unison. The officer inspected each man in turn, reaching out to straighten an angled hat, an idle sleeve, a drooping belt.

More orders were shouted as a black staff car swept through the gate. The soldiers jerked to attention. A senior officer got out, acknowledging the salutes. He in turn walked the ranks, pacing slowly with his arms behind his back. Occasionally he said something to the junior officer, who repeated it to the sergeant. An unfortunate soldier was upbraided. The inspection over, the guard was dismissed. The senior officer strutted into the guardhouse.

Yuri heard a sound from the bedroom. The noise of the parade had finally woken Olga. He found her propped against the pillows looking pale.

"Are you all right, my love?" he said taking her in his arms. "Such a bad night. Do you feel rested at all?"

"No, not really. There were no more dreams, but my head still hurts. I'm going to have a shower after you've brought me tea. And then it's a book by the fire till lunch-time."

Yuri didn't ask about the nightmare. Perhaps Olga couldn't remember the details. In any case it was over now. How weird, though, for it to be so violent. In their year of married life, not once had he seen her so disturbed. She normally slept peacefully. She might occasionally murmur or toss and turn, but suffer a nightmare? Never.

They spent a relaxed morning on the sofa in front of the fire. They read and Olga slumbered for minutes at a time. They heard the melting snow drip steadily onto the windowsills. A car drove fast up the estate road. Yuri closed his book.

"I'm just going to get a little fresh air," he said. "I won't go far, just a walk round the *dacha*s." He kissed Olga and saw her smile. Although the snow was fast turning to slush, Yuri still needed his coat, but could dispense with the hat. "After all, they will need to recognise me," he said to himself as he met the cold on the *dacha* steps. He walked off, his hair tousled by the wind.

Yuri spent the next half an hour going up and down the estate road from the main entrance to the largest *dacha*. Every few minutes a car would pass carrying some senior official or officer to the reception. As each one went by, Yuri ensured he was fully visible to the important personage in the back. Once or twice he got too close and slush was spurted from the wheels over his coat and boots. Much to his disappointment, no one paid him the slightest attention.

From the *dacha* window, Olga watched Yuri perform his little ritual. She did love him dearly, but there were times when he was incredibly foolish. Did he actually believe someone was going to stop and invite him to jump in and accompany them to the reception. "There are days when I despair of him," she muttered.

Olga returned to the sofa but could not concentrate on her book. When she awoke, she could recall little of the nightmare. Now the wind in the trees jerked something in her mind and images began to reappear. She shivered as the sensation returned. She saw and felt the branches of the trees envelop her, transforming themselves into repulsive arms which mauled and groped her. Then worst of all, as she tried to break free and run and run, the arms became those of Fat Alex, drawing her ever closer and closer into him.

Olga jumped up and tried to shake the disturbing dream from her head. How she wished Yuri would return to comfort her. But she could not tell him what had frightened her. He would not understand. She walked round and round and waited. Soon she heard footsteps on the path and then boots stamping on the doorstep. Yuri ran in out of breath.

"You will never guess who stopped," he said excitedly, "General Abramtsev, he's a friend of my father. I've met him a couple of times before. He's invited me to the reception as his guest. Can you believe that? And just when I was giving up all hope of getting noticed."

"That's very clever of you," Olga said, making no move towards her husband.

He looked at her, annoyed she was not more enthusiastic about the invitation. "Are you all right? You look as if you've seen a ghost." Yuri caught her as she toppled forward. "I'm so, so sorry, my darling. I shouldn't have left you alone. It's the nightmare, it came back to haunt you, didn't it?"

"Those trees," Olga began to sob. "They were chasing me, just like Fat Alex imagined they would. It's silly really, but so horrible."

"Look, I'll stay here. I don't really need to go. Abramtsev will understand. He invited you too, but I said you weren't feeling well. I can easily get a message to him."

"No, you must go. I'll be fine. Just don't stay too long and don't drink too much." Olga kissed him and released herself from his arms.

By the time Yuri arrived at the reception, the room was already crowded. All the men and women present were quite unknown to him, but without exception they had an awareness of their own importance. The faces of one or two of them were turned in his direction, already flushed from vodka and champagne. They registered curiosity if not irritation that one so young should be amongst them. Yuri was beginning to feel uncomfortable when to his relief General Abramtsev came over to welcome him.

"Glad you decided to come," he said with a smile. "You must find this gathering of your superiors rather daunting. One day, Yuri, you'll enjoy these privileges. But let's get you a drink and find you some people to meet."

The General was as good as his word, leading Yuri round the room and pointing out who was who and introducing him where appropriate. Most conversations were perfunctory, but Yuri felt elated to be in the company of such eminent people. His head was dizzy with the possibility of recognition and advancement.

In one corner of the room Yuri was introduced to two other guests: Deputy Minister Kondrashin and Mr Lokutin, both from the Ministry of Commercial Affairs. As they shook hands, Yuri was aware that someone else had joined them.

"Popov, Deputy Director External Department," he said introducing himself. "Poliakov works in my Internal Section."

"Well, in that case, I will leave him in your capable hands," replied the General, nodding to the other guests. "I'll circulate." As he moved away, Popov closed in on Yuri.

"What the hell do you think you're doing here?" he murmured under his breath. "This reception is for seniors and middle rankers, not for you juniors."

"I was invited by General Abramtsev as his personal guest," Yuri answered. "I'm staying here for the weekend in one of the *dacha*s."

"Are you now? Well, in that case you're off the hook this time, Poliakov. If I'd found you had sneaked in here of your own accord, I would have personally thrown you out on your ear." He smiled unctuously at Kondrashin and Lokutin.

"Tell me, Poliakov," Kondrashin said. "What exactly is your work in the Internal Section?"

"Sir, I keep a record of the movements and activities of all foreigners who are working in our country, other than diplomats. My colleague looks after those whose surnames begin A to L and I am responsible for the remainder."

Kondrashin nodded, liking the logic of the organisation. "We met some foreigners last week, English businessmen they were. One was visiting to see how his comrade's work was progressing." He turned to Lokutin. "What was his name? Carbuncle, wasn't it or something similar?"

"Yes, Deputy Minister, Carbuncle is correct, I believe. The Englishman he came to see was called Standridge. I remember him. I have met him a few times before."

Yuri was taking a sip of champagne and almost choked on Lokutin's words.

"This Standridge is a very busy man," Lokutin added. "He's always going everywhere. He must know our country better than we do. You've got him on your books, haven't you, Poliakov?"

"Yes, of course," Yuri replied. He looked across at Popov

to see if he had registered who this Mr Standridge was.

"You have to be very careful with these foreigners travelling all over the Motherland," Kondrashin said. "There has been a very large increase in their numbers this year it seems. And Poliakov, you need to keep a very close eye on this Standridge. He may seem quiet and reserved, but they are often the ones to watch."

Yuri found it difficult to believe he was hearing this and in front of Popov too. He had recorded all his suspicions in his reports and here was a Deputy Minister strongly supporting everything he had written. He was delighted to see Popov continuing to search for the connection.

"We must have another look at his man," Popov said after some thought. "If he is up to no good, rest assured Deputy Minister we will have the evidence in Poliakov's files."

Yuri decided it was time to leave. So much had been achieved, he didn't want to push his luck. He excused himself and sought out General Abramtsev.

"I'm sorry, but I must get back to Olga. Thank you very much for inviting me."

"Good to see you young man. Give my regards to your father and take care of that wife of yours. Goodbye."

Yuri made his way to their *dacha* and found Olga still curled up on the sofa.

"I wasn't expecting you back so soon. Bad party was it?" she asked.

"On the contrary," Yuri said kneeling down beside her. "It was very useful for work. Pompous old Popov was there, but I think I made a very favourable impression with him and with some of the other senior people. Good promotion prospects all round, I would say."

Olga stroked his face, loving him even more for his innocence.

CHAPTER 8

The office lights dispelled the greyness of the Moscow morning. After his brisk walk through the cold, Peter appreciated the brightness and artificial heating of the building. His face coloured, adjusting to the warmth.

He watched Ruth Rumbelow search through the files in her in-tray. She delved deeper but failed to find what she was looking for. Flustered, she started to rummage in the pending tray. A couple of files slipped off the top of the pile and Peter bent down to retrieve them.

"Oh, thank you," Ruth said. "This is becoming embarrassing. The letter's here somewhere. I can't believe it's being so elusive."

"I'm in no hurry," Peter reassured her. He settled himself more comfortably in the office chair and sipped his coffee. It was so much better than the thin tasteless stuff the hotel produced. One of the pleasures of coming to talk to Ruth was her coffee. The filter machine hissed softly in the corner and he looked forward to a second cup.

It was uncommon to see Ruth disorganised. She was very able and, in Peter's opinion, one of the most efficient members of the Commercial Section. It wasn't exactly *schadenfreude*, but he wasn't displeased to see that even the fastidious Ruth could have moments of disorder.

He looked at her as she leaned over the desk. Mid-thirties was where he put her. She was short and round with a taut, unsmiling face. Despite a good dress sense and paying close attention to her appearance, to Peter's eye she was not attractive. He was glad she had made no attempt to engage him in anything other than his work.

The search for the letter continued and Ruth became

desperate. Strands of hair started to fall across her face and Peter suspected she was close to tears. He wondered whether to assist her, but decided it would be pointless. She would refuse his offer as a matter of principle.

"Ah, at last," Ruth exclaimed, walking round the desk and handing Peter a sealed envelope. He caught the scent of cream soap and perspiration.

The letter was addressed *Personal for Mr Peter Standridge* and stamped *Confidential* in red ink. In case this was insufficient, an additional instruction was printed across the top *To Be Opened By Addressee ONLY.*

Peter slit the envelope and removed the single sheet of paper inside.

> *Dear Peter*
>
> *I want to thank you for all you did to make my recent trip to Moscow so worthwhile and productive. You prepared a very good programme and none of my time was wasted. I now have a much better idea of our business there and how the current projects are progressing.*
>
> *My impression is that the job is going well and you're enjoying it. I'm glad you have agreed to extend your tour until next summer. The appointment and promotion I mentioned is still yours if you want it. No decision yet on where we are going to site the office. Bear with us on that one for the moment.*
>
> *I have also been looking into the matter of your information gathering activities. It is acceptable from the firm's side for you to continue with what you are doing, provided it does not interfere with your work. It appears you have struck the right balance so far. Be careful though. We cannot afford any embarrassments.*
>
> *I am off to Hungary tomorrow, but I'll let you*

know how things develop when I return. Don't
forget to come and see me when you're back in
London over Christmas.
It was good to catch up with you, and thanks
again.
Yours ever
Derek

Peter read the letter a second time before replacing it in the envelope. He was disappointed with Derek's comments on his work: he had hoped for more praise and recognition. But at least the Senior Consultant appointment for Eastern Europe was still on offer. He had already made up his mind to accept it, assuming he hadn't blown his chances.

He was surprised he could carry on with his information gathering as before. Judging by Derek's reaction to his confession at the monastery, he was convinced he would be told to stop and might even receive a reprimand. Although he now had the all clear, he still felt he had not been given a satisfactory explanation. Who had Derek spoken to in the MOD? Had he met the mad Major and what was in it for the firm by allowing him to continue? He felt uncomfortable that these questions remained unanswered.

Peter looked at his watch. "Ruth, I'm sorry but I am due to see Chris Burroughs at ten. Was there anything we needed to talk about today?"

"Nothing that can't wait," Ruth said, rearranging her hair.

"I'll be off then," Peter said, getting up.

"You're not going anywhere with that letter. It's classified Confidential. It came in an outer envelope addressed to me with my letter of thanks from Derek. I've booked it in. You can't just walk out of here with it stuck in your pocket." Ruth had become rather heated. Her pale face ran with streaks of red, her hands trembled as she gripped the pending tray. "Do you understand what I'm saying?

Derek was in the wrong. He shouldn't have included a letter to you in my mail. It's violating the rules for the use of the diplomatic bag. It's abusing the privilege and the protocol. I thought he would have known better."

Peter reeled from Ruth's onslaught. "Look I'm very sorry. I didn't realise the use of the bag was so sensitive. Here, I don't really need to keep the letter any more. Please have it."

"In that case I shall destroy it and you must witness its destruction." Ruth got up and went over to the shredder, feeding the letter into the waiting teeth of the machine. She invited Peter to watch her strike through the entry in the register and initial it.

"Right," she said. "That's that dealt with. Now you can go and see Chris."

The combination of the letter and Ruth's outburst put Peter in a grumpy mood. He slouched along the corridor to Chris Burroughs' office and knocked. James Fortune's name was still on the door and he thought it strange he'd never met him. A cheery "Come in" lifted his spirits.

"Peter my dear good fellow, haven't seen you for ages, thought you might have claimed political asylum," Chris said, finding his own humour amusing. He waved him to his usual chair and tossed him an eraser board. "Good visit from your boss, was it?"

"Yes, it seemed to go pretty well. Can't believe it was almost three weeks ago. Anyhow, I don't expect to see him back here for a while."

Chris Burroughs produced a mug of coffee, which Peter accepted out of courtesy. He wondered how much he knew about Derek's investigations in London. As he was Peter's Moscow contact, it would be unusual for him not to know that questions had been asked. Peter also guessed that Chris would have been informed about his six-month extension in Russia. But he decided to say nothing; he would wait and see if Chris himself raised either of these matters.

They sipped their coffees and the routine exchange of information on the eraser boards commenced. Chris asked the predictable question: *Where and when next?* Peter wrote: *Stambov, Wednesday for 2 days*, Chris: *Where the hell's that?* and Peter concluded: *God knows!*

Chris laughed and to prolong the joke, went to his cabinet. He pulled out a large atlas of the former Soviet Union, opening it on the town index page. Humming to himself he ran his finger down the list of towns until he found Stambov. He flicked through the pages to the area map.

"Charming little place, middle of nowhere, probably dead boring," he said and slammed the atlas shut. "More coffee?"

"No thanks. I had a cup with Ruth just now." Peter cleared his board and wrote: *Anything special in Stambov?*

Chris Burroughs shook his head. He scribbled: *Just eyes and ears as usual. Americans call it a dirtbag town. Enjoy.* He held up his board and chuckled.

Stambov did indeed turn out to be a different kind of town. Peter wondered why the officials in Moscow had wanted him to go there. He knew there was some scope and money in the Handsome Fund for looking at the infrastructure of some of the smaller towns. Even so there were many larger and more important projects which required his expertise and immediate attention.

For all its adverse publicity, Stambov had the charm of a traditional provincial town. There were new industries and some gross architectural additions, yet there remained a feeling and atmosphere so well described by the great 19th-century novelists. It was a sense of the true Russia untainted by foreign influence, hard yet warm, dull yet full of soul. The air smelled of fields and woods not streets and houses, as if the soil was reluctant to yield to structures of brick and stone. It was proud and introspective, content with the settled rhythm of its life.

To his surprise and satisfaction, Peter also found a rare enthusiasm for his advice amongst the local officials. They seemed genuinely interested in his suggestions, impressed by what could be achieved at not too great a cost. He became excited about the possibilities for this little town. The meetings and site visits began to overrun. It seemed in Stambov, time was only of passing interest.

The hotel in the town centre was a disappointment. It was a new, six storey block of steel and concrete. Regimented windows all precisely aligned top to bottom and left to right gave the building a penitentiary look. Peter suspected his room was furnished exactly the same as all the others, right down to the missing bath plug. In keeping with the rest of the hotel, the restaurant food was dire.

It was not an unusually cold evening for mid-November in Stambov, but Peter was well wrapped up for his short walk. The pavements were clear but piles of grey-streaked snow were stacked against the kerbs awaiting the collection trucks. Peter held the symbolic town plan in his hand and navigated his way down a couple of streets until he found the restaurant. The interpreter had recommended it, even volunteering to accompany him, provided Peter paid. His offer was politely declined and a reservation for one confirmed.

It was quite early and the restaurant half full. Peter was the only person dining alone and he tried to ignore the looks cast in his direction. Further interest was shown as he tried to make the waiter understand his order. Feeling more conspicuous than usual, he perversely wished for the anonymity of the hotel restaurants he normally frequented. He removed a copy of *Anna Karenina* from his coat pocket and started to read.

"Please excuse my interruption, but for me it was not possible to be deaf to your conversation with the waiter. You are of course from the West and from Britain, I believe."

Peter looked up from his book. A tall, spare man showing signs of middle age stood beside his table. He was dressed in a dark blue suit and wore a rose in his buttonhole.

"Yes I am English. I am afraid my Russian is not very good. It was my fault the waiter could not understand."

"And I, I am from Hamburg. You must forgive me for my English as the Russians do for my Russian." The man smiled. "I am sorry to see you as a foreigner in this town having your dinner with yourself. Will you make me the honour of accepting my invitation to join me and my companion at our table? Today it is my birthday. My fortieth one, to be precise."

Peter was taken aback by such unexpected hospitality, but was grateful for a chance to avoid the continuing stares of the Russians.

"That's very good of you, and congratulations on your birthday. Are you sure I'll not be intruding on the evening for you and your friend?"

"Of course not. It will be our pleasure."

Peter got up and followed the man from Hamburg to his table. He signalled to a waiter, speaking to him quickly in Russian. The waiter nodded and as if scenting a healthy tip, hurried to rearrange the place settings.

Seated at the table was a handsome woman some years younger than the man. Where he was slim and neat, she was full and sumptuous. She wore a shimmering dress and dazzling necklace. Her make up was thickly and theatrically applied.

"Permit me to introduce my friend. This is Lydia Kuznetsova." The man pronounced her name with reverence and glanced at Peter for some reaction.

"I am delighted to meet you," Peter said, shaking her outstretched hand. "It's very kind of you both to ask me to join you, especially as you are having a private birthday celebration."

"Is pleasing, much pleasing for us," she said, her voice deep and sonorous. She smiled and lowered her eyelids. "And what they call you?"

"Oh, forgive me. My name is Peter Standridge." The man came between them and clasped Peter's hand.

"And I," he said, "I am Herr Rudolf Metzinger."

Peter and Herr Metzinger took their places at the table. They all discussed the menu in English and Russian with Herr Metzinger acting as translator. A decanter of vodka was brought for the *zakuski*. A bottle of sweet Russian champagne was opened to much acclaim. They drank to each other's health and to Herr Metzinger's fortieth birthday.

Dishes and courses came and went. The vodka decanter was sent away for a refill. Another bottle of champagne arrived.

"And so, Herr Standridge, why do you come to Stambov?" Metzinger asked.

Peter explained as best he could. They nodded, looked puzzled, but unanimously drank to the future prosperity of the little town.

"Music is our business," said Herr Metzinger proudly. "I am a percussionist with a speciality in the glockenspiel. My companion's a violinist. In March she will perform in Moscow at the University. A very difficult piece. You must come Mr Standridge."

"I should like to very much."

"You have heard of her of course. She is very famous."

Lydia Kuznetsova looked coy, but soon recovered. She beamed, waiting for the expected words of adulation.

"Um, I regret most profoundly my ignorance of good music and knowledge of the world's finest performers," Peter said emboldened by the champagne and vodka. "But I am delighted to say that I consider Lydia Kuznetsova to be one of the most brilliant players of the violin this century."

"Bravo," Herr Metzinger shouted, raising his glass to the restaurant. "Herr Standridge, you speak the truth. You do not know the ignorance of the critics in this country. They are mules and monkeys, quite unable to recognise talent when it is playing right in front of their ears."

Lydia Kuznetsova continued to smile her seductive smile. Her face flared and glistened, her make-up forming a perfect mask. "You good, you lovely," she slurred. She thought to raise her glass too, but overtaken by emotion, she stood, swayed and kissed first Herr Metzinger and then Herr Standridge. Peter felt the sweetness of her face paint, the stickiness of her lips.

It was obvious to everyone in the restaurant, who had not drunk as much as those on Herr Metzinger's table, that stupid things were now being said and done. They enjoyed the show, awaiting some further indiscretion or disaster.

Lydia Kuznetsova re-seated herself and beamed at Peter. He smiled and tried to avoid her eyes without causing offence. Herr Metzinger inspected his *plombir* with apprehension. "Why do I become an ice cream? Such desserts make me sad," he announced solemnly.

"Let me cheer you up then. I will buy some more champagne for your birthday," Peter said. His head was thick and heavy, his voice distant and distorted. Metzinger did not respond but focused on his watch.

"We must go soon. You, Herr Standridge, must come with us. We attend a party at our Institute. There you can buy champagne, much more champagne."

Peter wanted to make excuses and return to the hotel. He assembled the words in about the right order in his brain but then failed to locate them. Instead he blurted out, "Zounds good to me" and feared he would be sick.

Somehow the bill was requested by Herr Metzinger whilst Lydia Kuznetsova edged closer to Peter and stroked his thigh. Metzinger got himself in a tangle with his money, spilling notes onto the table, a few fluttering to the floor. In his confusion, the tip was evidently over-generous, for the waiters found their coats, escorted them out of the door and into a waiting taxi.

Peter rode in the front. The two friends sat in the back snuggling and bickering in melodic Russian. The driver grinned at Peter and turned the radio up. He drove fast with one hand on the wheel while beating the other on the dashboard in time to the music.

It did not take long to reach the Institute. As they struggled out of the taxi, Peter realized he had absolutely no idea where he was. Metzinger and Kuznetsova leaned on each other and mounted the steps. Peter paid off the driver and followed, invigorated by the cold air.

A concert room had been taken over for the party. It was brightly lit and tables and chairs were grouped at the end nearest the entrance. A temporary bar had been set up in one corner, its white cloth covered in bottles and glasses. At the far end a band was assembled on a raised platform with an area for dancing below. Attempts had been made to decorate the room with balloons and streamers, but several had already come adrift. Some hung loosely from the ceiling, others shimmied across the floor.

"You wonder, Herr Standridge, for why we have this party," Herr Metzinger enquired. "It is a dance for the Faculty of Music at the Institute. It happens each year at this time. They call it The Rite of Autumn. You understand the joke?"

"Naturally," Peter replied, unwittingly sending Herr Metzinger into yet more peels of laughter. He quickly recovered and translated for Lydia Kuznetsova, who smiled and looked at Peter approvingly.

At the bar Peter bought some champagne and mineral water. They found a small unoccupied table close to the dance floor. The room became busier.

Peter opened the champagne and toasted the hospitality

of his new-found friends. He studied them as they surveyed the other tables to see who was sitting with whom. Herr Metzinger was not in good shape and slouched with fatigue and drink. Lydia Kuznetsova sat with poise and continued to glow. There was no doubt in Peter's fuddled mind that she had come to enjoy herself.

The band crashed into life with a cacophony of sound. Even to Peter's untrained ear, they were playing wildly out of tune, but no one seemed to care. Soon the dance area was dangerously overfull. How ironic he thought that a Music Faculty were able to hire such an appalling band.

Lydia Kuznetsova stood up and like a ship's figurehead sailed onto the dance floor to join the throng. It wasn't obvious to Peter whether she had intended to take Herr Metzinger with her or not. Perhaps she had somehow forgotten him. He remained bent forward over the table, taking occasional sips of champagne.

"Call me Rudolf, you must always and forever call me Rudolf." Herr Metzinger fixed his reddened eyes on Peter. "Forty years… forty years… it's not right to be here in the Motherland and not in the Fatherland for such a birthday. And you, Herr Sandwich, how many years have you seen? You are so young. You make me cry for my youth."

Peter was unsure whether he should admit to his paltry twenty-six. He was on the point of doing so when Lydia Kuznetsova reappeared and pulled Rudolf onto the dance floor.

The band was playing furiously. The dancers responded by gyrating in a frenzy, flailing arms and legs and contorting to the rhythm. Once or twice Peter caught sight of his companions; Rudolf jerking and shaking like a skeleton, Lydia rotating with grace and ease. One moment they were together, the next far apart, bobbing back and forth like puppets on a stage.

They returned to their table out of breath and Peter topped up their glasses. Rudolf collapsed into his chair,

Lydia remained standing. There was no respite from the music as the band tore into another frantic number.

"Dance. You dance with me," Lydia ordered, grabbing Peter by the hand. Others parted to let them in. They reeled and writhed to the thudding beat. Peter felt better for the movement, though his head resounded to a pulse of its own. At last the band relented, playing a slow, melancholic tune. Couples moved together, humming the well known melody.

Peter believed he had done his duty dance with Lydia and made a move towards their table. She blocked the way and came towards him, enveloping him in her arms. She started to sway to the music. Peter shuffled his feet to follow her steps, holding her loosely. Lydia subtly adjusted her arms, sliding them beneath his jacket. Peter felt her hands run up and down his spine as if over the strings of her violin. Whose exquisite notes were being indented by those delicate, darting fingers? Was it Beethoven or Tchaikovsky she was playing? He was irresistibly excited by the thought, clasping her more tightly. Lydia sensed his arousal and pressed him closer in the slow rotation of the dance. She laid her cheek against his. He breathed the richness of her body.

"Is good, is very good," she whispered in his ear.

The music stopped. They drew apart, touching only hands. They found Rudolf slumped across their table.

"Rudi, Rudi!" Lydia called. Rudolf stirred but did not raise his head. She gently poured a glass of mineral water over his face and down his neck. He started, angrily wiping the water off him. He swore – first in German, then in Russian.

"Please, you help," Lydia said, turning to Peter. Between them they managed to get Rudolf to his feet. They each took an arm and supported him out of the hall.

"Sleep for him now," Lydia puffed. Peter tried to take most of Rudolf's weight as they descended the steps and crossed the road to the apartment block. A stationary police car watched their progress from a distance. They entered the building and propped Rudolf in the corner of the lift as they ascended to the fourth floor. Lydia took a key from Rudolf's pocket and unlocked his apartment door.

Rudolf was laid on his bed like a corpse. Lydia undressed him, hiding his nakedness under the blankets. Rudolf briefly opened his eyes, said "Bugger off, English," and fell to snoring loudly. They closed the door on him.

On the main road they found a taxi. They eased themselves into the cramped back seat. Instructions were given to the driver. The taxi sped off and Lydia threw herself on Peter with the ferocity of a Siberian tigress. She wrestled him flat on the back seat and drove her hands through his clothes. He felt those fingers again, now racing over his skin prestissimo.

"*Nyet, nyet,*" he said as he succumbed to the pleasure of her touch.

"*Da, da,*" she gasped and clamped her lips hard on Peter's mouth. The taxi careered over cobbles and pot-holes, dislodging Lydia's mouth from his. He felt her lips bounce on his cheeks, eyes, and nose before finding his mouth again. Peter tasted her desire. He ran his hands over her, enjoying the tightness of her well-tuned body. His excitement was unbounded.

The taxi swerved and came to a shuddering halt. Lydia lifted herself off Peter and adjusted her dress and hair. He could see her profile against the lights of the residential block. He wondered which apartment was hers.

"I come with you now?" he asked slowly.

Lydia leaned across and kissed him. "Not good come in my house. Husband kill you." She ran her hand across her throat and made a gurgling sound. "I go now. You... beautiful boy." She kissed him again. "*Spokoyny nochy.*"

"*Spokoyny nochy.* Good night."

He watched her as she walked towards the front entrance. She didn't turn to summon him. She opened the swing door and disappeared from view.

CHAPTER 9

It was snowing heavily on Moscow. Peter lay on his bed in Hotel Leskov looking at the ceiling. The external whiteness paled his room, revealing magnolia brush strokes on the painted plaster in all their imperfection. There was an unusual silence as the deepening snow smothered all sight and sound of the bustling city.

Snow had lost its attraction. Peter's childlike enthusiasm to stand under falling snowflakes or crunch over crusted powder had waned. Snow was now an inconvenience, a nuisance which interfered with plans and a busy schedule. He dreaded the delays at airports and stations, the extra night or two in some uncomfortable provincial hotel. The resignation of the Russians to the caprice of nature only annoyed him more.

Saturday was a good day for a snowstorm, if there ever was a good day. It meant some restriction on what he did, but at least he was not about to set off to some distant town. He understood from the television forecast that the blizzard would continue until late evening. A bright weather sign was shown for Sunday but also a daytime temperature of Minus 12. He wondered idly if it was also snowing in Stambov.

Since leaving the little town just over a week ago, Peter had been unable to get Lydia Kuznetsova out of his head. Her image appeared each morning when he woke and danced around him until he slept. Even then his night-time dreams were seldom without her and memory played its tricks. Where she had been merely handsome, she was now beautiful, where rounded, now sensual and where playful, now serious.

His obsession disturbed him. He found he was weaving a fantasy, a fairy story of a Russian princess searching for her English prince in the deep, cold snow. She was going to be waiting to surprise him with a long mystical embrace: perhaps in the woods, on the corner of a street, on the Number 2 tram, or best of all here, in his very own bed.

"My God, this is ridiculous," Peter exclaimed and rolled off his blankets. He stared out of the window at the swirling snow. The Kremlin walls had become a frosted mirage. He knew they were there and was convinced he could see them; but he looked again and they were gone. The glorious churches too had disappeared, their golden cupolas mantled by the settling snow. An unseen hand had drawn a white shroud across the familiar scene of brick and stone.

Peter pondered the long winter ahead. He doubted he had made the right decision by agreeing to extend. Had he not done so, he would be going back to England in a few weeks time, unlikely to return. Perhaps that was the better option with hindsight. But he had committed himself to staying and it was now too late to change his mind. He had to make the best of it, snow and all.

The mystical figure of Lydia Kuznetsova appeared in front of him. He kissed the air as if her lips were there and ran his hands over the outline of her imaginary body. Would he ever hold her again? Of course he would go to her concert and hear her play. But it would be a torment to see and listen and know he could not touch. He would watch her darting fingers press the strings of her violin and sense them on his skin.

He would go further: he would arrange to see her after the performance. But what if she did not recognise or remember him? She had to feel something after the way they had kissed; desire, surely, would still be there. And Rudolf, lucky old Rudolf, he'd see him too, he'd get him drunk again and lock him in a cupboard. Now it would be his turn, yes Peter's turn, to slide into bed alongside the lovely Lydia.

The telephone rang, making Peter jump. Could it really be Lydia wanting to say how much she loved him and would he fly to Stambov this very moment? Then he remembered it was Saturday. It must be the *Hooligany* confirming the arrangements for the evening. He lifted the receiver.

"Hello?" There was no answer. "Hello?"

"Krotkin speaking. Is that Mr Standridge?" The line crackled but the voice was unmistakable. Peter was taken aback. Somehow he had completely forgotten about the professor.

"Yes, it is."

"I hope you are well, Mr Standridge."

"Yes, I am. Thank you. And how are you?"

"I too am well. Can you hear me correctly? This connection is making some noises."

"Yes I can, but it's a bad line. You must be phoning from a long way away."

"No, I am in your hotel lobby. I have come to see you, Mr Standridge."

Peter was still in his dressing gown. He hadn't intended to see anyone, at least not before lunch. He glanced at his watch. It was 10.45.

"I can't see you straight away. I'm not ready, I'll be about fifteen minutes. Is that alright?"

"It's no problem. I shall wait for you in hotel café."

Peter made for the shower. How damn inconsiderate of Krotkin. He must have known he was coming to Moscow at least a day ahead. Why hadn't he phoned in advance? He did seem to keep turning up like a bad *kopek*.

The so-called café in the hotel was an extension of the bar area, but some attempt had been made to give it a Parisian feel. It seemed a little incongruous with the snow piling up on the pavements outside, but the atmosphere was cosy enough. Peter saw Krotkin immediately. He was

111

sitting at a corner table reading a newspaper.

"Hello, Professor Krotkin," Peter said in greeting. "You've not chosen a very good day to come to Moscow with all this snow."

"Mr Standridge," Krotkin replied, getting painfully out of the little bistro chair. "It's a great pleasure to see you again. But I came to Moscow two days ago, so the snow has not affected my travelling. Please, have a seat."

Krotkin nodded to a waiter. Peter asked for coffee and a pastry, Krotkin ordered tea.

"You have been making your journeys again, Mr Standridge?"

"Yes, I've been quite busy. It's the nature of my work."

"And where were you for the last time?"

"Oh, I just went to a little town called Stambov. Do you know it?"

"I have, of course, heard of it, but no, I have never been there. Did you like Stambov at all?"

It was fortunate the waiter returned at that moment, placing the tea, coffee and pastry on the table. Peter had time to consider his reply.

"Yes, it was a pleasant and very hospitable little town." He imagined the wraith-like Lydia slip into the chair beside him and place her hand on his knee. He caught the perfume of a passer-by and believed it was hers. The sensation was real enough for him to reach out and pull the vacant chair closer to him. No one could sit there now. Krotkin noisily tried his tea.

"Soon you must be leaving us for England, Mr Standridge. I remember when first we met on that long train journey, you said you were in Russia for six months only. It must be close to your time to go, am I not right?"

"Yes, you are indeed right. You have a very good memory. Certainly I shall go to England in about a month's time for Christmas and the New Year. There is a possibility that I might come back to Moscow again after that." Peter realized he may have said too much, but Krotkin seemed indifferent to the news.

"You will always be welcome here as a friend of my great country," he said. "You must tell your friends in England to come here too. They must see Russia for themselves."

Peter had missed breakfast and ate his stale pastry with haste. The coffee was up to its usual insipid standard. He noticed Krotkin was waiting for him to continue the conversation.

"Have you come to Moscow on business?" he asked, wiping his mouth.

"Yes, there are always things I must do here. But also I come to see my friends and to speak with them." Krotkin leaned closer. "And you, Mr Standridge... you are now one of my friends."

"I feel honoured," Peter said, slightly bowing his head. No, he was definitely not one of Krotkin's friends. He knew that and despised him for saying it. Krotkin would not contact him without a better reason than spurious friendship.

"Would you like another coffee, Mr Standridge? I shall have some more tea."

"No, thank you. I'm fine for now." Krotkin ordered his tea. When it arrived, he made a ceremony out of adding the sugar and stirring it thoroughly.

"Mr Standridge, I have from you a small favour to ask," he said, adopting an unconvincing pose of supplication and slight embarrassment. "I know now that you will go to England soon. Could I request you take a gift to a good friend of mine in London?"

"But I don't live in London."

"Your aeroplane lands there, does it not?"

Peter was stunned by Krotkin's logic. "Yes, of course, I shall pass through London. If I can, I will take a gift for you, provided it's not too large."

Krotkin seemed delighted by Peter's response. "No, no

it is not large at all, just very delicate. That is why I could not post it. In any case, too many parcels disappear within our system." Krotkin bent down, picked up his briefcase and laid it across his knees. He opened it, taking out a small package wrapped in brown paper. "This is not the gift. The gift is not quite ready yet, so I could not bring it today. But it is like this one." Krotkin returned his briefcase to the side of his chair, laying the package on the table. They both stared at it in silence.

"Aren't you going to open it?" Peter asked.

Krotkin showed surprise at Peter's bluntness. "If that is your wish," he answered after a short pause. He undid the wrapping and removed a small painting from the soft tissue paper inside. He held it up for Peter to see. "An icon, Mr Standridge, an icon. Not an old one of course, they are too valuable and must stay in Russia. They belong here, this is their home. But this painting copies the old style. It was done by a friend who is an icon painter by profession. Beautiful, do you not agree?"

Peter had not expected anything like this. A painted wooden *Palekh* box or piece of blue and white *Gzhel* porcelain perhaps, but not an icon.

"It's exceptional, it really is," Peter said. His eyes took in the dazzling colours, the richness of the paint, the gold frame. It was one of the most exquisite works of art he had ever seen. "It must be as good as the original," he said.

"I am very much pleased that you like it. But it is my friend's composition. There is no original for this painting. It's a pastiche. He likes to paint angels and saints in the old way. As you can see, this one is an angel."

Peter studied the painting more closely. As he did so, he found the serene features of the figure became those of Lydia. How little change was necessary for this transformation. He wanted to dispel the image of her, but the more he looked, the more she was there. He tried to hide his emotion but turned away, blinking back a tear.

"I see you feel for the painting very much," Krotkin said softly. "Now perhaps you will forgive me for asking you to take an object as beautiful as this to London. It cannot go any way except in the hand of a trusted friend."

Peter recovered as best he could. "I'll be leaving Moscow on the 20th December. Try and deliver it to me a day or two before."

"Of course," Krotkin said, folding the icon back into the wrapping paper. "And next time I will give you more warning of my arrival."

They stood up, shook hands and said brief goodbyes. Krotkin put on his thick coat and fur hat and limped out into the blizzard. Peter went to the bar and ordered a large vodka.

The hotel was particularly quiet for a Saturday. Peter assumed the storm had marooned people in their flats, believing no one would bother to emerge without good reason. Most of the foreigners who lived in the hotel also seemed to be away. They heard the snow was coming and made their escape on Friday afternoon flights. Peter sipped his vodka, leaned back in his chair and had a moment of introspection.

His life, he decided, was going well. He hadn't planned or mapped out his progress in the same detail as most of his colleagues. They were always anxious to be doing a specific job at a certain stage in their careers. He knew they couldn't understand his relaxed attitude to promotion, even resenting his easy-going approach. He simply didn't share their priorities, that was all.

On occasions they had tried to take him in hand. *"You've got to do this Peter. It may be the most tedious grind in the most God awful place, but it will really help you get ahead. If you do it well, you'll be sure to catch the selector's eye and you'll be on your way."*

Peter accepted that for a number of his colleagues, this strategy had been successful. Only slightly older than him, they were already holding down much more important jobs. He also knew that for others, the plan had failed. Despite their best efforts, they had been passed over for promotion. For his part he was comfortable steering a middle course and taking what came his way. Such limited aspiration suited his temperament better.

His appointment in Russia was indeed regarded by some as a poisoned chalice. It was too risky and too much out on a limb. But it had worked very much in his favour. It would be interesting to hear their reaction to the announcement of his own promotion to Senior Consultant Eastern Europe. They would be dumbstruck.

Peter felt the experience of living and working abroad had made him more self-reliant. He suspected his parents and friends back in England would notice quite a change in him. And what about Deirdre? Would he want to take up with her again? They had mutually agreed to stay apart whilst he was here. Now, though, there was his extension for a further six months, which neither could have foreseen.

He should meet up with her over the New Year. He was still fond of her and they had shared much together. But her simple niceness could never compete with the exotic sensuality of someone like Lydia. In those brief moments in Stambov, she had aroused a latent passion in him. It could not be extinguished easily, nor could his feelings revert to those of his hesitant youth. Lydia had stripped him open and released the inner man.

Peter nodded to an acquaintance who looked into the bar, smiled and left. He was tempted to order another vodka. The first one had made him feel good, but a second would have the opposite effect and spell disaster. It would be too easy to mope around the hotel all day. He needed to get out, regardless of the snow. A little lunch and shopping on the Arbat was the answer. Hadn't he presents to buy for Christmas? Better to do so now rather than rush around at the last minute. If he had learned anything during his time in the Motherland, it was to get things whilst you could.

The hotel might have been quiet, but the Arbat was as busy as ever. Peter expected to have the street to himself but it was full of snow-covered figures bundling in and out of shops and cafés. There was a festive air about the place. Lights remained on, street sellers were calling from their decorated stalls and the smell of roasting nuts and grilled lamb *shashlik* filled the air. People laughed in the snow, rejoicing in a real winter's day.

Peter visited several shops and despite the scrum of people, managed to buy some useful gifts. He was unsure who was going to get what, but at least everything he purchased was genuine Russian and would be appreciated for that. The cold and effort of shopping made him hungry, though. He sought out Café Vostok whose light meals were good and cheap. He perched on a high stool by the window and had some *borsch* and doughy *pelmeni*. Once revived, he set off into the snow again. He had saved the best for last.

Knizhni Magazin Stolitsa was quiet and calm. An attendant brushed the worst of the snow off the shoppers as they came through the door. They were also encouraged to shake their fur hats vigorously and to stamp their feet on the matting to remove the snow from their boots. Once presentable, they were admitted through an inner door into the hush of the bookshop proper.

It was probably the best in the whole of Moscow. It had a comprehensive stock and excellent foreign language sections. A couple of the staff spoke good English and unlike assistants in other shops, they were knowledgeable and helpful. But this Saturday Peter needed no guidance. He made his way directly to the Fine Art Section.

There were several books on icons printed in English. Some were lavish with glittering reproductions, others more modest. He took a large, expensive edition from the shelf. He turned the pages, concentrating on the delicate portraits. Lydia had to be exorcised; he couldn't allow her image to distort and disfigure the beauty of these paintings. He looked into the faces of the Madonna and the angels. They wavered before his eyes, their features became unsteady. They must not change. He continued to stare at them intently: they gazed back unaltered. Peter smiled, carefully closed the book and replaced it on the shelf. Lydia couldn't presume to be an angel. She had to remain her ravishing, earthly self.

He was confident he had won his little battle, but needed to maintain his superiority. He searched the shelves and was particularly taken by one book. Although its illustrations were not the best, it did have an excellent historical summary and description of the techniques used by the icon painters. It would give him sufficient knowledge to discuss icons with Krotkin the next time they met. He decided to buy it as a Christmas present to himself.

"I didn't know you were into Russian Art," a voice laughed behind him. Peter spun round and came face to face with Chris Burroughs.

"I didn't know you were either," he countered.

"I'm not. I spied you across from the travel and sports sections despite the disguise of your winter clothing." He laughed too loudly for the bookshop and heads were turned in their direction.

"What are you looking for then?" Peter asked.

"Nothing in particular. Just nosing about. I see you've been spending your salary in advance," he added, glancing at Peter's carrier bag of parcels.

"It seemed a good day to get the Christmas presents, that's all. As you probably know, I'm going back to England for Christmas and the New Year."

"And never to be seen here again," he said grinning. Peter was unsure how to reply. Had Chris not heard about his extension? He decided to hint at the possibility of returning, without revealing too much.

"You never know, I may come back sooner rather than later."

"Yes, I had picked up something about you staying on. Not general knowledge, I assume." Peter felt Chris was being a little reckless discussing such matters in a public place. He was also surprised Chris clearly knew more about his official work than he had expected.

"No. Even those in Head Office have yet to be informed," Peter said with irritation.

Chris moved closer to Peter. "Well, I'm very glad you're going to be around for a while longer. You're becoming, how shall I put it, indispensable to us." He coughed and said more covertly, "Good time in Stambov was it? These little places are often full of interest."

Peter fought to keep Lydia out of his mind. He needed to sound convincing. "Nothing unusual. Hardly seemed worth coming to see you."

"Even so, you ought to pop in. Try next week. I'm going to be away a bit after that."

"I'll do my best, provided the snow's not too deep."

Chris laughed. "They'll have the roads cleared by tomorrow. Work all through the night they will. But it's a shame it's come today. Jean and I had great plans for our weekend. All been cancelled. How about you?"

"I'd arranged nothing special. Most of the Westerners in my hotel have fled the snow."

"Look, if you're at a loose end this evening, come round for supper. Don't know what you'll get as Mrs B doesn't know I'm inviting you." Chris again laughed too loudly.

"Well that's kind," Peter said. "I'd like to very much."

"You know where we are. Kutz, Block B, Flat 38 in case you've forgotten. See you at 7.30."

With a grin he placed his hat back on his head, gave half a wave and set off for the main door. He hadn't bought a single book.

The bookshop was too absorbing to leave. Peter walked round the other sections and hoped no one else was going to interrupt him. He looked at a number of books, but kept thinking about Chris Burroughs. He still didn't know what to make of him. He always gave the impression of being something of a comedian with his constant jokes and laughter. Nothing wrong with that of course. But Peter saw it more as a kind of disguise, a pleasing front for a scheming mind. He didn't dislike him but he didn't trust him either. As Chris had such a hold over him through his unofficial duties, Peter needed to keep on the right side of him.

The broad Kutuzovski Prospect stretched out westwards from the city, straight as a ruler. Echelonned apartment blocks lined each side of this great boulevard, standing square and solid on the edge of the city proper. One of the small group of blocks, set in its own compound, was reserved for foreigners.

Peter got off the trolleybus. The snow was lighter and the visibility better, but he became disorientated once inside the foreigners' quarter. All the blocks looked identical and it was impossible to read the identifying letters, especially in the dark. He blundered around, approaching two blocks in error before finding the entrance to Block B.

Peter received a jovial welcome from the Burroughs. Their accommodation was not generous but Jean was obviously a tidy person. She was proud that she managed to take 'home' with them wherever they went in the world. The apartment had the feel of a semi-detached in suburbia. It was as if Russia stopped at her front door and England took over: glass vases on the sideboard, porcelain birds on the shelves, signed prints of Bexleyheath on the walls. Past copies of *Good Housekeeping* and *Home and Garden* were arranged neatly on the coffee table. There was no sign of anything Russian in the apartment at all.

Peter settled himself in an armchair and through the doorway could see the dining table laid for four. Chris brought him a beer in a pewter tankard.

"We've asked Ruth to join us. Like you, she seemed to have little planned for the weekend. After supper I thought we could have a game of cards. Something simple, whist or rummy. You do play, don't you?"

"Sufficiently badly to make it worth your while," Peter quipped. Chris as usual roared.

Peter stood up as Ruth entered the apartment, removing her thick coat and revealing an attractive dress. She apologised for her lateness, but gave no excuse. The thought that she had spent too long preparing herself crossed Peter's mind. She was well presented as usual, her hair falling into place as she took off her hat, her make-up patiently applied. He remembered the smell of her cream soap as he kissed her politely on both cheeks.

Jean's supper of shepherds pie was bland and filling, the conversation slow but easy. Chris kept Peter and himself supplied with beer and topped up the ladies' glasses with Valpolicella, Ruth's more frequently than Jean's.

Peter sat opposite Ruth. He acknowledged his judgement might be impaired by the beer, but he was sure Ruth was behaving out of character. She held his eyes one second longer when she spoke to him, she mouthed her words with a hint of flirtation and she stretched her short legs under the table to make contact with his. Away from work, the organised and efficient Commercial Secretary was clearly a more exciting woman than he had imagined.

The card table was set up in the main room. Peter and Ruth were again seated opposite each other and Ruth's legs continued to explore under the table. At one point she obviously discovered the ankles of Chris Burroughs, who jerked back in his chair as if bitten by a snake. The inevitable embarrassment and apology followed.

"You're not having much luck this evening are you

Ruth," Jean said. "That's the third bad hand you've had in a row."

Ruth glared at her. "No, Lady Luck doesn't seem to be smiling on me."

"Nor on me," Peter said. "Chris, you seem to be the only one who's winning consistently. It hasn't got anything to do with your having the name Fortune on your office door, has it?"

There was a slight pause and a darting glance from Ruth.

Chris laughed. "Nice idea, but no." He paused for a moment. "It's rather sad actually. James Fortune was my predecessor, but was taken seriously ill and had to be flown back to England. That was over six months ago. I came in on a temporary basis to cover for him. James is getting better and we all hope he'll be fit enough to return. To help in his recovery and to encourage him back, I kept his nameplate on the office door."

"I'm sorry to hear about his illness. At least now I know why I haven't met him," Peter said.

The card games continued until midnight without much enthusiasm. Ruth announced she ought to go and Peter did likewise. Chris took him to one side.

"Don't talk about James Fortune, will you. It's still upsetting for some of the embassy staff. They don't like to be reminded about his illness. Anyhow, I don't know why I am saying this to you. You're a sensible chap and know when to keep lips sealed."

"I won't breathe a word."

"By the way, be a good fellow and see Ruth back to her apartment block. It's the furthest one from us in Kutz unfortunately. Apparently it used to be safe round here under the old regime, even at night. Now you can't take any chances."

"Yes, of course I will."

A severe frost had set in after the snowstorm. The paths

linking the apartment blocks had been partially cleared, but were now icy and uneven. Ruth tottered, reached out and tucked her arm tightly into Peter's. She clung to him for support as they walked carefully through the dark.

"You'd better know the truth about James Fortune," Ruth said. Her voice was muffled by her scarf and Peter bent closer to catch her words. "Wasn't taken ill at all. He got himself into some difficulties here... you know, compromised. Blackmail would have been the next step. Had to be removed as quickly as possible under the guise of serious illness. Chris stupidly thinks he might come back, but I know for sure he won't. James was a fool, but a lovely fool."

"You were particularly fond of him, were you, Ruth?"

"He was a delight. Good looking, amusing, cavalier. But also overconfident and a wee bit careless." Ruth was silent as they passed another foreigner on the path. "Fell for a young Russian girl," she snarled. "She got herself pregnant, usual story. Unfortunately she was also working for their Secret Service."

They walked on in silence. Peter felt an additional chill as he thought about his own unofficial duties. Would *they* try and set him up too? Had *they* already done so? His mind was drawn back to Lydia. Her image returned more strongly. This time she was dressed in a soldier's uniform and looked magnificent. She beckoned to him with a wave of her pistol. What did she want from him now?

Peter was so distracted by his own thoughts that he hardly registered they had entered Ruth's apartment block and climbed two flights of stairs.

"Here we are," Ruth said, disengaging herself from Peter's arm and searching for her keys. "Care for another coffee or a nightcap? You can use my phone to call a taxi when you're ready."

"It's late and I ought to be going. But a whisky would be nice."

Ruth's apartment was comfortable and well furnished with some excellent pictures, many of them by Russian artists. It provided a real contrast to the sterile Englishness of the Burroughs household. But like Ruth and her office, it was immaculate. To have an organised office was one thing, but to live a personal life in such order seemed unnatural. Peter could not believe it was like this all the time. Perhaps it was not and she had tidied up in case she managed to get him through the door. No, not Ruth. Theirs was strictly a working relationship.

Ruth poured generous whiskies for them both. Peter had deliberately chosen to occupy the only armchair. Ruth sat down on the side of the sofa closest to him.

"Cheers," she said, taking a large gulp of whisky. Some missed her mouth and dribbled onto her dress. She seemed neither to notice nor to care. "You know in my fifteen years or so in the Service, I've always been amazed just how stupid and weak-willed men can be. They invariably fall into the honey trap, completely ruining their careers as a result. We're talking about exceptionally bright and clever men who know the dangers, the pitfalls, the warning signs, yet still seem unable to resist temptation. They lose their heads and much more besides."

"Yes, I know what you mean. I suspect they reckon they can get away with it because they are so brilliant and successful. But there are others way down the scale who also get compromised, so it's not just the high flyers."

Peter hadn't thought where he fitted in. He was doing well for his age and might be regarded as someone on the fast track. So was Lydia out for more than a good time that Thursday night in Stambov? If they were going to fix him, surely a young Natasha would be used rather than the mature Lydia. Perhaps in Stambov they were short of young beauties and Lydia was the best they could find. He didn't care: she was wild and seductive and such a contrast to the prim, ordered Ruth who continued to look at him so strangely.

"But there is another side to this of course," he said. "There are just as many highly intelligent and capable women in the Service these days with promising careers. Some must fall for the same techniques and succumb to a Romeo or Boris. The thing is, we rarely hear about them."

"Perhaps they show greater self-control and presence of mind," Ruth said, draining her whisky. She put her glass down and came over to Peter's chair. She stared at him, swaying gently. "That's why I think it's much better and safer to keep such things in-house."

Ruth toppled forward into Peter's lap. She grasped him round the neck and clumsily sought his lips. Peter was caught unawares and for a brief moment Ruth succeeded in kissing him voraciously. She gnawed at his mouth, thrust her breasts into him and tugged fiercely at his hair. Peter wrestled her away, grasping her wrists firmly. She lay askew on his lap.

"Ruth! Please, please stop. This is embarrassing, for both of us."

Ruth started to sob and crumpled feebly against Peter. He released her wrists and held her gently like a father would a daughter. Her sobs turned to wails, then to moans. She gradually reasserted some self-control.

"Very silly of me," she sniffed. "Don't know what happened. Whisky must have taken over. Very foolish. I'm so sorry. Lots of apologies."

Peter gave her a handkerchief.

She mopped up the remaining tears and started to repair the damage to her face. "Trouble is you wouldn't understand how awful life is here for a single person, especially a woman. And it's not just Moscow, it happens in all the posts. It's so desperately lonely. I've almost given up all hope of ever finding a man. And that's the only thing I really, honestly want. I'd sacrifice the bloody job, the money, the lot for a man. Sad thing is I thought I'd got one, but then he went away."

"Who went away, Ruth?"

"James, you idiot. James Fortune. I was completely in love with James, but he didn't know it, didn't have a clue. Never will now. When he disappeared back to England, I thought I was going to die. There was I, a mature professional woman behaving like a lovesick teenager." The memory appeared too much for her. She tried to stifle a sob but it burst out unrestrained. She fell against Peter again and buried her face in his shoulder. Her whole body shuddered as she wept.

Peter continued to hold her, letting the storm of agony and distress rack her as a harsh but necessary purgation. He felt a deep sadness for her.

Ruth slowly sat upright and dabbed her mottled face with Peter's handkerchief. "I'll buy you a new one. This one will carry too many painful memories." She uncurled herself from him and stood up. "Never mention anything about this to anyone. Remove it from your mind and destroy all trace of it. Just like a confidential document." She gave a watery smile.

"No, of course. You have my word. But if you're alright now, I'd better go. May I use your phone?"

Ruth nodded and Peter made a short call.

"I'll be off then. I'll pick the taxi up on Kutuzovsky," he said. He put on his coat and Ruth came to the door with him. They kissed each other lightly. He sensed her pain through the softness of her cheek.

CHAPTER 10

The Monday morning after their weekend at the *dacha*, Yuri Poliakov had bounced into the Interior Ministry building full of boyish excitement. He felt so elated he could have danced round his office if only he had the space. He would have liked to do a Cossack dance, throwing his legs and arms out in sheer exhilaration. Instead he rotated between the desk and filing cabinet in a cramped, slow waltz, pretending to hold Olga in his arms.

The memory of that morning now depressed him. The whole business was a disappointment. He had such high hopes, only to witness them disappear one by one. Top of the list was the failure of Dr Wang Ho to come good. It all looked so promising until the report on his sudden return to China appeared in Yuri's in-tray. Illness was the alleged reason. The agency suggested he had picked up an infection through his over-zealous observation of the animals on the farm. Quite possibly a form of swine fever or bird flu, was the report's only comment.

Now Yuri was left with only two collaborators. Perhaps he had been overambitious, yet his analysis had been impeccable, his logic faultless. Could those upstairs not read, could they not follow the most obvious of signs? Evidently not. How was he, the most junior official in the Ministry, going to tell them they had missed such important leads? No he, Collator Third Class Poliakov, could not be held responsible for the stupidity of his superiors.

It was already three weeks since his hopes had been raised at the grand reception out at the *dacha*. Pompous Popov had sounded serious about pursuing a line of enquiry into Mr Standridge. Deputy Minister Kondrashin had met this Standridge and instinctively distrusted him. It seemed only reasonable, if not advisable, to follow up on what the Deputy Minister had said. But the reality was that Popov had done no such thing. The momentum had been lost. All Yuri's reports were being read by people with blindness in their eyes.

Matters though were still proceeding on the ground. Mr Standridge continued to act suspiciously on his travels and now he was associating with some very undesirable characters. There was of course Professor Krotkin, who only recently had met him again in Hotel Leskov. From the agency report, there seemed to be much discussion over a brown paper package. Regardless of what it contained, it was an incriminating article in itself.

The second and in a way more interesting piece of evidence was that Mr Standridge had not only met up with Herr Metzinger, but also with Lydia Kuznetsova. It was not possible that in the vastness of Russia their meeting was pure coincidence. The Stambov report gave him some vital information. He re-read it, as he had every morning that week.

CLASSIFICATION VERY CONFIDENTIAL
INCIDENT REPORT NO ST7935/B STAMBOV
ACTIVITIES CONCERNING MR P STANDRIDGE
(GREAT BRITAIN) 15 NOV 1992

19.30: Metzinger and Kuznetsova make contact with Standridge in Restaurant Kolodets, 23 Krasnoarmeyskaya Street, Stambov.

19.45: Targets eat meal (large) and drink champagne and vodka (much). (Comment. Source counted 2 bottles champagne and 2 decanters vodka. Comment ends.)

21.30: Kuznetsova embraces (ie kisses and hugs) both male targets (one after the other not together).

22.00: Metzinger has hundred rouble notes

to pay bill. Money spread on table. Counts with difficulty. Kuznetsova puts her hand on Standridge leg. (Comment. Unable to observe if hand moves into Standridge pocket. Assessment grading : probable. Not known if hand contained unseen item. Assessment grading: possible. Comment ends.)

22.15: Targets leave restaurant in taxi.

22.30: Targets arrive Institute of Advanced Education. Walk up steps diagonally.

22.45: Kuznetsova dances by herself. Male targets converse in English. Words Motherland, Fatherland and Sandwich identified by Source. (Comment. First two words known and understood. Third word not previously encountered. Suggest male targets using codeword. Assessment grading: Very Probable. Comment ends.)

22.50: Kuznetsova dances with Metzinger but without contact.

23.05: Kuznetsova dances with Standridge. Metzinger sleeps on table. (Comment. Close dancing by male and female targets. Proximity of heads permitted exchange of information. Movement of hands especially under outer and inner garments suggest passage of items between targets. Expression on faces interpreted by Source as satisfied. Assessment grading : Probable. Comment ends.)

23.30: Kuznetsova wakes Metzinger with water. Disagreement observed. Metzinger helped from Institute to apartment by other two targets.

23.45: Kuznetsova and Standridge take taxi to apartment block of Kuznetsova. Source follows and observes fighting between targets in taxi. (Comment. Subsequent interview with Source and taxi driver established that fight

129

did not take place as recorded above. Wrestling witnessed by Source was a misidentification. Corrected Version to read : Targets involved in embracing, see earlier definition above, and associated actions. Comment ends.)
23.59: Standridge returns to hotel alone in taxi.

Yuri had learned to identify the footsteps of everyone who worked on his corridor. Those he heard now, getting steadily louder, belonged to his Section Head Zagarin. He put the Stambov report away in its correct file and tidied his desk.

Zagarin, who was dumpy with a red face and lank dark hair, entered Yuri's office. "Poliakov, the Deputy Director wants to see you. Bring a copy of your latest weekly summary. From the way he spoke on the phone, he didn't sound very pleased. You're probably in trouble."

Zagarin had been Head of Internal Section for decades, a fine example of an official promoted to the level of his incompetence. With only two subordinates, he bullied Yuri and his Ivan relentlessly. Neither of them took much notice of him, other than count the days to his retirement.

Yuri said nothing. He assembled the papers he needed in a folder, locking the remainder in his security cabinet. He closed his office door and followed Zagarin as he waddled along the corridor. Yuri thought his Section Head might manage one flight of stairs, but not the six to Popov's office. They took the lift.

Popov's expansive office was the one Yuri had described to Olga as his own. It was grand enough in its own right, but Yuri had added embellishments to impress his wife. He liked the thick carpet and panelled walls, but most of all he coveted the wide desk with its bank of coloured telephones. One day all this would be his.

Deputy Director Popov sat writing at his desk. His secretary indicated they should arrange themselves either

130

side of a large table which occupied half the room. Zagarin seemed agitated in the presence of his Deputy Director, shuffling his papers and running a hand through his greasy hair. Popov finished what he was doing and joined them at the table.

"We have some interesting business to deal with," he said, opening the red covered file his secretary put in front of him. "Zagarin, you have been following in detail the recent summary reports from Poliakov?"

"Yes of course, sir," Zagarin replied in the ingratiating tone he reserved for his Deputy Director. "I always read them extremely thoroughly before I allow them to come up to you. I often have to make some alterations, improvements I should call them, to Poliakov's submissions. His reports are not – how shall I say – of the best quality."

Yuri boiled with indignation, but could say nothing. He knew Zagarin was a downright liar. He rarely read his summaries and, when he did, he never changed a word.

"I did wonder about that. I could not believe that someone of Poliakov's intelligence was regularly producing such clear, well written reports. So helpful and encouraging to have an attentive and discerning Section Head. Don't you agree, Poliakov? You are indeed a fortunate young man."

Zagarin nodded and smiled with satisfaction. Yuri looked down at his papers, wondering whether Popov expected an answer. It seemed he did not.

"Well, I am relieved to hear we are all up to date with the latest information on our foreign guests," Popov said, pleased with the irony of the phrase. "As you know, they are not always grateful for our hospitality and often breach the privilege of coming to our country. In short, they involve themselves in matters which do not concern them."

Zagarin nodded his head at the end of each sentence. It was not within his grasp ever to disagree with anything his Deputy Director said. Yuri listened intently, considering where all this was leading.

"I don't think I have told you this, Zagarin, but I came across Poliakov at the Ministry's *dacha* Reception. You know the one I mean, the big, important one held out at the estate each year. Naturally, Zagarin, you were too junior to be there. But Poliakov got in, guest of a General he was."

Popov enjoyed Zagarin's discomfort for a moment before continuing. "I instructed Poliakov to check out a particular Englishman whose name was mentioned by a Deputy Minister at the reception. I am pleased to see Poliakov for once has done what he was told to do. With your attentive reading of Poliakov's reports, you know of whom we speak, Zagarin, do you not?"

"Yes Deputy Director, of course, but there are several who would fall into this category," Zagarin blustered. "Poliakov is continually drawing our attention to the unusual behaviour of foreigners, the English in particular." Zagarin was now sweating heavily and dark stains appeared down his shirt. He scratched at his pile of papers, his eyes flitting wildly over the pages searching for the one name he needed.

"The person you mentioned is naturally well known to me through Poliakov's reports. Only last week I said to myself that this is a man who should be watched more closely. I... I remember rewriting part of the report myself as it was so important. This Englishman is quite an old man, is he not? And... and he spends a lot of time fishing, yes fishing in the Moscow River. Very suspicious the amount of time he spends fishing..." Zagarin's voice fell away to little more than a whisper.

"You don't have a clue, do you, Zagarin? You've not the first idea who we're talking about."

Zagarin was unable to reply. He hung his head like a victim awaiting the executioner's axe as drops of sweat plopped onto his papers.

"Poliakov," Popov said, issuing a sharp military command. "Tell us please, and especially your Section Head, the name of this Englishman."

"His name is Standridge, first names Peter Arthur."

"Now, Zagarin, does that name ring a loud bell in your thick head or is it the first time you've heard it?" Popov demanded.

"No, Deputy Director. I remember the name now. I apologise very much for not being able to recall it. I had a moment of confusion. There are so many foreigners to keep track of these days."

Popov appeared to grow tired of his harassment of Zagarin. He turned to Yuri. "Poliakov, I have been following your reports on this man Standridge. They are good summaries of the liaisons he is making with some of our citizens. I congratulate you, especially as it is now obvious your reports are coming to me without amendment by your Section Head."

"Thank you, sir." Yuri enjoyed the moment, although chose not to look at Zagarin. The Deputy Director could be a difficult man but there were times when Yuri admired his guile.

"I have also decided, Poliakov, that you should become more involved with this particular target," Popov said, closing the file in front of him. "I am assigning you to one of the close surveillance units. Some training will be required, but you will be working with the real professionals. They will keep you under tight control."

"Yes, sir. Thank you sir," Yuri said.

"And you, Zagarin. You will have to cover Poliakov's work whilst he is away on this task."

Zagarin's red face paled as he took in Popov's words. He said nothing.

"Well, thank you, that's all. Meeting over." Popov turned to his secretary, smiled and patted her arm.

Zagarin and Yuri stood up, bowed slightly and left the

office. Once in the corridor, Zagarin headed for the lift, Yuri for the stairs.

The narrow road cut through the thick forest like the blade of a sabre. On either side, tall trees, their boughs shaken free of heavy snow, stood sentinel in the darkness. Snow-covered strips ran between the road and the tree line, scarred by the wheel marks of passing vehicles. The taxi's tyres vibrated on the concrete surface as the driver sped towards the hidden barracks.

The waving headlights picked out the red and white barrier across the road. The driver slowed, dipping his lights to signal their approach. A floodlight came on high above the barrier, blinding them with its brightness. A soldier, his rifle slung across his chest, emerged from the shadows. He rapped sharply on the windscreen.

Yuri lowered his window, breathing in the fresh night air. He wondered for a moment what he should do. Was this where he should get out? There was no sign of the barracks; all he could see was the road and the impenetrable forest. He looked at the sentry, anxious for some direction.

"All identity cards, passes, documents," the soldier snapped.

The taxi driver, used to the routine, had his papers ready. Reaching over Yuri, he presented them through the window. Yuri found his Interior Ministry pass. He placed it in the outstretched hand of the sentry, who turned his back on the car and inspected their documents under the glare of the overhead light.

The sentry took his time, showing more interest in Yuri's pass than the driver's papers. Yuri suspected his pass would be unusual, different from those issued to the soldiers. As it was a special training establishment, they would require a special type of pass. He rather hoped they would provide him with one for the duration of his stay.

He liked the notion of special.

"All in order," the sentry said, returning the papers in a bundle. Yuri extracted his precious pass and handed the rest to the driver.

"Report to the duty officer in the guardroom," the sentry said. "The taxi must turn round at the entrance. Non-military vehicles are not permitted in the barracks. You'll be on foot after that."

The sentry went over to the barrier and, leaning on the counterweight, raised the bar to let the taxi pass underneath. As the driver accelerated through the gap, Yuri wound up his window. His excitement now changed to apprehension.

Yuri realized he had made the whole journey in the winter dark, not knowing where he was going. He had only received his instructions from Popov's secretary that afternoon, together with a rail ticket to Vozlodansk. He had not even had time to look at a map, not that he had anything of a helpful scale. He was travelling blind, with only the sketchiest idea of his destination.

"It's about another two kilometres," the driver said. "You'll see all the lights before you get there. I don't like coming up here, especially at night. Gives me the ghoulies. You should hear the rumours down in the town about what goes on here. Never believe it, you wouldn't." He hummed to himself as if enjoying Yuri's unease. "There are the lights now," he added. "Pretty, aren't they?"

Looking ahead, Yuri could see a glow above the trees against the night sky. The barracks did seem particularly well illuminated and perhaps the effect was exaggerated by the surrounding blackness. But as they turned the last bend, huge floodlights came into view.

The Interior Ministry's Special Training Establishment Number 5 was carved out of the deep forest. From what Yuri could see, it seemed to consist of older style wooden huts, mixed in with the newer two storey brick and concrete buildings so beloved of the Ministry. It was laid out on geometric lines with a gridiron of roads and paths linking the different sections.

Around the whole complex, which must have covered several hectares, was a high floodlit perimeter fence, topped by coils of barbed wire. Every hundred metres a guard tower overlooked the fence, with well-trodden patrol paths beneath. At the end of the approach road, the main entrance to the barracks resembled a fortress gatehouse.

Yuri paid the taxi driver, obtaining a scribbled receipt. He grabbed his bag from the back seat and walked towards the main gates. An armed sentry demanded his pass before easing open the pedestrian entrance. Yuri squeezed himself through.

"You not been here before?" the sentry asked.

"No, that's right."

"Report to the guardroom then and get yourself signed in," the sentry said, pointing to an adjacent building. "You'll find the duty officer in there somewhere, unless he's out on his rounds."

Yuri opened the door to the guardroom. He was met by a wall of heat and immediately started to perspire in his heavy coat. A sergeant at the desk looked him up and down, before clicking his fingers for his pass. Like the sentries, he scrutinised it for some time, turning it over in his fingers and holding it up to the light. Satisfied, he handed it back.

"Fill this in," the sergeant said pushing a heavy ledger towards him. Yuri found his ballpoint and standing before the tall desk like a schoolboy, he completed the rows of columns on the page. "And now this," the sergeant said giving him a blue form with boxes to tick and questions to answer. "If you do it right, you might get one of our special passes. Having one will save you a lot of hassle whilst you're here, so it's worth doing properly."

As a civil servant, Yuri was no stranger to forms and form filling. He accepted that several forms asking for the same information needed to be completed before any action could be taken. In that respect, if in no other, his Ministry was very thorough, for no chances should be taken with the Internal Security of the State. Yuri was rightly proud of his Ministry's reputation for correctly completed documentation.

The sergeant seemed impressed by Yuri's efforts. It wasn't every day he had a trained official filling out his forms. He looked at Yuri's handiwork with admiration. They certainly knew their stuff, these men from the Ministry. They did a lovely form. What a change from the rough and ready soldiery whose writing needed the services of a cryptographer to decipher.

"It's Major Kantimirov you want to see. He's in charge this evening. Next floor, office in front of you. I'd leave your bag here."

Yuri mounted stairs and knocked on the door marked *Duty Officer (Night)*. He thought he heard a cough and a gruff "Come in". He opened the door, wincing as it scraped across the floorboards.

Slumped in an easy chair in the corner was a grey-haired major. His tie was loosened, his tunic unbuttoned around his large belly. He emitted short snorts and grunts. Awakened by the noise of the door, his bloodshot eyes blinked open. Yuri feared he had roused a sleeping dragon.

"You young bugger," he said fiercely. "Who the hell are you? What do you think you're doing barging in here when a chap's having a snooze?"

"I'm very sorry to disturb you. The sergeant said I needed to report to you. I did knock and I thought I heard you say come in."

"Bollocks," Major Kantimirov said, pushing himself out of the chair. "I never talk in my sleep." He tightened his tie, did up his tunic and moved to the chair behind the desk. From his trouser pocket he produced a toothless comb which he ran vigorously through his hair. He drank the remains of some liquid in a stained mug. He looked at Yuri with the charm of a grizzled bear.

"Now you've bloody well woken me up, you'd better tell me your name and what the hell you want. I'm not the duty officer for nothing," he growled.

"I'm Yuri Poliakov. I'm an official in the Interior Ministry. I work in the main building in Moscow. I've been sent for some training here by my Deputy Director."

Major Kantimirov continued to fix Yuri with a fiery glare. It appeared his mind was gradually starting to function after the oblivion of sleep and a few shots of vodka. He rubbed his eyes and bending down, took a file out of the desk drawer. He turned the pages. "Poliakov, Poliakov," he murmured to himself. "Ah ha, I have you now. You're here till Saturday.... not on any specific course... need to report to the Chief Instructor tomorrow morning at 0800... billet allocated in block Z23, wherever the hell that is..." He looked up abruptly. "What's your job title and service grade?"

"I'm a Collator Third Class," Yuri replied proudly.

Major Kantimirov took a book out of the drawer. Yuri caught its title: *Protocol For Military Ranks And Civilian Grades*. "Now let me see. Third Class Collators. Have they officer status or not?" Major Kantimirov mumbled, consulting the tables at the back of the book. "Um, not too sure about that, looking a little shaky I'd say. Could be bad luck on you, my lad." He stood up and walked around the small office engrossed in the book and still shaking his head. "Oh dear, oh dear," he kept repeating. "This could be quite a problem."

He turned another page, stopped and grimaced. "No, here we are. You Poliakov as a Collator Third Class have the equivalent rank of Junior Lieutenant. They don't come any lower than that."

Yuri had not imagined for one minute he was not equated to an officer rank. But Junior Lieutenant was altogether too demeaning. He would have to do better than that. He wondered briefly what old Popov was as a Deputy Director. Colonel perhaps or even Major General? Yes it would certainly be worth getting promoted to gain such an exalted equivalent rank.

"You can use the officers' facilities while you're here," Major Kantimirov continued. "I'll get one of the soldiers to show you to your billet. In the morning get yourself to Building 9A for the meeting with the Chief Instructor. Someone in your block will tell you where to find him."

Yuri felt the Major study him more closely. He hadn't been invited to sit down, so remained standing near the door. His coat was open, revealing his dark suit, white shirt and Ministry tie.

"You'll definitely need to visit the quartermaster tomorrow," Major Kantimirov said. "We can't have you wandering around the barracks looking like a bureaucrat. There'd be a mutiny."

"So I'm to get a military uniform?" Yuri asked excitedly.

"Good heavens no. You're not a soldier, are you? You'll be kitted out in something more appropriate. We won't want you to go crawling around in the dirt in your best suit, will we?"

Major Kantimirov stood up and Yuri followed him down the stairs. The sergeant ordered a young soldier to escort Yuri to his accommodation. Major Kantimirov said a gruff goodnight.

They set off down a narrow path, their boots scrunching on the snow. The soldier lit a cigarette, concealing it in his cupped hand. Yuri trudged behind him with his bag slung over his shoulder. He tried to keep his bearings, but the similarity of the buildings in the glow of the floodlights disorientated him. The shadowy barracks seemed designed to confuse.

The soldier stopped at the entrance to one of the wooden huts. He nodded in the direction of the door and without a word marched back down the path. Yuri went in. A notice in the small entrance hall listed the room allocation. He found his name against Room 12.

Yuri's room was small, with a bed, desk and chair. He looked at his watch. Almost midnight. He felt hungry, but realised he had not asked about the Officers Messroom. Locked at this time of night, he guessed. In consolation he nibbled the chocolate bar he had brought with him.

The bed was too hard to encourage immediate sleep. Yuri thought of Olga, wishing she were here, pressing her soft body gently against him. Her absence hurt. Was she asleep or perhaps awake like him, saddened by their separation?

There were unfamiliar sounds, a door opening and closing, the heating system clicking and wheezing. Outside he heard the marching steps of troops softened by the snow, shouted orders carried in the clear, still air. In the distance, guard dogs barked, fell silent, barked again. He drifted off to sleep.

CHAPTER 11

A purposeful Olga Poliakova set off for the University, wrapped up against the morning cold. She had resolved to keep busy, to press on with her work, to push Yuri's absence to the back of her mind. She would use the extra time to her advantage. There would be no need to rush home; she could eat a quick supper in the cafeteria and stay in the library until it closed. Old friends could be phoned and encouraged out midweek. She would find many things to do, inconsequential things, anything to avoid returning to the apartment until late.

Only the previous evening Olga had arrived home to find Yuri there before her. That was the first surprise, a pleasant one, especially as he seemed unusually excited. The second rendered her speechless. He spoke quickly, apologetically. "Olga darling, I've got to go away for a few days. It's work. There've been some developments. I'd like to tell you, but you know I can't. They want me to go straightaway. I've packed my things. I... I love you." They had kissed all too briefly and the next moment he had vanished.

It was the suddenness of it all. The few minutes they had together seemed so mean. Perhaps if there had been some warning, or if she knew where he was and when he would be back, she could have coped better. Her unhappiness overwhelmed her. At night her cold bed was barren, her arms empty, her body unfulfilled. Her dreams were irrational fears; what if he disappeared as they had in the past? Would he ever return? She wept silently in her sleep.

Once Olga reached the University, she went to the library to continue her research. As usual everything was as it should be: she had her favourite place by the window, her reference books beside her. She started on her work but concentration seemed elusive. The view from the window over the snow covered woods distracted her. The trees looked so beautiful in the sunlight against the backdrop of an ice blue sky. There must have been days like this in the Central Asian mountains as the Tsar's armies marched and probed their way further and further south. What would it have been like to be a soldier then? She tried to resist imagining Yuri in a smart cavalry uniform, but there he was sitting up high on his fine horse, handsome and dashing. She felt the tears pushing into her eyes and looked back at her books. It was pointless sitting here. Her studies would have to be suspended.

The librarian accepted the books, looking quizzically at Olga. She made no comment, but found it surprising that the normally diligent researcher was leaving so early. It was also annoying as much effort had gone into assembling all the volumes she requested. At least she asked for them to be reserved for her again the following day.

Olga wandered along the long corridors without any clear idea where she was going and what she was going to do. It was not even midday and the thought of the empty hours before returning home filled her with dread. All her friends were working or away, so there was no prospect of company and conversation to help pass the time. It was no good; she would just have to take a bus into the centre and find something to do. A film perhaps or maybe some shopping. She was resigned to accepting whatever fate put her way.

Although it was cold outside, Olga continued to amble. She was enclosed in her fur coat and, like a wild animal, she could endure far lower temperatures than Minus 10. If she missed a bus, that was of no consequence, there would soon be another. She actually hoped to see one drawing away as she approached; more time would elapse whilst she waited for the next.

Three huddled figures stood at the bus stop, shielding themselves from the cutting wind. They had no furs to protect them, only rough felt coats and scarves. They pressed close together, sharing their warmth with each other. Olga stopped a few metres away, turning her back to the wind. She admired the University building with its tall tower and steeple, displaying the distinctive wedding cake architecture of Stalin's rule. The capital had other grandiose public buildings in the same style, but in her eyes none enjoyed as fine a setting as the Moscow State University.

She heard the roaring engine as the bus climbed the last metres of the incline. She watched the driver brake skilfully, slewing the long vehicle obliquely across the ice towards the stop. Its rear wheels bounced against the kerb before the gasping machine slid to a halt in front of the waiting queue. Olga got on, finding a seat near the back. She rubbed the window to get a better view for her journey into town.

The bus moved off, its rear wheels skidding before finding their grip. Another passenger sat down on the adjacent seat. She shuffled across to make more room, squashing herself against the window. Her fellow traveller breathed heavily.

"Olga Nikolaevna, I am greatly heartened to see you and to note you dutifully punched your ticket."

Olga quickly glanced at the person beside her. "Alex, my God, what a surprise. Are you all right? You're puffing like an old train!"

"Quite, quite well and even better for seeing you so unexpectedly and fortuitously on this delectable omnibus." Fat Alex shifted uncomfortably, but Olga could move no closer to the window. She knew that less than half of Fat Alex was actually on the seat, the balance hanging awkwardly in the aisle. He needed a double seat to

143

himself, but there was none available. She also suspected he liked being pressed close to her. He leaned across, kissing her sloppily on the cheek.

"You've been spying on me haven't you, you naughty man?" she said playfully. "Following me around like a *borzoi*, tracking me like a bloodhound, eh?"

Fat Alex gave a chesty wheeze. "Yes of course. You've got it in one, sussed me out first time. Trouble is I can't help myself; you're just too damned attractive. You're my lodestar. I'm like a bit of old metal drawn by your irresistible magnetism. What a fate for one such as me."

Olga giggled. She felt better for the gentle banter, well able to hold her own with their harmless repartee.

"I'm dying for a fag," Fat Alex gasped. "What other country forbids its noble citizens to smoke on a municipal bus? Bloody police state. No smoking, no boozing, and no smooching either." He squeezed Olga's thigh through the thick fur of her coat. "More's the pity for that."

"And what may I ask were you doing in the vicinity of the Moscow State University in the first place?" Olga asked, hoping to move the talk away from smooching. "You've strayed a bit off your usual patch coming up here, haven't you?"

"Ah well, my dear, dear Olga Nikolaevna, I know you think, with perhaps some justification, that I, Alexander Petrovich, should never be allowed within fifty versts of a seat of learning, but the fact remains that I actually count some of the most brilliant academics amongst my friends. In their turn, they are greatly honoured to be associated with such an esteemed and revered figure as me. I even have it on excellent authority that there are many who would wish to be included in my inner circle, but regrettably there is insufficient room. What it is to be so wanted, so much in demand by the finest brains in the land. You, too, must consider it an honour to be able to sit on this very bus next to such an eminent personage." Fat Alex raised his arm in mock salute, catching the headscarf of a *babushka* on the adjacent seat. She cursed and beat him with her stick. He made an extravagant apology. She cackled and forgave him.

"But you still haven't told me who you came to see today," Olga said. "I know I'm only a humble research student, but it's possible I might know them."

"Top secret, can't say. Your husband would know all about that."

Olga did not want to be reminded of Yuri, well not him of course, only his absence. She was in danger of feeling morose again unless she kept the conversation moving. "Don't talk such rubbish. Other than creeping around after me, what were you doing here?"

"All right, all right, I'll confess under such duress. If you must know, I came to sell some goods and services to the man who runs your kitchens."

Olga laughed out loud. "Nonsense, you can't mean that? You wouldn't be seen dead in some measly kitchen, unless of course you were up to something illegal. Black market business was it?"

"What it is to be so clever: so beautiful and so clever. Do you not now have some sympathy for my infatuation, you gorgeous thing? But seriously, deadly seriously, do not eat one grain of bread, one morsel of meat, one leaf of cabbage in that students canteen of yours, not, that is, until I give the word. You have no idea what goes on in that inferno. My time in there was a hell, knowing that wretched students would, from sheer hunger, eat this food which even a starving dog would spurn. No, Olga, until my fine produce and quality service is accepted by that sweltering cook, do not pass through the portals of that unsavoury place."

Olga was unsure how to take Fat Alex's remarks. It was always a dilemma with him. He could be outrageously amusing and wicked one moment, then without warning change to being serious and honest. Where was he now? Olga didn't know.

The bus rattled on towards the centre. The streets became busier and the progress of the bus slower. More passengers were now in the aisle, many abusing the protruding Fat Alex for taking up so much of their standing room. He took no notice.

"Come and have lunch," he said without warning. "I know a good place where I guarantee you'll not be poisoned."

Olga glanced at him. There was a moment of indecision before she answered. "Thank you. I'd really enjoy that."

They got off at the next stop. Olga slipped her arm inside Fat Alex's, pre-empting his attempt to clasp her to him like a lover. They walked along the crowded pavement feeling the fresh air in their faces. Fat Alex lit a cigarette.

"Where are we going, Alex?" Olga asked. She was in an unfamiliar area. The shops looked poorer and less well-stocked, the passers-by more furtive. She felt a little nervous.

"Don't you like surprises, my little beauty?" Fat Alex chuckled. They turned a corner into another shabby street. Two ragged children ran towards them with hands outstretched. Fat Alex batted them away. They swore at him in language which brought a blush to Olga's cheeks. Whilst she clung tighter to him for protection, she felt nothing but pity for the wretches.

"It's hard, I know," Fat Alex said, "but giving them money only makes it worse. It's a problem out of control." He stopped and added, "What do you think?"

Olga's thoughts were still with the street children. She took some seconds to switch her mind back to where they were. Fat Alex was gesturing to a building on the opposite side of the road. Amongst the rundown façades was the brightly painted front of a new restaurant. Curved above the door was its name: *Olga's House*.

"You old ruffian," she said. "I'm unsure whether to be flattered or offended. How on earth did you know it was here, in an area like this?"

"Because I own it. Well, some of it. Half of it to be strictly accurate." Olga was impressed and even more so, once they got inside. It had been decorated and furnished very artistically and was scrupulously clean. The waiters and waitresses, whom Olga quietly noticed were all young and attractive, wore immaculate peasant costumes. *Balalaika* music played softly in the background.

A particularly beautiful girl greeted them, giving a grinning Fat Alex a warm kiss on each cheek. She showed them to their table, the best in the room.

"Alex this is really lovely. How long has it been open?"

"Just two days. I wanted you and Yuri to come for our opening night on Saturday, but the receptionist had let all the tables go. It was quite an evening. And see, even now on a Tuesday lunchtime, it's almost full."

Olga looked round the restaurant. Fat Alex was right, it was very busy.

He sat and beamed at her. "Olga comes to have lunch in Olga's House. That is a special occasion. Let me order for you. There's nothing you don't eat is there?"

"No. I'm sure I shall be delighted with whatever you choose."

Fat Alex called the waitress who arrived with a bottle of wine. She poured it skilfully, listening as he ordered a series of courses.

"Here's to Olga," he said, raising his glass. "May she and her house have all blessings showered upon them." They smiled at one another. Olga had not tasted such excellent wine in years.

"You may think, Olga, that I named this restaurant after you. A very logical assumption given the deep love and respect I have for you. But no, Olga was also my mother's name. It is after her that I have named it, God rest her

147

soul. It's a year almost to the day since I lost her."

Olga noticed a tear run down Fat Alex's face. He made no attempt to wipe it away.

"I'm sorry Alex," she said, reaching over to hold his hand. "She would be so proud of you and this place." Fat Alex nodded. He enjoyed Olga's hand and stroked it gently. He turned from grief to love without shame.

The first of many courses was served. Fat Alex set to as if he had not eaten for a week. Olga ate more slowly, relishing the exquisite tastes. She felt content and relaxed. Fat Alex, though, was irrepressible. He devoured huge platefuls of food, drank the wine like water and kept Olga entertained with hilarious stories. He was sometimes desperate to talk and eat simultaneously, which only added to her amusement. As the last course arrived, the chef paid him a visit and was congratulated effusively. All the time they were attended by the beautiful waitress, assisted by a young man in training. Fat Alex made a point of caressing their bottoms whenever they came close.

Olga realized too late that she had drunk too much of the delicious wine. She knew that most of the two bottles had been consumed by Fat Alex, but even so, she had had far more than normal. Once she acknowledged her state, she decided not to let it spoil the rest of the lunch. She felt fine, if a little distant.

She studied Fat Alex as he launched into another story. What was it about him? Gross he certainly was: overweight, ugly, with pale sweaty skin. An unpromising prospect for any girl. And yet there was something undeniably attractive about him too. The more she'd got to know him, the less his physical appearance seemed a deterrent. Nothing had changed of course, she knew that, but his personality had steadily become more important to her, more appealing. She laughed so much in his company and felt the shiver of pleasure as he sprung yet another delightful surprise. She liked the power he exercised over others and the confident way he coped with life. She felt safe and secure with him. Deep, deep down, she was intrigued by the outrageous sexuality of this extraordinary man.

Olga laughed as Fat Alex finished his tale. He smiled with satisfaction and called for yet more wine.

"I mustn't have any more," Olga said. "You'll have to drink the whole bottle yourself."

"No problem. In a manner of speaking, it's mine already. I own it." Fat Alex laughed heartily and lit another cigarette.

"Alex, I need you to be completely honest with me for a moment. I want you to tell me the truth, no evasions, no fabrications. Did you or did you not come up to see someone at the university, someone official like this catering person?"

Fat Alex thought for a moment. "Indeed I did. Why did you think I should wish to deceive you?"

"I wanted to be sure you didn't come up specifically to engineer a meeting, a meeting with me. That's why I asked."

"You want me to be honest and I shall be. I know Yuri is, how shall I put it, away. Yesterday evening from the panorama window in my apartment, I saw him leave in a hurry with a suitcase. He got into a taxi. Although it was dark, I could see him clearly through my night vision scope." He drew heavily on his cigarette. "And how did I come by that sophisticated device? Gift from a friend in the military. I did some favours for him in return. I just happened to be using it to get a closer look at the young lovelies when all of a sudden there was my old friend Yuri scurrying along and filling the frame." Fat Alex leaned across the table towards Olga. "Everything all right at home is it?"

"None of your bloody business," Olga retorted angrily.

"Forgive me, forgive me. I only enquired in case I could be of assistance. But to continue with my rare saga

149

of honesty, I have to confess to searching for you at the university. I had my appointment there with the catering buffoon in any case, but afterwards I came to the library to offer you a coffee and a break from your studies."

Fat Alex was interrupted by the proximity of a young woman moving to a nearby table. He raised his hand ready to feel any part of her within reach, but thought better of it. He returned his attention to Olga. "Sadly in the library, I saw you packing up and, not wishing to interfere with any arrangements you may have made, tracked you from some distance to the bus stop. I had to hide in a shed for many freezing minutes as you stared at the building. Appalling architecture, you must have been thinking. The bus came, you got on, I ran, almost died, found the seat beside you, revived."

Olga looked at her hands. It sounded plausible but she still had an uncomfortable feeling. She felt like a forest deer being stalked by a wolf. The waitress brought the wine.

"You do believe me, don't you Olga?" Fat Alex pleaded, grasping the waitress round the waist. "Be my witness you gorgeous daughter of Bacchus, that Alexander Petrovich speaks the truth to his goddess Olga Nikolaevna on all matters relating to his pursuit of her within the university precincts."

The waitress giggled and tried to work her way out of Fat Alex's clasp. He refused to release her until she gave him a noisy kiss.

Fat Alex tasted and approved the new bottle of wine. Olga wondered whether she should leave before he got very drunk. She didn't want to offend him though. There was also the problem of the unfamiliar area with its threatening streets. Would she find her way back to the centre on her own? Perhaps it would be better to stay, despite the lascivious look on her companion's face.

Fat Alex shifted his body to the edge of his chair, tried

to drop onto one knee, but found it impossible to do so. He grasped Olga's hands instead. "Princess Olga," he said imploringly, "the flush in your cheeks, no doubt induced by this priceless wine, becomes you greatly. Were I not such an honourable and upright man, I would invite you to spend what is left of this winter afternoon in the comfort of my apartment, where I would administer solace and tenderness, thus to comfort you in the unforeseen absence of your dear husband, the valiant and noble Yuri. How heart broken you must be, how bereft, distraught and cold you must feel without him. Would that I were such a man who could take his place alongside you until his much yearned-for return."

Olga listened to the fluency of his words, trying to dismiss the innuendo. But his seductiveness was compelling, the force of his presence again overcoming the obstacle of his ugliness. She felt at the mercy of the wolf as he closed for the kill. She hid behind her silence.

Fat Alex released her hands and leaned back in his chair. He studied the other diners whilst enjoying a cigarette. He coughed and turned to Olga. "I want you to know I've not forgotten the interest you showed in my apartment when we went on that forest walk," he said, somewhat formally. "Am I correct in assuming you still wish to accomplish an exchange or have you changed your pretty little mind and decided to stay in your cosy love nest on the third floor?"

Olga was cross with herself for not anticipating this question, particularly as Fat Alex sounded more business-like. She was ill-prepared to answer, but did not want to lose the chance of finding out if he was serious. She struggled to sound clear headed.

"We are still interested to know if you would consider an exchange of apartments. There would be advantages for all of us. At the moment we would just like to hear your views."

"My views, at least those from my apartment window,

are unrivalled," Fat Alex said, laughing at his little joke. "But since you last visited my apartment, some weeks ago I remember, I've had a platoon of cleaners, polishers and painters sorting the hovel out. I preferred it as it was, but a young man with whom I have a pleasing relationship was horrified by the mess and chaos. He said he would never honour me with his company again unless it was cleaned and ordered like Heaven. Dear, sweet Olga, what could an infatuate like me do, faced with such an ultimatum?"

"Poor deviant Alex," Olga mocked, glad they were back to their verbal sparring. "It's amazing what it takes to get an apartment refurbished."

"So you must come and see it. You may not recognise it at first, but when you take in that view again, you'll know it's mine. Let us go now whilst the idea is fresh, to say nothing of the desire. Come, I'll get a taxi. Let me take you my fair, fair one to my cavern of delights."

Fat Alex was already on his feet, calling for their coats and hats. Olga stayed seated, anxious to show some reluctance, some indecision in the face of his unbounded excitement. She should at least attempt to resist his invitation, even if in the end she knew she would succumb. She was caught up in his enthusiasm, in that beguiling charm of his. He was like a little boy, who could not wait to show her yet another of his toys. She also suspected that, like a wolf-man, he could not avoid enticing her into his lair.

Without further protest, Olga allowed herself to be bustled out of the restaurant and onto the street. Where normal people would wait or walk some distance for a taxi, Fat Alex the magician had but to wave his arm for one to appear. No ordinary, scruffy Moscow taxi either, but a clean, shining Western car with comfortable seats and a sweet murmuring engine. Olga imagined she was indeed a princess being driven through the snow in a sparkling carriage. But sadly beside her rode a frog awaiting his transformation into a handsome prince. Until that happened, she decided she should return the hand which impatiently groped her thigh.

Fat Alex chatted loudly to the driver. Their conversation about flashy cars bored her. Olga looked out of the window. She took in the passing street scenes, recognising where she was with some relief. She distrusted Fat Alex sufficiently to suspect he might try a detour to some place he knew and she did not. So far they were going in the right direction for their apartment block.

But once there, what should she do? Should she go up to the eighth floor with him or should she perhaps plead a bad headache and lock herself in her own apartment? That would avoid any embarrassment, any explanations to Yuri. But there was the issue of the apartment swap to discuss. Also, wasn't she, Olga Nikolaevna, quite capable of looking after herself, should Fat Alex become too demanding? He was after all only a friend. He may talk stupidly about his desire to bed her, but that was all a charade. He didn't mean it for one moment.

Fat Alex paid the driver, whose voluble thanks spoke of a generous tip. Olga went ahead and summoned the lift. It shuddered down, arriving as Fat Alex came through the outer door to the apartment block. He entered the lift first, his huge girth covering the control panel. Olga hesitated for a moment before squeezing herself in beside him. He slipped an arm around her and, rotating the upper part of his body, pressed a pudgy finger on the button for the eighth floor. The lift groaned slowly upwards, as if objecting to the load.

Fat Alex took some time to find his keys and select the one for the apartment door. Olga stood back, watching him fumble and grunt. He succeeded at last and the door was pushed open.

"Now, my angel of the departing day, please enter my new Winter Palace," Fat Alex said waving his arm with a flourish. "I have every confidence you will desire it even more once you are inside."

Olga went in with a little fear but a greater curiosity. She was astonished. It was impossible to believe it was the same disgusting, chaotic apartment she had seen only recently. It had been completely transformed. Everything was new: furniture, carpets, curtains, and not just new but expensively new. It all matched and held together in a way which Olga could only covet. Nothing was out of place either; no piles of books on the floor, no dirty washing on the chairs, no un-emptied ashtrays on the tables. It smelt clean, pristine. There was no strong sense of Fat Alex at all. It was as if a stranger lived there now.

"Incredible, unbelievable," was all Olga could find to say, still gawping in amazement. "But who did all this and where did you get it from? You didn't mention these new things at all."

"Friends, good friends arranged it. I just said I wanted it changed and left them to it. They know me well, so guessed I would like it. And I do, I definitely do, very much indeed."

"But Alex – how will you keep it looking like this? It's not in your nature to live in this way. How long will it be before it becomes a shack again?"

Fat Alex appeared offended. He didn't answer immediately, but went over to the large window. "You haven't mentioned the view have you? I thought you were only interested in the view from my apartment."

Olga realized she had been negligent. She'd hardly glanced at the window since coming in. Normally she would go straight to it and just stand there for several minutes absorbing the magnificent scene before her. "I was saving that for last. Surely you wanted me to admire the transformation of your apartment first? The view's still there, isn't it? It hasn't changed or gone away has it?" Olga made her way across the room to join Fat Alex by the window. "No, it's still as enchanting as ever."

They stood side by side, gazing in silence. The light was going quickly, turning the sky from a brilliant blue to the deep ultramarine of dusk. Streetlights stuttered into life, forming linear markers for the probing lights of vehicles. Windows at different levels made chessboard squares of white and yellow, some already subdued by blinds or drawn curtains. The ice strewn surface of the broad river reflected the myriad lights of the city. Olga let Fat Alex take her hand as they watched the fading day from the darkness of the room.

"You haven't seen the bedroom yet," Fat Alex said.

"I'd rather see the kitchen."

"Ah yes, the kitchen. More important to a young wife than the bedroom perhaps."

"Sometimes you talk more nonsense than a *troika* driver. I'm curious to see what your friends have done to your kitchen, that's all. Don't forget that ours is the same size as yours."

Olga detached her hand from Fat Alex's, made him turn on some lamps and lead the way across the main room. As there was no space for them both in the cramped kitchen, Olga brushed past him in the doorway. She felt him press himself against her.

Again she could not take in the changes. There were new worktops, cupboards, a stove and a complete set of shining kitchen equipment. "Where did you get all this from?" she gasped with envy. "It's foreign isn't it?"

"German mainly. Some bits also from Finland and Italy. A United Nations kitchen I call it." Olga laughed for the first time since entering Alex's apartment.

"And now would you like to see the bedroom?" he asked.

Olga looked at him. He was grinning as he so often did. She liked it when he smiled. She liked his dancing eyes too and the way his dark hair wound itself in curls. She felt drawn to him, his large powerful body inviting,

155

comforting. But he was still the cunning, stealthy wolf and she needed to beware.

"If you like. It's no doubt as fine as the rest of the place," she replied.

Fat Alex went into the bedroom and beckoned Olga to follow him. She remained in the doorway.

"It's beautiful Alex, really beautiful," she said, admiring the quality and workmanship of the room. Fat Alex sat down on the huge bed.

"Come and feel this for yourself," he said patting and smoothing the counterpane. "It's English. Best quality of course."

"I expect you sleep on it like a man without sin," she said tentatively.

"I do and I make love on it like a man without restraint."

Olga did not move from the doorway. She again fixed her eyes on Fat Alex. A devil in her head urged her on, an insistent voice persuading, cajoling, tempting. Surely at this moment she wanted nothing more than to go to him. Didn't she wish to enter into his arms, into his embrace, into his power? Didn't she long to be gently, slowly undressed by him, to feel his desire? And didn't she crave to strip him naked, to see and feel that vast body and to have him take her on the newness of the bed? Her lips parted at the thought, her eyes found no focus, her limbs trembled as if she were already in his grasp.

"Come Olga, my loveliness. Come and put such temerity as you have behind you. It's a beautiful bed made for beautiful people. It was designed with you in mind. Come and lie your silken body on this blissful place."

"I need the bathroom," Olga blurted out, finding the will-power to back away from the bedroom door. She turned and walked unsteadily to the sumptuous bathroom. She locked the door firmly behind her. She shook with fear and confusion.

Fat Alex was sitting on the sofa in the main room when Olga emerged several minutes later.

"The bathroom is impressive," she said, her voice subdued.

Fat Alex nodded and continued to smoke a Turkish cigarette. He indicated to Olga to take a seat, not insisting she join him on the sofa. She remained standing, shifting her feet uneasily.

"No, you cannot go yet," Fat Alex said curtly. "We have some business to conduct. Come and sit down and stop bobbing about like an old hen."

Olga moved to one of the armchairs. "So what's this business you want to talk about?"

"May St Cyprian save us. The apartment, dear lady, the apartment. You do still want to exchange, don't you?"

Olga silently swore at the wine for muddling her mind. She had been so overwhelmed by both Fat Alex and his apartment, she'd almost forgotten about the proposal to exchange. Subconsciously she had perhaps dismissed the whole idea. "Yes of course we do. But do you, after all this expensive work's been carried out? I mean this place is indeed a palace compared to our apartment."

"Dear Olga," said Fat Alex, mellowing a little. "This looks wonderful, you're right. But as you pointed out yourself earlier, this is not the kind of place where I can live. Well... I could, but not happily, not contentedly. I shall therefore be willing to exchange apartments with you, provided we can agree the terms and conditions."

Olga wanted to jump up and kiss him but restrained herself. She didn't want another misinterpretation. In any case, his conditions might be unacceptable. "That is wonderful news for us. When were you thinking about doing the exchange?" she asked excitedly. "And when will we know about your terms and conditions?"

"We should move in the Spring. That's always a good time to do such things. And the terms, well, I have not finally decided on them yet. When Yuri returns, I shall have them ready."

"I can't wait to tell him. He'll be delighted."

"And when does he intend to grace you with his presence? I'll be bound that no man could willingly stay away from you for more than half a day."

"I'm not quite certain. He didn't know exactly either. By the end of the week for sure," Olga answered jerkily. "Anyhow I must be going, Alex. Thank you very much for the lunch. Your restaurant and this apartment are superb."

Fat Alex eased himself off the sofa and found Olga's coat. He went with her to the door.

"Thank you again," Olga said, giving him a quick kiss on the cheek. He unexpectedly gripped her by the arm.

"I shall have all the terms and conditions typed out in duplicate by Friday. There will one other condition which will not be on the list. It is, my lovely Olga, that you come to me between now and Friday and share my bed for an hour or two. You resisted me today, but you will not refuse me a second time."

Olga looked at Fat Alex. For a moment she thought he was up to his usual tricks, pushing the limits of his humour too far. But the more she searched his eyes, the more she was convinced he wasn't joking.

She tore herself away and ran down the corridor past the door to the lift. She skeltered down the stairs to the third floor, bouncing off the walls in her haste. Once in her apartment, she threw herself on the bed, sobbing like a child. "Yuri, Yuri," she cried, "for God's sake come back, come back now."

CHAPTER 12

The invitation was lodged in the corner of the mirror. Formal functions were not Peter's style: he always felt gauche and out of place, unable to engage in the small talk required on such occasions. He hoped there might be some good excuse he could make. Perhaps he could arrange to be away, undertaking some vital business in a far corner of Russia. But his attendance was expected: he had been in the country long enough to merit an Ambassador's invitation. He was obliged to go.

He stood in front of the mirror, putting the finishing touches to his new tie, which failed to knot as well as he wished. He had one eye on the impressive invitation, working out what time he ought to arrive. Not too early of course, but not noticeably late either, particularly as he planned an early exit. It said 6.30pm in the raised gold script, so 6.40 would be appropriate.

Relieved of his hat and coat in the Embassy's entrance hall, Peter joined the line of guests waiting at the head of the staircase. The queue moved steadily forward, making dignified progress towards the host and hostess. The welcome was short and businesslike: brief words of introduction accompanied by a quick handshake. Beyond the double doors, waiters stood with trays of drinks. Feeling in need of encouragement, Peter selected a whisky and moved cautiously into the reception.

In the magnificent surroundings of the White and Gold Room, the Embassy staff were busy greeting guests and exchanging pleasantries. Peter stood awkwardly to one side, admiring the huge chandeliers and those oil paintings not obscured by the crowd. He hoped to catch sight of someone he recognised from Commercial Section. Instead a young man he had not met before came across, shook his hand and spoke to him in perfect Russian.

"Actually I'm British," Peter told him.

"Terribly sorry. I've only been here a week. Still finding my feet and getting to know who's who. Nice to meet you anyhow. I'm John Metcalfe, Third Secretary Political."

"Peter Standridge. I've been in Russia for almost five months doing some work under the auspices of the Handsome Fund." Peter took a gulp of his whisky, by which time John Metcalfe had moved on, burrowing into the mass of people in the centre of the room. A waiter with a tray of canapés appeared, pleading with his eyes for Peter to lighten his load. He demolished two in quick succession and was on the point of having a third, when he saw Jean Burroughs detach herself from a group to his left. She spotted him and came over.

"Hello, Peter," she said, casting a suspicious eye over the canapés. "You look a bit lost. Don't you know anyone here?"

"No, I can't say I do, other than you. It's not my scene really. I can't see the purpose of it all. A lot of inconsequential chit-chat. A bit futile."

"That's rather a strong opinion, isn't it? These formal occasions may seem old-fashioned to outsiders but a lot of work gets done, you know."

"I'm sorry. I spoke out of turn. I didn't mean to be rude."

"Apologies accepted. Just cheer up and stop looking so damn miserable. Whilst you're here, you may as well enjoy yourself. Not too much whisky though." Jean sipped her orange juice as she surveyed the room. "In any case, I shouldn't be talking to you. I ought to be circulating and looking after our guests."

"But I am a guest, a British one, but a guest all the same."

Jean stared at him for a moment. "Yes, I suppose you are. You've been around so long I keep thinking you're Embassy, but you're not. So I can chat to you for just a few minutes without someone senior giving me the stare. They always do you know, as if to say time's up, move on, find a really tricky guest to talk to."

Peter laughed. He felt better for Jean's company. She was relaxed and easy, someone without pretence and self-importance. He hoped she wouldn't rush off too soon. Another waiter replenished Peter's glass. "To change the subject, many thanks for supper the other night. It was a delightful evening. If you and Chris hadn't invited me over, I'd probably have got nastily drunk all by myself."

"Well, it was good to see you, but don't expect me to believe that a nice-looking young man like you was going to be alone on a Saturday night in Moscow. In the old days, that was probably the case, but not now. There's lots going on here, no shortage of entertainment of every type... that's if my dear husband is to be believed."

"I'm sure he's right about that," Peter said, recalling the exploits of the *Hooligany*.

"You know, I don't think I've seen Ruth this evening," Jean said. "Maybe she's not here. She does have to attend an awful lot of official receptions and dinners. Perhaps she's been given the night off." She looked back at Peter. "It was good of you to walk her home after our little soirée."

"It was my pleasure," Peter mumbled, hoping Jean would not dwell on the matter.

She regarded him more closely. "I was a little worried, as she did seem to be drinking quite a lot. Was everything all right? No dramas were there, like her passing out and you having to put her to bed?"

Peter tried not to blush. Why was Jean being so inquisitive? What business was it of hers to pry into his affairs? He swallowed his whisky before replying. "No, she was fine. To be honest I haven't seen her since. Is she all right?"

"As far as I know. It's just that she has a reputation for having a bit of an appetite when it comes to men. I didn't wish to see you being devoured against your wishes, that was all."

Before Peter could respond, Chris Burroughs stalked over. He wasn't smiling, which was unusual for him. "Jean, you mustn't stand here in full view of the whole room talking to someone you know, and British at that. The Head of Chancery has just had a word with me. He's not happy. You're letting the side down."

"Oh dear," Jean said, only partly concerned. "But Peter is a guest you know. He's not one of us." She turned to Peter, giving him a wink. "Nice to chat all the same, but I'd better toddle along and seek out some boring old buffer to flatter with my atrocious Russian." Jean bustled off and introduced herself to a clump of serious men on the far side of the reception room.

Peter finished his whisky and thought about leaving.

"Come with me," Chris said. "There're some people you might like to meet."

Peter dutifully followed as he snaked through clusters of guests to the far side of the room. He stopped beside a group of younger people, who were chatting gaily. They paused and made room in their circle for the two of them.

Chris introduced Peter briefly and turned to go. "I'll leave you to it then. Just thought you might like to meet some people of your own age."

An older waiter arrived with a tray of fresh drinks, drawn no doubt by the vivacity of the group. He made a few jokes, fussed around the young women and took pleasure in their laughter. He withdrew with a promise to return once he'd attended to the "old soaks".

Peter eyed the others diffidently over the top of his glass. From their conversation, he established two of them were British: David, a young businessman like himself, and

Paula, a secretary in Commercial Section. The other two were Russian, Vladimir and Anna, both of whom worked for Intourist and spoke excellent English. John Metcalfe completed the circle, but quickly made his excuses and moved on.

"So, Mr Standridge, what is it that you do here in Russia?" Anna from Intourist asked.

Peter told her as sensibly as he could. He tried to make it sound interesting and exciting, but accepted urban renewal and infrastructure did not have glamour on their side. As he spoke, he prayed her wide brown eyes would not glaze over.

She looked at him, a faint smile on her lips. He began to talk quickly, almost gabbling in his haste to impress, his voice running ahead of him. He was mesmerised by the beauty of her smile, the purity of her complexion. His eyes moved admiringly from the cut of her hair to the grace of her body. A sweet agony rose inside him as he finished saying all he had to say. He continued to stare at her oafishly: she seemed amused, entertained.

"Mr Standridge, with all this travelling around our country, you must know more about it than we do in Intourist."

Peter tried to reassert some control over himself. "No, it would be impossible for me to do that. I only touch the surface of your country. You, on the other hand, understand it."

"No, we believe in Russia, but we cannot explain it. Was it not a famous Englishman who said Russia was a riddle wrapped in a mystery inside an enigma?"

"Yes, of course! Winston Churchill. I agree, it's an accurate description." Peter wanted both to look and not look at Anna. He longed to feast his eyes on her but feared to do so. He had to resist betraying such an obvious interest. Apparent indifference was required.

He was relieved when others joined their conversation. There was a lot of laughter, voices raised more than usual for such a formal occasion. Glances were thrown in their direction, more envious than reproving. The waiter returned as promised, but no one wanted more. Guests started to shuffle, preparing to take their leave.

None of the young group made any suggestion about continuing elsewhere. Peter kept his silence, foolishly already wanting Anna for himself. But perhaps Vladimir was there before him. Better to put her out of his mind. What would one so beautiful ever see in him?

Polite goodbyes were said all too quickly. Some hopes of further meetings were ritually expressed. Peter watched Anna and Vladimir thank the Ambassador and leave the room. They laughed together. She took his arm. She didn't look back.

"Are you Peter Standridge?"

"Yes, I am," Peter said, turning to find a tall, elegant man with a slender woman beside him.

"Jocelyn Misterton. I'm the Cultural Attaché. I'd been hoping to meet you earlier, but the paths of commerce and art seldom cross. Oh – my wife, Candida."

"Nice to meet you," Peter said shaking her delicate hand.

"We were in a little town last week making some arrangements for a cultural exchange," Jocelyn continued. "For a small town it has a very good music school. Candida's a pianist, so she was particularly interested in accompanying me to see it, if you'll excuse the pun." He chuckled at his little joke with Candida smiling in support.

"Where did you say you went?" Peter asked.

"I'm not sure I did. Anyhow, it was called Stambov. I understand you were doing some work there quite recently."

"Yes, I was. I grew quite fond of the place."

"There is a very fine violinist teaching at the school called Lydia Kuznetsova. We heard her play. Exceptional she was. She is coming to Moscow this weekend at short notice. She's agreed to stand in for someone who's been taken ill. The concert is at the Conservatoire on Saturday evening. You ought to go."

Peter could not believe what he was hearing. "I'd very much like to," he said with a smile. "I'm fairly certain I'm free that evening."

"Excellent, excellent. Such talent, as well you know," Jocelyn said whimsically, glancing at his wife. Candida put her glass down and clasped her hands excitedly.

"You see, Kuznetsova mentioned she'd met you whilst you were in Stambov. She said the two of you had played together, but somehow your instrument got lost in translation. She said you were very good, very experienced for someone so relatively young. If only I'd known before, you and I could have had many pleasurable sessions together here in Moscow. So I've been dying to ask, what do you play?"

Peter could not disguise his embarrassment, nor his amusement. The combination of Anna, the whisky and now Lydia Kuznetsova had made him dizzy. "There was indeed some confusion in translation. I don't play any musical instrument. I can only think she was referring to us dancing together at the Faculty party. It's quite funny really, the *double entendre*."

Candida's face turned to stone as she realized what a fool she had made of herself. Jocelyn looked equally appalled. "Well at least you've cleared up that little misunderstanding. You must excuse us, Mr Standridge."

Once alone, Peter faced the curtained window and laughed. He could not decide what had entertained him most. Whatever it was, there was no doubt in his mind that this was the best diplomatic reception he had attended.

It was time for him to leave. The room was thinning out: he had already stayed longer than he intended. He said his polite farewells and collected his coat and hat.

Putting on his overshoes in the entrance hall, Peter set off into the night.

As the cold was not too intense, he decided to walk. It wasn't far. He only needed to cross the river and follow the embankment below the Kremlin walls to get to Hotel Leskov. With any luck it would not snow. Pulling his heavy coat tighter, he made his way briskly along the pavement towards the bridge.

Peter skirted round a heap of dirty snow spilling from the gutter. He passed a parked car, its engine running, the faint sound of a symphony drifting from its radio. So what about Lydia? He was excited by the thought of seeing her so much sooner than expected. In only two days time he would hear and watch her play. And afterwards? Well, who knew what might happen later.

He found it more difficult to visualise her now. There was an overlay of Anna which distorted his perception. She looked younger than he knew she was, lithe instead of statuesque. But for all the frustration of her changing image, his desire was still intact. He wanted to feel her again, to breathe her in and have her envelop him in the way she had before.

So what about this Anna? He could only think of her as Anna from Intourist. He had missed the surname, but it would make no difference. He had only set eyes on her about an hour ago, talked to her for minutes. Why bother? Their paths would not cross again, but there would be no harm in imagining. He would allow himself to indulge in a little fantasy of his own.

Peter walked more slowly up the rise to St Basil's Cathedral and crossed the end of Red Square. He had only been twenty minutes in the cold, but he welcomed the warmth of the hotel foyer. The receptionist waved an envelope at him as well as his key. His crazed mind suggested a *billet doux* from Anna. Peter took the envelope and finding a seat, tore it open.

Dear Mr Standridge,
A friend of mine has come to Moscow and delivers this letter to you at your hotel. I myself shall come on Tuesday to bring the gift for my friend in England. I am honoured that you will take it to him from me. I shall arrive at your hotel at 13.00 with the package. If this is for you a bad time, leave a message at reception with a more convenient time. I shall be in Moscow for a few days so a meeting will be possible.
I shall take pleasure in seeing you again.
With my best wishes,
Dimitri Krotkin

Krotkin's letter reminded Peter he had only a week before his flight to England. There was much to do before he left. It was good a trip to Pavlozavodsk in the north had been postponed until his return in January. Quite what he was supposed to achieve at this time of the year in the frozen wastes of Northern Russia eluded him. There was some suggestion of him appreciating the difficulties the authorities faced at first hand, but three days close to the Arctic Circle was not appealing. In any case, surely it was dark for much of the time in mid winter? What would there be for him to see?

Peter put Krotkin's letter in his pocket and made his way into the hotel restaurant. He was not particularly hungry but decided to order the meatballs. When they arrived, he felt even less inclined to try them. They sat in grease which seeped into the accompanying chips, turning them limp and grey. He picked at the surface of the meatballs with his fork and selected a couple of the drier chips beached on the rim of his plate. It was no good, the whisky would not let him continue. He pushed his meal away, contenting himself with bread and reviving mineral water.

* * *

Saturday evening came soon enough. Peter had a busy Friday, not helped by a sore head from the Embassy reception. He was equally committed for much of Saturday. He had found out more about the concert from the hotel's tourist bureau, discovering that tickets could only be purchased at the door. Arrangements were also made for Peter to catch up with his colleagues after the concert. The normal Saturday night out had been cancelled due to lack of interest. A small group had decided to go out for a meal; Peter would join them later if he could.

The Moscow Conservatoire would require a suit. The newly dry cleaned one and laundered blue shirt would do. He dressed with care, conscious of the need to make a good impression. But, as he put on his clothes, he visualised Lydia removing them one by one with the dexterity of an accomplished artist. Lest it impede her, he even decided against the trouser belt he had planned to wear. He looked at himself in the mirror and imagined her fingers gliding through his hair.

It was snowing again as Peter took a taxi to the Conservatoire, the short journey taking longer than expected. He fretted about the delay and the taxi finally drew up with only five minutes to spare. To his relief there was no queue inside the main entrance, but the ticket office was closed. He could hear an orchestra tuning somewhere in the building and hurried towards the sound. Reaching the door a little breathless, the hall looked completely full. Lydia was obviously very popular.

"*Bilety*?" Peter asked, turning to two women sitting at a desk by the entrance.

"*Nyet*," one of them answered. She looked at Peter. "*Inostranets*, foreign man?"

"*Da, da*, English," Peter said, becoming flustered. As the two women bickered, he removed some dollars from his wallet and laid them on the table. The women paused to look at the notes before one of them bent down and produced a ticket from a tin.

"You, special," she said, scooping up the notes. "Good chair, very good chair. Ten dollar chair." Peter took the ticket. Row D was near the front and he walked quickly up the aisle, finding his seat as the conductor entered to applause.

Peter looked at the programme, deciphering the Russian as best he could. In a way he had hurried for no purpose as Lydia was performing a Prokofiev Violin Concerto in the second half. He jumped as the orchestra launched into a Mozart symphony.

There was not much to do in the short interval while the orchestra's chairs and music stands were rearranged. Most of the audience remained in or near their places, chatting amongst themselves. Peter felt privileged to have one of the best seats in the hall with an excellent view of the platform. It was an enviable position. Most of the surrounding seats were occupied by distinguished concert goers of middle age. He realized he was also the object of some interest to those nearby. They studied at him as if trying to remember which promising young musician he was. Some even nodded to him knowingly. Peter smiled in response. *Good chair* indeed it was.

Peter glanced behind him. No one was as young as him until at least Row M. But several rows back he was sure he caught sight of Candida Misterton. She looked away the moment Peter caught her eye.

The orchestra reassembled, the audience resumed their seats. More fine tuning from the leader, followed by an expectant hush. Peter felt his heart racing. The side door opened. Lydia strode across the hall to the centre of the platform, the conductor in her wake. The audience clapped enthusiastically.

Lydia looked magnificent. She stood majestically to acknowledge the applause, her fine head thrown back, a confident smile on her lips. Her long shimmering dress contoured the curves of her body, highlighting her ample breasts. Her bare shoulders glistened in the light of the chandeliers. She placed the violin under her chin, its dark polished surface contrasting with the whiteness of her skin. Peter was transfixed.

The music of the concerto sounded strange to Peter's ears. He had no idea of its movements and structure, or whether it was a difficult piece to play. Such matters were of no consequence. It was sufficient just to listen and admire.

Lydia attacked the music. She turned and twisted, coaxing sublime notes from the strings, imparting meaning to the sounds. Peter sat motionless, only his eyes shifting to follow her every movement. He loved the passion on her face, the energy of her body. He watched her supple fingers race across the strings, longing for them to caress his naked skin. He wanted her to play and play, and then for him alone.

The concerto finished triumphantly. There was an imperceptible pause before the hall exploded. The applause was tumultuous, the audience rising to its feet. Even the dignified roared their approval. Lydia smiled and bowed, withdrew and made a second entrance followed by a third. A huge bouquet was presented. She took a final bow and disappeared from view. The applause gradually subsided.

The audience was reluctant to go; they wanted more and would stay all night to hear her play again. Gradually they started to leave, accepting their disappointment. Peter sat down overcome with emotion. He yearned for her. Some well dressed members of the audience gathered near the platform. Perhaps if he waited, she might reappear.

"Glad you came?" Jocelyn Misterton said, standing two seats away.

"Yes, very much so. She was stunning."

"I thought you might say that. Anyhow we're on our way, but I expect you'd like to wait."

170

"Yes, I think I will. But thanks for telling me about the concert. I'd never have forgiven myself if I'd missed it."

"No doubt, no doubt. But I'd better go now," Jocelyn said with agitation.

Peter nodded a goodbye. Turning his head, he saw Candida waiting impatiently at the back of the hall.

The side door opened. Lydia and the conductor emerged. They received more applause from the group of dignitaries before hands were shaken and kisses given. Peter rose to his feet. He had to see her. He moved forward to join the waiting group.

No one seemed annoyed at Peter's presence. As a famous young musician, he had every right to be there to pay his respects to such a virtuoso. He waited his turn. Lydia smiled as he came towards her.

"Wonderful, superb, fantastic," he said, hoping she would understand. She smiled even more. He kissed her formally on both cheeks. He felt her warmth, her softness.

"Good boy, you come see, you come hear," she said stroking him. "Very good for me." She ran her fingers lightly down his cheek. She caressed his neck, drawing his face gently towards her. She delicately kissed him on the lips.

Peter looked into her eyes. He desperately wanted to say something more, something loving but no words came. A man moved between them, ushering Lydia on. Peter thought it best to go. He looked at her one more time as she laughed and talked to others. He walked out of the concert hall like a man bereaved.

Standing outside the Conservatoire, he adjusted his hat and buttoned his coat. The snow was still falling, covering the city in a grey white mist. The swirling snowflakes masked the lights, rendering them mean and feeble. The gloominess obscured the buildings, disrupting the traffic and muffling the figures on the streets. He crossed Bolshaya

Nikitskaya and braved a side road, his shoes crunching on the compacted snow. It would be safer trudging along the pavements of the boulevards, but he wanted time alone to replay the concert in his mind.

The taste of Lydia still lingered, but was now less powerful, diluted by the melting snowflakes on his lips. Yet the memory of her was stronger. He saw her again on the concert platform, glowing with the exertion of playing. And she had remembered him, appearing more than pleased to see him. He in turn had not been disappointed. If anything she was even more alluring than she was in Stambov. He worshipped this woman whom he hardly knew.

Peter stopped. But where was his rival Herr Rudolf Metzinger, where was he, that jousting Rudi? Surely he must have accompanied Lydia to Moscow? Even if Peter had missed him at the concert, he would have seen him afterwards for certain. So where was he? And what of Lydia's husband, might he be around, anxious to keep an eye on his wife in this exciting city? And was he not the man who would be keen to slit Peter's throat if he went too far with her? He shivered more at the thought of cold steel than the penetrating frost. He started to walk more briskly.

Tverskaya Street was busy with pedestrians and traffic. Snowploughs and salt trucks kept the roadway clear, whilst small bands of women shovelled and swept the snow. Peter was close to the restaurant by Pushkin Square and trusted his colleagues would still be there. He felt hungry.

"Ah, so how is our music lover, our *Meistersinger*?" one of them joked, as Peter shook hands round the table.

"It was very good, excellent in fact," Peter replied.

"I went to the Bolshoy once," said another. "Some opera was on. Did nothing for me. I had to go. I mean, there is no way I could go home after weeks in Moscow and say I hadn't been to the Bolshoy. The wife would have killed me."

They all laughed. The five of them were close to finishing their main course and several bottles of wine as Peter joined them. He knew none of them well. They were acquaintances, people he would not have bothered with, had they not been thrown together in Hotel Leskov. Peter certainly regarded them as a social convenience.

They made room for him at the table and continued their conversation. Peter was poor company and he knew it. His thoughts were elsewhere. Perhaps he should not have come. It was a mistake to join a party half way through, particularly when he was hardly in the mood. The others seemed not to mind. They were quite happy getting drunk and telling their outrageous stories. Peter said little as he concentrated on his steak, laughing only when he sensed he should.

His colleagues were keen to make a night of it. After much argument, they settled on a nightclub and urged Peter to come along. He declined, making some excuse, which they clearly did not believe. They were not insistent. They said their goodbyes.

It was close to midnight when Peter reached Hotel Leskov. He had decided to walk back from the restaurant, making his way down Tverskaya Street and across Red Square. The snow had stopped and the temperature was falling. He went up to his room. Taking off his suit and tie, he kicked his shoes under the bed and slumped in a chair. He felt more emotionally drained than physically tired. He poured himself some mineral water.

He was angry with himself for not asking Lydia to join him for a drink or even supper after the performance. If she had been committed to accepting the hospitality of the Conservatoire, he could at least have tried to make some arrangement to see her later. That must have been possible despite her bad English and his worse Russian.

Peter got up and looked out of the window at the

Kremlin. The settled snow covered every roof, cupola and battlement like crafted icing. Long shadows from the emerging moonlight stretched over the inner courtyards, silent in the cold. A sentry moved slowly on his patrol, his rifle swinging on his shoulder. The bell of the Spasskiy Tower tolled midnight.

There was a sharp tap on Peter's door. Were his colleagues back so soon, the nightclub a disappointment? If they had come to plague him, he would give them a piece of his mind. He went to the door in irritation, knowing he was a sight in his socks and open shirt. He slipped the chain off and swung the door open. Lydia stood there, a champagne bottle in her hand.

Peter gaped. Lydia appraised him and laughing, pushed into the room. Peter locked the door and turned to face her. She was still dressed as she was for the concert.

Lydia emptied his water glass into the basin and over-filled it with foaming champagne. She drank it down and topping up the glass, handed it to Peter.

"*Za vashe zdarovye...* drink all," she said.

"Cheers," Peter said, taking two quick gulps.

Lydia unzipped her dress which fell to the floor like a crumpled sail. For a moment only the rigging of her underwear covered her naked body. She moved towards Peter and drove her hands through his open shirt. She kissed him long and hard. He was helpless in his arousal. Lydia tore off his clothes and thrust herself on him. They fell onto the bed, rolling like a ketch in a surging sea.

Lydia groaned as they lay entwined. "Very nice, very good," she whispered. They adjusted themselves on the narrow bed, pressed together in the afterglow of pleasure. She sighed and murmured. She closed her eyes.

Propping himself on his elbow, Peter looked at the sleeping Lydia. She was no longer magnificent, immaculate. Her hair hung in sticky strands, her lipstick was smudged and faded. Her face unprotected and masked by her make-up showed its imperfections. Her body, only seen before in the stricture of a flattering dress, billowed more naturally now it was less restrained. Peter felt a twinge of disappointment. She began to breathe heavily.

He lay back quietly, wondering how she'd managed to find him, to track him down. Perhaps she too was staying here, unable to secure a room anywhere cheaper at short notice. But he didn't care, he had enjoyed her. He shut his eyes, letting a shallow sleep overtake him.

When he woke, Lydia still lay exposed beside him, her mature body relaxed and unimpeded. He stroked her breasts and ran his fingers lightly over her skin. He touched her limp hand, caressing the fingers which had pressed those strings, marvelling at their softness. Yet somehow she seemed a different person, no longer the exciting, alluring violinist playing exquisite music on the stage. She was only a sleeping woman, vulnerable in her nakedness like any other.

She stirred, opened her eyes and smiled. He rolled across, stretched himself over her body, and arched into her with vigour.

They lay moulded to one another, exhausted by their passion. Their hands continued to explore but now moved with languid gentleness. Gradually they unwound and Peter raised his body from her. He reached out to the table and filled their glass with the rest of the champagne. Lydia rested herself against him. They kissed, taking alternate sips from the tall glass, enjoying the decadence of the moment.

"Rudolf in Moscow?" Peter asked.

"*Nyet*. No Rudolf. Rudolf end. Rudolf finished." Lydia moved her arm briskly in a chopping action. "Rudolf no good." She twisted her head, staring in disbelief at Peter's alarm clock.

"*Bozhi moy*. My God," she shrieked and scrambled over Peter and off the bed. She found her underwear, wriggled into her dress and slipped on her shoes. Peter was bewildered.

"What's the matter? Is there a problem?"

"Problem? Problem for me." She looked at Peter. "And big problem for you."

"What problem?" Peter asked, standing naked beside the bed. Lydia pressed herself against him, kissing him frantically.

"Husband problem," she whispered. "Husband in hotel, husband wait for me." Peter shuddered. Might the husband force Lydia to tell him where she had been and come after Peter with his carving knife? He felt sick at the thought, but Lydia was already by the door. She threw Peter's coat at him.

"You look, you see," she said, miming how Peter should check the corridor was clear. Peter put his coat round him, catching sight of his ridiculous appearance in the mirror. He unlocked the door, pulling it open slowly. He peered up and down the passageway. No one was there.

"No husband," Peter said.

Lydia brushed past him, forgetting to give him a farewell embrace in her haste to leave. She turned back and stifled him with her lips. She hurried down the corridor.

Peter locked the door, put the chain across and wedged his desk chair firmly under the handle. He was not having Mr Kuznetzov paying him a visit in the dead of night.

CHAPTER 13

It was the worst week in Olga Poliakova's life. Nothing had gone right from Monday to Saturday. Yuri's sudden departure, his absence, his silence from wherever he was, were almost too much to bear. She missed him even more than she had imagined. But she was angry too. Why was he not here when she needed him most?

Olga continued with her routine as best she could. She still trembled and often broke down in tears whenever she thought of Fat Alex and his demands. It was bad enough knowing he was there five floors above waiting in lusty anticipation for her arrival. Worse was the possibility of her bumping into him on the stairs or in the lift or at the entrance to the apartment block. What would she say, what would she do. Or more to the point, what might *he* do?

She took sensible precautions. She left her apartment very early each morning, listening for footsteps before descending the stairs to the exit. She would walk fast in the darkness to the bus stop, keeping an eye on shadowy strangers. If one of the figures remotely resembled Fat Alex, she would move away and keep her distance. She did admit to being ultra cautious. After all he did have a silhouette like no other, unmistakable even in the dark. Rarely, too, did he appear from his apartment before the winter sun had risen.

Her diligence in the University library was remarkable. It would not be unusual for her to spend a full twelve hours at her place by the window. She was waiting at the door when the librarians unlocked and had to be reminded of the time when they came to close up. But her restlessness was noted too. She would settle for a while, apparently absorbed in reading and writing. Then she would spend a long time staring out of the window or going for a slow walk round the book stacks, lingering here and there, inattentively thumbing an occasional volume.

Yet for all the hours spent in this great seat of learning, Olga achieved surprisingly little. The squandering of such an opportunity annoyed her intensely. She knew she could have done so much, forging ahead with her project with so few commitments to distract her. But the willpower to concentrate had deserted her. It was an absurd, indecent waste of time.

To add to her frustration, Olga found herself contriving to extend the breaks from her work. She would go for long walks through the building and, if the weather were not too bad, she would take to the grounds, keeping a careful eye on others. She would go off to the canteen and watch the door to see who came in. On occasions she would impose on those she knew, insist she buy them coffee and sit and talk till their patience was exhausted. They would make their excuses and leave, concerned that the sensible Olga Poliakova was behaving so oddly.

Going home at the end of the day presented the greatest danger. It was always late in the evening and, if she could not persuade a friend back to her apartment for a drink or light supper, she would creep into the building as silently as a soldier on patrol. She would check out the foyer, identify the sounds and, if she sensed no ambush, make her way softly up the stairs. She had become adept at unlocking her apartment door without a sound. Once inside, she was assiduous in double locking and chaining the stout door. It took all her courage to check each room, especially the bedroom. She looked in all the places where Fat Alex could conceal himself, which, in her saner moments, she would admit were very few.

Each day seemed longer than the one before. If Wednesday had but twenty-four hours, Thursday had thirty-six and Friday twice that number. And still no word from Yuri. The telephone did ring each evening, making Olga's heart race more from fear than anticipation. Each time she hesitated before lifting the receiver, sick at the thought of hearing Fat Alex's voice the other end. But it never was, nor was it Yuri's: only a couple of friends, her father and two wrong numbers.

Olga's sense of guilt depressed her even more than Yuri's absence. She was honest enough to admit her fascination for Fat Alex. She knew in some primitive way she was attracted to him. She could not help it, but were it not for the relaxing effect of the wine, she could have controlled her emotions better. It would have been so pleasant to continue with their mild, innocuous flirting, but Alex had ruined it all. Olga remained in no doubt that he was not his normal playful self when he had made his wishes known to her. What is more, she believed that, given the opportunity, he would force himself on her if she did not submit to his demands. Everything had changed. She could only view him now with trepidation.

At some point she would have to confess to Yuri. It would take all her ingenuity to explain what had happened and why they were not going ahead with an apartment exchange. She would want to dissuade Yuri from immediately tearing upstairs to attack Alex with whatever came to hand. That would achieve nothing and cause endless trouble.

What worried Olga more was how Yuri might react to her. She hoped their love for one another would be strong enough to survive this gathering storm. The last thing she wanted was distrust and suspicion to enter their marriage. She had been faithful and loyal to him and, as far as she knew, he had been likewise to her. He would be devastated if she told him how close she had been to succumbing to Fat Alex on his new English bed. His nagging attraction would have to remain her closest secret.

It would not be helpful either to blame her behaviour on the influence of the wine. She knew Yuri would condemn her for agreeing to have lunch with Fat Alex in the first place and for not showing more self control. He would also berate her for being so keen to get Fat Alex's apartment. Did she not think he would want something extra from the deal? *Foolish girl*, she could hear him say.

Now Saturday was here to be treated as yet another working day. She had convinced herself Yuri would be there when she came home the previous evening. But he was not, nor did he ring with news of when he would be back. The hours of Saturday were waiting to be filled.

Unsurprisingly, Olga sought sanctuary in the University library yet again. The cafeteria was half-empty at lunchtime. Olga joined Maria, a friend from her course, who made some unconvincing excuses for also being at work. Olga too spoke half-truths about Yuri's absence and her need to catch up with a backlog of research.

"I've heard there is an exceptionally good concert at the Conservatoire this evening," Maria said. "Lydia Kuznetsova's playing. She's apparently standing in at short notice. I'm going. Why don't you come along too, if you've got nothing better on?"

Olga took little persuading. They met up at the Conservatoire and joined the long queue for tickets. They were lucky to get two together and quite reasonable ones at that. Many hopefuls behind them were turned away.

Olga felt strange sitting in a concert hall without Yuri. He was not very musical and she felt it was her duty to enlighten him. To his annoyance they would always arrive early so she could talk him through the pieces to be played. She would also comment on the merits of the orchestra, the conductor and the soloists. She would playfully ask him questions on what she had said to check if he had listened. There were tears in her eyes as she wondered where he was and what he was doing instead of sitting here beside her.

The concert hall was full, every seat taken as far as Olga could see. The orchestra finished tuning, the conductor was expected. A well dressed young man walked calmly to an expensive row near the front. He and his fine suit were foreign, almost certainly European. He was good looking with attractive dark hair which curled at the ends. She had not seen him before, but suspected he was a talented musician. He took his seat amongst the senior figures of the Conservatoire.

Kuznetsova was brilliant. Olga agreed with Maria how disappointing it was not to have an encore. But they were in no hurry to leave, content to enjoy the atmosphere and relive the music. They sat and watched as the audience slowly thinned, Olga subconsciously waiting for the foreigner to leave his seat and pass them by, affording her a closer look. But he did not, at least not until Kuznetsova had appeared and he had gone forward and embraced her. When he turned and walked slowly down the aisle between the seats towards them, he looked deliciously distraught. Olga felt a flutter in her heart.

It was not difficult for Olga to get Maria to come back for supper. Even with her, Olga felt tense approaching the apartment block, but there was no sign of Fat Alex. In a way she was relieved the Friday deadline set by him had passed. Whilst it was there, she prayed she wouldn't weaken and try to secure a retraction or some compromise to preserve their friendship. Not that she was in any way going to satisfy his crude demands, now or in the future. On that point she was adamant.

Once she had seen Maria safely on her way soon after midnight, Olga again secured herself in the apartment. She undressed and slipped into bed. The space beside her was still vacant, the sixth night she had lain unloved and alone. And there was also that beautiful man at the concert, that enigmatic foreigner with sorrow in his eyes who, Olga had to admit, made her want her Yuri all the more. She tossed and turned, eventually finding sleep.

Olga woke with a start. There was an insistent banging on the apartment door interspersed with long rings on the bell. She was rigid with fear lest Fat Alex with his strength and in his rage forced the door. The noise continued, enough to wake her neighbours. She crept into the hallway.

"Go away, for God's sake go away, I don't want to see you. Go away or I'll call the *Militsia*," she cried. The banging and ringing stopped. There was a short silence.

"Olga? Olga? Are you all right? It's me, Yuri. For heavens sake open up."

Olga threw herself against the door, fumbling in haste to release the chain and turn the lock. She heaved the door open and collapsed into Yuri's arms. They fell into the apartment and she cried incessantly against him. He caressed and kissed her.

Olga watched Yuri sleep beside her. He lay very still, his breathing soft and rhythmic. His young face bore the lines of fatigue with deep black smudges under his eyes. She noticed with alarm how his healthy skin had turned pale and blotchy, how his usually firm mouth drooped at the edges. She wanted to run healing hands over him, but worried he would wake to her touch.

She felt guilty as she studied him, for he returned an exhausted man. She saw it more plainly now in the grey morning light, but hours earlier she had been too emotional to realise his state. He had appeared drawn and dishevelled but at that hour of the night it was only to be expected. Yet she should have detected his slow, mechanical movement, his slurred, confused speech and how, in only a week, he looked a decade older. He did not want any food, just plain water and a thorough shower. In bed she had felt his naked body, touching the faint foreignness of its surface, even wincing from the staleness of his kiss. Their lovemaking had been urgent, desperate. Almost before he had removed himself from her, he seemed heavily asleep.

Olga lay her lips on Yuri's forehead. He did not stir. She rose quietly from their bed, found some clothes and tiptoed into the main room. She fussed about the apartment, telling herself Yuri was home, they were together again, life was back to normal. She longed to rejoice openly, but feared she might disturb him. And in the silence, Fat Alex still prowled around her mind.

Of course she had her explanation ready. It would be truthful up to a point, but Yuri would still be angry. There would be no alternative but to take his scolding and promise not to be so gullible in the future. She would also have to convince herself that she would never want to see Fat Alex again, that he held no attraction for her. That, perversely, would be the hardest part.

At midday Olga decided to check on Yuri. She had heard no sounds but he had been asleep for almost nine hours. Surely she thought he must be rested now. She peered round the bedroom door to be greeted by his open eyes and broad smile. She ran to him, slipping out of her clothes as she did so. She threw herself on him. They kissed and laughed and loved.

"This is so good," Yuri whispered.

"I was convinced I would not last another day," Olga murmured, tucking herself into him as tightly as she could. "I know it was less than a week, but it felt like a century. I've never been so miserable. Don't you dare go away again." She ran her fingers over his body as if casting a spell to keep him forever by her side.

"I'm here now," he said kissing her. "A bit of a shattered wreck, but here."

"So what kept you?" Olga said a little peevishly. "You've only ever had a Monday to Friday job before, but now without warning, it's turned into twenty four hours a day, seven days a week." She paused, searching Yuri's eyes for some explanation before continuing more stridently. "Just what has changed, what on earth have you done to deserve this extraordinary routine? Promotion can't be this unpleasant."

Yuri, surprised at his wife's accusatory tone, became defensive. He withdrew his arm which lay across Olga's body and lowered his eyes, refusing to meet hers. "You are being unusually inquisitive," he said quietly. "I can't understand why you are probing me like this." As Olga showed no sign of relenting, Yuri adopted a more serious tone. "Do I have to remind you that all matters relating to the work of the Interior Ministry are classified confidential at the very least. Most of our work is of necessity graded secret. That means I cannot tell you what I am doing or where I am doing it. You know all this only too well, so I am surprised you have even bothered to enquire."

Olga, stunned by her husband's harsh words, burst into tears. She pushed Yuri's conciliatory hand away, allowing herself to cry alone. "You are a heartless, uncaring man," she blubbered for full effect. "Don't you see I only want to know what you're up to because I love you. I don't want all the ugly, dirty details, just some idea of what you're doing when you disappear and abandon me for days on end."

Yuri made no attempt to console her, failing to sense that Olga was now ready to be consoled. She looked at him through her tear-soaked eyes, pleading for some understanding. She willed him to meet her half way at least. He seemed reluctant to do so.

"I know why you are being so difficult, so insistent on finding out what my new duties involve," he said. "You suspect I'm hiding something important, holding back on something you feel you have a right to know. You think I'm being unfaithful, don't you?"

Olga was astonished. Nothing could be further from

her mind, but was clearly not from his. Was he trying to provoke her and if so why? Was he perhaps suspicious in his own turn, had he heard rumours about her and Fat Alex? Had someone in the Interior Ministry tipped him off? She feared unseen eyes had been watching her.

"Oh, Yuri my love, let's stop this skirmishing. I know you're tired and I'm all uptight and emotional about your being away. Sorry I said what I did. I was being selfish, unreasonable. Let's just forget it."

Yuri reached out and drew Olga to him. She succumbed to him, enjoying the pleasure he gave her. She promised to herself never to raise the issue of his work again. Perhaps now he might like to hear what she had been doing in his absence.

"I've been very conscientious, you know, these last few days," she said coyly. "You'd only have to ask the librarians at the university to find out how busy I've been. The thesis is coming along very well. I think the end's in sight."

"That's excellent. I wondered what you would be doing without me to distract you," Yuri countered with a smile. "Released from domestic responsibilities, you could return to your former life of independence, your carefree existence. Surely it wasn't all work and no play in my absence?"

"I did spend long days in the library for sure. But I did take in a really good concert with Maria at the Conservatoire last night. I wish you'd been with me. I was so sure you'd be home when I got back from the university, but you weren't. You missed something very special."

"Sounds as if I was spared the agony of sitting through a musical performance I wouldn't understand or enjoy. But I'm just pleased you didn't pass the time moping around here all day."

"I'd have gone mad doing that. This place, although it's home, can be depressing. It's so low down and without any view, as well you know." Olga studied her hands. "And it looks as if we're going to be staying."

"Decided not to move then? Suits me, if that's the case."

"No, it's not that at all," she said. "You see, I bumped into Fat Alex on Tuesday at the university. Well not actually at the university but on a bus from the university. You remember we did talk about swapping apartments briefly when we were all out at the *dacha*? Fat Alex told me he wanted to go ahead. It quite took me by surprise. He said he wanted to move in the Spring and he would produce a set of terms and conditions by this weekend. Sadly he hasn't, so I think he must have changed his mind."

"Well, I hope he has. I have never been keen on the idea of living in a place previously inhabited by Fat Alex. It would take a year to clean it out. He lives like a pig."

Olga shivered slightly as if some spectre had passed by, a fat one which mocked her for her secrets. She clasped herself for courage. "I want you to know that we discussed all this over lunch. Fat Alex invited me to a new restaurant he part owns. It was an incredible place with wonderful food and wine."

Yuri's ponderous mind was still dwelling on his good fortune of not having to move into Fat Alex's apartment as Olga broke her news. Normally he would ignore such an unimportant detail as his wife's lunch companion, invariably a woman friend, since little of interest rarely emerged. But one aspect of his intelligence work, which surprisingly was not lost on him, was a well-developed curiosity. A red alert now flashed across his brain. "Wasn't that a little reckless, Olga?" he said.

"Oh, for God's sake Yuri! I can look after myself without you having to hold my hand all the time. In any case I thought it was very generous of Fat Alex to invite me." Olga hesitated. "Don't you trust me?" she added nervously.

"Of course I trust you my love, it's just that I don't

trust Fat Alex. He's a clever and unprincipled man. He's the devil's work. I don't doubt he tried to get you back to his apartment having plied you with a good lunch and lots of wine."

Olga blushed. She had planned to admit she had gone back with him, but in her own time and in her own way. Now Yuri had pre-empted her and she had to confess. "Yes, as a matter of fact he did, but it was not for the purpose you imagine," she lied feebly. "He wanted me to see the apartment as it had been completely refurbished and transformed. Really Yuri, you'd never believe it was the same place."

Yuri observed his wifely coldly as she struggled with her explanation. He wanted to know more. "And do I assume he made some improper suggestion to you once he'd got you through the door and dazzled you with his shiny new décor?"

"Oh, darling. You know Fat Alex and the way he talks. Of course he said some stupid things like he always does, but I just laughed them off and told him not to be such an idiot." She stared defiantly at Yuri. "So for heaven's sake stop being so suspicious. Nothing happened, honestly."

Olga put sufficient emphasis on her words to make Yuri recoil. He did not doubt his wife, but felt her protests overdone. Something had happened in that apartment, not as dire as her being unfaithful to him but something too delicate for her to reveal. One day he would find out. But for the moment he was relieved she had not done anything so awful as to shatter their lives.

He took Olga in his arms. He sensed her relax. She responded to him with a strong, physical passion. She was totally with him in body but, behind her closed eyes, the sensual image of Fat Alex refused to leave her mind.

Coming home was a strange experience for Yuri. Although he had only been away for six days, he had difficulty in readjusting to the more normal routine, to the predictability of domestic life and to Olga. Whilst they had put their earlier quarrels to one side, there remained a discrete sensitivity between them. Neither wished to resurrect any argument which would mar their pleasure of being together. Olga for her part pampered Yuri, flattering him, grooming him back to his old self. He enjoyed the feel and scent of her, her laughter and her love.

Despite his pompous outburst about the secrecy of his work, he regretted he could not tell Olga more. He would have loved to share with her the excitement of it all, to boast about his success, to enjoy her surprise and admiration. But he was right to be so firm. It was impossible to tell her, forbidden to mention even the smallest detail. No doubt, he excused himself lamely, if he were able to let her into the secret, she would not believe the half of it.

Yuri felt less tired by late Sunday afternoon but still ached. Whilst Olga busied herself in the kitchen preparing his favourite *blini* for supper, he stretched out on the sofa. He closed his eyes and relived his week away.

Special Training Establishment No. 5 of the Interior Ministry had lived up to its motto 'No Soft Centre'. Yuri had noticed it that first morning emblazoned on the flag flying above the headquarters and repeated on the sign-board by the entrance. He still had no idea what he was going to do in the barracks, but the words of the motto were not encouraging. He worried he would fail to make the grade and be returned to Moscow in disgrace. He remembered wishing at the time that he could indeed be back there, making his usual way to his basement office, browsing his familiar, unthreatening files. Instead he was trudging along the snow covered paths between the huts, hoping he would not take a wrong turning and be late for his appointment.

The office of the Establishment's Chief Instructor was on the first floor of the headquarters. It was not difficult to find, once Yuri had been through the security check and pointed in the right direction. At 0800 exactly, he knocked on the half open door, entering after a hearty "Come in".

A tough man in his late thirties sat at his desk. He was dressed in uniform and carried the rank of Lieutenant Colonel on his epaulettes. His well weathered face had a long sunken wound on his right cheek. It looked to Yuri like an old fashioned duelling scar and it pulled his right eye slightly lower than his left, giving him a crazed look. He greeted Yuri, still bizarrely dressed in his Ministry suit, with a disabling handshake.

"Poliakov, got special instructions for you. You're going to be busy this week, by God. Like being busy, do you?"

"Yes sir."

"And are you fit?"

"Yes sir, quite fit, for a desk officer that is."

"We'll see, we'll see. Collators Third Class are not known for their fitness, not that I've ever met one before." He roared with laughter. "And you know what? You're the first person who's ever come into my office dressed in a suit. You look like the Government Inspector." The Chief Instructor could hardly contain himself so amusing did he find his joke.

"Now to business," he said, recovering his composure. "Here's a copy of your programme. You've got a lot to learn and little time to learn it in. Your Deputy Director Popov says you are to be attached to Special Surveillance Unit No 68, codenamed Meat-Hook. And we've got to train you up in just five days so you don't make too many cock-ups when you join them. Tall order I have to say. But I've put you with the best man I've got. He'll teach you everything you need to know."

There was a knock on the door. A fit young man entered, wearing a roll neck sweater, leather jacket and moleskin trousers. He had quick, alert eyes and a sharp, mean face.

"Here you are, Poliakov," the Chief Instructor said, "meet your trainer, Krov."

Yuri half extended his hand, but Krov did not reciprocate. Instead he looked Yuri up and down, his face showing no sign of what he might be thinking. Yuri felt like an animal at auction.

"You know what you've got to do, Krov, so you'd better get on with it." Yuri half expected to be put in a painful armlock and frogmarched out of the office, or grabbed by the nose and beasted down the stairs. Instead Krov turned on his heels and signalled to Yuri to follow.

They walked briskly along a narrow track in the sub-zero temperature. Turning onto a wider path, Krov headed for a green painted hut, larger than the rest. A metal stove pipe pierced its roof, belching smoke into the morning air.

"Quartermaster's Clothing Store," Krov said looking at Yuri disapprovingly. "We're going to put you in something better than that stupid suit."

Under Krov's exacting gaze, the Senior Sergeant checked Yuri's measurements and kitted him out. He called out the items to two storemen who ran to the shelves, returning with armfuls of clothing. Yuri watched as a rising pile of socks and vests, sweaters and trousers, jackets and coats was stacked on the long counter in front of him. Cold weather outfits and wet weather outfits were added, thick gloves and scarves. Finally the sweating storemen slammed two pairs of boots on the counter, topping the pile with three types of hat.

Yuri obediently signed the issue voucher, trusting the Senior Sergeant had got it right, whilst the storemen packed the items into two large holdalls. Krov led the way back to Yuri's billet with the storemen lugging the holdalls behind them. Once in his room, Krov pointed out what he wanted Yuri to wear and waited for him in the corridor.

Yuri found his new clothes fitted surprisingly well. He

worried about the fur lined boots, but as he set off behind Krov through the camp, they felt instantly comfortable. Similar to the rest of his clothing, they were top quality, quite unlike anything he had ever seen in the old shops or had the money to buy in the new, flashy boutiques. The most remarkable thing was that, although made from the best materials, all his issued items were subtly disguised to look just like everyday clothes worn by ordinary citizens. Apart from the invisible quality, he would be dressed the same as them.

Yuri began to puff, trying to keep up with Krov. It did not appear that Krov was walking particularly fast, but his steady loping stride was misleading. It was not a normal walking pace, nor was he pushing himself like a speed walker, but Yuri found the rhythm of his steps was more than he could manage. Embarrassingly he had to break into a run every twenty or so metres to close the gap, conscious of his panting and noisy intakes of breath. Yuri suspected Krov knew exactly what was happening behind him, but never once turned his head to check.

They walked for about ten minutes before Krov stopped outside a shoddy hut near the perimeter fence. He unlocked the main door, entering a small room with an unlit stove in one corner. He man-handled a badly stained table into the middle of the floor, motioning to Yuri to draw up a wooden chair. Krov produced an angle poise lamp from a metal cupboard and adjusted it to shine on one of the blank walls. Yuri made himself as comfortable as he could in the freezing cold. Krov kicked the door closed.

"Normally, Poliakov, I have a group of six or eight to train and several weeks to get them up to standard. But this morning I've just got you and five days to do the same. Tough one that for me, but more so for you. Let's hope you're up to it." He made a sucking noise through his teeth. "Can't say first impressions are very encouraging."

Yuri said nothing. Krov stared intently out of the

window, as if addressing an unseen audience in the dense forest beyond. In profile he looked as uncompromising as he did face on.

"So let's waste no more time," Krov said, turning to Yuri. "Surveillance is the name of the game, and game indeed it is."

For the next five days and for much of each night, Yuri was subjected to the most intensive training he had ever experienced. Krov started with all the rudimentary skills Yuri needed to understand and acquire, before introducing him to the more difficult techniques. He taught Yuri how to observe, how to follow a suspect, how to patiently endure long periods of waiting. He showed him where to stand, how to work a street, how to memorise what he had heard and seen. And most important of all, he demonstrated how to abort a task in case he was rumbled.

Krov, as Yuri thought he would be, was thorough and relentless, pushing him to his physical and mental limits, probing his tenacity and resilience. He explained, he examined, he had Yuri practise and practise, making him repeat procedures over and over again until they became second nature. Krov cursed him and bullied him, working him till he was ready to collapse. He would deprive him of food, of rest and leave him out in the cold for hours, judging finely when to relent and rescue him from his agony.

"Instinctive reactions, Poliakov, instinctive reactions. You won't have time to think and decide, you'll just have to do, to act, sometimes fast, sometimes slow, now openly, now covertly. You've got to become undetectable, a man in the crowd, one of the masses. Nobody is to give you a second look. And you've got to get the information without them having a clue you've got it."

Yuri couldn't like him and undoubtedly Krov would have regarded himself a failure had he done so. But despite wishing to kill him on several occasions, Yuri developed a grudging respect for his tormentor. He knew no other man who could have taught him all he needed to know in such a short space of time, and done it so effectively. Despite the rough time Krov gave him, Yuri acknowledged there was that side to him which made him the excellent instructor he was. He encouraged and congratulated, he advised and supported and, for so stern a man, he even managed a sardonic sense of humour. He was a perfectionist in every way, instilling into Yuri the futility of second best.

Krov took him into the local town of Vozlodansk for his final test. He worked him hard, setting him one task after another. He would stick Yuri in a doorway or at a busy tram stop and make himself the target. He would tell Yuri to identify him, to take a picture when he entered a building or stopped to talk to a passer-by. Or he would point out some innocent pedestrians, and get him to trail them, report on their movements, where they went, what they bought, who they spoke to, what they said. One time he would select a busy street, another a half deserted park, always varying the location.

Yuri had to keep up his disguise, changing his headgear, reversing his coat, wearing a scarf, taking it off, glasses on, glasses off, walking fast, walking slow. Krov would in turn track him, checking on what he did and how he performed. Yuri knew he would be there, and several times he turned suddenly to spot him in the crowd or on an empty road, but never could. For Yuri, Krov was always the invisible man.

By the end of the training, Yuri was confident he had sufficient skills not to be an embarrassment to the surveillance unit. He could follow a target on foot, in a car, on public transport. He could watch and not be noticed, he could listen and record without suspicion, he could photograph and film without attracting attention. He could operate by day or night. He would never be as good as the real professionals, but he would not let them down.

Late on the Saturday evening, they went to see the Chief Instructor. Krov marched him in and delivered his official report. "Sir, Collator Third Class Poliakov is competent to join a surveillance unit provided he is at all times accompanied and supervised by an experienced officer, sir."

"So, it seems you've succeeded, Poliakov, against all our expectations," the Chief Instructor said. "Well done. You'll receive further orders when you get back to Moscow. Your issued kit will be sent on to you. Now clear off, and don't forget to take your government suit with you."

Outside the office, Krov turned to Yuri, "One last task. Track me back to Moscow."

Krov used every trick in the book to confuse Yuri, appearing and disappearing, changing disguises and laying false trails. Yuri stuck with him whether on the road, on the Moscow train, or on foot. Once in the capital, Krov quickly descended into the metro, making one of the last trains with Yuri close behind. At the final stop, Krov raced out of the station, leading Yuri through a maze of side-streets and across a huge estate of apartment blocks. On the edge of a park, Yuri lost him.

The footprints in the snow were too many for Yuri to identify which belonged to Krov. He retraced his own steps, checking out the entrances to the nearest apartment blocks. No sign of him. He returned to the park and leant against the railings in the freezing cold, exhausted. There was a tap on his shoulder.

"Game's over, Poliakov. I win, you lose. Remember next time you're out, it's for real." Krov gave a mock salute and disappeared into the darkness.

Yuri had no idea where he was. He felt almost too tired to move, but knew if he did not, he would roll over and quietly expire in the snow. He dragged himself back through the estate to find a main road. A late-night taxi at the end of its shift was his salvation.

Yuri gradually surfaced from his shallow sleep. It took a few moments for him to adjust to his surroundings. He smiled at the sound of Olga laying the supper table.

The telephone went, jerking him to his feet. He took the short call.

"Who was it?" Olga called from the kitchen.

"Only the Ministry," he replied nonchalantly.

CHAPTER 14

The building was the grubbiest in a street of grubby buildings. The recent heavy snow covered many of its imperfections, yet couldn't conceal its dilapidated appearance. If passers-by gave it a second glance, they might consider it possessed a kind of romantic charm in the winter sunlight, but nothing more. To Yuri Poliakov standing on the pavement on the opposite side of the road it presented an inscrutable façade.

Although the instructions were perfectly clear, he checked again to ensure he had the right address. There was no doubt this was Starogradnaya Street No 13, and, according to his orders, he would find entrance B off the inner courtyard. He hesitated a minute more before crossing the road and approaching the building. He walked through the arched entrance, picking his way carefully over the icy cobbles. A rat dived behind the stout double doors which were held back against the side walls with rusting metal hasps.

The three storey building displayed more of its faded glory in the courtyard. Yuri guessed it was late 19th-century from its design and crumbling stucco. An old woman sweeping the steps in one of the doorways eyed him warily. Higher on the building, flapping pigeons dislodged snow from the railings of the remaining balcony. Scars on the outer walls and heaps of snow covered rubble in the courtyard showed others had once adorned the building. Yuri moved with caution lest the frost worked more masonry loose, checking the doorway lintels for entrance B. He found it on the far side of the courtyard next to a parked *Zhiguli*. Watched by the old woman, he opened

196

the door and climbed the stairs to the third floor. On the landing, he turned to his right and faced the front door of an apartment. He pressed the bell three times.

No one responded nor was there any sound from the other side of the door. Yuri felt he was acting in a play. There had been the single phone call from the Ministry, he had collected his written instructions from a disinterested clerk and now he stood in a decrepit building waiting for the next scene to begin. Unfortunately no one had thought to give him the rest of the script. He had no idea why he had been sent to this place, who he was going to meet, what he was going to do. He even wondered if this was still part of his training: had they perhaps set him up to see how he performed? Were they, even now, observing him?

Yuri started as the door behind him opened and a man about his age stepped onto the landing at the head of the stairs.

"Name?" he demanded.

"Poliakov, Yuri Pavlevich."

"Identity card."

Yuri went to reach inside his coat for his documents when the young man leapt across the landing and gripped his wrist. "I've changed my mind. I'll find your card, just in case you're not the Poliakov we're expecting."

It was pointless to resist, but Yuri couldn't prevent his body tightening as he was frisked. The young man deftly removed the card holder from his jacket pocket, checking the documents thoroughly before returning them.

"You'd better come in," he said directing Yuri towards the open door.

They entered a small apartment now converted into an office and storeroom. Yuri put his briefcase on the only table and hung his hat and coat on a rack close to a bookcase filled with maps. In one corner the open doors of a cabinet revealed shelves of photographic equipment. A large cat stretched along the back of a tatty sofa by the only window. From what must have been the kitchen came the sound of washing-up.

"Welcome to the Meat-Hook team. I'm Valery, the team leader," said the young man shaking Yuri's hand firmly. "Let's go through and I'll introduce you to the other players." Yuri followed him into the galley kitchen, where an older man was rinsing mugs in a dirty sink. A limp cigarette hung from his mouth. "This is Sergei. He's been watching people since before I was born."

Sergei continued with his washing up, bending his short, thickset body over the sink. He nodded his head in greeting, flicking the ash from his cigarette into the water.

Valery ushered Yuri out and led him to what he guessed was the bedroom of the old apartment. He tapped a couple of times on the door. "You decent? Come and meet our new recruit."

The door opened slowly, revealing an attractive woman in her early thirties with freshly painted lips.

"Tania, this is Yuri Poliakov. Just remember to keep your hands off him."

Tania appraised Yuri from the doorway before coming up to him and putting her face close to his. "He'll do nicely," she said. "I bet he's wasted behind a desk." She turned back into the bedroom, closing the door behind her.

"So that's the team. Just the three of us with the occasional add-on like you. And this is our set-up," Valery said waving his arm round the apartment.

"But I don't understand why I was instructed to ring the bell on the door across the way," Yuri said naively.

"Just a precaution. We own the whole of this floor. Our sitter lives in there but his door is sealed on the inside. He comes and goes through here. But when we're out, he bars himself in, just in case someone tries to pay an unannounced visit." Valery indicated the thick steel bars which lay on the floor beside the front door. "Take a tank

198

to break through those," he added with satisfaction.

Sergei shuffled into the main room with glasses of tea which he slopped on the table.

"Tania, you old boot!" he shouted towards the bedroom. "Breakfast." He chuckled, lit another cigarette and spooned sugar into his tea.

Tania joined them, sitting down beside Yuri on the sofa. The cat shifted its position and surveyed the Meat-Hook team through half closed eyes.

"Let's get briefed up," Valery said. "It seems, Yuri, that you've got a special interest in one particular foreigner. An Englishman, sort of mid-twenties if I recall."

"Yes, that's right. His name's Standridge, Mr Peter Standridge."

"Sorry, codenames only. He's Pumpkin to us. Been up to no good has he, this Pumpkin?"

"From the excellent reports I've been getting from you and other agencies, I have deduced that Standridge, sorry Pumpkin, is involved in gathering intelligence. There is no concrete evidence as yet, but his activities and the company he keeps are both very suspicious. My superiors believe he is using the cover of his job as a foreign consultant to undertake his espionage. They consider him a clever and dangerous agent who should be unmasked."

"So is that why we're going to concentrate on just him for the next few days?" Tania asked. "Sounds very tedious. My observations make me think he's a very boring man. I hope you've got this one right, Poliakov, or I won't love you at all – and just think what you'd be missing."

The other two Meat-Hook regulars smiled, but Yuri stared at Tania blankly. With her dark hair and soft brown eyes, his Olga would look quite like her a few years hence. She was about her height and shape too, but unlike his dear Olga, Tania seemed rough-edged and earthy. Her harsh, assertive voice unnerved him. He couldn't see himself working with her too readily.

"It's my belief that Pumpkin presents as dull and uninteresting in order to hide his illegal activities," Yuri continued ponderously. "He doesn't like to attract attention, he has predictable routines and he spends a lot of time by himself, apparently doing very little."

"You can say that again," Tania butted in for a second time. She got up and walked into the centre of the room. "I remember monitoring him once in a hotel in some bog awful town. I had the evening shift, six to midnight. Mr Pumpkin was a big disappointment, I can tell you."

Tania moved closer, impersonating Standridge as she spoke. "He sat, read a book, then a thick magazine, not even a dirty one, picked his nose, scratched his bum, inspected himself in the mirror." She finished by leaning against the table and extending a shapely leg like a dancer.

"Did you know, Poliakov, I once trained for the ballet," she said, stepping back from the table and rotating gracefully round the room in a series of pirouettes. "I so wanted Pumpkin to throw his knickers in the air, to dance naked in his room, to move his body, to show a bit of style." She stopped and balanced beautifully on her toes. "But he didn't. He went to bed, fell asleep and snored like a peasant." She pattered forward and twirled into the sofa. She lifted the cat onto her lap and stroked it. "Mind you, he's an attractive-looking bloke."

The men smirked, but Yuri was concerned Tania's mockery might undermine the seriousness of their surveillance operation. Even so, he was amused by her description of the man he had spent so much time and effort on. He tried hard to visualise him in different situations, not least as Tania saw him, but found it impossible to do so. He was impatient to meet him for real, to watch him, to hear him talk. He wanted to know more about Standridge than any of those agency reports in his files could tell him.

The cat purred, Sergei coughed and shifted on his chair. "It's possible that this Pumpkin has been deliberately misleading us, as our new comrade Poliakov has indicated," he said in a slow drawl. "He's perhaps not as bland or as unadventurous as he pretends to be." Sergei stubbed out his cigarette which was close to burning his lips. "And I have some recent evidence of this."

"How come?" Valery asked.

Sergei selected another cigarette from his crushed packet, lighting the drooping end with care. "I too did a late shift, just last Saturday. Pumpkin went to a concert alone, at the Conservatoire no less. He's not done that before, has he Poliakov?" Yuri waggled his head in agreement. "He dressed up quite smart, fancy suit and tie, that kind of thing." Sergei took a slurp of tea. "He looked good Tania, he really did. Shame you missed him." She scowled at Sergei but said nothing. He took his time before continuing. "At the end of the show, Pumpkin hung around with some of the bigwigs. The conductor and soloist returned to be congratulated by this crowd of seniors. Then our Pumpkin got in on the act. He didn't bother with the conductor but started some kind of kissing game with the soloist. She was a woman by the way. I got a copy of the programme. Name was Lydia Kuznetsova."

The others saw Yuri tense at the mention of her name. "Saturday night was it, just last Saturday night?" he asked excitedly.

"Of course," Sergei said, "You got any other Saturday nights in mind?"

"No, no, it's just that it's so recent. The report on this meeting wouldn't reach my desk for at least another week. And it's so important." They all looked at Yuri.

"Pumpkin," Yuri explained hurriedly, "met Kuznetsova in Stambov last month. They had a few cuddles there too, with information passing between them without doubt. She is also having some kind of an affair with another foreigner, a German called Metzinger. He's an expert on the glockenspiel. He's under surveillance by a local unit with encouraging results."

"There's more," Sergei said quietly as Yuri stopped for breath. "Do you want to hear it?"

"Yes, of course, sorry," Yuri said, embarrassed by his interruption.

"Pumpkin left the Conservatoire, still by himself, met some other foreigners for supper, all grade E, and returned to his room in Hotel Leskov. I went there to watch him on the CCTV. It was almost the end of my shift so I hoped Pumpkin would just turn in. True to form, he started to undress, but then he sat in a chair for a while doing his usual nothing. I was about to switch the video machine to remote when he leaps up, opens the door and there – surprise, surprise – is Madame Kuznetsova, nursing a bottle of champagne."

Sergei inspected his cigarette. "They had a good rumble tumble on the bed. They didn't say much but the translators have got the tape. You'll hear if there's anything useful on it. I reckon they were having too good a time to worry about state secrets, but there's no telling in this game."

"Did she stay with Pumpkin till dawn?" Yuri asked.

"No, about two in the morning she left in a big hurry. I kept the video turning and ran down to track her. I found her in the foyer talking to a big ugly bloke who didn't seem too happy. Probably her husband," Sergei chortled.

"Not so boring after all," Tania said optimistically. "Haven't we underestimated him."

Yuri's mind was whirling. So much was going on he found it difficult to keep up. But how gratifying it all was. He had started with only a modicum of suspicion about Standridge, yet now he had a definite case of espionage on his hands. Standridge was clearly running Kuznetsova as an agent. He wondered for a moment whether he should not be back in his office summarizing all these sensational reports. But no, he told himself, he had been assigned to this special surveillance unit for a purpose. He was on the front line now and close to getting his first glimpse of the man whose trail he had been following so diligently.

"Well, that was a useful breakfast meeting," Valery said. "Now to work. We are stepping up our coverage of Pumpkin from today. We already know he has an appointment in the British Embassy Commercial Section in about an hour. We have to be able to account for all his movements and contacts round the clock. We should be able to manage that between now and Friday when he flies back to England."

"If we are all here, who's watching him now?" Yuri asked.

"The night staff are doing a bit of overtime," Valery said. "Pumpkin's ordered a taxi from the hotel for 9.30. One of our men will be the driver. We'll be in position by the time his meeting's over. Let's go."

The team went down to the courtyard. Valery got the old *Zhiguli* started, whilst the others cleared the snow and scraped the windows free of ice. Valery produced the wiper blades from the glove compartment, clipping them back into position. They piled into the car and skidded out onto the street. The windows steamed up as the whirring heater sucked in the traffic fumes. Yuri sat squashed in the back with Sergei, who smelt of smoke and damp blankets. Tania's rich perfume reached him each time she moved her head.

As they barged their way through the morning rush hour, Yuri felt his excitement mounting. He could not believe his good fortune to be in the field, nor could he control his imagination either. Already he regarded himself as an experienced operator, able to outwit the cleverest foreign agent. He pictured difficult situations from which he extricated himself skilfully, tight corners from which he emerged unscathed. He saw himself returning with vital information, with the key to unsolved cases. In his mind he anticipated the admiration of the other team members, smiling to himself as he heard their congratulations. Most of all he liked the appreciation Tania showed him.

Yuri was brought quickly to his senses as the car left the tarmac and bounced down a cobbled back street. Reality was very different from fantasy. The inside of the car had become hot and fetid, the atmosphere stifling. Yuri tried to wind down the window, but the handle was jammed. He felt himself sweating in his fur hat and layers of clothes. He could see little through the misty, dirt-streaked windows and wondered where they were. The others seemed unconcerned. Sergei continued to smoke his foul cigarettes, Tania prattled on about her latest conquest, whilst Valery cursed every Moscow driver. Yuri gripped the team's briefcase balanced on his lap and wished they would soon arrive.

Close to the austere building housing the Commercial Section, the team split. Sergei and Yuri were dropped off to work on foot, whilst Valery and Tania remained in the car. They took up their positions, covering the entrance to the building and the surrounding side roads. Valery sent a short crackled message to confirm Pumpkin had arrived. They lay in wait for him to reappear.

Yuri checked his watch: 10.45 and still no sign of Pumpkin. They could not have missed him, not these professionals. Yuri's impatience was getting the better of him. He wanted to get on with it, to put into practice all he learned on the course. But instead of action, it was standing around trying to look inconspicuous, taking a short walk along one street and back down another, never straying too far from the target building. It was frustrating.

Then Yuri remembered Krov and the discipline of waiting. He stamped his feet, sharpened his eyes, steeled himself against the cold. At least it was not snowing, no blowing white haze reducing the visibility and hindering their vigil. He envied Valery in the car; he would have the heater on and Tania for company. He had Sergei.

"What do you think he's doing in there?" Yuri asked to pass the time.

Sergei continued to puff on the misshapen cigarette affixed to his lips. His veiled eyes didn't move from the street corner he'd been watching for the previous fifteen minutes. He shuffled his feet. "Touching up First Secretary Commercial, I shouldn't wonder," he mumbled.

"Oh, come on. Why on earth do you say that?"

"Don't you young buggers read anything in your cosy offices?" Sergei said, throwing his cigarette into the snow in disgust. Yuri was embarrassed since he could not recall any report linking Standridge with a member of the Embassy staff. After all he was primarily interested in the contacts he had with Russians and what he did on his travels. Perhaps, though, he had missed something by paying insufficient attention to internal liaisons.

"I'm not sure I quite follow you," Yuri said nervously.

"Last month I filed a report on Pumpkin having an amorous grapple with this First Secretary Commercial, codenamed Blossom. It took place in her apartment on a Saturday night. Blossom has been in our sights for a while. Her previous boyfriend fell into a neat little trap we set with one of our close liaison dollies. Got him we did. The English shipped him out faster than a missile."

Yuri tried to understand what Sergei was telling him. He did not like to think he had failed to register some important information about Standridge. It was all about connections and he hoped he had not overlooked a vital one. Were there, he wondered, any plans to do to Standridge what they had done to the boyfriend? If there were, Yuri did not know about them.

"You'd think Blossom would have had a word with Pumpkin and warned him off the local totty," Sergei growled. "But seems she didn't bother, judging by his antics with that fiddle player."

Yuri was on the point of asking Sergei if he knew of any

scheme to compromise Pumpkin when the radio buzzed. Sergei grunted an acknowledgement.

"He's on his way," he said. "We'll catch him on the corner." They set off down the street they had been watching so attentively.

"How did you know he'd come this way?" Yuri asked.

"Creature of habit. If he's on foot, he always turns left out of the entrance, crosses the road and walks past the end of this street. After that, where he goes depends on what he's up to."

Yuri was excited knowing he was about to have his first proper sighting of Standridge. He accepted he would not be able to see that much of him, given the heavy coat and hat he would be wearing. Even so he would get a sense of the man, how he stood, how he moved, how he carried himself. He would need to be able to distinguish him from all others in the future.

"There he is," Sergei said quietly.

For the ten seconds or so Standridge was in view, Yuri had the picture of a man about his height and build, with a fresh face partly muffled against the cold. He strode with purpose, a steady upright walk with a slight swing in his arms. He crossed over the road junction and disappeared round the corner.

When Sergei and Yuri turned the same corner, Standridge was about thirty metres ahead of them. There were other pedestrians about, but too few to impede their surveillance. At the next junction, he took a right turn and started to cross one of the bridges over the Moscow river. At the half way point he stopped and leaned over the iron parapet staring down at the jostling lumps of ice on the river below. Sergei and Yuri sauntered by him.

"Keep an eye on him from that bench over there," Sergei said as they reached the end of the bridge. "I'll be the other side of the road by the kiosk. When Pumpkin moves, trail him."

Yuri settled himself on the bench beside a mother with her child and looked back across the river. The angle of the sun was excellent, illuminating the south side of the bridge with its weak midday rays. Although many people were watching the movement of the river, Yuri identified Standridge without difficulty. There was something about these foreigners which made them stand out from the Russians. It had little to do with the coloured scarf Standridge was wearing, or the fine cut of his clothes, although both were helpful. It was just that he walked, stood, even leaned in a different kind of way. Yuri could not explain it properly; these distinctive characteristics were just that and there was little Standridge or any other poor foreigner could do about it.

Yuri smiled at the little boy wedged between him and his mother. The only visible part was his face and even that was half covered by a scarf. He sat motionless, unable to move arms or legs in the padded clothing. Only his flickering eyes showed he was awake, only the damp patch on the scarf proved he was breathing. Yuri pulled a funny face and heard a snuffled gurgle of amusement.

Yuri returned his attention to the bridge, relieved that Standridge was still in the same position. He tried to imagine what might be running through his mind. Was he going over the new intelligence instructions he had just received from his controller in Commercial Section? Could that controller be Blossom or was there someone else? Perhaps he was considering his trip back to England. Would he get a fresh briefing there about new areas to focus on, new contacts to make? Was he day dreaming about Kuznetsova? If he was, she did not make him look very happy.

After about five minutes, he saw Standridge move and continue over the bridge. Yuri prepared to follow him, gathering his newspaper and briefcase together. He was aware this would be the first time he had tracked a real target on his own. It was no longer a training session, nor was he going to have Sergei beside him to tell him what to do. Sergei would follow for sure, but more to see how he coped going solo than to monitor their target.

Yuri scratched his nose to hide his face as Standridge passed close by. He waited half a minute before getting up from the bench. He turned and saw him standing by the side of the main road with a group of pedestrians. Yuri strolled over and crossed the road behind him.

Once on the other side, Standridge started to walk faster, taking a number of side roads winding up a slight rise from the river. Yuri kept close behind him. At one point he was forced to pass him, as he stopped to buy a bag of roasted nuts from a street vendor. Yuri lingered by a notice board, watching Standridge amble past, selecting nuts from his bag and discarding the shells. After a few more streets, he entered a café. Yuri followed him in.

Yuri found a seat which allowed him to see Standridge in profile. He heard him order a tea in passable Russian. Yuri asked the waitress for a coffee and unfolded his newspaper, holding it up in the prescribed way. He observed Standridge as he pretended to read.

Unlike most of the Russians in the café, Standridge had removed his hat, enabling Yuri to get a good look at him. He had a more interesting face than his photographs suggested. He had a fine head of dark hair, which curled over his collar, a thin straight nose, a tight mouth and pink boyish complexion. But it was his eyes which Yuri found most revealing. They were a weak blue in colour and shimmered like a woman's. They seemed defensive, unsure, nervous.

How strange, Yuri thought, that his face should tell so much about his character. He even wondered whether he would have bothered to pursue him if he had seen him looking so ineffectual. That would surely have put him off. Boring and unexciting in the reports, vulnerable and diffident in the flesh made an improbable combination for a cunning, successful undercover agent. And yet this is what it increasingly appeared he was and Yuri had been the one to spot him first. How proud he felt as he sat just metres from his quarry.

Standridge spent much of his time reading a letter. It was in longhand but the writing was neat. His expression did not change as he read through the two pages. He appeared serious, preoccupied. A couple of times he paused and looked round the café, his eyes moving quickly, avoiding the gaze of others. Yuri caught his glance momentarily before he looked away.

Standridge got up and left the café. He took a bus to the Manezh and walked across Red Square to his hotel. Yuri watched as he collected his key from reception and headed for the stairs. He felt a light tap on his arm.

"Not bad for your first outing," Sergei said. "Come on, I'll show you to our room."

Sergei took Yuri up in the lift to the ninth floor. He led him along a corridor until they came to a door marked *Domestic Cleaning Staff Only*. He inserted a plastic card in the lock and pushed the door open. They entered a walk-in closet with shelving piled high with cleaning materials, soaps and liquids and smelling strongly of disinfectant. Sergei went on through, past well-used mops and metal buckets, knocking twice on a door at the end. He looked up into the lens of a small camera above the doorway. Yuri heard locks being turned before the door was opened by Valery.

"Pumpkin's back in his box," he said pointing to one of three TV monitors on a desk by the wall. Yuri moved closer to get a better look, aware that Tania was watching the screen intently. He saw Standridge sitting in a chair, unlacing his boots.

"I hope he keeps going," Tania said, swinging her legs provocatively. "I prefer to see my targets in the raw." Valery joined them by the desk.

"So far we have very little for our efforts, Yuri," he said. "A pretty negative morning. I hope your Pumpkin isn't going to disappoint us. There's a danger he could bore us all to death."

By the evening, Yuri felt deflated. Standridge had let him down badly. The other members of the Meat-Hook team took little trouble to hide their frustration, making pointed remarks about their superiors for sending them on such an unproductive mission. Yuri suspected their comments were intended for him, since he was to blame for diverting resources to this speculative target. He felt guilty. He had hoped for more activity from Standridge to support his suspicions and add to the evidence, but regrettably he had not obliged.

Other than going for a quick lunch and an early supper, Standridge remained in his room. He had not stripped bare as Tania had hoped but slopped around in an open necked shirt, trousers and socks. He spent much of the time writing. They realized the static hidden camera was not fitted with a strong enough lens to focus on the desk. Valery cursed the technical section for such an oversight, particularly as Standridge seemed determined to get it all word perfect.

Several times he ripped up his drafts, tearing the paper into small pieces and placing them carefully in an envelope. Valery commented that he was at least pleased to see Pumpkin was following the correct procedures. He pointed out to Yuri that he would take the envelope with its contents to Commercial Section for proper disposal; until then he would keep it on his person. They all agreed this was another indicator that Pumpkin was a well trained agent. But when, oh when, was he going to do something exciting, get up to some mischief?

Occasionally Standridge would get up, stretch and stare out of the window. He would yawn, have a scratch, mumble to himself. He brewed himself several glasses of tea on a little boiler. Sergei queried why the hell he did not call for room service instead of messing around like a housewife. Sometimes he would also take a break from his writing to move to the armchair and read a book. As the hours passed, his lethargy communicated itself to the Meat-Hook team. They sat around lazily, taking it in turns to watch Pumpkin on the monitor, but finding little to excite them.

"Aha," Tania said. "Looks as if the naughty bear is snuggling down for the night."

"But it's only 9.30," Sergei grumbled as they all crowded round the screen.

"Being boring is obviously very tiring," Tania added. "Maybe he's got a big day tomorrow. I hope to God he has, or I'll go nuts."

Standridge took off his shirt and trousers to a wistful gasp from Tania. He disappeared into the bathroom where there was no CCTV coverage. The team were left gawping at Pumpkin's empty room on the flickering screen. He soon returned fully dressed in his pyjamas, much to Tania's disappointment. As he placed the envelope of shredded paper under his pillow and zipped the final draft of his work into his pyjama pocket, the Meat-Hook regulars exchanged knowing smiles. Standridge got into bed and turned the light out.

"Looks like that's it for today," Valery said. "Sergei and I will wait till the night owls take over. You two push off, but be here by 0700." He went over to his briefcase. "Yuri, you'll need one of these to get in." He handed over a key card for the outer door. "You got a wife to go to?"

"Yes sure. I did tell her I might be late, so she won't be worrying."

"Sometimes husbands and wives give up on us in this profession you know," Tania said eyeing Yuri. "You need to make the most of your free time or the whole neat little structure gets blown away. It happens, I know."

"Go on, shove off," Valery said pushing them out of the door. "Remember 7 o'clock. Don't be late or it's ten years down the mine."

CHAPTER 15

The stars were fading as the first light of dawn outlined the city. Yuri walked briskly towards Hotel Leskov, beseeching the Kremlin clocks not to strike seven before he reached the foyer. He increased his pace, his boots losing their grip on the frozen surface, the cold air searing his lungs.

"Cutting it a bit fine, aren't we, Poliakov?" Valery said as he opened the inner door to the operations room.

"The metro was all screwed up. I left in plenty of time, but we sat in a tunnel for ages. Sorry." Yuri removed his hat and coat. "Is Pumpkin rolling yet?" he enquired, hoping to avoid further criticism for his late arrival.

"Yes, he's up and showered. He's now giving Tania her early morning thrill in front of the camera." Yuri glanced at the monitor. Standridge was unwittingly facing the lens, drying his back with a sawing motion of his towel.

"There are some advantages which go with the job," Tania said, her eyes riveted to the screen. "Not many, but a full frontal is one of them. More fulfilling than a pay rise if you want my opinion, but you probably don't."

Yuri turned away, leaving Tania to ogle the monochrome figure of the naked Pumpkin cavorting in his room. Pouring himself a glass of tea, Yuri found a chair beside Sergei. He was leafing through the morning papers, a cigarette affixed to his lips. The hot tea tasted good; perhaps Yuri should have taken Olga a glass before he left.

He had to admit, Tania was right. He ought to make the most of his time with Olga. Last night she was angry he arrived home so late. They talked, kissed, made love, but it wasn't as it used to be. Everything seemed rushed, super-ficial, distracted. She was indignant and unsympathetic, he guilty and anxious. She hated the unpredictability of whatever it was he was doing, the lack of openness, the inconvenience of it all. He pleaded patience.

Valery's voice interrupted his thoughts. "Yuri, go and have breakfast with Pumpkin. Use 113 for meal and drink purchases. Here, take a paper to look at." He tossed him a copy of *Izvestia*.

Yuri didn't have long to wait in the foyer before Standridge appeared. He followed him into the restaurant, settling himself at a table some distance away. He caught up on the world and local news as he ate his yoghurt, bread and jam, keeping half an eye on his target. But Standridge was in no hurry. He ate slowly, frugally, checked his watch and sipped his tea. After half an hour he got up and went back to his room.

"Anything?" Valery asked as Yuri returned.

"Nothing. Had a table to himself, spoke to no one, except a waiter, ate a small breakfast, stared into space. That's all, I'm afraid."

The other Meat-Hook members showed no surprise at Yuri's report. They had already lowered their expectations. There had been many a similar case. Urgent orders from a very high level, a lot of running around, several days of close observation, but in the end, nothing. *Well done team, but it was a wrong call*. A nice way of saying someone had blundered. What a demoralising waste of time. They sensed their pursuit of Pumpkin was not shaping up any differently.

"It looks as if he's preparing to go out," Valery said, nodding towards the monitor. They saw Standridge ferreting around his room, gathering things together and dressing for the cold.

"Right, let's get going. Yuri you're working with Tania today. Sergei's coming in the car with me. We're using channel twenty." Valery handed out the radios. They tuned in to the frequency.

"We'll go down and wait in the car. Yuri, you cover the foyer. Tania, you stay here until Pumpkin exits his room. Okay?"

They donned their hats and coats and collected the rest of their equipment. Yuri found he was the bag man again for the duo on foot. At least this time it had a shoulder strap.

Standridge arrived in the hotel foyer at 8.30, carrying a briefcase and a bulging plastic bag emblazoned with a Union Jack. The doorman waved at the cab rank with one hand, accepting Standridge's tip with the other. The car with Valery and Sergei pulled out behind the taxi as it accelerated away. Tania joined Yuri at the hotel entrance.

"We'll hang around outside till they call us," she said. They stood apart, Tania content to be alone. Yuri noticed she wore a fresh hat, but the same elegant coat. She looked striking, yet seemed indifferent to the leers of the waiting drivers. Yuri suspected she secretly enjoyed the attention, but did wonder why she dressed so flamboyantly. Surely something less attractive would be better for following Pumpkin around the streets of Moscow. Perhaps this was simply the way she operated: today arrayed in finery, tomorrow dressed as a tramp.

The radio had been silent for twenty minutes. They walked up and down, trying to keep their circulation going. Despite his good coat, Yuri could feel the frost steadily penetrating his layers of clothing. He willed Standridge to hurry up and get to wherever he was going. He also prayed the Englishman would come up to expectations and not fail him a second time.

"He's in the Ministry of Commercial Affairs," Valery's voice rasped over the air. "Get yourselves here in a cab. Go and sit in Café Belka on Zubovskaya, you know the one, Tania. Have a coffee on the firm. Just the one between the two of you." He laughed into the mouthpiece.

Café Belka faced the side entrance to the Ministry building. They were lucky to get a small table by the window and shed their hats and coats. The seats were cramped, Yuri finding he couldn't sit down without his knees resting against Tania's. He kept very still, hoping she wouldn't notice.

The café was a popular place, almost full despite the early hour. Many of the habitué were trenching into large breakfasts; others, like them, were content with coffee and conversation. There was sufficient background noise to hide their voices and the radio. Tania informed Valery they were in position.

Yuri looked out of the window. He studied the road layout around the Ministry building, working out the routes Standridge could take and how long he would remain in their field of vision. He concluded the café was an excellent observation point, very much in the best Krov tradition.

"Darling," Tania said loudly as the waiter brought their coffee. "I love the way you caress me with your eyes." She reached out, laying a hand firmly on Yuri's arm and giving him a ravishing smile. The waiter placed the cup midway between them and withdrew.

"Look at me," Tania hissed at Yuri.

"I can't. I'm supposed to be keeping watch on the Ministry building."

"I'll handle that, you goose. Don't forget I started doing this stuff before you were out of shorts."

Yuri looked across at Tania, but quickly lowered his eyes in embarrassment.

"Stop pissing about Poliakov," she spat angrily. "I call the numbers round here. You do as I say. One day you might discover what we learn on the advanced course, if you ever get that far."

"Such as?" Yuri retorted, finding the courage to look Tania in the face, but feeling utterly at her mercy.

"Such as when we're posing as a couple, and that, in

case you're too stupid to realize, is our little game right now, you've got to act it out. You have to do some holding, some hugging, some kissing and look like you're enjoying it, even if you aren't." Tania gave Yuri's arm a little squeeze and spoke more softly. "So, my young pioneer, I'm your sweetheart for today. Treat me good."

Yuri was too bewildered to do anything but smile at Tania and place his hand on hers.

"That's better, that's nice," she simpered. "It's so sexy to have a good working relationship, don't you think?" Tania pouted a kiss at Yuri, fluttering her eyelashes provocatively. Even as she did so, he realised that she had not let the Ministry's side entrance out of her sight for one second. She had it covered, despite everything else she was up to.

Yuri felt he was back in his surreal world. Was all this happening to him, was he a part of it or merely a spectator? Here they were, special government agents taking alternate sips from a single cup of coffee, whilst the waiter watched them with a curious look on his face. It really was bizarre.

"Here he comes," Tania said sharply as Standridge appeared from the side entrance. They saw him set off down Zubovskaya away from Valery's car. Tania placed several roubles under the coffee saucer. They threw on their hats and coats and fell into the street. Leaving the warmth of Café Belka behind, the cold enclosed them.

They started off at a good pace keeping Standridge in sight. Tania radioed Valery while Yuri pulled the street map out of the shoulder bag. She slipped an arm in his, clipping him tightly to her.

Standridge seemed in a hurry. He marched rather than walked with the thin briefcase tucked under his arm. He no longer had the carrier bag.

"Must have been stuffed full of expensive New Year gifts for the Ministry officials," Yuri suggested as they struggled to keep up with him.

"Bribes more like, though I suppose it amounts to the same thing," Tania said dismissively. "Anyway do you know who he goes to see in there, Poliakov? You should do, you know, or are you being a naughty boy and skimping on your homework?"

"A chap called Lokutin seems to be his main contact, but he's not that senior. My guess is Pumkin's presents or bribes were for the big men. It's always important to keep in with them."

"You don't say, my little cherub," Tania said caustically. "Just getting to learn how the big world goes round, are we? I've been taking my clothes off for directors, deputy directors and assistant directors since I don't know when. Sad thing is, I'm still waiting for promotion. But it will come, it will come."

Several empty taxis cruised past Standridge, but he took no notice. Each time he approached a tram stop, they expected him to join its patient queue, but he never did. Instead he continued to stride out purposefully, not stopping, not looking round, not showing any interest in anything except the road ahead.

"Where the hell's he going?" Tania said with a hint of alarm. "He's not on course for the Embassy nor Commercial Section nor his hotel. Nor for the red light district either, come to that."

Just before reaching a major intersection on Zubovskaya, Standridge turned right down a narrow street. They speeded up, rounding the same corner in time to see him enter a little church.

"This looks like trouble," Tania muttered. "What's he come to confess or is he after a bit of divine intervention?" She detached herself from Yuri. "I'll go in after him. You tell Valery where he's gone and loiter over there," she said, pointing to a rundown shop the other side of the street. She disappeared through the church door.

Yuri sent his message and stood looking at the pitiful display of cooking pots in the shop window. The reflection in the glass was poor, though adequate for him to see who entered and left the church. On the steps leading up to the door, two old ladies in dark coats and headscarves stood talking. An elderly man tapped his way into the church with his stick, followed by a black robed priest. A middle-aged couple came out smiling and tipped some coins into the waiting cap of a beggar. Yuri thought none of them seemed a likely contact for Standridge, but perhaps things were different for Tania inside that holy place.

Such was Yuri's concentration on what was unfolding behind him, he failed at first to notice the scruffy shop owner staring at him from the other side of the window. He was a slight, bearded figure, wearing a rough coat fastened with cord and clutching an old fur hat. He looked hopelessly optimistic that such a well-dressed young man might just come in and spend a princely sum on his battered pots and pans. Yuri smiled foolishly, which only seemed to encourage the elderly owner. Before Yuri knew it, he had appeared at his side.

"Your Excellency," he said with ingratiating servility. "Might you do me the honour of blessing my humble shop with your presence? What you see here in the window is but a small preview of my large inventory, most as fine, if not finer than these. And you, sir, if I might enquire, are perhaps shortly to wed... or are perhaps recently married? What greater gift can a young man present to his wife or betrothed, than an array of pots for good stews to warm his heart and stoke his ardour?"

Yuri turned away and thought of Olga. He visualised her in their little apartment kitchen, preparing dinner. He involuntarily nodded his head.

The owner, who smelt worse than Sergei, moved closer and whispered, "I see your temptation is getting the better of you, sir. If I need to convince you further, I have other desirable things for you inside, not merely metal and tin. Come sir, come now."

Yuri checked the window reflection to confirm that neither Tania nor Standridge had reappeared from the church. He reckoned he'd have a clearer and more discreet vantage point inside the shop from which to observe the church door. But was it worth the risk?

Yuri felt his arm being clawed by the mittened hands of the owner and winced at the odour of cheap alcohol on his breath. He looked at the shrivelled, pathetic man more in pity than disgust.

"Look, I'm on my way to a meeting. I can spend a minute, only a minute you understand."

"Sir, you are most gracious. You will not regret one second of your time," the owner said, leading Yuri into the shop and locking the door behind him.

The shop stank on a par with its owner and seemed even colder than the street. Its shelves were stacked with dented tin and brass ware, all thick with dust. The floor of rough planks seesawed under Yuri's boots. In a back room, metal was being beaten with a hammer.

"Is there anything which attracts you, sir, anything that you find, may I suggest, irresistible? A fine kettle perhaps, a deep cauldron or a well-rounded pot?"

"No, nothing does immediately," Yuri said, wondering how long he could last without passing out in the stench.

"Then a moment, sir, a moment of your patience," the owner said, disappearing behind a thick curtain at the rear of the counter. Yuri looked over to the church. The two old ladies were still gossiping on the steps, the beggar remained hunched on the pavement. There was still no sign of Standridge or Tania.

The owner reappeared clasping a dirty vodka bottle containing a colourless liquid. Yuri immediately guessed it would be an illegally made spirit, some form of *samogon*.

"My own distillation, sir," the owner announced with

obvious pride. "I make it in the village. It is indeed highly thought of and much praised by many. Would you be so kind as to sample it?"

"No, thank you. I don't drink spirit, especially *samogon*. It upsets me."

"Oh sir, I do understand. In that case you may wish to try this potion, homemade again of course." The owner produced a small medicine bottle from under the counter. It was half full of a dirty brown concoction. "This is more beneficial and even more highly regarded than my *samogon*. It is much in demand by young men such as your esteemed self, sir. Neither you nor the young women you know will be disappointed," he leered. "Only twenty *roubles* too."

Yuri glanced out of the window to see Standridge already walking back down the narrow street towards Zubovskaya. He went quickly to the shop door. As he tried desperately to pull it open, he noticed Tania helping the old man with his stick down the steps of the church. What brilliant cover, Yuri thought, tugging more frantically at the shop door. In a moment of panic, he realized Tania would expect him to be hard on the heels of Standridge already.

"Open this stupid door, you old fool," Yuri shouted at the owner.

"No need to be abusive, sir. You may decline my generous offers, others do, not often to be sure, but they are always most polite," he said, advancing with his keys. "So what's the hurry, sir, do you think I'm going to put a spell on you? Ah, you're a strange one, indeed you are."

"Just get a move on. I'm already late for my meeting." Yuri stumbled on the pavement in his haste to leave the shop. As he got to his feet, he saw Tania advancing towards him.

"Just what do you think you're playing at, Poliakov? I told you to stay out here on the street. Pumpkin's gone

221

and could be anywhere. You've lost him by poncing about in that metal shop."

They were walking fast now. Tania gripped Yuri's arm, determined he would never stray again. They reached Zubovskaya in time to see Standridge board a tram just metres from the junction. They broke into a run, managing to cram themselves into the crowded tramcar as the doors slammed shut behind them.

Yuri needed to make amends. He searched through the heads of the swaying passengers for Standridge. At first he could not see him, but as the tram lurched sharply to the right, the people shifted and he glimpsed Standridge's now familiar face. He was staring out of the steamed up window trying to get his bearings.

"I've got him," Yuri muttered to Tania, realizing how close he was to her.

"Just as well for you," she whispered, laying her cheek against his and giving his ear a tender nip. "Now you'd better tell Auntie Tania just what you were up to in that shabby little tinsmith's."

Yuri kept a firm hold on the shoulder bag as he attempted to wriggle away. But the other passengers, unable to move themselves, kept him wedged against her. He received a couple of elbow blows in the back for his efforts. Though uncomfortable and embarrassed, he was stuck where he was for the time being thankful for the layers of winter clothing between them.

"I thought I'd be less conspicuous inside the shop," he said quietly. "I had a good view from the shop window looking out across the street. The only problem was the bastard owner locked the door and disappeared out the back. I saw Pumpkin come out of the church, but couldn't get out to follow him." Tania give an earthy chuckle. She moved her head, brushing her lips across his cheek.

"Foolish boy. You should never put your trust in a stranger in this game, especially a seller of crummy kitchen pots and naughty potions."

"How did you know he was into those?"

"Do you think that old tinker could make a living from all that junk? He'd have to find other ways to survive. Nothing is off limits now." Tania kissed Yuri delicately on the cheek. "You should get out of your pen more, piglet."

Yuri could feel the blood rushing to his face as Tania's warm lips sent an unwelcome thrill through his body. He tilted his face away and sought Standridge in the jostling medley of hats and headscarves. "He's still with us," he said. "Shouldn't we tell Valery what's happened, where we are?"

"Don't be a dunce. We're not radioing anyone from this tramcar. Valery won't be worried. He'll expect us to be close on the trail of Pumpkin. You're with professionals, remember?"

It was a relief when the tram stopped near Red Square and the majority of passengers shuffled towards the doors. Standridge, whether intending to get off or not, was caught in the surge and carried out onto the street. Tania and Yuri pushed and shoved their way through the mass of people trying to board the tram. Despite the mayhem, they succeeded in keeping Standridge in view. He led them, as they thought he would, straight back to his hotel.

"Predictable as ever," Tania said in exasperation as the Meat-Hook team regrouped.

"Except he made that detour to the church," Valery said. "Tell us about it."

"He spent much of his time looking at the icons. He just stood there, hardly moving. He didn't seem interested in any particular one. He just gazed at the whole iconostasis for about ten minutes. He did light a candle for St Demetrius, though, before he left."

"No contact then?" Valery queried.

"He didn't speak to anyone and nobody approached him. Everyone noticed him of course, knew he was a foreigner but left him alone. He didn't drop anything for collection either."

"So why did he go there?" Sergei asked.

"There's no record of him showing any interest in churches or priests or icons on my files," Yuri volunteered. "But he didn't call in there by chance. He seemed to know the church was there beforehand. He went straight to it from the Ministry."

"Perhaps he's cleverer than you imagine," Sergei said impassively. "If he's an intelligence gatherer, he'll know all the tricks and ruses as well as we do. I suspect he went into that House of God to spring you two." He looked at them. "Exposed yourselves did you, failed to follow the rule book. Tradecraft a bit rusty was it, Tania?"

"Shut your face, you old goat," Tania retorted. "Your mind's going... you're past it... they should put you out to grass."

"Okay, okay, you two, just calm it," Valery ordered. "We're not going to get very far trading insults. Our business is cracking Pumpkin not each other."

They all instinctively looked towards the monitor. Standridge was pacing round his room, gesticulating like an actor rehearsing his lines.

Keeping Standridge under observation, the Meat-Hook team settled into their stand-by mode. Tania, as usual, volunteered to watch the screen, while the others relaxed in the cramped surroundings of their room. Valery wrote up the unit log of the morning's activity.

At 12.30pm Standridge stripped to the waist and went into the bathroom. He reappeared towelling his chest and arms. He dressed, putting on a clean shirt, jacket and tie. He picked up his briefcase and left the room without his hat and coat.

With a nod from Valery, Tania and Yuri slipped out of the operations room, taking the lift down to the foyer. They arrived to see Standridge making himself comfortable in an armchair facing the hotel entrance. They put their hats and coats on a stand and settled on a sofa behind him.

By 1.10pm it was obvious that whoever Standridge was hoping to meet was late. He kept looking at his watch, glancing at the hotel clock and returning his attention to the entrance. By 1.30pm he was visibly agitated; by 1.45pm he looked ready to abandon his rendezvous.

Yuri had deliberately allowed Tania to sit down on the sofa first, before positioning himself a safe distance away. He understood that they needed to be seen conversing, chatting quietly about this and that, and he tried to be as relaxed and natural as he could. As the time passed and their vigil became longer, Tania gradually edged her way towards him. Once she was close enough, she leaned her head against his shoulder.

"There's a bloke in the corner who keeps looking at me," she said, interrupting their discussion about the latest political scandal. "He's sitting by that artificial palm reading a foreign newspaper. I'm trying to work out if he's one of Pumpkin's minders or whether he just fancies me."

Yuri waited a moment before chancing a look at the man. He had his head in the newspaper, but raised it as he turned a page. The face was instantly familiar; the colour copy of a black and white photo in Yuri's files. The man was, without doubt, Herr Rudolf Metzinger.

Yuri calculated that even if Standridge turned his head, a pillar would obstruct his view of Metzinger. He, however, by looking in their direction and moving his eyes further to the right could see Standridge in profile. But why the stand off? If Metzinger was the person Standridge had come to meet, why on earth hadn't they got together?

"What do you think of my adoring fan?" Tania asked. "Not really my sort of man." She gave Yuri a quick kiss on his cheek.

"Just as well. He's not got eyes for you, he's fixed

225

on Pumpkin. I know who he is, he's on my books. It's Metzinger, he's the German who's also tied up with Kuznetsova. Remember?"

"Hey not bad, my beautiful Yuri. You're good and getting better. We've got ourselves some action at last. I bet Metzinger's here to spoil Pumpkin's pretty face for cuddling up with Kuznetsova. We'll have to think up a codename for this guy. How about Gooseberry? I'll suggest it to Valery."

Although Tania was now running her hand over his thighs, Yuri tried to concentrate. He had to sort out what was going on between these two foreigners in the foyer. He still believed Standridge and Metzinger could be working together, as well as sharing the pleasures of Kuznetsova. But somehow that theory didn't seem to make so much sense, now that Metzinger was playing hide and seek with Standridge. The German's behaviour introduced an unwelcome complication. Yuri returned his attention to the main doors and grabbed Tania by the arm.

"That's not possible," he whispered in disbelief. "It's crazy he's here too."

"I didn't realize you cared so much," Tania said, laying her hand on Yuri's and following his gaze to the hotel entrance. They both watched as an older man with white hair made his way into the foyer. He took off his hat and looked around. Standridge was already on his feet, going forward to meet him. They shook hands, the older man appearing to apologise for his late arrival. They walked slowly towards the coffee shop chatting. Metzinger got up from his chair in the corner and followed.

"So who's your ancient friend?" Tania asked, standing up.

"Professor Krotkin. He heads the Institute for Foreign Languages. You know, the one in Nizhny Novgorod. He and Pumpkin have met three times since September. I'm convinced Krotkin is passing information to Pumpkin.

This meeting just before Pumpkin goes to England could be the big one."

"You're getting more impressive by the minute, my little duckling," Tania said admiringly.

"Have we camera cover in the coffee shop?" Yuri asked.

"Not that anyone's told me."

They hurried across the foyer. Most tables in the coffee shop were full, but they managed to get onto a table for four. A middle aged couple already seated did nothing to hide their resentment at having to share. Tania gave the man one of her smiles. He blushed with pleasure, his wife scowled.

Their table was quite central, but they were not close enough to eavesdrop on Krotkin and Standridge. Yuri, though, had a good view and was able to see their faces and expressions. Glancing round the room, he spotted Metzinger grumpily sharing a corner table with three ladies in enormous hats.

Yuri watched every movement on Standridge's table. Krotkin was doing most of the talking. There appeared to be much to explain. Standridge too seemed to have some questions to put to Krotkin, who nodded, then shook his head. A document was passed to Standridge, which he placed in his briefcase. Krotkin opened a carrier bag and produced a parcel. After much discussion and gesticulation, this too was handed to Standridge.

"Having a nice time are you, darling?" Tania said, sipping her tea. She smiled at the couple opposite as if to excuse her intense and silent lover.

"Yes, of course," Yuri answered sharply.

"We can go now if you're bored. You do look bored, you know. Haven't you eyes for me anymore?"

Yuri turned to look at Tania, conscious of the need to play his part in the irritating little scene.

"I'm sorry. I'm not being very considerate, am I? Too

227

distracted, too lost in thought," he said convincingly. He intended to return his attention to Krotkin and Standridge, but Tania took his face in her hands and kissed him longingly on the lips.

"That better, my love?" she said releasing him. "You can go back to your daydreaming now."

Yuri caught the disapproving looks of the couple opposite, but also saw the envy in the man's eyes. Yuri, too, had to fight hard to suppress the pleasure he felt from Tania's kiss. Just acting, just a play, he kept reminding himself.

A little dazed, he refocused on his targets. They had evidently finished their business and Standridge was signalling to a waiter. Back in the foyer they spent a few minutes in conversation before Krotkin said goodbye. Standridge waved him off and made for the lift.

"Pumpkin looks to be heading back to his room. It's important we follow Krotkin," Yuri said urgently. Tania radioed Valery for permission to switch targets. They collected their coats and hats, putting them on as they flew out of the door.

With his strands of white hair and limping gait, Krotkin was easy to spot in a crowd. They picked him out as he walked past GUM, where he paused to admire the displays in the windows, and trailed him down to the bottom of Petrovka. He started to walk up the street, but after a short distance, he abruptly turned round. They joined some shoppers in a queue as he passed close by.

Krotkin appeared indecisive. He was displaying, as Tania pointed out, the classic signs of a man anxious not to be followed. He took the metro from Teatralnaya, travelled two stops before resurfacing, walked up and down a street, jumped on a tram, alighted and rested on a bench. Finally he stood up, strode round the corner and entered the courtyard of the Tretyakov Gallery. He disappeared through the main door in its ornate façade.

Yuri was full of admiration for the way Tania operated.

Following Standridge had been easy by comparison, since he had behaved like an innocent. In contrast Krotkin acted to confuse, to lay false trails, to flush out anyone tracking him out of malice or curiosity. Tania though played it by the book, walking arm in arm with Yuri, chatting to him loudly when required and whispering instructions. Were it not for her irrepressible sexiness, he would have felt like a child in the capable hands of a governess.

"We'll give him a chance to sort himself out and then we'll go in after him," Tania said as they stood in a doorway facing the gallery. Although operationally no longer necessary, she continued to hold Yuri's arm.

"He's drawing a lot of attention to himself by being so devious," Yuri said.

"Don't be so dim, Poliakov. We may see him that way, but for anyone else, he's just an old white-haired bloke with a wonky leg and a cartload of confusion. There's lots of them about – or haven't you noticed?"

"Yes, of course I have. But hopefully he's unaware we're pursuing him, because, well, he wouldn't expect to be of interest to the Interior Ministry in that way. Perhaps it's something or someone else he's worried about, someone who wants to settle a score with him, someone with a grievance." As he spoke, Yuri appreciated he fitted the bill in that respect, but that was a personal matter. He mustn't let such considerations intrude into his official work.

"More likely he's got a little popsy tucked away somewhere near. He takes this dizzy route and all these precautions in case his old lady has put the dogs on him. He's marking time in there with all those pictures till he's sure the coast is clear. Maybe it's the nudes and naked cherubs he likes, just to get him in the mood." Tania gave another of her gravelly chuckles and squeezed Yuri's arm. "Let's go and check him out."

Yuri remembered being taken to the Tretyakov on a school trip but had never returned. At the entrance to the gallery, very little seemed familiar. But as they walked through the rooms, the paintings brought back pleasant memories. He became absorbed by the landscapes and the scenes of a Russia which had long disappeared. Tania annoyed at his distraction, merely glanced at the walls, alert to everything other than the art.

The gallery was comfortably busy offering excellent cover for Tania and Yuri to spot Krotkin from a distance. There was however no sign of him on the first floor. They moved on, splitting up, coming back together, systematically working the rooms, ensuring he could not slip out behind them. They prepared to adopt the appearance of art lovers once they had him in their sights.

It was Yuri who saw him first. They had covered about half the gallery when he glimpsed the telltale head of white hair. Krotkin had his back to him. He was walking very slowly, taking his time in front of every painting and reading the text beside it. Yuri moved closer to Tania.

"He's in there," he said waving his gallery guide in the direction of the adjoining room. Tania took Yuri's arm as they went through the doorway, pausing at the first painting they came to. Krotkin was still on the far side of the room, apparently transfixed by a classical nude. Yuri was impressed by Tania's presentiment when it came to the Professor's tastes.

As they ambled to the next painting, Yuri caught sight of a man with an all too familiar shape entering the room. He walked straight across to where Krotkin was standing. Yuri checked again and went very pale.

"What's up, my little chicken?" Tania whispered. "Just seen Rasputin?"

"That man," Yuri gasped, "he lives in our apartment block. He mustn't see me, he mustn't."

Fat Alex and Krotkin had shaken hands and were asking loudly after each other's health. Tania gripped Yuri and steered him back into the previous room, stopping in front of a large 18th-century portrait of a prince.

"Now you just stay here and admire this bloke with the funny hairdo and fancy trousers while I go and take a look at your professor and his big fat friend. You do keep strange company, Poliakov, you know."

Yuri did as he was told. He continued to shiver from the shock of seeing Fat Alex. What in the world was he doing with Krotkin? The two of them were surely incompatible. The one a professor, an academic, a public servant; the other, well just what was Fat Alex? An entrepreneur maybe, an opportunist, or even a Class A villain? Perhaps he was all of them and more. Yuri had no idea what he did, where he went or what brought him and Krotkin together. Where was the common ground? Yuri's brain was unable to cope with so much thinking.

Yuri felt someone's eyes on him. He glanced round to see an old woman staring at him from her chair by the door. The room was her responsibility. Perhaps he had been standing in front of the portrait too long and she had become suspicious. He moved slowly to the next painting. After what seemed an age, Tania reappeared, sliding an arm around his waist.

"The gross one has buggered off, so you can relax. The hoary professor is hanging on here for half an hour, till it's time to get his train back home."

"What went on between them?"

"They sat on a couch and talked about paintings."

"They what?"

"Just that. Lots of chat about Repin, Savrasov and others."

"Was it a sort of code then? You know, using the painters' names to indicate something?"

"No, they were just bleating on for my benefit and anyone else who cared to listen."

"You heard it all?"

"Of course, every word and it's all on my lovely little

tape as well."

"You're amazing, you really are."

"Yes, I know, darling. I can do other tricks too, if only you'd let me try."

"Was there anything else of interest?" Yuri asked, ignoring the invitation.

"Fat one gave old one an envelope. I guess that was the whole purpose of their little picnic. Nothing was said about it. They just continued to discuss some wizard with a paint brush when the envelope was slipped across. The Prof got so excited, he almost dropped it between his knees."

"I don't understand. What could Fat Alex be handing over to Krotkin. Just what information or intelligence could he have to pass on?"

"Yapping up the wrong tree, my sweet," Tania said stroking the back of Yuri's neck. "It's nothing to do with the security of the State. Payment no doubt for a little local favour, that's all. The key connection still has to be between the Prof and our English Pumpkin."

Yuri began to feel incredibly tired. He yawned and, unthinking, placed his head on Tania's shoulder.

"Come on, my weary rabbit," she said. "We can back off now and leave your learned friend to catch his little puffer train all by himself. In any case, I've seen quite enough pretty pictures for one day. I feel in need of a serious drink. Care to join me?"

The china mug thudded into the wall close to Yuri's head. It was followed by a plate, which ricocheted off his shoulder and smashed to the floor. Olga fired out of the kitchen, her face red with fury. She tore into Yuri, thumping him with her fists and hacking at his shins.

"You bastard, Yuri Pavlevich, you cheating, lying bastard," she screamed at him. "I'd never believed it of you. To think I trusted you, you little swine."

Yuri, taken completely by surprise, tried to defend

himself. He parried Olga's blows and jigged to avoid her flailing legs. But still she came at him, gaining mounting strength from her rage. He fought her back, finally seizing her trembling arms and forcing her against a wall.

"Olga, Olga," he shouted, "what the hell's going on?"

Olga was panting like a animal, her eyes wild with distress. For a moment she had no breath to talk. Her whole body shook, her taut muscles quivered, cold perspiration covered her skin. She continued to squirm and struggle, occasionally freeing a leg or arm to lash out at him. But he held her firm, pinning her tightly by the wrists, overcoming the violence of her temper. Gradually her face lost its colour, her body stilled, some calm returned. When she found a voice, it sounded high pitched and anguished, barely hers.

"You were seen today... by Maria... with a woman," Olga stuttered. "You were walking arm in arm... you were smiling... laughing together... like you... like you belonged to each other." Tears ran down Olga's cheeks. She spoke faster. "Maria was behind you, she thought at first it was you and me, but then the woman turned her face to kiss you and she saw... she saw it wasn't me at all." Olga broke down, her slender body racked by weeping, her resistance ebbing away.

Yuri held her to him, gently stroking her hair. He kissed her forehead as he would a child's. "I can explain my darling, it's not what you imagine. It's all a misunderstanding on Maria's part."

Olga shook her head in disbelief, unready for excuse or explanation. She seemed to collect herself. "That won't do, Yuri. It actually seemed very plain, very clear to Maria. She gave me all the details, she told me how you looked at her, clung to her. She said you couldn't hide your enjoyment, your pleasure. We women can sense these things, you know." Olga sobbed some more, a deep sadness displacing her anger.

"Look, it's my job. It's what I'm doing now," Yuri said in desperation.

"Your job? Oh come on. One moment your working in some Ministry, the next you're out pimping on the streets."

"Olga, for God's sake be sensible. You know I can't tell you everything, but being with this woman is just part of my work. There's a small team of us. Most of the time we operate in pairs. Yesterday I was on duty with a man. Would Maria have got excited about that if she'd seen us?"

"That's pathetic, Yuri. Don't try and make stupid jokes. Lots of men and women work together, but the married ones don't have affairs in the open. They're more discreet. It's degrading what you've done, you don't know how much you've wounded me. For the ultimate humiliation, you chose Red Square to parade on; the most public sodding place in all of Moscow."

"Look, Olga. You've got to listen," Yuri said more firmly. "I'm not trying to wriggle out of anything or deny Maria saw me with this woman. It's just that our duties, the tasks we have, require us to behave in a certain way. You can say we're sort of actors, pretending to be people we're not. It has to be realistic, we have to do things to be convincing, otherwise it's all a waste of time."

Olga said nothing, but her sobbing became more spasmodic. Yuri wanted her to enclose him in her arms, to hear her say she understood, to kiss him the way she always did. But he sensed she was still seasons away from forgiveness. She continued to hang in his arms like a linen doll.

"Maria said she was very beautiful, very sexy," Olga said at last. "Why can't you be paired with someone who looks like a stove? I might still be angry, but I wouldn't be so jealous."

Yuri chanced a brief laugh to see how far he still had to go for reconciliation.

Olga moved her head up slowly and looked him in the eyes. "Yuri, if you're lying to me, if you're cheating on me, I will never, never forgive you. For the moment I'm allowing you the benefit of the doubt. I have always thought you a man of honour, someone I can rely on, depend on, someone I can trust, whatever temptations cross your path. Don't disillusion me, don't disappoint me. You have always had my love. Don't lose it now for the sake of some high class, painted whore."

Olga detached herself from Yuri. She went into the bathroom. Yuri heard the shower being run. He picked up the pieces of the broken mug and plate and threw them in the bin. He looked around the kitchen for something to eat, doubting he'd been catered for. He found a lump of cheese and a tail end of bread. He gnawed at them like a ravenous arctic fox.

There was no love in their bed that night. Olga, her body wound in the bedclothes, lay tight on her side. When Yuri tiptoed in, she sounded deeply asleep. He kept his dressing gown on, wrapped himself in a blanket and lay down on the open sheet. Although exhausted, he couldn't get comfortable. He twisted and turned, hoping not to disturb her.

Staring into the darkness, he swore at Maria for seeing him. Why didn't she just keep her big mouth shut, instead of running to Olga? It was all so unnecessary. After all, was he not intending to tell Olga himself, this very evening, how he had to work with a female colleague throughout the day? He was sure he would mention some of the things they had to do together, things which were, of course, all show and all part of the deception. But no, Maria had to stick her nose in and cause a major upset.

Okay, he could not pretend he was not impressed by Tania, but that did not answer the question of where Olga was with Fat Alex. She had never fully explained that incident in his apartment. Was she feeling guilty? Did she think he, Yuri, had exacted some revenge by playing away with another woman in broad daylight? Perhaps she had told him a half truth about that afternoon, suspecting he had now done the same to her in retaliation.

Still, there would have been even bigger problems if he had taken the predatory Tania up on the offer of a drink. That would have been way beyond the call of duty. He had still to work out where Tania's undoubted professionalism ended and her self-interest began. He was sure, if he gave her half a chance, she would whisk him into bed. However exciting that prospect was, he was more resolved than ever to resist her. There was far too much at stake.

Despite seeking the oblivion of sleep, Yuri could not help running over the day's events in his mind. For all the disappointments, he still believed he had a good case against Standridge. Yet the main players seemed adept at adding complications. They were all linked in some way but, for the moment, he failed to see how. It was as if he had all the jigsaw pieces in his head, but could not get them to fit together to complete a coherent picture. He needed time to think it all through. It would fall to him to decide what should be done to guarantee success. Two more days and Standridge would be gone. That would be his chance to lay a trap for his return.

CHAPTER 16

Peter was pleased with the final draft of his letter to Deirdre. He had finished it off after his meeting with Krotkin and let it marinate overnight. By the morning he felt no alterations were required. It flowed well and he admired the way he had finally set out his feelings about their relationship. It was important to use just the right words, just the right phrases and he sensed he had. The letter was gentle and considerate, but nonetheless firm. It could stand as it was.

Nevertheless he was cross she was so tardy in writing. She had known for months he was coming back for Christmas, yet only now told him she was going to be away. *The deal was too good to miss. Saved pounds by booking early. Be back for the New Year though. I'm sure you won't be rushing to return to that horrible old Russia, so we'll still be able to see loads of each other.* There was an apology, her usual words of affection, a bland assumption they would pick up where they were last summer. Peter didn't know what Deirdre had been doing in his absence, but he had undergone a transformation. He had moved on from the closeted world of East Grinstead.

Peter looked at his watch. Almost midday. He had a meeting in Commercial Section with Chris Burroughs in a couple of hours. He would take along the torn up drafts of his letter and dispose of them there. They were hardly compromising material, but he would not want anyone going through his waste bin, digging around in his private life.

Going to his desk, Peter took Krotkin's well-wrapped package from the drawer. He weighed it in his hands;

it was surprisingly light. He was not concerned about exceeding his baggage allowance, but even so expected it to be heavier. What if it were not an icon, but something different, like priceless amber or dollar notes?

Although Krotkin was a curious character, Peter had no specific reason to doubt his honesty. *Handle my precious painting with great care and deliver it to my good friend, the Doctor Homilly, as soon as you can* were his parting words. No, Peter was sure it was an icon. That, after all, was the item stated on the export licence.

Peter opened the brown envelope again. The certificate was written in both Russian and English and had official stamps from the appropriate Ministries. It appeared genuine enough. Krotkin had said the Russian Customs would definitely want to see the document, but did not know how interested their British counterparts would be. He did reassure Peter that previous gifts requiring such a licence had all been delivered without a problem. Peter had to accept his word.

The package itself was tantalising. He was tempted to open it there and then. To do so would mean untying the string, cutting through the adhesive tape and tearing the neatly folded paper. Once unwrapped, he would have to repack it, making it appear indistinguishable from the original. Surely the good Doctor Homilly would notice immediately it had been tampered with. It might be more prudent to act merely as a courier for Krotkin and go without the benefit of inside knowledge.

Yet he badly wanted to see this work of art, remembering how affected he was by the previous one Krotkin had shown him. Since then he had visited a number of museums and galleries to see their rich collections of icons. He found he had become more and more drawn to them. Good old Jocelyn Misterton had also told him about the Church of the Resurrection, which had a fine iconostasis. Peter was delighted he had taken the trouble to visit the little church on his way back from the Ministry. It was only a short distance off Zubovskaya. It had been a moving experience.

The telephone rang. It was Reception informing him he had a letter delivered marked *urgent*. Would he like someone to bring it up or would he prefer to collect it himself? Peter said he was planning to come down, so he would pick it up on the way.

His name on the envelope was in long hand, though the writing was not familiar. He crossed the foyer to a vacant chair and opened the envelope. He drew out the sheet of paper, unfolding it as he did so. It was blank. Peter turned it over only to find the reverse was likewise. He flicked it back in case he had missed something. He checked the envelope again, but there was nothing else inside.

"How extraordinary," he muttered in disbelief, aware a figure had stopped in front of him.

"Mr Standridge, I presume." The man clicked his heels as he stood to attention and bowed respectfully. "Please excuse my intrusion."

"Good heavens, Herr Metzinger," Peter said with astonishment. "What are you doing here?"

"Indeed it is a most strange way to meet. But I have my history right, yes? Only instead of coming across one another in the middle of Africa, we meet here in the centre of Moscow, midway between Europe and Asia."

Peter was bemused by Metzinger's analogy. "You're quite right. I congratulate you on your history and your geography," he said, rising to his feet and shaking Metzinger's hand. "How are you?"

"My health is not of the best. This coldness is bad for my lungs. It is a problem from my early days. Always I wished to be a brass player, but my breathing would not permit it. So I become a percussionist instead. It is most strange how these things happen, would you not say?"

"Indeed, life does not always turn out as you would

wish. Some disappointments, occasional success, many surprises. Please, do have a seat."

Herr Metzinger drew up a chair. "But I have been most ungracious and not asked you how is your health in this difficult climate," he said sitting down.

"Very good thank you. I seem to have adapted to the cold successfully."

They both fell silent, studying each other behind their smiles. Metzinger seemed so much older than forty. Despite his semi-drunken state in Stambov, Peter recalled him looking more youthful, more vital. Now he appeared tired and drawn. His face was pale, his hair dishevelled, his well-made suit stained and creased. Peter wondered what had happened since that night in Stambov.

"I feel embarrassed," Peter said. "I have never thanked you properly for inviting me to join you for your birthday dinner, to say nothing of your hospitality at the Rite of Autumn celebration. It was very generous of you. I wished to write to express my gratitude, but I had no address."

Metzinger waved his hand dismissively. "You were, of course, most welcome. But it is I who must make the apology. I had too much champagne and vodka and was not a good host to you. For my shame, I remember very little of the finish of the evening. I hope there was no unpleasantness and no difficulty in finding your hotel?"

"No, it was fine. I shared a taxi with your companion. She was dropped off at her apartment and I went on to my hotel. I expect she told you."

Herr Metzinger's expression changed from mild pleasure to something close to anger. Peter stiffened. He immediately regretted raising the matter of Lydia and hoped he wasn't in for a difficult time. Was she the reason Metzinger had sought him out in Moscow? He quickly changed the subject. "This envelope addressed to me, did you leave it at Reception?"

Metzinger nodded. "You will, I hope, forgive me for a

second time. Yesterday I tried to meet with you, but you were busy with a friend. So today I have, without grace, resorted to a subterfuge. I believed that, for some reasons, you would not wish to see me and talk with me. If I phoned to your room, I was thinking you might tell me to go away. So, yes, I am the guilty man who drew you here by false pretending." Metzinger looked contrite. He edged his chair nearer to Peter's, staring intently round the busy foyer. Peter followed his gaze, half-expecting Lydia to sail loftily through the entrance.

"We must take some care here," Herr Metzinger whispered, beckoning Peter closer. "There are some things I must say, but say them only to you."

Their chairs were set against one of the foyer walls. Two middle-aged men on a nearby sofa were deep in conversation. A child was worrying its mother a little further away. There was no Lydia, though an attractive woman sat opposite reading a magazine. She put a hand into the bag beside her, rummaged and removed a handkerchief. She returned to her magazine.

"It is of Kuznetsova that I must speak," Metzinger continued in an undertone. "She is the purpose I have come here to see you. I have come to warn you from her, Herr Standridge."

Peter maintained his composure but was ready for Metzinger, should he try to grab him by the throat.

"Kuznetsova is a good musician, a very good musician. She was also for me a kind and helpful friend, especially when first I was in Stambov. We did many things together." Metzinger thought for a moment, as if considering whether to continue. "After some months, she has taken me into her bed. I believe, Herr Standridge, you have also had that experience."

Peter nodded, surprised at Metzinger's frankness.

"She told me about the difficult times there are in Russia and how she has not enough money. I, like a *Dummkopf*, said I would like to help her. I started to give her money. She said thank you, but always asked for more and for bigger sums. I give her thousands of *Deutschmark*, but it is never enough. So I tell her, no more. But she says I must or she will tell the authorities, the German Embassy and my wife. How do you say it in English? Blackmail – am I not right?"

"Yes, quite right. But honestly, I cannot imagine you have broken any laws," Peter said reassuringly.

Metzinger studied his hands, then spoke very softly. "Information, Herr Standridge. Information. Kuznetsova gave me some information for which I asked. Nothing secret of course, just some information about people – music people – which is most useful to me. You see this information is held in a part of the faculty into which I cannot go. But Kuznetsova, she can go there." Metzinger put his head in his hands. "Now she says I bribed her with all this money to get this information, that I pestered her, but that is not the truth. She has made herself the victim, but it is I who has been wronged, very much badly wronged." He seemed on the point of tears.

"I am very sorry to hear all this," Peter said. "It must be very difficult for you. What are you going to do?"

"I go this evening to Germany. I shall tell my director in Hamburg and confess to my wife. She is a lady of much understanding and forgiveness. My director must decide whether I can return and what to tell the Russians if I cannot. I have still six months of my contract to fulfil."

"But I don't understand why are you telling me all this?" Peter said. "I am a stranger to you, you hardly know me, yet you are sharing these confidences."

"You are right, Herr Standridge, but I come to you mainly as a messenger… as a prophet. You are yet a young man. There are many in this world who will wish to take some advantage from you. Kuznetsova is one of these people. She will try you next for money, I know. She has

242

made you love her, now she is ready to make a bad life for you like she has made for me. This is my warning and my advice. Do not see her again. She is a rapacious woman."

There was a moment when Peter had the uncharitable thought that Metzinger's story was a ploy to scare him off. Perhaps he wanted to ensure he could enjoy Lydia in peace, without the worry of a younger man competing for her affections. But what he had said and the way he had said it convinced Peter he was telling the truth. There was also a question he wanted to put to him. "Is she actually married?"

"Yes, that also is a bad problem. He is not a good man. I have seen him, but I do not speak with him. I think he makes Kuznetsova take my money. She says he will make an accident for me if I do not pay more. *The revenge of a husband*, she says." Metzinger sat back in his chair, looking relieved to have unburdened himself. With their mutual link to Lydia, Peter suspected he was perhaps the only foreigner in the whole of Russia who could fully understand Metzinger's dilemma.

"So now, Herr Standridge, I must go for my flight. It was a duty for me to see you, but also a pleasure." He stood up and shook Peter's hand. "I wish you a Happy Christmas. Perhaps I shall see you again in the New Year, or perhaps not. Goodbye and may the God of Russia keep you safe."

Before Peter could wish him well, Herr Metzinger had turned, crossed the foyer and left the hotel. Peter checked the time, realising he would be late for his meeting if he didn't hurry. He set off for his room. The woman sitting opposite followed him to the foot of the stairs.

Although Chris Burroughs was surrounded by Christmas cards, Peter found him in an unusually sombre mood. His in-tray was overflowing and instead of an initial chat, he abruptly handed Peter a sheet of paper.

"Be so good as to read that, and then I'll destroy it," he said.

Peter began to read.

I thought it easier to write this out rather than use our eraser boards. I know you are scheduled to go to Pavlozavodsk on 6th Jan. London is very keen for you to do your normal information gathering whilst you're there. But they would also like you to take some radiation readings. I've got the bit of kit here for you to use. It's very small and discreet and you'll only have to wander around the edge of a particular installation to get what they want. Come in and see me on 5th Jan before you get the night train.

I'm telling you this now so you'll have a chance to practise your technique whilst you're back in England. I've got a mock-up of the device for you to take with you. Try using it in your coat pocket and also in a carrier bag. Now I'll show you the real device and how it works.

Chris Burroughs placed two plastic cases on his desk. Saying nothing, he demonstrated how to activate the device, how to direct the nozzle and how to read the special dial without being detected. He pushed it towards Peter, encouraging him to try.

Peter did not have time to appreciate fully what he was being asked to do. It was certainly a departure from his normal collecting. But would London expect him to do anything which could get him into serious trouble? He assumed not, particularly after Derek Carbonnel's intervention.

Peter played with the device until he felt confident he could use it properly. He realized the most important action would be to record each reading accurately, noting the location and the time. Other than that it all seemed straightforward. As Chris had said it was neat and compact and would be unobtrusive in an overcoat pocket.

"Anything else?" Peter asked as he placed the mock-up in his briefcase.

"No, I don't think so... except for this from Jean and me," Chris said, handing over a Christmas card.

"Thanks, mine's in the post. Oh, may I use the spare office for a moment? There are a couple of things I need to do before I go."

"Of course. Let me have the key back when you've finished."

Once in the room, Peter took Krotkin's parcel out of his briefcase. He also removed the envelope with the torn up drafts from his inner pocket and started the shredder. He fed the scraps of paper into its chattering jaws and watched as they were devoured. He switched the machine off.

The office door flew open. "My God, I'm sorry," Ruth Rumbelow said. "I didn't know anyone was working in here."

"No problem. I'm just doing a few last minute things before I leave on Friday. I think everything is tidied away, so there shouldn't be any loose ends for you to worry about. Are you staying here for the holiday period?"

"Sadly yes," Ruth said, her eyes focusing on the desk. "Presents for the parents or the girlfriend?" she asked, moving closer and fingering the wrapped parcel.

"This one's for a friend. It may have to be posted in UK, so I was just making it secure."

Ruth seemed in no rush to leave and lodged herself on the edge of the desk. "You know Peter, I've not really had a chance to say sorry for what happened in my apartment a couple of weeks ago. It was most unfortunate. I assume you've kept your side of the agreement and not told anyone?"

"I haven't told a soul," Peter replied. "To be honest, I'd

forgotten all about it."

"Yes, I suppose you would have done," Ruth said with a hint of disappointment. She adjusted her position on the desk, her skirt riding higher. "But I did want you to know that if you ever decided to change your mind, I would be very happy to accommodate you."

Peter stared at Ruth in astonishment. She had spoken in a very matter of fact way, as if discussing some routine commercial matter. But he sensed danger. By the look on her face, she appeared ready to launch herself at him, given the right signal.

"No, Ruth. I'm fond of you, but only as a friend. I'm sorry, but that's the way it is."

Ruth stood up, smoothing down her skirt and giving him a lopsided smile. "See you next year then," she said and sashayed out of the office with an amateurish swing of her hips.

Peter let out a soft whistle of relief. He could not believe Ruth still had designs on him. He continued to admire her efficiency and ability, but that was as far as it went. Their regular office meetings had been examples of rectitude, with no hint of any lingering, suppressed desire. He did feel sorry for her, but he had no wish to get involved. He went to the door and turned the key to prevent further interruptions.

Returning to the desk, he stared at Krotkin's package. Despite his misgivings, he ought to know what was inside. Did not the current concerns about security require him to say he had packed it himself? He started to untie the cord and remove the outer layers of paper.

The image of the icon was visible through the clear protective covering. He knew he had seen enough to confirm the parcel's contents, but he could not resist going further. He painstakingly unwound the transparent sheets until the icon was fully revealed. He held it reverently in his hands.

The icon was very similar to the one Krotkin had shown him a month earlier. It was superbly painted with lustrous colours. Even under the fluorescent office lights, it glowed magnificently. Peter studied the face of the angel, whose serene eyes looked deep into his. He was exultant that the image of Lydia had not appeared to distort its beauty. Her exorcism was complete.

He turned the painting over. There was a white envelope taped on the back addressed in longhand to *Doctor Stephen Homilly*. In the top right corner, *Personal and Confidential* had been written in the same hand, but in red ink.

Krotkin had failed to say much about the Doctor. Peter did not know if he was a doctor of medicine or philosophy, or indeed what he did or where he lived. *He is moving house in London*, Krotkin had told him, *but you can reach him on this telephone number. He will always answer. He likes to receive these gifts from his Russian friend.* Mindful of his obligation, Peter re-wrapped the icon with the utmost care.

It was dark by the time Peter got back to Hotel Leskov. A German tour group had debussed at the entrance, their luggage blocking the foyer. The hotel staff were busy attaching labels to cases, exchanging names and room numbers loudly with Reception. The bewildered tourists were marshalled by their tour guide, as inquisitive Russians circled them like wolves. Some calm was restored. Peter made his way round the group, stopping at the desk to collect his key.

"If I am not wrong," came a female voice, "I believe you are Mr Standridge from the British Embassy."

He swivelled round to find Anna from Intourist smiling at him. He opened his mouth to speak, but was unable to utter a word.

"It is part of my work to remember people and their names," she said. "So although you seem reluctant to speak with me, I know who you are. Perhaps the fault is on your part. You, Mr Standridge, do not remember me."

Sweat dampened Peter's shirt. His mind searched for words. "No… I mean yes… of course I remember you," he stammered. "You're Anna. We met, briefly, at our Embassy reception."

"Ah, at last I see you can talk. I thought like the old days you were *nemoy*, dumb, quite dumb," she said.

A besotted Peter wanted to go down on his knees and kiss the delicate hand she offered. Instead he grasped it awkwardly, giving it a formal shake.

"It's nice to see you again," he said. "But what brings you to Hotel Leskov?"

"Tourists. Looking after them is what I do," Anna said mischievously. "This is my group for the next week."

"So you speak German too?"

"Of course. I would not be much use with German tourists if I did not, would I now?"

Peter was angry with himself for appearing so stupid. The effect Anna had on him made it impossible for him to relax. He was behaving like a tongue-tied adolescent with nothing sensible to say. She seemed aware of his predicament.

"And you are living here in this place all the time, Mr Standridge?" Anna asked.

"I'm afraid so, but I've got used to it. It's convenient, if nothing else." Rediscovering his voice made him bolder. "Are you too busy to have a coffee or something?"

"Yes, I am. But in about one hour, I shall have a short break whilst my guests have their supper. I shall meet you here again at reception, Mr Standridge." Anna smiled at Peter and walked gracefully away.

Peter spent a frantic hour in his room. He rushed around trying to make up his mind what to do. Should he bother to change, take a shower, reappear downstairs as if he had made a major effort? Or should he just be nonchalant, arrive a few minutes late dressed as he was, pretend it was nice to see her, but nothing more? He could not decide.

With the clock ticking away, Peter finally dived into the shower. He dried in haste and spilt the contents of his wardrobe on the bed. He tried on, inspected himself in the mirror, he took off. Was the shirt better with or without a tie, would he need a pullover, should he wear a jacket? He panicked at the thought he could blow the whole thing. Why could he not just stay calm? Would it really matter what he wore? Oh yes, it would. It was essential he appeared looking at his best.

With five minutes to go, Peter left his room dressed smart but casual. He took the stairs, knowing he would arrive in the foyer with a minute to spare. He had butter-flies in his stomach, wild fantasies in his head. His imagi-nation led him delightfully astray. Only two more floors and there Anna would be waiting, gazing up at him with her beautiful eyes. Already she loved him.

He re-entered the real world. A large woman, made larger by her winter coat, barged Peter out of the way as he stepped into the foyer. He glanced across to Reception; no sign of Anna. He decided to sit down a short distance away, ready to go forward once she appeared. It would be unwise to show his interest too soon.

Peter slouched in his chair, hoping his anxiety and expectation were adequately concealed. As he knew from experience, Russian rendezvous were always flexible. There had to be quite a margin of time before an apology became necessary. So far Anna was only ten minutes late which was well within the limits of acceptance.

"Hiding from me again are you, Mr Standridge?" she said, tapping him on the shoulder. "As an English gentle-man, I expected you to be waiting at Reception at least five minutes early, ready to greet me with beautiful flowers."

"Well, er, yes I was on time," Peter said quickly getting

to his feet. "It's just that Reception was busy, so I sat over here to wait for you."

"Poor Mr Standridge, I believe you were probably fretting and wondering whether I was going to turn up at all. I mean look, oh dear, it's almost 7.15. How late is that!"

"I did think you might be a little delayed because of your tourists," Peter suggested.

Anna smiled. "Whenever I arrive is always the right time. So where are you going to take me?"

"I thought to the coffee shop or the hotel bar. I assumed you couldn't go out anywhere."

"I hate these dreary hotel places. There're so boring, so without soul or spirit. No imagination, Mr Standridge, no imagination." For a moment Peter thought it was he who had no imagination, rather than the hotel management. But Anna quickly continued. "You're right though. I must stay here. Just this once, you can escort me to the coffee shop of Hotel Leskov."

Anna walked beside Peter across the foyer. He had succeeded in getting off to a poor start with her again. She seemed to be totally in control, leaving him to catch up as best he could. So desperate was he to make a good impression, he ended up performing badly.

Peter found a table for two in the corner which seemed to meet with Anna's approval. He glanced at her to confirm she was comfortable. It seemed she was.

"Did you know the English are much easier than the Germans, as tourists that is," she said. "I have just spent half an hour dealing with a particularly demanding German woman. That is the reason I kept you waiting and was, how do you say, very 'grizzled' when I met you. It was not you, Mr Standridge, who has upset me. It was this woman who found everything was wrong and she had only been here for two hours."

"I'm very sorry," he said lamely.

"And what is more, this bitch insulted me and my country, my Russia. How dare she speak such terrible words. She's an uncultured peasant." Anna was becoming quite emotional, almost tearful.

Peter immediately felt protective, ready to defend her against anyone who came near. Deciding he had nothing to lose, he stretched out his hand and laid it on her arm.

"Thank you, Mr Standridge, thank you," she sniffed. "Forgive me for making a burden of these things. They happen sometimes, and by now I should be used to them. Perhaps I am too proud, too sensitive. Come, let us talk of other, better things."

Peter was ready to tell her how incredibly beautiful she was, how he adored her. Common sense, though, intervened. "Your English, it's impeccable," he said. "You didn't, by any chance, attend the Institute for Foreign Languages in Nizhny Novgorod?"

Anna laughed, displaying her lovely white teeth for Peter to admire. "What a curious question, Mr Standridge. I did, as it happens. But how did you know there was such a school, and in Nizhny Novgorod too?"

"I met the Director, Professor Krotkin, on a train in Siberia."

Anna laughed some more. She laid her hand on his, giving it a little squeeze. "That is an extraordinary coincidence. He was the Director when I was there, though we didn't have much to do with him. But wasn't it quite a relief to find an English speaker on a train in such a remote area?"

"Yes, it was. But his drunken friend caused a few problems for me and some of the other passengers. I've seen the Professor a couple of times since, here in Moscow. He turns up when I am least expecting him."

"Yes, that I understand. He always appeared to me like someone full of surprises. I thought he looked what you English might call 'a little shady'. He certainly associated with some people whom you wouldn't expect a person of his standing to know. Perhaps I am being unfair, but that was my impression."

Her opinion made Peter feel uncomfortable. He thought fleetingly about his relationship with Krotkin and where it might he going. He drank the rest of his tea.

"Will you spend the New Year here in Russia, Mr Standridge?" Anna asked. "We do have a very good party you know."

"Sadly not. I'm going to England on Friday and not coming back until after the New Year. It's a long-standing arrangement I have with my parents and friends."

Anna released his hand as if signalling her disappointment. "You should enjoy our winters whilst you have the opportunity. I don't expect you have done *langlauf*, I think you call it cross country skiing, and what about a snow barbecue? Have you been to one of those?"

"No, I've missed out on both counts I'm ashamed to say."

"In that case I shall invite you when you return. We always do these things with our tourist guests. You shall join us."

A member of the hotel staff came over to Anna. There was a quick conversation and she stood up.

"I am required, so I must go now,"she said smiling at him. "It has been very pleasant to talk with you again, Mr Standridge. I will contact you in January about a winter sports day,"

He was tempted to kiss her lightly on the cheek, but knew the moment was not right. Instead, he clasped her hand, managing to impart a faint caress. He was completely lost to her. "Goodbye. Have a happy New Year. By the way, my name… it's Peter."

"Yes, I know," Anna said smiling. "Goodbye, Mr Peter."

CHAPTER 17

There was little to disturb the passengers in the half-empty aircraft. The business class meal had been cleared and a laconic announcement from the Captain confirmed they would land in Moscow on schedule. Peter relaxed, thankful for the smooth flight and the vacant seats around him. He glanced out of the window at the crumpled mass of cloud stretching to the horizon like rucked ice on the surface of a frozen river. With still two hours to go, he closed his eyes and dozed.

He was glad to be returning. Though it had been good to see the parents and catch up with his friends, it had been an unexceptional Christmas and New Year. Somehow he had found it difficult to settle. He was restless, occasionally irritable. His one satisfaction was walking the streets of East Grinstead with the mock Geiger counter in his pocket, pretending he was in Pavlozavodsk. He had practised so thoroughly, his technique was now near perfect.

Yet even with this distraction, disillusionment had set in. He could not cast off the surroundings of his boyhood, but now he had the wider world to put them in perspective. They no longer seemed so special and ceased to offer that close, secure feeling of belonging. Perhaps his visit was too brief, the change too abrupt. Maybe it would be better the next time he came back, whenever that might be.

But deep down he was alarmed by what he felt. England seemed strange to him, almost foreign. Things were easy, life so organised, so straightforward, so dull. There was none of the daily fight for survival, no raw, rough emotion, no struggle, no soul. And he loathed the temperate weather, the warm, damp greyness of the days. How he missed the hard frosts, the snow in all its forms, the coldness of the air. With the aircraft heading for Russia, he took a guilty pleasure in thinking it was now he was going home. The country with its new freedoms seemed on the verge of an exciting era. He would never have the same challenges in England, nor face the same difficulties and problems. It was a time of opportunity; it was where he wished to be.

Peter was roused by the passing trolley of duty free. He shook his head, glad he had spent time at the airport choosing a suitable perfume for Anna. He hoped she would be pleased. Even if she disliked it, she would still be more gracious than the doleful Deirdre.

She had lowered his spirits. He had taken his letter round to her house the day after his arrival. They were a family of routine and Peter was sure nobody would be in. He slipped it quietly through the letter box, but the twitch of a curtain showed he had been spotted.

It was a painful hour with her mother. He could not refuse the glass of sweet sherry, poured from a bottle still two-thirds full from the previous Christmas. He had to tell Mrs Thwarton all about Russia, knowing she could never comprehend what he was saying. He, in turn, had to hear all about them and, of course, Deirdre.

She still had her job in the insurance office in Crawley and played her tennis at the club. She had such a nice group of friends, but, as Mrs Thwarton emphasized – leaning forward and tapping him on the knee – no one to compete with him. It was bizarre listening to her talk, as if they were to be engaged and married by Easter, whilst all the time she toyed with his fateful letter on her lap. His replies, if she heard them, were polite and diplomatically evasive.

His actual meeting with Deirdre on a wet day was a very different matter. She turned up at his front door, looking tanned from her skiing. She was more angry than sad. They walked through the kissing-gate up to the woods, scuffing through the fallen beech leaves in silence. Once there she cried, shouted, called him names, accused him of having *a little Natasha in his head and in his bed.* The encounter ended as miserably as it had begun. The recollection was uncomfortable. He was not so uncaring to feel no twinge of guilt, but it was too late for recriminations. The deed had been done, there was no going back.

The showdown with Deirdre had put him in a fragile mood for his meeting the following day. Doctor Homilly had answered the phone promptly when Peter dialled the number Krotkin had given him. They had a short conversation, agreeing to meet at midday on Thursday at the entrance to the National Gallery. Doctor Homilly said he would wear a daffodil in his buttonhole, carry a pinstriped umbrella and have a copy of the *Financial Times* folded under his arm. Peter felt rather dowdy confirming he would be there in his fawn raincoat holding a plain black briefcase.

Peter arrived on the steps of the Gallery just after Big Ben struck twelve. He walked up to the entrance, convinced he would find the Doctor waiting for him. He scanned those standing around on the terrace and the constant stream of people going in and out through the main doors. No one remotely fitted the description of Doctor Homilly.

"Excuse me, could I trouble you for the time?"

"It's just gone twelve, five past to be exact," Peter said consulting his watch.

"Thank you, Mr Standridge. Most kind of you."

Peter looked at the stranger in front of him. He was a short, spherical man wearing a long hooded coat. With his tonsured head and benign expression, he looked ready to intone the Benedictus.

"I'm sorry, but are you Homilly – Doctor Homilly?" Peter asked.

"Indeed I am. Delighted to make your acquaintance," the man said, extending his hand.

255

"But you're not wearing or carrying anything you said you would."

"Am I not? Oh dear, what a regrettable oversight. I must have a word with my wife. She takes responsibility for my appearance." He placed a hand on Peter's arm. "Shall we have a drink? I quite like The Reluctant Volunteer. Do you know it?"

"No, I'm afraid not," Peter said, as he was walked down the steps and steered along Northumberland Avenue to a small pub tucked down an alley.

"Pint?" Doctor Homilly asked as they settled on a bench seat.

"Just a half thank you. I've a meeting with my Director this afternoon."

"Have you indeed? How most unfortunate for you," Doctor Homilly laughed. He scuttled to the bar, returning with Peter's half pint and a Guinness for himself.

"Your good health, and thank you," Peter said. "By the way, I've got your gift in my briefcase when you want it. Have you anything to carry it in?"

"Hands and arms are adequate for the task," Doctor Homilly replied with a smile. "And tell me, how is my honourable friend Professor Krotkin?"

"He seemed well when I last saw him. Have you known him a while?"

"Oh yes, we met on some conference years ago... can't remember which one, may have been Zurich, or was it Zagreb. It's unimportant. How about you?"

"On a train in Siberia."

"Ah, Siberia. Not his favourite place," Doctor Homilly said glumly. "He told you about it, I expect."

"About what?"

"His banishment. Sadly I've always believed it was I who was responsible for his unplanned stay in that little corner of the world. An untidy business with foreign currency it was." Doctor Homilly took a sip from his glass. "Did you know he was there for three years teaching singing in a primary school? What a humiliation for such a brilliant linguist."

"Singing? He never told me he could sing."

"Oh, but he can't. Not a note. That was the whole point of the punishment," Doctor Homilly said gleefully. "So Mr Standridge, learn a lesson. Don't you be a naughty boy in Russia or you could finish up playing the violin beside the Bering Strait." Whilst Doctor Homilly enjoyed his joke, Peter wondered why it was the violin he should be condemned to play.

"Of course, you might like the violin," Doctor Homilly continued, "and you may also like the virtuoso who can play it with such brilliance, especially if it's a woman." He turned to Peter, his inquisitive eyes exploring his face. "In my experience of dealing with the Eastern Bloc, it's always advisable to be very cautious, very wary. Beauty is often a shroud for devilry." He drained his Guinness, smacking his lips with satisfaction.

"Like another?" Peter asked keen to change the subject.

"No, no, one at lunchtime is adequate. I mustn't exceed my norm or my wife, who, as you realize, keeps a very close eye on me, will impose a sentence of hard labour. I'll be condemned to toil in her garden until I can lift a spade no more."

Peter laughed and bent down to pick up his briefcase. "Well in that case, I'd better give you your gift from the Professor. This is it and here's the export certificate, should you need it."

Doctor Homilly prodded the parcel, even holding it to his ear and giving it a shake. "I wonder what it could be?" he said like a child.

"Don't you know?" Peter cried, alarmed that the precious icon might get damaged.

"Of course not. Professor Krotkin likes to surprise his

friends. Knowing would defeat his object."

"Well, handle it with care. I've got it this far in one piece. It would be a shame if anything happened to it on the last lap."

"Ah, so you know what my present is? I shall follow your advice and take a taxi rather than the Tube. Now, if you'd do me a favour in return, please deliver this personally to the great Professor." Doctor Homilly handed a plump envelope to Peter, who went to put it in his briefcase.

"No, no, you must keep it on your person day and night until you can give it to Professor Krotkin. It is most important that nobody including yourself opens it. He is the only one who should see it. Top secret you know," he said, tapping the side of his nose.

With that Doctor Homilly stood up, shook Peter by the hand and darted out of the pub.

Peter wriggled in his airline seat to get more comfortable, patting his pocket to ensure the Doctor's envelope was still with him. What a bizarre character he was, quite a joker too. How absurd to suggest his letter for Krotkin was top secret. And then there was his reference to violin playing: such a strange coincidence. He could not possibly know about Lydia. As for his warnings about dealing with Russians... well, after nearly six months in the country, Peter reckoned he knew enough about the pleasures and the dangers of that.

The memory of that meeting made Peter smile. He regarded it now as light relief, sandwiched as it was between his painful break with Deirdre and a grumpy session with Derek Carbonnel. Why his director had been so short with him remained unclear. Peter accepted Derek was a busy man and pressed for time, but still felt he could have shown him more consideration.

Peter had not had a chance to talk to him seriously since their walk round the lake at the Novodevichy Monastery at the end of October. He needed to know how things were progressing with his promised new appointment. When would it be officially announced, when would he take up the post and where was the office to be located? Derek Carbonnel failed to give him proper answers to any of these questions. *Don't worry, it's all going ahead, only need to do some fine tuning before we go public. For the moment just keep soldiering on, you're doing a great job. I'll make sure you get a medal at the end of it.*

Peter knew he was justified in expecting more information, not only on that but also about his unofficial duties. Clearly Derek did not share the same view and all his attempts were rebuffed. He left with no more knowledge than he had when he arrived. It was frustrating, to say the least.

The plane started its descent and touched down at Sheremetyevo Airport on time as the captain had predicted. It then took Peter almost two hours to negotiate passport control and customs. He endured a thorough baggage check, worrying all the while he might be randomly selected for a body search. If that were to happen, he would have to admit to not knowing what was in Doctor Homilly's envelope. But no official seemed particularly interested in him and he emerged intact. He set off across the main concourse to find a taxi.

"Welcome back, Mr Peter," Anna said, materialising in front of him like an immaculate apparition.

"Anna! What a surprise to see you," Peter stuttered. "Are you meeting a new tour group? There wasn't one on my flight, I'm afraid."

"It is possible, but I would not describe one person as a group," she said as Peter gaped at her. "You do look like a puzzled little boy. Are you not pleased I am here to say hello to you?"

"Do you... do you mean you came here to meet me?"

"Of course. Is that not allowed?"

"But you didn't even know when I was returning or on what flight?"

"In my business it is always possible to find out such things if you want to." Peter dropped his bags and stretched his arms out to Anna. "Forgive me, please forgive me, I'm the biggest idiot in Muscovy."

Anna took his hands in hers but kept him at arms length. "It is not permitted to be any closer when I am on duty. It is one of the rules of the Company," she said laughing.

For a moment Peter thought he was still daydreaming on the aircraft, but the softness of Anna's touch reassured him everything was real.

They took a taxi to Hotel Leskov, Anna allowing him to hold her hand for the journey. She asked him about England and his holiday. She had been there once and would like to go again. He in turn hoped she had enjoyed a good New Year. Oh yes, she had, she definitely had. Such a wild, all night party, lots of dancing, drinking, special things to eat. She had slept for most of the next day. Peter prayed she had slept alone.

They spent some minutes together in the hotel foyer. Peter clumsily presented her with his gift of perfume. Anna seemed mildly pleased.

"I must go now," she said. "I have responsibility for a group in another hotel. Soon it is my time for duty there. Tomorrow I take them to the airport in the morning. In the afternoon I shall be free, but more tourists will come on the evening flight. Let us have a winter walk in Sokolniki Park, if of course you would like to go with me."

Peter wanted to sweep her into his arms and kiss her to exhaustion. But all he could find to say was "I would love to."

"Here at 2pm then. And, Mr Peter, no hiding from me this time please." They shook hands like friends.

Peter took the lift up to his room, which smelled of too much cleaning. Leaving the door ajar, he took off his coat and unlocked his suitcase. There was the sound of shuffled footsteps in the corridor and a brief cough. Krotkin's head appeared round the side of the door.

"Please, Mr Standridge, you will forgive me," he said, stepping into the room. "As a precaution I have come to meet with you here. There are too many inquisitive eyes in the public places."

Peter recovered from his surprise. "Of course, come in, you're most welcome, although as you can see, I have only just arrived."

"No matter, I stay only for a short time. So, you have something from Doctor Homilly for me? A letter I believe?"

"Ah, yes," Peter said, removing the envelope from his jacket pocket. He held it out to Krotkin, who snatched it like a thief.

"Good, and I trust my gift of the painting was safely delivered also?"

"Yes, it was. It was a pleasure to meet Doctor Homilly. He sends you his best wishes."

Krotkin grunted and examined Doctor Homilly's envelope, testing the seal with his thumbnail to see if it had been opened. He nodded with apparent satisfaction. "Thank you. You are a good messenger for me. But now I will disturb you no longer. Goodbye, Mr Standridge, until our next meeting."

Krotkin hurried out of the room, closing the door behind him.

The bus took Peter and Anna to the southern entrance to Sokolniki Park. He had not been there before, but recalled other foreigners in the hotel saying it was the best park in Moscow. He did not care if it was the worst, provided Anna was beside him.

The temperature had fallen since the previous evening. Sensing the frost in his nose, Peter guessed it was at least

Minus 10. They were well wrapped against the cold, the shape of their bodies hidden deep in their coats. Anna held onto Peter. He longed to feel her properly, but it was fur touching fur, leather against leather.

They followed a main avenue through the trees. Many people were out, couples, families, the occasional solitary walker with gloved hands cradling a novel or book of poems, all enjoying the freshness of the air. Motionless bundles of small children were pulled on sledges, whilst older siblings raced ahead. An energetic skier swished past with marching arms and elegant strides.

"That's what you've got to do," Anna said. "You can't have your snow barbecue until you've completed at least two kilometres."

"Oh, come on. That's very unfair for a complete beginner."

"No, you'll manage to do it. I shall be in front of you and I expect you'll want to try and catch me."

"Put like that, I'll probably do fifty. When is this going to happen?"

"Next Saturday if you like. Maybe there will be some other opportunities if you wish to come another time."

"No, Saturday will be fine. I assume ski kit and clothing will be provided?"

"Of course, of course."

They walked on in silence. There were fewer people about as they went deeper into the park. The path they chose was narrower, its edges poorly defined. The sun cast long shadows over the snow, creating a stark contrast between light and dark. There was a deep silence with only the distant shouts of children and the squabbling ravens in the trees. Occasionally the birds would descend to strut and peck the frozen ground, leaving wandering imprints in the snow.

"Will there be lots of people at the skiing?" Peter asked.

"Normally we have about twenty tourists who want to do it. Then there's the ski instructors, the cooks, the people in charge of the vodka. We bring some other Intourist staff also. Vladimir will be there, he always comes. Probably you remember him from your Embassy party. He's an excellent skier, you know, and a very fit man. He's a champion at biathlon."

Peter did not care what Vladimir excelled at, provided it was not making Anna happy. He remembered him all right and the way he and Anna had left that reception arm in arm. The winter sports day was beginning to look less attractive.

"Yes, I do recall him," Peter said gruffly. "Sadly I didn't have a chance to talk to him very much. Seemed a nice chap though."

Anna peeked round the side of her fur edged hood and giggled. "Oh yes, but he's not just a nice chap. Vladimir is a guy of heroic proportions. He's like a god from Ancient Greece. Does that not make you just a little jealous, Mr, ever so English, Peter?"

Peter stopped in the middle of the path. He enveloped Anna in his arms, seeking out her face through the furs. She moved forward to meet his lips. Her kiss was gentle, lingering.

"Naughty Mr Peter," Anna whispered softly. "Where have you put your famous reserve?"

Peter did not want to break the spell by uttering a single word. They stayed wrapped together, his whole unseen body alight with desire.

"I think we should retrace our steps now," Anna murmured. "It's boring I know, but I have to change and go to the airport."

"I understand," Peter said, reluctantly releasing her from his embrace. They ambled back along the forest paths making the most of their remaining time.

"Are you going to be in Moscow this week?" she asked.

"Not initially. I'm going to Pavlozavodsk Monday evening on the night train. I should be back on Friday."

"That's a shame. On Wednesday I have a spare ticket for the Bolshoy. I thought you might like to go."

"Of course I would have loved to. But duty calls. Will you be able to find someone else to go with you?"

"No, there's only one ticket. I won't be going. Already I have seen this production. If you could go, you must go on your own."

Peter was unsure how to interpret Anna's offer. He hoped she was just being generous rather than signalling a retreat. Perhaps it was her subtle way of telling him not to go too fast, not to assume too much, too soon.

He glanced across at her, making sure she could see him round her hood. She smiled and squeezed his arm. He felt encouraged.

"Have you been to Pavlozavodsk?" he asked.

"No, of course not. It is not a town for tourists. I don't understand why you are going there, especially in the middle of winter."

"Nor I, except I might get a better idea of how difficult it is to keep things running in the dark and the cold."

"Rather you than me. They are a rough people in those sorts of towns, so just you take care of yourself." She paused. "For my sake, if not for yours."

They took the bus back into the centre of town. Anna had to get off before Peter. She touched his hand as they approached her stop. "This is where I must say goodbye. I will leave a message for you about next Saturday. I wish you a very safe journey." She stood up, making her way to the door. She gave him a quick wave before she disappeared.

Peter sat morosely in his seat for the rest of the journey. A young couple got on and sat in front of him, adding to his anguish with their cuddling. He looked out of the window. Pavlozavodsk sounded an unattractive place from both his own research and Anna's comments. He would rather be closer to her rather than the Arctic Circle. There was also that task to complete with the Geiger counter. He was now more anxious than ever that this coming trip should pass off smoothly.

CHAPTER 18

Saturday was not the best day to hold a conference, tucked as it was between New Year's Day and the balance of the weekend. Most of those summoned needed time to recuperate from their excessive celebrations and had planned on a few relaxing days before returning to duty the following Monday morning. It was accepted, though, that working for the Interior Ministry was a privilege which had its obligations. They understood, too, that even Deputy Director Popov would not call a meeting at 3pm on such a day, unless it was essential.

Once Yuri Poliakov heard he was required to attend, he faced the urgent task of getting up to date with his office files. There would have been developments which he would need to know about, particularly relating to Mr Standridge. Unfortunately it would mean going through the latest reports on his case with Section Head Zagarin. It was not a session he looked forward to with any pleasure.

"There you are, Poliakov. Everything's in here, set out chronologically and cross-referenced," Zagarin said, handing him a pink file. "I'm not going to hang around and hold your hand. You can read it all yourself. You'll find I've recorded every detail," he added with a self-satisfied air.

"Thank you. I really appreciate what you've done."

"But I want you to know, Poliakov, that I've hardly enjoyed doing all your work, as well as my own, whilst you've been out having a good time on the Moscow streets. One half of me wants you to make a real balls up at Popov's meeting and have your halfwit suspicions shown up for what they are. I've taken a long hard look at all the reports in your files and I'm not convinced."

Zagarin shuffled round the side of the desk, putting his sweaty face close to Yuri's. "You've no proper evidence have you? It's all supposition, a neat little theory. You've got nothing concrete at all. You're relying totally on your targets coming good for you out of the blue. Well, in all my years of experience, they just don't behave like that. They tend to let you down."

Yuri did not respond. It was obvious Zagarin resented the special attention he and his project were receiving from Popov and others more senior. But Zagarin's words did worry him, for in his heart of hearts he knew hard facts on Standridge's espionage activities were rather scarce.

"On the other hand, Poliakov," Zagarin went on, "I hope your little wheeze is successful and all the big cats shower congratulations on you. And you want to know why? Because, of course, as your Section Head, I shall receive much of the credit for your achievements. It will be noted that you would have done nothing without my good management, encouragement and direction. It's called reflected glory, something I greatly relish."

Zagarin glowered at Yuri for a moment before shambling off down the corridor. Once he was out of sight, Yuri fanned his stale smell out of the office and started work on the pink file. As he read through the copious notes, to his surprise he found Zagarin had done an excellent job. All Yuri needed to know was there and clearly indexed. He would at least have the satisfaction of arriving at the meeting fully briefed, despite Zagarin's scepticism about his methods.

Three of the participants had already assembled by the time Yuri entered the conference room. He quickly took his place on the far side of the long table set for nine. He nodded to Zagarin who deliberately ignored him. He decided not to interrupt the two men opposite, neither of whom looked keen on introductions.

Popov bustled in with his secretary, closely followed by

Tania. She sat down on Popov's left, running her eyes over the men she had not met. She gave Yuri a broad smile and skimmed a folded note across the table towards him. As Popov sorted his papers, Yuri read her message. *Hello little pigeon. Got all your ducks in a row for your big boss man? You know you have my support whatever you say. I've got some plans for your Mr P too!!! Love you to distraction. T.*

Yuri heard Popov clear his throat. "Good afternoon, everyone. Let's get started. Introductions first. You all know who I am," he said, beaming a rare smile round the table. "Over there is Zagarin, the Internal Section Head," – he waved an arm casually in Zagarin's direction – "and one of his collators, Poliakov. Poliakov is currently working with Meat-Hook, our best Close Surveillance Unit."

Yuri nodded deferentially to the others, aware he was the most junior official present.

The door opened and a man and a woman entered, apologising to Popov for their late arrival. They quickly occupied the vacant places at the end of the table. Popov let them settle. "Just so there is no misunderstanding, the colleagues who have joined us are observers from the Minister's Private Office who wish to remain anonymous. They will not take part in our discussions this afternoon."

Popov turned to Tania next. "And here on my left is Kalashnikova, whom I'm delighted to say is representing Meat-Hook. Her leader is otherwise engaged on another mission." Popov glowed as Tania devoured him with her eyes.

"And sitting on the far side are two gentlemen from our security agency, Mr Yegorov and Mr Rogozhin. Thank you for joining us." The two men raised their heads from their papers and stared defiantly round the table. With their austere suits, heavy rimmed glasses and stony expressions, they appeared to have emerged from the same mould on a human production line. Yuri avoided their direct gaze, since he always had a cautious respect for any representative from this agency. He was prepared to believe they knew more about him than he did himself.

Popov adjusted his glasses and read from his brief. "The purpose of this meeting is to examine the evidence surrounding the activities of a British national called Standridge, codename for field purposes, Pumpkin. He arrived in our country in July last year, using the cover of his work as a consultant to carry out illegal activities." Popov raised his head to ensure his introductory speech was having the required impact.

Satisfied, he continued. "Pumpkin's work requires him to travel widely, thus giving him opportunities to collect information prejudicial to the security of the State. Initially it appeared he was a low level operator, taking his time to adapt to a new country and environment. More recently he has extended the scope of his activities by befriending Russian citizens. It is on this aspect that I wish to concentrate today."

Each person around the table quietly took in Popov's words, gradually coming to terms with the severity of Pumpkin's crimes. Not satisfied with stealing secrets, this enemy was determined to subvert honest citizens and pollute their minds. No one had any doubt that this Pumpkin was a well trained and dangerous agent.

"Poliakov will now give us details of Pumpkin's contacts," Popov said.

Yuri fingered his notes in front of him. It was important for him to perform well. He started nervously.

"The first contact Pumpkin made was in Moscow in early October with the Director of the Nizhny Novgorod Institute for Foreign Languages, Professor Krotkin. We had no warning of this meeting and were unable to request proper surveillance in time. However we do know that they went to the New Confidence restaurant for dinner."

Zagarin raised a hand. Popov nodded to him.

"This restaurant is well known to us," Zagarin said.

"In the year or so it has been open, there have been many incidents involving foreigners and some of our less worthy citizens. It has acquired a bad reputation. Poliakov is unaware of this fact as it is sensitive information and not for release to lower officials such as Collators Third Class." Zagarin smirked at Poliakov before turning back to Popov. "The food's very good there though, Deputy Director," he said, patting his stomach.

"I do not see the relevance of that last remark. If you cannot contribute sensibly to the debate, I shall expect you to remain silent. Poliakov, continue."

Yuri remained impassive in the face of Zagarin's humiliation. He was a fool and deserved to be embarrassed. But as he had provided Yuri with the information he needed for the meeting, he was not inclined to be too harsh on him. He found his place in his brief and continued more confidently than before. "Since then, there have been two more meetings, the most recent of which was on the 18th December. On this occasion a package and envelope were given to Pumpkin by Krotkin. Also on the same day, Krotkin liaised with a man identified as Alexander Stroynov, using the Tretyakov Gallery as a meeting place. This man, Stroynov, is known to the police."

It was strange for Yuri to hear himself refer to Fat Alex by his full name. He almost felt he was reporting on someone other than the gross, indecent lump he had come to detest. Alexander Stroynov sounded too dignified, too refined, and quite unfitting for the Fat Alex he knew. It gave him an air of respectability which under no circumstances did he merit.

It was the turn of one of the two men from the security agency to catch Popov's eye.

"Please Mr Rogozhin," Popov said unctuously.

"That meeting you mentioned in the Moscow restaurant was not the first between Krotkin and Pumpkin," Rogozhin said quietly, getting everyone's attention. "They met earlier, the 12th September to be precise, on a train in Siberia. It seems that Krotkin made contact with Pumpkin and not vice versa, and he did so by using the services of a drunk." There was a snigger round the table. "This conflicts to some extent with the view that Pumpkin is responsible for initiating contacts with Russian citizens."

"How did you miss that encounter, Poliakov?" Popov asked sharply.

"I don't know, sir. I'm not sure we received a report on any such incident," Yuri said, blushing with embarrassment.

"It is true that some source material is not disseminated outside our agency for certain reasons," Rogozhin said. "It is possible this report was for internal use only."

"Quite so. Quite understandable," Popov said relaxing. "But thank you for bringing this to our notice. You can carry on now Poliakov."

Yuri felt undermined by Rogozhin's intervention and continued hesitantly. "The other contact was one that Pumpkin made in Stambov with Lydia Kuznetsova, a musician. He met her again recently after a concert she gave in Moscow. They are also both involved with a German, Herr Metzinger, codename Gooseberry, who visited Pumpkin in Moscow on 19th December. It would appear that this is another espionage ring masterminded by Pumpkin and separate from the one he controls via Krotkin, involving Stroynov and probably others." Yuri finished breathlessly and glanced up to see Tania touching Popov affectionately on the arm. He gestured for her to speak.

"Poliakov is right," she said. "I taped the conversation between Pumpkin and Gooseberry. Kuznetsova is being given money by Gooseberry to obtain information. She is now asking for some big sums so the information must be difficult, if not dangerous, to obtain. Gooseberry put on an impressive performance, pretending to be the victim of blackmail by Kuznetsova. He's a good actor, as, by the way, is Pumpkin."

There was a murmur of assent around the table. Why allow facts to interfere with obvious conclusions? Despite the slight complication over the incident on the Siberian train, they all agreed that Pumpkin was the main instigator of trouble. He was clearly a menace and should be taught a lesson.

"I also think Poliakov is right concerning Stroynov," Tania continued. "At the time I believed he and Krotkin were only involved in some illegal business. But I have seen other reports since their Tretyakov meeting and I'm convinced Poliakov's interpretation is the correct one." Tania flashed a dazzling smile at Yuri, much to Popov's obvious annoyance. Although he couldn't be certain from where he was sitting, Yuri suspected Tania quickly placated Popov by a sleight of hand under the table. Whatever she did to make amends, Popov shone with delight.

Rogozhin coughed. "If I may expand on Stroynov. Poliakov also will not know this, but Stroynov was once in an air force supply squadron in Siberia. During his service with this unit, he was accused of selling aircraft de-icing fluid to the local people, watered down and bottled as a spirit drink. The court let him off for lack of evidence, but everyone knows he was as guilty as hell. They still talk about it out there."

"That makes it even more important for us to watch this man along with Professor Krotkin," Popov said. "He also did some time in Siberia; three years exile for smuggling foreign currency. Together they may be involved in both criminal and espionage activities at the same time." He signalled to Yuri to carry on with his report.

"The most recent contact has been with an Intourist guide, Anna Lebedeva. Pumpkin met her in Hotel Leskov. They had a drink and a chat in the hotel coffee shop. The Meat-Hook report did not thrown up anything suspicious at that stage, but there was talk of another meeting on

Pumpkin's return from England—"

Tania interrupted. "I can inform this meeting that Lebedeva showed up at Scheremetyevo Airport to meet Pumpkin yesterday evening. The other half of the Meat-Hook team are trailing the two of them round Sokolniki Park as I speak."

Rogozhin cleared his throat. "Again I must make clear that this was not the first meeting between Pumpkin and Lebedeva. They met at a reception at the British Embassy on 22nd November. One of our people reported this, so it is Grade A information." He looked at Yuri who was beginning to hope the floor of the conference room would part and allow him to disappear.

"That again is information which was not passed to us," he said helplessly.

"How can you be so sure, Poliakov?" Popov asked in irritation.

"Because I have spent more time on Pumpkin than any other target. I know his file inside out. That piece of information did not come to me."

"Deputy Director," Rogozhin said smoothly, "it is certainly possible that Poliakov is also correct on this point. Only the most significant pieces of information are released from such a large gathering as an Embassy reception. The meeting between Pumpkin and Lebedeva in a group of other guests would not have been considered worthy of dissemination." Rogozhin returned his attention to Yuri. "But I can, however, confirm we have no negative information on Lebedeva. She is, of course, subject to security checks by our people and regularly debriefed for information on her foreign guests, so we have a good profile of her. She is clear. There are no entries by her name."

Yegorov fidgeted, seeking Popov's permission to speak. He received the required nod, although Popov's eyes kept straying back to Tania. "My Department can go further should it be necessary," Yegorov said. "If there is a development between Pumpkin and Lebedeva of the friendly, amorous sort, we can bring her in for some discussions. When we do this, we can offer her the usual options. She can either cooperate and extract all we need to know from Pumpkin; or if she decides not to assist us, she will lose her job and find it impossible to get another. It's not difficult for us to arrange these things."

Yuri felt uncomfortable with what Yegorov had proposed so routinely. Yet he knew that sometimes it was necessary to take such action for the sake of security. It was often hard to accept, but the interests of the State still came before those of the individual.

"Thank you for your offer of assistance in such a matter, Mr Yegorov," Popov said acknowledging his contribution. "For the moment however we will wait and see what happens between Pumpkin and Lebedeva. But it will always be helpful to know that these other means are available to us." Popov turned to Yuri again. "Poliakov, do you know who Pumpkin's controller is?"

"Not for sure, sir. There is some evidence that it is a Rumbelow, codename Blossom. She is the First Secretary Commercial in the British Embassy. I shall need more information before I can confirm this."

A long roundabout discussion followed as everyone put forward their views. Normally such an exchange would last a while, but Popov appeared anxious to foreshorten this meeting due to the attention Tania was giving him. She had changed his priorities, but he seemed at a loss to know how to conclude without disappointing the others. All meetings had to record some progress. In this case, a plan for dealing with Pumpkin was the obvious solution. His dreamy eyes settled on Yuri. "Poliakov, we are all interested in stopping this Pumpkin before he does more damage to the Motherland. How do you suggest we proceed?"

Yuri had anticipated that this question might be asked. He had spent a long time in his office working up an answer. His proposal was ready. "Pumpkin will no doubt continue with his own observations in addition to running his contacts. I believe that, if we gain good evidence of him collecting this low grade information, we can arrest him. Under questioning he will be persuaded to tell us about his clandestine dealings with our citizens." Yuri's mouth felt very dry. He took a gulp of mineral water. "It is my opinion, sir, that we should place Pumpkin under close surveillance on his next trip. Up to now he has only had local teams tailing him and, with respect, they do not have the same expertise nor the same knowledge of him as the Meat-Hook unit. We know that Pumpkin is due to go to Pavlozavodsk on the Monday night train, returning to Moscow early Friday. I propose that Meat-Hook is given responsibility for Pumpkin on these train journeys and during his visit."

There was a nervousness round the table. A very junior collator had suggested that a unit operate out of area. Such a deviation from accepted practice was almost revolution-ary and the repercussions from such an operation could be severe.

Popov, eager to be on his way, seemed to view things rather differently. "Excellent Poliakov. I will telephone Pavlozavodsk myself and perhaps Mr Rogozhin you will also speak to your colleagues there. Poliakov, you must see my secretary about the administrative arrangements afterwards. Everybody agreed?"

There was no dissent. Gathering their papers and files, the participants started to leave. Popov placed a detaining hand on Tania's arm.

Yuri walked down the corridor with Popov's secretary, well satisfied with the outcome of the meeting. Despite the misgivings expressed by some, he had been given a final opportunity to prove Standridge's guilt. Much now depended on Standridge himself and what he got up to in Pavlozavodsk. There was always the risk that, for one reason or another, he might decide to behave himself and do nothing suspicious or illegal. He could in any case still be arrested and questioned but, without some reasonable proof, he could justifiably claim his innocence. Yuri needed him to cooperate more than ever in the coming week: like a true Englishman, Standridge had to play the game.

Yuri emerged from the front entrance, disappointed that the brightness of the day had already given way to the dark, sinking cold of dusk. Where the full sun had melted the snow, the frost now cemented the crushed surface into frozen, brittle ridges. People stepped with care, seeking out the cleared sections of pavement, steering round the treacherous patches of sparkling ice. Joining the evening crowds, Yuri set off through the Moscow streets towards his rendezvous with Olga.

They had agreed to meet at 6.30pm. He had no idea how long Popov's conference would last, but said he would ring if he was going to be delayed. As it was he had half an hour to spare, but there seemed little point in his returning to the apartment before their promised dinner. Perhaps they both hoped the excitement of meeting in the bar like lovers would repair the damage they had suffered.

For both Yuri and Olga, the previous three weeks had been a torment. The disruption to the harmony of their life had been savage on the surface and harrowing beneath. The doubt and suspicion, the sadness at what had been lost, the fear of the future gnawed at their minds and bled their hearts. They hated how they behaved, how there was thrust and parry, quick tempers and resentful silence. When they spoke, they spoke with care, choosing clear words and phrases, yet each found innuendo in their interpretation. They seemed incapable of expressing those vital inner thoughts and feelings. They wanted to share their secrets but somehow could not, they wished for forgiveness, but shied away. Their relationship had become an edgy coexistence.

Yuri found a seat in the bar from which he could see the entrance. He smiled to himself as he realised he was almost subconsciously using his newly acquired tradecraft to watch for his wife. He ordered a beer and waited.

Olga arrived respectfully late and breathless. Yuri was stunned by how beautiful she looked. He kissed her with passion.

"Good meeting?" she asked, removing her hat and loosening her coat.

"Not bad at all. We were through in a couple hours, but then I had one or two things to do in the office. I've only been here a short time."

The waiter brought a cocktail for Olga. The colour in her cheeks rose as she sipped her drink and enjoyed the warmth of the bar. She told Yuri about her day, a sweet account of simple pleasures. Yuri listened, smiling and laughing where appropriate and occasionally interjecting. All the while he watched her, wishing he could take her into their bed that moment and love her like a tsar.

"We ought to go," he said. "The table is booked for 7.30. It's a good ten minute walk from here."

The icy pavements slowed them down. They arrived a few minutes late and pushed their way through the crowd at the restaurant entrance. A relieved receptionist showed them to their table.

"Yuri, my love, are you sure we can afford this?" Olga asked anxiously as she surveyed the menu. "It's very pricey."

"We – particularly you – deserve it. It's our private New Year celebration. It's to welcome a good year ahead for the two of us."

Olga looked at her husband quizzically, but decided to go along with his optimism. "I'll drink to that," she said, raising her glass.

The meal was excellent and the bottle of Georgian wine relaxed them both. It softened their words, the way they looked, the smiles they gave. They chatted with a rare gaiety, sensing the coming release of their suppressed desire. They welcomed the approaching reconciliation.

Olga leaned back in her chair and watched the waiters rushing back and forth through the swing doors to the kitchen. She was wondering whether she ought to have a dessert when an unexpected movement caught her eye. A narrow door in the seemingly continuous back wall of the restaurant opened, throwing a rectangle of light onto an assemblage of artificial plants. Through the door stepped the unmistakable shadow of Fat Alex. He surveyed the crowded restaurant before setting off towards them.

"Oh my God, Yuri. It's Fat Alex and he's coming this way," Olga whispered in panic.

"What?" Yuri turned his head, horrified to witness the huge bulk moving on a direct course for their table. Olga's face had lost all its colour, her mouth hung open.

"My dears, what a fortuitous and felicitous coincidence to find you dining here in another of my worthy enterprises," Fat Alex said once he was within range. "How generous of you to come. Let me welcome you most heartily." Fat Alex wanted to embrace them in his usual fashion, but as they remained seated, he was unable to bend down far enough to reach them. Thwarted, he placed a sloppy kiss on Olga's proffered hand and slapped Yuri on the shoulder.

It became immediately apparent that Fat Alex had arrived to stay. Lined up behind him were three waiters: the first carried a chair, the second champagne and glasses, the third a dish of ice creams and chocolates. It was a rude and unwarranted intrusion on their evening.

Yuri looked at Fat Alex with disdain and a certain superiority. Matters were very different since he had found him with Krotkin in the Tretyakov Gallery. He had always disliked him for his overconfidence and showmanship, to say nothing of his constant flirting with Olga. But now he was involved in more serious matters which required Yuri to regard him as a villain and an enemy of the State. He was no longer someone with whom he, Yuri Poliakov of the Interior Ministry, could associate. He hoped Olga would rebuff him too. For the moment, she looked like a terrified rabbit unable to run or utter a sound.

Fat Alex seated himself clumsily in his semi-drunken state. He seemed keen to get Olga into an embrace but she recoiled from him. Yuri's normally placid face was full of contempt. Fat Alex was indifferent to their displeasure. He ordered the expensive French champagne to be poured.

"To the New Year and to us all," he said raising his glass.

Yuri and Olga followed suit, exchanging glances only they could understand.

"Please, please, they're for you," Fat Alex said, waving at the desserts. "They're on the house, of course."

Neither Yuri nor Olga made any move to help themselves.

"I trust you enjoyed your dinner," Fat Alex continued. "Olga of course recently had a lunch with me at another of my restaurants, when you, my good sir, were out of town on a secret mission," he said, fixing his gaze on Yuri. "And now you're back, although I have not seen you personally, there have been some sightings of you scurrying around the streets of Moscow instead of sitting in your warm, little office. New job is it, Yuri, or just a bit of recreation?"

Somehow Yuri maintained his composure, refusing to rise to the bait. "It's a busy time of year for us. Lots of meetings in different buildings. That's all."

Fat Alex showed no interest in Yuri's reply. "Look, you are both intelligent young people, intelligent and very beautiful, so you will know that our meeting here is not entirely accidental, at least not on my part. I knew of course from the book of reservations that a Poliakov had a table for two this evening. Using the special spy hole in my office wall, I made it my business to check if that Poliakov was indeed you, my dear Yuri, and I was delighted to find it was. I wouldn't want you to come to any place of mine and not be properly looked after, now would I?"

Fat Alex took a large slurp of champagne. "Furthermore, it was a great pleasure and relief to see that you were escorting your gorgeous Olga and not another lady companion."

Yuri wanted to smash his fist into Fat Alex's face with all the strength he could muster. But he controlled the impulse, knowing he might have the greater pleasure of seeing him put away for several years. For now he would rely on an inner fortitude to ride out the insults and provocation as Fat Alex rambled on.

"So having ascertained you were here, I said to myself, Alex, you have not seen these good people for some time, at least not together. It is time to make amends for your shameful and unwarranted neglect. Take a bottle of your best champagne and toast the New Year with them. And this is what I do." He raised his glass again.

"Thank you for your generosity," Yuri said, grudgingly lifting his glass in return.

"Of course, there remains an unresolved matter between us," Fat Alex continued, "and it concerns my apartment with its magnificent view. As you well know the Princess Olga visited it most recently and has no doubt given you a full account of its fine furnishings and delicious décor. It has indeed undergone a metamorphosis so profound that no one believes it is I who still lives there." Fat Alex laughed loudly.

Yuri permitted himself a smile and glanced at Olga. She remained as motionless as a stone.

"And it is on this account that I owe you both an apology," Fat Alex said penitently. "I have thought most deeply and seriously about your proposal to exchange apartments, but I cannot agree to it. I have become too fond of my refurbished home to leave it. I cannot abandon all the good work my friends have done in that place and let others occupy it, even such sensitive and desirable people as your lovely selves. I am ashamed at my behaviour, I ask forgiveness for leading you on, for raising your hopes and then dashing them like a glass on the frozen ground." Fat Alex put his hands out in despair.

"Perhaps you never did intend to exchange," Yuri said boldly.

"Oh, what cruelty you show, dear Yuri. What lack of compassion. Please don't doubt me in that way. I was fully prepared to proceed, I even had the terms and conditions drawn up before I was assailed by these second thoughts. My greatest sin was not to have informed you the moment I changed my mind."

"And these terms and conditions, were they likely to be acceptable?" Yuri probed.

"Naturally. They offered all the usual legal safeguards. There was nothing in the document which was unreasonable or improper," he said in a rare flash of sobriety.

Fat Alex had addressed his remarks to Yuri. Olga had not said a word since he had imposed himself upon them. She had made no effort to disguise her resentment. She now leaned forward slowly and grasped Yuri's hand. "I think we should believe what Alex is saying, my darling. Whilst I was visiting his apartment, he made no suggestion which we would find difficult to agree to. If I'd got a place like his, I wouldn't want to move either."

"I'm sure you're right," Yuri said squeezing her hand.

Fat Alex nodded his appreciation and filled up his champagne glass. He looked more sombre as his drunkenness took hold. "There always comes a time when it is advisable to assess the regard we have for one another," he said tortuously. "For me, my acquaintance with you both has given me the greatest pleasure. You, Yuri, are a most upright and honest man. You, Olga, an intelligent beauty who understands the power you have over men. Together you are a fine couple, an example to all and especially to those who prefer the decadent path of immorality. I salute you individually and collectively." He brandished his glass and drained it. He lit a fresh cigarette, drawing deeply on the sweet Turkish tobacco. "And now we must decide what to do for the best," he slurred. "It is the evening of the day when the light is failing, it is the point at which the made-up road becomes a rutted track, a time when, what we have known hitherto, comes to an end." Fat Alex coughed on his cigarette.

"We have reached a junction, a bifurcation of the ways. Do we go on together by taking the same road or do we go separately… you into the meadows and I the lone traveller into the dark forest? Or is there some reordering of our intimate relationship, so it is not I who walks alone into the forest, but one of you?"

There was a hush at their table amidst the restaurant hubbub. Yuri frowned, puzzling to understand.

Olga looked at Fat Alex. "If you're suggesting we conclude our acquaintance with you, then I think we should do just that. You have been generous towards us, but we can't compete at your level. We will never be able to repay you in the way you most desire, either jointly or individually."

"Never have I heard a woman speak with such decisiveness and clarity. It seems that my dreams must wait to be fulfilled. You are one, dear Olga, to try the patience of the blessed saints, but I shall never abandon hope. Never will there be any diminution of my intent." Fat Alex stared at his glass. He raised it shakily to his thick lips, before realising it was empty. "No, this is not the end for me. I will not be kicked aside like a wild dog," he said angrily. "But this evening, I shall keep my counsel and bother you no more.

Drink and eat what you will. I bid you both good night."

A waiter was at hand to assist Fat Alex from his chair. He swayed as he stood but he made no attempt to embrace or shake hands. He was steered towards the mysterious door in the back wall.

"What was that all about?" Yuri said in astonishment.

Olga picked up the champagne bottle and filled their glasses. She took Yuri's hands and looked steadfastly into his eyes. "You may find this distressing, my love, but Fat Alex was asking me to go with him and abandon you. It was to be a parting of the ways in more than one sense."

Yuri's sluggish brain responded even slower after the wine and champagne. "I'm sorry Olga, I'm still not with you."

"Look Yuri, I hate to have to say this, but Fat Alex is an attractive man. I know he's nothing to look at, but women find his personality and power very sexy. He's only too aware of his appeal, and that makes him even more reckless." Olga stopped for a moment, as if concerned she had already said too much. She gathered herself. "It's only when you get to know him better that you realise he's an absolute bastard."

Olga's words now began to register with Yuri. He tried to withdraw his hands from her grasp but she wouldn't release them. She kept her eyes fixed on him. "After that lunch in his restaurant, Fat Alex tried to seduce me in his apartment. I had been drugged by all his wine and that was the closest I came to finding him irresistible. Thank God I didn't succumb. I would never have forgiven myself, had I done so." Olga let a couple of tears run down her cheeks. "I'm sorry I lied to you about what happened that day. I didn't tell you the whole truth when you returned from your course because I was afraid you would overreact and do something rash. I hate him for trying to take advantage of me."

"This is so humiliating," Yuri snapped. "How could you

even consider him attractive? He's disgusting, repulsive."
In his anger, Yuri was ready to punish his young wife but
was afraid he'd go too far. "I suppose there were other
demands?"

Olga nodded slowly. "As I was leaving, he said he
wanted me to come to him before the end of the week and
spend some time in his bed," she said tearfully. "It was one
of the unwritten conditions for swapping our apartments.
I lived in fear of him, Yuri. In deep, deep fear."

Yuri's self righteous indignation subsided as he remembered Olga was not alone in facing the beckoning arms of
infidelity. Had he not tasted the temptation of Tania and
almost succumbed himself? In a perverse way it helped
him understand Olga's predicament. Through a shared
guilt there might be a shared salvation. "Is there anything
else you've got to tell me?" he asked quietly.

"No, I've made a full, though belated confession. I
never, ever want to see that evil beast again. I'm so sorry
Yuri. I was very foolish, very unloving. I'm guilty in every
way. I repent, but I don't deserve your forgiveness."

Yuri leaned across and kissed Olga's tears. Those closest
to their table were enthralled but neither of them cared.

"You shall have it nonetheless. I've never trusted Fat
Alex," he said shaking his head. "He tried to buy our
friendship, make us beholden to him. He wanted to get
you into his bed and triumph over us both. I never believed
he'd sink quite so low. Olga, you must forget about him,
remove him from your mind. He's come too close to blowing us apart."

"I will, I will! I promise. But I just can't bear the thought
of bumping into him again. That would be so awful."

"I feel we may have seen the last of him, whatever he
may think."

"Oh God, my darling, I only hope you're right."

"And we've got our own catching up to do. Let's just
go home."

Olga shuddered. "Yes, yes, we must. This place makes me feel unclean." She dabbed the remaining tears from her cheeks, wondering whether they would ever untangle themselves from the web Fat Alex had spun for them.

CHAPTER 19

On the surface there was nothing unusual about Peter Standridge's trip to Pavlozavodsk. The overnight train was not particularly late, the local hotel not distinctly uncomfortable, the town's authorities not overly keen to see him. He had made many similar journeys to other middle-sized Russian towns and was accustomed to the routine of these official visits. He found the apparent normality reassuring in view of the extra task he was obliged to perform.

Pavlozavodsk was cold and full of snow. Peter alternately froze in the open air and roasted in the overheated buildings. The representatives of the town council whisked him around in a fuggy car, pointing out on the ground all the places they discussed in their meetings. If ever there was a town in need of *perestroika*, it was Pavlozavodsk. It had such deficiencies, Peter was at a loss to know where to begin. It seemed they had to wage a constant battle against the elements and cope with decades of haphazard planning, shoddy construction and poor maintenance. Sorting out Pavlozavodsk would be a major undertaking. He could spend months offering his advice, but suspected there would be little to show for it in the end.

By lunchtime on the second day, Peter sensed his hosts were anxious for him to leave. What turned out to be their final meeting stuttered to a close as long silences were interspersed with brief questions and even shorter answers. *Glasnost*, it seemed, had its limits. A tray with glasses and a bottle of vodka was brought in on cue. Toasts were drunk and the senior official stood and thanked Peter for his assistance. He hoped he would have a pleasant return journey to Moscow.

Not wishing to appear ungracious, Peter in turn expressed his thanks for the welcome he received and for the opportunity to appreciate the many difficulties confronting the town. He trusted the early conclusion of his visit was not due to the quality of the advice he had given. Indeed it was not, he was assured. Perhaps, Peter suggested, the council might wish to facilitate his departure by changing his train reservation, since he was now to leave a day earlier than scheduled. This they would do with pleasure and a junior official was dispatched to make the necessary arrangements.

In the car to the hotel, Peter considered the alterations to his plans. He was elated by the thought of arriving in Moscow the very next day. Would he be able to see the delicious Anna or would she be too busy with her tedious tourists? He would enjoy thinking about her on the way back in the train, but for the moment he must concentrate on the vital task he had to complete before leaving Pavlozavodsk. Time was limited and there was not much daylight left.

Peter sorted himself out in his room. He removed the Geiger counter from its case and slid it into the right hand pocket of his coat. He unclipped the top of the plastic casing, exposing the battery switch and the face of the meter. From a special section of his briefcase he extracted a notepad of soluble paper, a pencil stub and a miniature torch. These he tucked into an inner pocket.

On the rickety table, Peter laid out the basic town plan he had purchased the previous day. It was schematic in form, offering a rough diagram of the major streets and principal facilities. Like other such plans of Russian towns, it would require some imagination to interpret. Fortunately Pervomayskaya Street, which ran past the front of his target installation, was marked as a main road. It was some distance from the hotel, but at least it would give him a start.

Peter heaved on his thick coat, wrapping a scarf tightly round his neck. He wedged his fur hat firmly on his head and put on his gloves. Fully prepared and equipped, he held a dress rehearsal. He paced up and down and caught his reflection in the mirror. He convinced himself he looked quite Russian. He lifted the flap of his coat pocket to read the dial on the meter and gave the plastic covering a little polish with his finger. Still walking and turning about, he pulled out his notepad and scribbled down a few random numbers. Finally he practised illuminating the dial with his torch in case the daylight was too poor. Satisfied, he strode into the corridor, locked his room and went in search of a taxi.

According to the town plan, the museum was located on a street parallel to Pervomayskaya. Peter got the taxi to drop him there, although the driver seemed reluctant to do so. Only when he walked up to the entrance, did he notice the sign *Na Remont* and discovered it was closed for repairs. He stood on the steps to get his bearings. Despairing of a return fare from this stupid foreigner, the taxi sped away.

Peter set off down a side street, hoping to come out close to his installation. The town plan was as inaccurate as ever. What appeared on the map to be a short walk down a straight road took over ten minutes down a winding alley. When Peter did emerge onto Pervomayskaya, he had no idea which way to go.

On the other side of the street where his installation was alleged to be, there was a row of small shops and a shabby apartment block. In the poor afternoon light, he was unable to see very far down the street in either direction. The town plan indicated he would come across a major intersection, whichever way he went. Each was named on the plan, so provided he walked far enough, he would eventually discover his location. He decided for no particular reason to turn left.

There were many people hurrying in the cold. Most, like Peter, had heads bent as they chose their route along the pavement, weaving round heaps of discoloured snow. They either took short shuffling steps on the firmer patches or strode out like skaters across the glacial surface. There was many a slip and stumble.

Peter felt frustrated and not a little apprehensive. The promised intersection, so boldly marked on the plan, failed to appear. So where was his target? Surely he would have spotted it by now if he was going in the right direction. It was supposed to be a factory of some sort and there would be a signboard, but he had no further details. What if the signboard had been removed? Abort, abort now, kept running through his mind.

Five minutes later he reached an intersection. A cobbled street, admittedly a little wider than the other minor roads he crossed, bore the same name as the broad boulevard marked on the plan. It had to be it; there were not going to be two Friedrich Engels Streets in Pavlozavodsk. He reluctantly turned round and started to retrace his steps. He had come the wrong way on Pervomayskaya.

Peter trudged back to his starting point and continued on in the direction he should have taken in the first place. He walked for another ten minutes, noting the area was becoming more rundown with fewer pedestrians about. He felt exposed and self-conscious. The cold too was now getting to him. He could feel the frost on his face, the hollow chill in his body. With each breath he took, his temperature edged lower.

Although it was only 2.45 pm, it was starting to get dark. He wondered whether it was wise to continue. Would it not be sensible to give up and go back to the hotel? He decided to give it five more minutes and, if there was still no sign of the place, then it would be curtains for Mr Chris Burroughs, Major Pomfrey (Retired) et al.

The change from squat buildings to a long wall of

concrete sections drew Peter's attention to the other side of the street. Further along a gap marked an entrance with stout double gates, beside which a signboard displayed the word *Tekhnika*. He had found his installation at last.

He stayed on Pervomayskaya, deciding to circumnavigate the complex anticlockwise. Without altering his pace, he continued to observe. A couple of trucks went in through the entrance, stopping at the internal barrier before being allowed to proceed. Behind the wall he could make out buildings and workshops, puffing steam and smoke into the freezing air. It looked similar to hundreds of other small factories all over Russia. What made it so special that they needed to send him here?

The perimeter of the installation turned a right angle at the next road junction. Peter crossed the main road and walked down the small side road close to the wall. He put his hand into his coat pocket and switched the Geiger counter on. It gave a sharp crackle and fell silent.

There was no one in front of him on his side of the road. He hazarded a glance behind him, but again the pavement was deserted. On the opposite side a couple were walking slowly in the same direction. At the end of the road Peter turned left beside the perimeter wall as it ran along the rear of the installation. The couple went straight on. In the fading light, he found himself completely alone on a rough tarmac road with no pavement.

Anxious as he was to get to the end of this minor road, he found it impossible to go quicker. He was forced either to walk close to the perimeter wall through the accumulated snow or to chance his luck on the slippery road surface. He tried both, but in the end felt safer in the gutter by the wall. On the other side, squat dark houses began to show an occasional light in their square, mean windows. A parked van was the only vehicle in sight. Peter had the road to himself.

The Geiger counter remained silent in Peter's pocket.

Using his torch, he confirmed the little device was still functioning. He wondered whether he would record a zero for all his efforts. He had already walked half the factory perimeter and it was not much further along the rear wall either. His progress was still pitifully slow. A truck roared past spattering him in loose, dirty snow. He brushed off the worst and continued.

A short grunt came from the Geiger followed by more intensive crackles. Peter checked the time: 3.05pm. He kept going, periodically glancing down at the Geiger's dial to see the arrow dancing up and down in time to the crackles. He stopped, shone his torch to get an accurate reading and memorised the figures. Before moving on, he noted a particular whitewashed building close to the perimeter wall. As far as he could see, it had no windows nor leaded lights in the roof, neither chimneys nor ventilation louvres. Security lights beamed down from under the eaves. A notice in unintelligible Russian was fastened to the wall.

As Peter walked beyond the building, the Geiger's crackling gradually subsided. He took two more readings and under the orange glow of a solitary street lamp, recorded the numbers in his notepad. By the time he reached the next corner, the Geiger had fallen silent. He continued up the far side of the installation before doing a final walk along the front and past the entrance. There was no further response from the Geiger.

Peter crossed the main road, switching the machine off once he reached the pavement. He walked back along Pervomayskaya and made his way up the side street leading to the museum. He felt relieved and pleased with himself. He was happy no one had taken the slightest interest in him or his activities.

Diligence was the hallmark of the Meat-Hook team. They had boarded the train in Moscow, taking it in turns to keep Pumpkin under observation. It was a thankless task: other than one brief walk along the corridor to the toilet, Mr Peter Standridge of Great Britain had failed to emerge from his compartment. He had the two berth, 'soft class' compartment to himself, as they thought he would. Their checks revealed he had paid a double premium, a bottle of vodka and five packets of Western cigarettes to secure this unusual reservation. He was conscientious in locking his door throughout the journey.

None of the Meat-Hook team was prepared to admit going to Pavlozavodsk before. As the long hours passed, it became something of a game to guess which of them could be lying. Might Valery have visited as part of his university course, or Sergei looking for contraband cigarettes, or young Yuri keen to find a wife? No, none of them. But what about Tania? Did she learn to dance in this bleak northern town, moving and leaping just to keep warm? No, she shook her head and laughed, she had danced elsewhere.

During spells of inactivity, Yuri thought about the future. He knew this would be his last outing with the Meat-Hook team. Popov would pull the plug on the special operation if they failed to get Pumpkin. If they were successful, he would be back at his desk in any case. Olga for one would like that. He had already told her this was going to be his final trip to out-of-the-way places. She even laughed when he said there would be no more running around town with mysterious women either. That Saturday night they had made peace in the sanctity of their bed.

At Pavlozavodsk station, Valery trailed Pumpkin to the hotel. The others loaded their bags and equipment into a taxi and followed on. They hovered around as Pumpkin attended his meetings and was driven round town by his official hosts. At the end of the first day, he did nothing other than eat supper in the hotel restaurant and retire early to bed.

The Head of the Pavlozavodsk Interior Ministry Section resented their arrival. They were trespassing on his patch and they might discover things he would rather they did not. Only under pressure did he agree to provide a grumpy driver as a guide and a wreck of a van for transport and observation. No one was attached to Meat-Hook for liaison. Valery had to bribe a female official in the council building to keep him informed of Pumpkin's programme. It was her phone call at lunchtime on the Wednesday which swung Meat-Hook into action. They had to move fast.

"Looks like he's dressed for a long walk in the cold," Valery said, as Pumpkin appeared from his hotel room and headed for the foyer. "You all know what you've got to do, so let's go."

Sergei stood by the solitary taxi at the hotel entrance enjoying a cigarette. Once Pumpkin had given his instructions to the driver, Sergei joined his companions in the back of the van. "He's going to the museum. It's closed, but he's not to know that. Perhaps he's arranged to meet a contact by the front door."

Their lugubrious driver, Grom, jammed the gear stick into first. The engine roared, its exhaust belching smoke like a nuclear cloud. He jerked the steering wheel round and the van rocketed onto the main street.

"She won't keep up," Grom mumbled. "She's not used to four passengers and all their kit. We'll lose them, I know we will," he added prophetically. As they rounded the first bend, Pumpkin's taxi was nowhere to be seen.

"Go straight to the museum," Valery said. "We'll catch up with him there."

"Might not get that far," Grom complained. "She doesn't like the cold, she doesn't."

Despite Grom's pessimism and the van's expiratory noises, they managed to get to their destination before Pumpkin. They parked a short distance away, tucking themselves into a group of vehicles. The van's engine gasped, issued a loud report and died. Tania and Sergei scrambled out of the back.

Pumpkin's taxi drew up in front of the museum. Yuri prepared their cameras and observation equipment and took a few practice shots of Pumpkin standing at the top of the museum steps. Valery established radio communications with the two on foot.

Grom meanwhile started to talk to the van. He cursed and cooed melodically before his voice broke into the wavering pitch of a peasant song. He got down from the cab and raised the engine cover. Singing a more strident tune, he began to beat the engine casing with a metal bar. He returned to the cab and turned the ignition. The engine exploded into life.

Pumpkin crossed the main street and set off down a side road. Tania and Sergei moved in behind him.

"Yuri, clean these windows up," Valery said. "We want shots of him with good sharp definition. No streaks of Pavlozavodsk grime on the negatives." Yuri did as he was ordered. He too was more than anxious to get the best quality photos of Pumpkin's nefarious activities, whatever they turned out to be.

Tania radioed in every five minutes. It seemed that Pumpkin had turned left when he reached a main road called Pervomayskaya. He was walking further and further along it, consulting his map and checking out the street names. He was definitely looking for something, though she had no idea what. Valery told Grom to go down onto Pervomayskaya and park up.

"He's decided to turn round," Tania reported breathlessly. "He's just passed us, he's retracing his steps, looks like he's coming back to where he started." Valery and Yuri stared at one another, each wondering what Pumpkin was up to. Was he going to disappoint them again? Yuri had a creeping sense of failure.

He took more shots of Pumpkin through the clean

windows as he passed. There was an assumption he would take a taxi from the museum back to the hotel. But to their surprise, he kept on walking. Whatever Pumpkin was after, he seemed determined to find it.

There was a flurry of activity as Tania reported Pumpkin was taking a lot of interest in a factory called *Tekhnika* much further down Pervomayskaya. Valery gave his orders and even the sullen Grom appeared to rise to the occasion. He drove madly through the traffic, managing to park the van on the small road behind the factory in record time. Valery told him to switch the engine off and lie down on the front seats out of sight. Grom grumbled, but did as he was told.

Tania said Pumpkin seemed to be walking the factory perimeter and would soon appear in their line of vision. She and Sergei would go straight on, then double back to pick him up again on the main road. In the gloom Yuri fumbled with the low light cameras. Valery whispered the angles they would need to get and which of the van's windows they should use. Yuri manoeuvred himself into position in the enclosing darkness and waited for his target to appear.

It was not difficult to spot Pumpkin as he walked cautiously round the corner. He was the only person on the road and despite his obvious attempt to look more Russian, he would always be identified as a foreigner, especially in a place like Pavlozavodsk. He also seemed unsure where he should walk, alternating between the middle of the road and the verge. In the end he seemed to go for the verge.

Valery took charge of the cine and started to film Pumpkin. Yuri with a larger lens fired off some shots with his motorised camera. His fingers were stiff against the metallic cold and the clunky camera mechanism sounded far too loud. Pumpkin though had the earflaps of his hat pulled down. He also seemed too preoccupied with the factory to pay much attention to the van.

They admitted it was a stroke of luck they had parked just where Pumpkin started to misbehave. He took a great interest in a building just inside the perimeter wall, he kept fiddling with something in his coat pocket using his torch and he stopped to make notes under the street lamp. Yuri and Valery recorded it all.

The whole incident was over quickly. All the time and effort had been worth it for those few brief minutes. Yuri felt elated and relieved; at last they had some definite evidence of Pumpkin's illegal activities. They had enough to bring him in for a chat, once the films were developed. He'd deny it all of course, such devious people always did. But their pictures would do the talking.

Pumpkin completed his circuit of the factory without further incident. He headed back towards the centre of town and picked up a taxi. Meat-Hook covered him all the way to the hotel. Once there they held a quick debrief over warming glasses of tea. Valery went to fix their train reservations, leaving the others to sort the equipment. After almost an hour he returned, waving the tickets in jubilation.

"Tonight's train is packed," he said. "It took the old stationmaster a while to understand who I was and what I needed. I even had to threaten him a little. Don't like doing that too often, but on this occasion his cooperation was essential. It was vital to get what we wanted and we did." He sat down, laying out the tickets on the small table. He drew the others round him.

"You'll be pleased to know we've all got berths in 'soft'. No slumming it down in 'hard class' for us. But we're a bit scattered. Yuri you're in with me, Sergei you're at the end of the carriage with someone who's getting on in Archangelsk."

Immediately Yuri pitied this unfortunate. It would be better to travel in a cattle truck than be billeted overnight with Sergei.

Valery looked more serious. "Tania," he said, "it was so very difficult to get you on the train. But you must thank me sometime for this favour. I worked really hard to arrange it. I've managed to get you a berth in with Pumpkin."

Everyone smiled, Tania included.

"I shall look forward to that," she said, giving them one of those looks which make men buckle at the knees.

"But won't Pumpkin recognise you?" Yuri said with alarm. "You've been pretty close to him a couple of times just recently." Tania picked up her bag and extracted a slim diary. She turned the pages carefully.

"Every day I record what I wear and how I look. If I'm close to a target at any particular time, I go into extra detail. For instance, Yuri, can you remember exactly what I looked like when we tracked Pumpkin down Zubovskaya on foot and in the tram? You know, the time I went into that church after him and you... you got yourself locked in with that metal basher? Well, can you?"

Yuri blushed to the amusement of the others. Oh yes, he could recall that day all right, and all the others when he had felt and tasted the sweetness of Tania. It was a mixture of excitement and guilt, pleasure and embarrassment. And how did she always look whatever she was wearing? Totally and utterly stunning.

"Not in any precise detail I can't, I'm afraid," Yuri said frowning.

Tania flicked over another page. "The closest I got to Pumpkin for the greatest length of time was in the Hotel Leskov foyer on 19th December when he met the German Gooseberry. Then I had my full make-up on, I wore a green dress, brown boots and a fawn beret. This evening I shall appear as a different person." She snapped her diary shut and returned it to her bag.

"We'll need to be at the station in good time," Valery said. "Two people are going to be bumped as we have taken

297

their berths. Tania it's very important you get into your compartment before Pumpkin. Sergei, you make sure you delay Pumpkin on the platform." Sergei gave a chuckle.

"Pumpkin's not going to like this," Yuri said. "He'll expect to have the compartment to himself. I've never known him share, not once in the whole six months he's been here."

"Then we'll just have to make him comfortable, won't we?" Tania said.

Peter Standridge packed his small suitcase carefully. He paid equal attention to his briefcase, wrapping the Geiger counter in a soiled shirt. He extracted the pages he had used from his soluble notepad and placed them in his wallet. The rest of the notepad together with the torch and pencil were tucked into the inner pocket of the briefcase. Satisfied, he went downstairs for a light supper before settling his bill.

The taxi dropped him off at the station. It was 9.30pm according to the station clock, a full half hour before the Moscow train was due. He made his way into the crowded waiting room to escape the cold, braving the aroma of stale bodies and strong tobacco. Round the cramped room passengers sat patiently in their heavy coats and hats watching each other with expressionless faces. A couple of old women shuffled along a side-bench to make a space for him. A rough voiced attendant sold tea and pastries from a counter. She also presided over a glass fronted chiller with its flickering neon light and grey chicken legs on display. A pair of drunks opposite shared a bottle. A nearby seat supported tight wrapped figures curled in sleep.

There was a rush towards the door as an announcement ruptured the air. It seemed too soon, but Peter gathered his bags and went out onto the platform. The crowd were hurrying towards a waiting train. No it wasn't his, too early, too few carriages. He decided to stay out in the cold.

The local train departed and silence returned. Behind him the diffused lights of the town arced into the night sky. Across the tracks the black outline of a deep forest fringed the station. Further down the line trucks were marshalled to the occasional hoot of an engine. The red and green lights of the signals patterned the darkness. The platform slowly filled with people.

The beam of the locomotive grew brighter as the Moscow train approached. Peter checked the carriage numbers whilst the train drew in, hoping his was somewhere near. They seemed unusually jumbled as if the shunter had played a game and shuffled them around. The train shook to a halt. To his surprise, he found himself opposite an end door to his carriage. He made for the steps.

Peter felt a tug on his arm. An older man, an unlit cigarette dangling from his mouth, was gripping the sleeve of his coat. He tried to shrug him off but he held on more firmly. Passengers around them cursed and barged.

The man said something unintelligible in Russian. Peter looked at him blankly. The man laughed, repeated "*Speechki, speechki?*" and pointed to his cigarette.

"*Nyet,*" Peter answered, irritated at being delayed for the sake of a match. The man released him. Peter made his way to the carriage door but found he was now at the back of the queue. There was a mêlée in front of him as passengers clambered up the steps, heaving their cases and bundles ahead of them.

Eventually it was his turn to climb aboard. The carriage attendant checked his ticket and pointed down the corridor. He passed several before finding his compartment. He slid the door open. A woman was seated on one of the bunks.

Peter was at a loss what to do. He continued into the compartment, putting his bags in the rack. He checked his reservation. As it had been altered, there was extra writing and official stamps all over the ticket. It was impossible to decipher. With the change of train, perhaps a mistake had been made. He should have the whole compartment. He had paid handsomely for it after all.

The woman was watching people in the corridor. Peter cleared his throat and out of politeness said good evening in his tolerable Russian. She smiled at him, a rather lovely smile he had to admit, and replied pleasantly. Peter showed her his ticket; she shrugged and smiled again.

Peter went to find the carriage attendant. She seemed equally unconcerned, but went from compartment to compartment in search of assistance. She returned with a short, bespectacled man, who bore a remarkable resemblance to a toad.

"Sir, my name Zhabin, Engineer Zhabin. I speak English little," he said. "What is matter? You problem? I help very much."

"My reservation is for this compartment," Peter said slowly, showing him the ticket. "When I get on the train, I find this woman is also in my compartment."

Zhabin looked puzzled. He studied Peter's ticket for a while, before having a loud discussion with the attendant. The woman in the compartment sat demurely reading a newspaper.

"I not understand problem," Zhabin said at last. "Two beds, two persons. One bed, gentleman. One bed, lady. One bed, English. One bed, Russian," he said pointing back and forth from one to the other. Hearing the raised voices, other passengers now crowded round in the corridor to see what the argument was about. The attendant briefed them with the aid of sweeping gestures.

Peter also used his arms to describe a wide circle encompassing the whole space in front of him. "But I have paid for all the compartment," he said in desperation. The other passengers now joined in, arguing and disputing the case amongst themselves.

Zhabin continued to look bemused. "Russian people have one bed only," he said. "Why Englishman wish two beds?" He looked hard at Peter. "You not fat man. You sleep one bed with... with comfortableness."

Peter realized he was getting nowhere. The woman had her reservation, she was not going to move. Judging from the number of passengers who had got on at the station, there would not be anywhere for her to move to. He felt the crowd outside his compartment was against him too. He had no alternative but to reluctantly accept the awkward situation.

"All right. No problem," he said.

Zhabin looked relieved, smiling for the first time. He bowed briefly, muttered a goodbye and departed. The attendant shooed the other passengers away, although one or two crept back to have a second look at the extraordinary foreigner.

Peter felt hot after the incident and removed his jacket. The woman was impassive and continued to read her newspaper. The train lurched forward, leaving the station lights of Pavlozavodsk behind.

A relative calm returned to the carriage. The attendant brought refreshments and had what sounded like consoling words for the woman. She seemed unconcerned but the attendant frowned at Peter, took the money for his tea and bustled on to the next compartment.

Once they had finished their glasses of tea, the woman tapped Peter on the knee. She mimed rather beautifully that she wanted to get ready for bed. She pointed at him and then at the door. Peter got up and went to stand in the corridor, finding himself in the company of several other men similarly banished. He heard the lock turn in the compartment door behind him.

After about ten minutes the woman opened the door, indicating to Peter he could come in. She had put her coat on over her nightdress and wore her boots. She sauntered down to join the queue at the end of the corridor. Peter, alone in the compartment, pulled the door across. He liked the fragrance the woman had left behind.

Peter saw his jacket hanging on the hook by the door. He felt a flush of panic. How could he have been so rash as to leave it in the compartment? He went straight for the inside pocket. His wallet was still there. He checked his money, his cards, he unzipped the inner section, removing his precious notes. They were all in the right order, seemingly untouched. Even the paper clip holding them together was exactly where he placed it.

He pulled his briefcase down from the stringed rack above his bunk. The integral lock was still securely fastened. He found his small key and undid it. Everything inside was as he had packed it. He confirmed the torch, pencil and notepad were there, he unfolded the shirt to check the Geiger counter. Nothing had been disturbed.

In his relief, he felt a slither of guilt for suspecting this charming woman of going through his things.

The other members of the Meat-Hook team had settled in quickly. Whilst Tania would naturally be doing the night shift, Valery and Sergei were the first on duty in the corridor, keeping watch in case Pumpkin had a contact to meet. Yuri sat in his compartment guarding the equipment and waiting.

It was not long before he heard the distinctive double tap. He let Tania in, locking the door behind her. She sat down on the couchette opposite him.

"How did it go?" he asked.

Tania did not answer immediately, but produced a miniature camera from her wash bag. "This one's got the photos of his notes. We were lucky to get them, but Pumpkin left his jacket in the compartment with the naughty literature tucked in his wallet. I had to be very careful not to leave any trace on the paper." She laid the little camera on the bunk beside her. She delved into the bag again and drew out a second camera. "And this one's got the rest of his kit. It was all hidden away in his briefcase."

"Wasn't it locked?"

"Of course, my little one, but it only had one of those clip locks which come with the bags. I've been opening those since nursery school."

Yuri stared at Tania in total admiration. Dressed bizarrely as she was, with her hair hanging limp and her face devoid of make-up, she was still a most ravishing woman. His admiration was veering close to adoration.

"One item hidden in the briefcase which I couldn't identify was a small box with dials," Tania continued. "It was concealed in one of his smelly old shirts. It wasn't the greatest fun undoing and doing that up again. Anyhow I've got the pictures, and the technos back at base will tell us what it's all about. My guess is that it's probably a recorder or sensor of some kind." Tania handed the two cameras over to Yuri. "You take great care of these," she said, zipping up her wash bag. "I should be getting back or Pumpkin might be wondering where I've gone. It's going to be frustrating lying in bed close to a gorgeous foreigner and not being able to touch him. Maybe he'll dream of home, do a little sleep walk and cuddle in with me. We live in hope, don't we, Poliakov?"

Yuri looked at Tania wistfully. "I think it's as well you and I are not sharing a compartment tonight. I might be tempted to do something I would regret. I know in a different life I wouldn't want to resist you."

Tania shook her head and laughed. "And you're a very, very sweet boy. I never do serious stuff when I'm on duty, but at playtime, I'm always ready for a game or two. Although not with you, my pretty Yuri, you've got your wife to love and cherish. I'm not coming in there to mess around."

They both stood up, finding themselves pressed close

together by the confines of the compartment. Yuri looked at Tania. She took his face in her hands.

"For the next ten seconds I'm off duty," she whispered and kissed him softly on the lips. "Good night, little bear cub. Sleep well." She stepped out into the corridor.

Peter heard the woman return to their compartment. He lay in his couchette, pretending to be asleep. He had turned the main lights out, leaving only the small reading lamp above her bunk for illumination. She hummed a soft Russian lullaby as she got into bed. She extinguished the light.

It was a strange experience. She was an attractive woman and he felt an adolescent thrill lying but a few feet from such a stranger. Perhaps there were unwritten rules about this situation, secret Russian protocols on how to conduct oneself in a compartment occupied by a member of the opposite sex. If there were, he did not know about them.

Peter drifted off to sleep as the carriage rocked from side to side like a baby's cradle. He dreamed lovingly of Anna, but her features slowly changed to those of Lydia. She appeared half woman, half ravenous beast, loving him, yet tearing him apart. He thrashed from side to side in his nightmare, waking with a cry. He lay disorientated in an uncharted hinterland of fantasy. A hand touched his forehead, a soft, cool woman's hand. A cautionary *shsh* was uttered.

"*Shsh, shsh,*" she repeated, "*shsh, speetye, speetye spokoyno.*"

Peter only half understood, but felt soothed by the sibilance of her voice. In the darkness he savoured her closeness, letting her hand caress his face. She bent forward, placing a kiss on his lips with the gentleness of an angel.

Drowsily he sensed her ghostly outline move back to her couchette. There was a rustling of sheets, the turning of a body seeking comfort. He thought he heard a sigh, the sound of quiet weeping. His dream had the redolence of a Russian fairy tale, of a maiden vainly seeking her lover in the whiteness of the snow.

The locomotive wailed, the carriage jolted, the train rattled on to Moscow through the clear, piercing night.

CHAPTER 20

The taxi from the station charged through the middle of Moscow passing close to Hotel Leskov. Tempted as he was to drop in, bath and change, Peter stuck to his procedure of going direct to Commercial Section. He did not need to be reminded how important it was to deposit his notes and equipment in Chris Burroughs' office before he did anything else. It would be particularly foolhardy to be compromised at the eleventh hour after all he had achieved in Pavlozavodsk.

The report on his unofficial duties in that cold northern town took longer to write than Peter anticipated. He went into some detail about the *Tekhnika* installation, even producing a sketch of the faceless building which excited the Geiger counter. He drew a diagram to show precisely where he took the radiation readings, putting the data in a separate key. He also included other information about the town collected during his stay. The report ran to three pages, the longest and most detailed he had submitted to date.

Chris Burroughs seemed impressed. He spent some time reading it through, nodding to himself at intervals. Once he had finished he scribbled, *Excellent, well done, London will be pleased*, on his eraser board, holding it up for Peter to see.

"Your return a day early is a surprise though," Chris said. "Were there some particular problems or did the locals just get fed up with you and your good advice?"

Peter laughed. "No problems on my side, but I can't speak for my hosts. It was certainly unusual to finish after just a day and a half. Perhaps as you suggest, they'd heard enough and couldn't take any more. It'll be an almighty task sorting that town out, whoever takes it on."

"In my experience they'll do whatever they want to do in their own time. There's never any merit in trying to push things in the provinces. They just dig their heels in. Anyhow, I'm delighted you're back in one piece." Chris stood up to put the report in his safe. "You know, one bonus of returning today is that you can join in our farewell party for Julie. She's done a lot of typing for you over the last six months, not that you'd be aware of it. Now's your chance to thank her. We're getting together at five in the conference room."

Peter returned to Hotel Leskov and relaxed in the familiar surroundings of his room. He told himself the trip he had worried about for so long was now over, the incriminating evidence securely locked away. A reward for a job well done might even be in order. He treated himself to a comforting bath, the warm water drawing the remaining tension from his body.

It had indeed been an unusual visit. He still could not understand why the local officials were so indifferent to his proposals. Perhaps they simply did not care to have the shortcomings of their town pointed out by a foreigner. They probably knew them well enough themselves and considered them insurmountable. If that were the case, no wonder they could not wait to send him on his way.

The bigger challenge was the business with the Geiger counter. It had gone so much better than he expected, despite the difficulty in finding the installation in the first place. But he had managed it and without attracting undue attention. Perhaps he would do something similar again if he were asked.

The nonsense over the train reservation was annoying. In the end it did not turn out too badly, but he was still confused about what happened in the night. He remembered having a bad dream, but did that attractive woman really speak to him, touch his forehead and kiss him fleetingly? Was his mind playing games, mingling wishful thinking with reality? Surely he must have imagined it all. What he did know for certain was that she was as pleasant and courteous in the morning as she had been the evening before. It would remain one of those delightful mysteries so beloved of the Russians.

Most of the members of Commercial Section were there for Julie's party, as well as a couple of business people like himself. Curiously Peter noticed Jocelyn Misterton was also present. He wondered what connection the urbane Cultural Attaché had with a secretary in Commercial Section.

After drinks, a couple of speeches and the presentation of a small gift, the party began to break up. Peter was now keen to get back to the hotel to see if Anna was around. He was about to leave when Jocelyn came over to him.

"Lydia Kuznetsova's in town," he said with a smile.

"Is she really?"

"Thought you'd be interested."

"But her big concert's not till March."

"Seems her performance at the last one went down particularly well. Standing in at short notice did her reputation no harm at all. Just the reverse in fact. She's playing tonight. It's a sell-out, I'm afraid."

"That's a shame."

"All's not lost. She's going to give a little performance in the Embassy tomorrow evening. Just invited guests. Knowing how much you admire her, you'll be one of the select few of course."

"Thank you, I'm honoured. I'm sure I'll be able to make it," Peter said, not wishing to be discourteous.

"She's agreed to do this since I've arranged for her to come over to England to give a couple of performances. She's generating quite a bit of excitement, as you can well appreciate from your favoured position."

Peter had no wish to discuss Lydia Kuznetsova, nor his relationship with her, especially with Jocelyn. "How come you're here for Julie's farewell?" he asked by way of a riposte.

"She paints, quite well in fact. Such things are of interest to Cultural Attachés. By the way, we're starting at seven tomorrow. See you there." Jocelyn moved away to say goodbye to Julie, who by now was a little tearful. They embraced with surprising tenderness.

As Peter had no means of contacting Anna, he spent much of the evening hanging around the hotel bar with one eye on the foyer. Since she had been so good at surprising him, he wanted to catch her unawares for a change. It was his chance to turn the tables, to see how she reacted when he appeared out of the blue.

By midnight, though, he had drawn a blank. He was a little tipsy after ordering a series of beers without counting. His black mood was not lifted by the receptionist handing him a note from Anna with his key. How had she slipped through unseen? He had wasted the whole evening. Even the note itself was brief. She would meet him in the foyer on Saturday at 11am. He must not be late. She had signed it simply, *Anna*.

Peter returned to his room. Even in his inebriated state he remembered he should bar the door while Lydia was in town. She knew where he was now and might try to pay him another late night visit. This time it would not be for love, if Herr Metzinger were to be believed. Peter felt his interest in her fading. But suppose it were Anna? Well, too bad. If she wanted to sneak around delivering notes and avoiding him, she did not deserve to come in either. He jammed a chair under the door handle and went miserably to bed.

With his muzzy head and grumpy mood, Friday was a difficult day. He spent much of it in Commercial Section writing up his official report on the visit to Pavlozavodsk.

He was as diplomatic as he could be, knowing that the Ministry officials could take it out on the Pavlozavodsk Council if he were too critical. Under normal circumstances, it would not be an easy report to write. In his present frame of mind, it became something of a chore.

But as he worked, Peter was tormented by irrational doubts about Anna. He was ashamed of his obsessive behaviour. Although desperately needing to see her, he dreaded the prospect of disappointment. He knew he should get a grip on himself, but could not find the necessary resolve. Partly out of pique, he decided he would go to the Embassy to hear Lydia play. He had intended to send an apology, conscious of Herr Metzinger's warning. But now he changed his mind, perhaps to be perverse, perhaps to pay Anna back for not being around when he wanted.

Peter arrived shortly before the little concert was due to begin. They had squeezed sixty or more chairs into one of the Embassy reception rooms, reserving a small playing area at one end. There were going to be three relatively short pieces, one requiring a piano accompanist. Jocelyn was waiting and waved him to the front where there was a spare seat. Peter suspected he had reserved it especially for him.

"This close enough for you?" Jocelyn murmured. "I know you'd rather be bouncing around on her bosoms, but that's not on the programme. Enjoy the music all the same."

Jocelyn made a pretty speech about Lydia before she swept in to polite clapping. She was as Peter remembered her in Stambov and at the Moscow Conservatoire. She looked immaculate, not a hair out of place. How different she had appeared lying beside him in his bed, smudged and unadorned. Was she really the monster Metzinger made her out to be? She smiled at the audience in appreciation, her eyes flickering on Peter for a second.

Her playing was as fine as ever. Sitting but a few feet from her, Peter felt her passion, her energy, her sensitivity. She was a magnificent creature producing magnificent sounds, her body and mind bound together in exquisite effort. The audience was transfixed, Peter cruelly tortured.

At the end of the concert after prolonged applause, the chairs were removed and drinks brought in. Lydia returned to be congratulated. Peter knew he should leave to avoid the complication of meeting her again. He was less bothered by what Metzinger had said about her than he was about his own feelings. As she stood glowing from her exertions and the praise, no man in the room would wish to deny her. Peter sensed his helplessness, his weakness in the face of her. Yes he should go, indeed he must go.

Jocelyn Misterton, though, had different plans. "Peter, the Head of Chancery has asked you to join us for supper with Lydia Kuznetsova," he said loudly.

Peter received looks of disapproval from the more senior figures in the room, especially from their wives.

"I really ought to be going, you know," Peter said as quietly as he could.

"Nonsense. You can't turn down an opportunity like this. Next door in ten minutes, alright?"

The audience began to thin. Peter stood to one side, partially obscured by others. Lydia spotted him.

"Good evening," she said, clasping his shoulders and appraising him with satisfaction. Drawing him to her, she laid kisses on each of his cheeks. "Good see lovely boy again," she murmured. Jocelyn interrupted to escort her into supper before Peter could reply.

There were a dozen guests round the table. The seating plan put Peter opposite Lydia and beside Candida Misterton. Using his fluent Russian, the Head of Chancery engaged Lydia in conversation as the supper was served.

Candida turned to Peter in her superior Kensington way. "The road to Stambov is now open," she said, skilfully forking a portion of chicken fricasse towards her mouth. "There are no obstacles barring your path."

"I'm not with you," Peter said, curious to know what she meant.

"The husband's in jail," she said none too discreetly. "Guilty of extortion. Your lady friend is dumping him. She's about to be a free woman, not that it'll make much difference as far as her dalliances are concerned."

Peter was astonished to hear Candida speak in such terms. He didn't know her well, but she'd always seemed so very proper. He accepted he had embarrassed her, offended her even, at the Embassy reception two months earlier, but it seemed insufficient justification for such gratuitous remarks.

"I'm not sure I shall be continuing my acquaintance with her," Peter said manfully.

Lydia looked across, her questioning eyes fixed on them both.

"Oh, but you should, you know. Now that Jocelyn has done all this hard work to get her to the UK for some concerts, she's become quite fond of the English. Surely you're not going to inhibit her performance by holding back now?" Candida dealt with the last piece of salad on her plate and took an unseemly quaff of wine.

Peter suspected Candida was taunting him. What was in it for whom if he rolled into bed with Lydia again? Jocelyn of course, who else. Peter disliked the way he was being manipulated. "I don't know why you're talking like this. I've no wish to continue discussing her in these terms."

Candida's cheeks reddened. Her normally placid eyes flashed like diamonds as she put her face closer to Peter's. "Don't think your high jinks with her have gone unreported. It's vital we keep her on board. She mustn't waver and let the Germans get to her. The men in homburgs and dark coats may come round to collect any time now. Her international career must be launched in England." She

312

sat up straight and smiled. "So you see, you've got to keep your end up and support the cause. Cooperation is the order of the day."

Peter was still stunned by Candida's outburst as the supper table was cleared and they stood with coffees. The representative from the Ministry of Culture, Mr Bozlov, seemed anxious to leave, but could not do so without Lydia. She brought him over to meet Peter and help with interpreting.

"I hope you come to my town again," she said, using Bozlov as a mouthpiece. "There's much to enjoy there."

"Perhaps in the Spring I shall have some more work in Stambov."

"But do not come for work. You come and see me. I will play for you, for you alone."

Peter was embarrassed. As Lydia did her usual enticing tricks with her eyes and lips, he saw Candida watching him over her coffee cup.

"I'm very flattered, but my diary is exceptionally full. Also I may have to go back to England again soon. It's difficult to make any firm arrangements."

Lydia nodded as if acknowledging Peter's evasions. She nudged Bozlov, who produced a plastic wallet from his jacket pocket.

"This my card. Any time you wish to make meeting with Kuznetsova, you must ring number here," Bozlov said, jabbing his finger at the card. "She also very busy and playing around a lot."

"Of course I will," Peter said relieved.

"And when I come to England," Lydia said, "I shall look and find you there." She stepped forward and kissed Peter fully on the mouth. "I go now. Goodbye until next I see you."

Peter mumbled good night. Out of the corner of his eye, he saw Candida smile approvingly.

Peter had been so wound up in his thoughts the whole

day he had hardly noticed the heavy snowfall. For him, snow had become such a part of the Moscow scene, it seemed unremarkable. It was like a permanent embellishment to the city's architecture, sometimes new, crisp and virgin, other times old, churned and discoloured. In whatever form, it was always there. Only now as he left the Embassy after the concert did he take an interest in the swirling snowflakes from his taxi window. If the storm continued, he worried tomorrow's planned barbecue and skiing would be cancelled. That would be a major disappointment.

Peter woke to find orange sunlight penetrating his curtains. He lingered in bed for a while, his mind full of doubt and nervous anticipation. He was looking forward to the day, but what if things went wrong? He chided himself for his pessimism.

Aware of his need to be prompt, he went down to the foyer in good time. The members of the German tourist group gathered, suitably dressed for winter sports. They joked together, the good weather raising their spirits. The coach drew up at the entrance and Anna came into the foyer. She wore a fashionable ski suit, highlighting the contours of her body.

"Good morning Peter. Are you ready for this?" she asked laughing.

"Yes, except I've no kit. I feel like an idiot standing here in my coat."

"Don't be stupid. I said I'd bring the things for you and I have. Just get on the bus and I'll sort you out when we get there."

Peter sat by himself near the back. Anna spent some time checking the Germans had everything they needed, before briefing them at length over the intercom. Peter did not understand a word. As Anna was so indifferent to his presence, he turned his thoughts defensively to Lydia.

314

He was a fool to go to the concert. Seeing her again had only tangled his emotions. What was it about her? Perhaps it was her music which, siren-like, bound him to her, or perhaps the sensuality she displayed as she produced those sublime, seductive sounds. He wanted to break free from her spell, but lacked the power to do so. Only Anna, if she cared, possessed the magic to release him.

They travelled some distance round the Moscow ring road before turning onto a minor road. A snowplough had preceded them, piling the snow into high banks on either side. They passed through groups of huddled houses, the wood smoke from their stoves climbing high into the frosty air. After several miles, the coach drew up on a cleared space close to woods and open fields.

The advance party had already pitched tents, laid out snow shoes, skis and sticks and lit two large barbecues. A brilliant red cloth covered a long table set with bottles and glasses. Peter recognised Vladimir, who was exercising with gusto in full view of the tourist coach.

Anna busied herself with the tour group, organising, joking and cajoling. Vladimir kitted out those who wanted to cross-country ski. Other helpers were fussing around, steering the least athletic towards the makeshift bar. Peter felt he had been assigned a low priority.

"Come on old misery," Anna chided him, thrusting a ski suit into his arms. "Go and change in the tent on the right, it's got a parrafin heater. Then see the handsome Vlad for your equipment."

Vladimir had been tipped off, greeting Peter like an old friend. He did a professional job on him too, ensuring his shoes and skis fitted well and patiently demonstrating the art of *langlauf*. Peter grudgingly warmed to him.

The skiing was more fun than he expected. He was pleased by how easily he got into his stride and, once he mastered the rhythm, he sailed along. The route was flat, the snow perfect, the cold air exhilarating. He felt an inner glow as they snaked through the woods and across the fields.

Vladimir as the leader moved up and down the column, assisting and encouraging. Soon the stragglers fell behind, left in the charge of another instructor. The remainder panted behind the intrepid Vlad as he forged tracks through the virgin snow for them to follow. Anna glided alongside him well ahead of Peter, her skiing a smooth, effortless ballet.

They could smell the roasting meat some distance away. It had never tasted so good, nor had the beer and vodka. They stood around, their faces glowing from exercise and cold, now flushed with drink and food. Anna moved from group to group, ensuring all was well.

They returned to the coach, fatigued by the fresh air, lunch and skiing. Most of the Germans dozed. Anna and her colleagues held what seemed like a debriefing at the front, with the driver joining in. There was some seriousness, but much laughter. They were right to be pleased: it had been an excellent day.

As they slowed for the central Moscow traffic, Anna came and sat down beside Peter.

"Good time, was it?" she asked.

"Well, I feel exhausted, if that's anything to go by," he said huffily, refusing to look at her.

"Come along now, my little boy. You're all grumpy because I didn't pay you much attention. I have my duty to do, you know. I can't just abandon my tourists, drop everything for you."

"I realize that. I suppose I was being too optimistic, that's all."

Anna was silent as Peter's emotions waged a war of attrition inside his head. Was his desire to smile and enfold her going to lose out to sullen obduracy?

As usual it was Anna who chipped the ice away. "I could make you supper this evening, if you'd care to look at me," she said.

Peter could restrain himself no longer. He turned, wrapping her in his arms. "There is nothing in the whole of Russia I would love more," he whispered.

At the moment of waking he wasn't sure where he was. A thin light came through the window, but somehow the window was no longer where it should be. He heard unfamiliar sounds, the bark of a dog, the cry of a child, the creak of floorboards. He moved his head and saw the sleeping face of Anna. She would be naked under the blankets, just as he was. He remembered now.

Peter smiled at his good fortune, yet his stupidity astounded him. He had come so close to throwing everything away, to losing what he wanted most. Where was the justification for acting the way he did, for laying bare his immaturity? He cringed at the very thought of it.

Anna, though, had appeared so understanding, so forgiving. She seemed able to read him like a book, knowing when and how to tease and when to stop, keeping him on his mettle lest he think her too easy, and when he had that hang dog look, raising him up to feel like a god. And most important of all, she seemed to enjoy him as much as he had her.

They made Sunday a lazy day. Her bed detained them till late morning, when the sun enticed them out to a café for tea and pastries. They took a bus out to the west of the city. They admired the stoic fishermen squatting over holes cut in the river's ice. They dodged falling icicles, kicked the snow, kissed the cold from their faces. They walked, laughed, talked, each seeking more about the other. There seemed a wide space before them, an unlimited steppe of future pleasure.

As the sun set and the cold closed in, they returned to the city. Anna had a late flight to meet and needed to leave at nine. They had an early restaurant supper.

"I know you want to come up, but you'll only make me

late," she said as they stood at the entrance to her apartment block. "And if you make me late, I'll lose my job and I'll not love you."

"I'm prepared to run that risk," Peter said.

"Well, I'm not. I want to love you, not be cross with you, so just do as you're told." She kissed him lightly. "Come round on Tuesday about six. I'm going to be busy until then."

Anna's apartment was quite central and, although it was now dark and very cold, Peter decided to walk back to his hotel. He set off with the lightest heart he'd had in years. All the worries and fears of the last few weeks were unimportant and readily banished from his mind.

Peter took Bolshaya Dimitrovka, which ran parallel to Tverskaya as far as Red Square. He walked quickly to stay warm, almost failing to see the beggar who hobbled into his path. He managed to avoid a collision and sought to side step the nuisance, but the old man was quick to waggle a tin mug in his face. Peter found some coins in his coat pocket, jingling them into the mug. He didn't see the men nor hear the car.

They were well practised and very thorough. His arms were seized, his body turned towards the open door. They forced him down, pulled his scarf over his mouth and propelled him horizontally onto the back seat. They piled in either side of him. He was the thin meat of a burger pressed between two slabs of dough.

The car took off at a ferocious speed. They removed the scarf, but clipped handcuffs on his wrists. With human shock absorbers either side, Peter rode out the tight corners. He sat bemused, unable to grasp what had happened, what was going on. But as his mind slowly caught up, his body began to tremble.

The guards at the entrance to the building paid little attention as he was escorted firmly through the doors. He was taken down a corridor and into a small room with a large desk. The men in heavy coats handed him over to the men in uniform. They searched him, removing his wallet, his watch, his pen and a handful of loose change. They wrote out a list of his possessions, undid his handcuffs and pointed at the place where he should sign.

"British Consul. I want to see the British Consul," Peter said, embarrassed by the tremor in his voice. They took no notice, merely shrugging at his outburst.

Two of them took him down a flight of steps. They walked along a passageway, unlocking and relocking a series of metal grilles. They came to a door, opened it and pushed him in. He heard the lock turn and the footsteps recede.

The cell was almost bare. A stained metal bucket stood prominently on the floor. Along one side lay a wooden bunk with two grey blankets at its foot. In the high ceiling, a light bulb buzzed out of reach. With no window, the stale smell of fear lingered in the walls. There was a creeping silence.

Peter paced the length and breadth of the tiny space, shivering more from terror than the cold. Pulling his coat tighter, he squatted on the side of the bunk. He stared at the door, wondering what lay beyond. He felt tears of desperation in his eyes.

He sniffed his clothes, his skin, seeking out the scent of Anna. He persevered, fighting through the foul smells of the dark coated men and the rankness of the cell. At last he found the comfort of her. He breathed the faint allure of her body.

A guard opened the door. Like a reluctant waiter, he thrust a tray at Peter. A tin mug, similar to the beggar's, steamed with tea, a slice of thick rye bread lay on a metal plate. The guard grunted in Russian and left. Peter clasped the mug, anxious to taste its warmth before it cooled.

Without his watch, he had lost all sense of time. He felt both weary and awake. He remembered he left Anna about eight and walked for a good ten minutes before they grabbed him. The car journey was fifteen or twenty minutes and he had been in this place for at least an hour. That made it only nine-thirty, but it felt like three in the morning.

He got to his feet again, walked over and booted the bucket hard. It clanged into the stone wall and fell on its side, rocking backwards and forwards. What was this place and why was he here? He hadn't broken any rules, he hadn't done anything illegal, well nothing beyond his harmless unofficial duties. Hell, they couldn't take exception to those.

But in the back of his mind was an unworthy, dispiriting thought. Had Anna done this to him, had she befriended him, slept with him, all out of duty to the State? And had she taken over from Lydia, so the men in those long, dark coats could track him all the way? He shook his head in anguish at the baseness of his thoughts.

Peter moved back to the bunk, lying down on the wooden slats. He kicked the soiled blankets to the floor, too squeamish to pull them over him. Later perhaps he would need them, but for now he would do without. He made a makeshift pillow out of his scarf and pulled the earflaps of his hat round his face, fastening the cord beneath his chin. The single light bulb in the ceiling seemed trained directly on his eyes.

He had no idea if he slept at all and doubted he had. He was certainly awake enough to hear the key turn in the door and the guards return. Thinking him asleep, one of the guards shook him roughly. He shouted something in Russian and pointed to the door. Peter got up and was escorted down the passage and up a different flight of stairs. He was pressed into a solitary chair in the middle of an airless room.

A lively looking man in a suit hurried in with a folder under one arm. He went to a desk facing Peter, pulling out an upright chair. He sat down and opened the folder.

"First you must confirm your identity," he said in almost flawless English. "You are Peter Arthur Standridge, are you not?"

"Yes, that is correct," Peter croaked.

"And you entered Russia on the 7th July 1992 and are resident in Hotel Leskov, Moscow?"

"That is also correct."

"You work for a British firm called Duggan Meade and you are in Russia under a British Government initiative called the Handsome Fund?"

Peter nodded.

The interrogator, as Peter came to regard him, closed the folder. He leaned back in his chair and stared at the ceiling. "Mr Standridge, I need you to help me. I cannot do everything by myself. I wish to have your assistance."

"And I wish to see the British Consul about this illegal detention."

"Ah, I see we have a lawyer in you, too." The interrogator paused. "And not just any lawyer, but one who knows all about the laws of Russia. Is that not clever of you, Mr Standridge, to know so much?"

"I have a right to see the Consul and, if necessary, to be legally represented."

"Have you really? Perhaps in Britain you have some of these rights, but not in Russia. Here things are different, as no doubt you know. You will of course meet with someone from your Embassy, but not yet, not until you have helped me."

Peter was torn between staying silent and responding. His main consideration was which course would get him out of the place quicker. He decided to see how the questioning went, taking care with the answers he gave.

"Now, Mr Standridge, we know you do much travelling around this country as part of your work. You always travel alone and you always ensure you have a compartment to yourself when you take the train. I am sure your work is of benefit to Russia. But on your journeys, do you also do some work for others?"

"I don't understand what you mean," Peter said nervously.

"You take a lot of notes, Mr Standridge. Not just at your destination, but also on your way to your destination. What are these notes, who are they for?"

"I don't take notes when I'm travelling to places. I don't know where you've got this from. And when I arrive, everything I do is related to my work."

The interrogator shook his head. "You make me sad, Mr Standridge. I ask for your cooperation, but I see you don't want to give it to me. But there is still time. Would you like some tea?"

Peter nodded automatically. One of the guards was sent out, returning with two lukewarm mugs. Peter took hurried sips from his.

"These notes you make on your journeys," the interrogator continued, "do they also contain information about the Russian people you meet?"

"As part of my job, of course I include some details of my discussions with officials in my reports. That is perfectly normal."

"Yes, yes, I understand that you do this. But what about the other Russians you meet, like Professor Krotkin and Mrs Kuznetsova? Do you make secret notes about them?"

Peter could not hide his surprise, aware the interrogator was looking at him and waiting for an answer.

"They were just people I met on my travels. They were kind and hospitable. I had no need to make secret notes about them." Peter immediately realized the trap he had fallen into.

"So you do admit to making secret notes, not about these two people perhaps, but about other people, other things. That is most helpful and obliging of you, Mr

Standridge. Thank you."

Peter's mouth opened and closed like a fish. He tried to say something but no sound emerged.

The interrogator smiled at Peter's discomfort. "And this Mrs Kuznetsova, who you say was very hospitable. In what way would you describe her hospitality?"

Peter shook his head, keeping his eyes fixed on the floor. "She plays the violin very well," he said.

"I think she has also played you very well. Has she not entertained you to your satisfaction? What secrets has she given you to send to London? And when she goes soon to England herself to play her violin, you will meet her there and hear more secrets, am I not right?"

"No, it's all nonsense, she hasn't given me any secrets, none at all," Peter almost shouted in exasperation.

"No secrets? So what does she whisper in your ear when she lies naked in your bed? Not sweet nothings surely, Mr Standridge?" the interrogator said, raising his substantial eyebrows.

Peter lowered his head again. "She passed no secrets to me, ever."

"How interesting this is. She gives secrets to your friend from Germany, but not to you. That is not fair, is it Mr Standridge? Perhaps Herr Metzinger gives her money for her secrets and you do not. Or perhaps, he is just the better lover, older but better."

Peter made a move towards the interrogator, but got no further than the edge of his chair. The guard's hands were on him, pinning his arms painfully behind his back.

"Now, now Mr Standridge, we don't want any violence or someone could get very hurt. Your uncontrolled anger is merely more evidence of your guilt. I shall record it." The interrogator wrote briefly on the papers in front of him. Only when he had finished did he signal to the guard to release him. Once free, Peter rubbed his wrists to lessen the pain and regain some circulation.

"So we have established from your reaction that this Kuznetsova has passed to you many secrets," the interrogator said. "Now tell me about this Professor Krotkin, what things does he make you do for him? A parcel for special delivery to a friend in England, I understand? Tell me, Mr Standridge – what was in that parcel?"

"Look, it was only a painting. It was all legal. There was an export certificate."

"Nothing else, Mr Standridge, nothing else inside the parcel?"

Peter remembered the white envelope taped to the back of the icon. He'd assumed it was just a letter. And then there was the bulky envelope Dr Homilly had given to him for Krotkin. He had no idea what either contained. "Not that I'm aware of," he answered quietly.

"I find it strange that a man who spends so much time observing cannot see things in front of his nose. You look at a picture but you do not look behind the picture. You see the surface paint but you don't see the meaning. Meanings are often in envelopes, people seal words and deeds in envelopes." He leaned forward. "That's why I like them so much and give them so much attention."

The interrogator opened the folder again, turning a couple of pages. Peter finished his tea, the liquid soothing his arid throat.

"Do you like the movies, Mr Standridge?"

"I used to go to the cinema in England, but I haven't here."

"Then I shall show you a Russian film."

There was sudden activity as a screen was erected and a projector brought into the room. The lights were dimmed and the projector started to turn. A flickering black and white image appeared on the screen. The film seemed to have been shot in semi darkness, but a snow-filled street and high wall were clearly visible. A figure well wrapped against the cold was walking towards the camera. Peter knew it was him.

The film lasted a couple of minutes. It recorded in good detail everything he did along the back wall of the *Tekhnika* installation in Pavlozavodsk. How had they managed such a professional job? Of course the old van, that rotten old van. He had been caught red-handed. He felt sick at the thought of what might happen to him now. The projector whirred to a stop.

"Did you enjoy the film, Mr Standridge? It's good, very good, don't you think? I thought you were very well cast as the villain. An excellent performance, such a skill, just what the director wanted. But now, I must know how you do these things. In your pocket you had something we cannot see in the film. What was this something, a little special camera, perhaps?"

"No, no I didn't have a camera with me."

"Not a camera? So what was it then?" The interrogator took an envelope out of the folder. "Not a camera, not a camera," he repeated, "perhaps these will help you recognise what you had in your pocket that evening."

The interrogator stood up and walked over to Peter. He placed a hand on the back of his chair and gave him a set of photographs spread out like a fan. Peter felt forced to look at them. He was shocked by the detail they contained, guessing they too must have been taken from the van. But for all the good definition and focus, it was still impossible to see what he was fiddling with in his pocket.

"There's nothing of importance there," he said defiantly. "I can't remember what I was doing. Probably trying to undo my hip flask. It was very cold that evening."

"Hip flask? What is this hip flask?"

"You put whisky or vodka in it. You have a sip when you need it."

"I see, I see. And you needed such a sip, didn't you Mr Standridge, just to calm the nerves as you did your spying?"

"That's not true. I wasn't doing anything improper or illegal there."

"So you don't know what this sign says?" the interrogator asked, pointing at one of the photographs.

"No, my Russian isn't good enough. In any case it was dark. I couldn't really see it."

"Let me translate for you then. It says, *Restricted Area, Photography Forbidden*. And here you are in this picture walking down a prohibited road and taking illegal photographs."

"I wasn't taking photographs," Peter insisted.

"Well, you can again assist me, Mr Standridge. If you were not taking photographs, what were you doing half way out of the town that evening? Will you tell me your presence there was coincidence, that you had no interest in this place you walked all the way round?"

Peter had no idea how to respond and remained silent.

"If you cannot help me, let me help you," the interrogator said, going back to his chair. He rummaged in his folder, producing another envelope. He spilled a pile of photographs onto his desk and started to sort through them. After discarding many, he got to his feet again. He paced up and down, shuffling the photographs in his hands. Peter wondered what he had now to incriminate him.

"This is the best," the interrogator said, thrusting one of the photographs into Peter's hands. Although fearing what it might reveal, Peter glanced quickly at it. He was horrified to see a finely developed enlargement of his Geiger counter. How on earth had they managed to get a picture of that? He had been so careful to secure it the whole time in Pavlozavodsk and on the trains.

"So, Mr Standridge," the interrogator said, standing over him, "can you please tell me what is this device? You will know, because we found it in your bag wrapped in a shirt with your name on it."

Peter wriggled in his chair. "It's a Geiger counter, that's

all," he said.

"Thank you, Mr Standridge, thank you. Of course I knew what it was, but it's so nice to have confirmation from a professional." The interrogator seemed to have more of a spring in his step as he returned to his desk.

"Do you know, we are very close to ending our little meeting. I'm sure you're pleased to hear this. But there is one more thing, a small thing, but something for which I must have the answer." For the third time, he came over to Peter with fresh photographs. "These are puzzling to me and my colleagues. Can you help us with an explanation?"

Peter stared in amazement at the photos which one after another recorded his jottings from the soluble notepad. The pictures were razor sharp, his writing and codes clearly legible. That woman, that charming woman, who had laid a kiss on his lips that very night, had deceived him. She had exposed him without mercy.

"They're the readings from the Geiger counter and also other observations I made," Peter said, accepting he had little to lose, but hoping to gain some credit from his confession.

"Thank you, Mr Standridge. You have been so cooperative, we have finished early. Sometimes these friendly talks can go on for hours, even days. Your help has been so extraordinary, I shall make a note of it. The judge at your trial will take such matters into consideration when deciding the severity of your punishment."

Peter was returned to his cell by the guards. He sat down on the bunk close to tears. He felt wretched, unable to fully comprehend what had happened. There were times during the interrogation when he thought he would be able to explain away many of the accusations levelled against him. But the film and photographs completely dashed any hope of denying his unofficial duties. They had caught him with all the evidence they needed. He was left with no defence.

He picked up the blankets and lay down on the hard bunk, feeling utterly helpless. Terrifying thoughts of Siberian prison camps, of perpetual cold and deprivation haunted him. But even that seemed mild compared with the worst they could do. He imagined the firing squad lined up, ready to raise their rifles as the blindfold was tied over his eyes. And all the while Anna watched, as if standing in judgement over a traitor, a betrayer of her trust. Peter shivered uncontrollably. The tears he held back so bravely began to drain into the foul fustiness of the blankets.

The cell door opened. Two guards entered and heaved him to his feet. He was in a state of confusion as he was led upstairs, uncaring what they did with him. They went into the small room where he had been searched on his arrival. His possessions were returned.

A flustered John Metcalfe from the Embassy appeared. "My God, what have they been doing to you?" he asked, looking at Peter. He turned to the guard sergeant, speaking to him in rapid Russian. He signed the document they gave him.

"Come on," he said to Peter. "They've released you into my protection, but you're not to leave the country. Let's go before they change their minds."

It was dark and a light snow was falling. Despite a dull elation at his release, Peter felt exhausted. "What's the time?" he asked, forgetting he now had his watch.

"Five past five in the bloody morning. What on earth have you been up to?"

"It's a long story, I'll tell you later. But thanks for rescuing me. I thought that was the Consul's job."

"Just my luck to be duty officer. Normally they wait till the morning when someone from Consular Section's available, but for some reason they wanted you out of there, pronto."

They drove straight to Hotel Leskov. "You look as if

you could sleep for a week," John said, dropping Peter off at the entrance. "We will be making representations to the Russians first thing. We'll demand some explanations. Suggest you come over to the main Embassy, not Commercial, early afternoon."

Peter took the lift up to his room. Although dog-tired, he couldn't go to bed without a shower. Once dry, he collapsed into a deep sleep.

CHAPTER 21

It was almost 2.30pm when Peter arrived at the British Embassy. The security officer signed him in, requesting he wait whilst John Metcalfe was contacted. Although he had slept for a good six hours, Peter remained disorientated. He sat on a chair in reception, startled by every voice and sound.

"Feeling more human now are you?" John Metcalfe asked anxiously.

"Thank you, yes, a little."

"Well, if you'd like to follow me, I'll take you somewhere more secure for a chat." John set off down a corridor leading to the back of the building. They went up two flights of stairs and along a short passage before stopping in front of a half open door. John ushered Peter into a sealed, air-conditioned room. Standing beside a table in the centre was Derek Carbonnel.

"Derek?" Peter said in disbelief. "What on earth are you doing here?"

"I'll go into that in a moment, but it's good to see you." He shook Peter's hand and went across to the door. "Thank you, John. We should be through in about half an hour." John Metcalfe nodded and disappeared down the passage. Derek pushed an internal lever down to lock the door. They took their seats on opposite sides of the table.

"Peter, I've got a number of things I need to discuss with you. But first, and most important of all, are you alright after your ordeal last night?"

"No, not really. I did sleep once I got back to the hotel, but the whole thing was a bloody nightmare. I'm just mighty relieved I'm not still in that cell."

"Yes, I can imagine it must have been very frightening. John Metcalfe said you looked dreadful when he collected you early this morning." Derek shifted in his seat. He bent down, extracting a file from his briefcase with Peter's name printed on the cover.

"But before we get down to business, I must apologise for not letting you know I was coming over. I did try to contact you, but it seems you were out from Saturday morning until, well, early this morning. Nice weekend away, was it?"

Peter was astonished at Derek's insensitivity. Did he not understand how horrific his experience had been? Yet, here he was asking whether it was a nice weekend, as if his incarceration in that lock-up had not obliterated the memory of everything he had enjoyed beforehand.

"Derek, can't you see that my arrest last night is the only thing that's important right now?"

"Yes, yes, of course. I'm sorry. I was just trying to cheer you up, rather ineptly it seems." Derek pushed Peter's file to one side, placing a clean sheet of paper in front of him.

"Do you want to tell me about it?" he asked. "You can talk freely in here. It's swept on a daily basis, electronically that is."

Peter spoke slowly, recounting everything in detail from his visit to Pavlozavodsk to his arrest, questioning and eventual release. Derek listened intently, making the occasional note and asking Peter to clarify a couple of points. By the end of his account, Peter felt he had relived his nightmare sufficiently.

"I don't think I want to say anything more about it," he declared. "I'm still technically a prisoner here, unable to leave the country. They may call me back in. With the evidence they've got, they're likely to put me on trial. It doesn't bear thinking about."

"I doubt they'll do that," Derek said reassuringly.

"Why ever not? I was caught red-handed doing that special task and carrying out my usual O and R stuff. Don't forget you said I should continue with these so-called unofficial duties, so you've got to accept some of the blame."

Derek didn't look as concerned as Peter thought he should. "I still don't think they will press charges though," he said.

"How can you be so sure?"

"The Embassy made representations to the Russians this morning. John went to a meeting just before lunch. It seems there is some confusion over identity. They are suggesting that perhaps they arrested the wrong man."

"The wrong man? That's ridiculous. The film and the photos I saw during the interrogation, they were all of me. The notes were mine, the equipment was mine, that stupid Geiger counter was mine. How can they now say it was somebody else? They're not that daft."

"No, I can assure you they're not. But I am also surprised at your reaction. Aren't you pleased to hear you're probably off the hook?"

"I would be, if it were true! But I don't believe it, I can't see how it could happen." Peter stared at Derek's impassive face. "Will you please tell me what the hell's going on here. Are you in league with the Russians or something?"

Derek got up. He walked slowly up and down the small room, tapping a pencil on the palm of his hand. After about a minute, he returned to stand behind his chair, resting his arms on its curved back.

"Some explanation is in order," he said. "However, you must not repeat a word of what I'm going to tell you. If you do, you'll be in serious trouble."

"More serious than the trouble I'm in already?" Peter queried.

"Yes indeed. It's very much in your own interest to stay silent."

"In that case, I shall do so."

"Very sensible," Derek said. He came round the side of his chair and sat down, placing his elbows on the table and clasping his hands.

"You're probably aware, Peter, that, since the rather sudden end to the Cold War, there's been a lot more contact and cooperation between East and West. For a start, the fact that you're here working for the Handsome Fund is ample evidence of improved relations. But the breadth of the cooperation is much wider, much more comprehensive than that. It extends to many different aspects of government and commercial work."

"Look, Derek, I'm not feeling particularly robust at the moment for obvious reasons. Can you just move it along a bit faster, please."

"I'm not telling you all this for fun," Derek said with an injured look. "It's important you understand the background. The rest of what I'm going to say won't make much sense unless you know what's been happening behind the scenes."

He adjusted his tie and recommenced his monologue as if addressing a Learned Society. "You may be surprised to hear that these contacts have even included cooperation in certain sensitive fields. One of the early initiatives in this area was to devise a scheme to test the responsiveness of our respective security agencies. It was decided that there should be minor, low level tests to start with, building up to bigger and more complex activities if these were successful. The first of these minor tests commenced last year."

Peter became more interested at the mention of security, wondering where Derek's little speech was taking him. He decided not to interrupt.

"Only those in a very senior position knew about this test and its purpose, since it involved the use of foreign personnel. The foreigners' task was to carry out minor information gathering in the respective countries under the guise of their normal work. It was hoped that the security services of the host nations would be able to identify the individuals and produce evidence of their illegal activities." Derek paused, unsure where to look, before finally focusing on the ceiling. "And Peter, you were chosen as the British undercover agent in Russia."

The low hum of the air-conditioning was the only sound in the room. Derek continued to concentrate on the ceiling, Peter on the patterned carpet.

"Why wasn't I told about this beforehand?" Peter demanded.

Derek leaned forward. "We couldn't let on, Peter. If you'd known what you were doing wasn't for real, you'd have behaved very differently. You would have been more cavalier, less security conscious and therefore much more identifiable to the Russian Security Service. It stands to reason you had to believe what you were doing was both sensitive and genuine. You would have been too relaxed, too casual if you'd known it was just a training exercise."

"Just a training exercise!" Peter burst out. "Are you telling me I took all those risks, lost a lot of sleep, worried about my safety and all for some poxy training scheme? I can't believe you'd do that to me."

"Sorry, but it had to be that way," Derek said, slightly shamefaced.

"It was so disingenuous. I never wanted to get involved in any of this. It was only your henchman Chris Burroughs who persuaded me to go ahead. After meeting that Major Pomfrey in London, I intended to wash my hands of the whole business. In any case, the military surely don't employ madhatters like him anymore, do they? I know you denied any knowledge of him, but where did you find him?"

"He's an actor."

"An actor? Oh, come on Derek."

"The MOD were very helpful. They let us have a couple of rooms they weren't using and we fitted them out to look like offices. Pomfrey was really rather good, although he almost overdid it."

"Are you going to confess to any more actors in this charade?"

"Doctor Homilly of course. The real Doctor Homilly was already in police custody."

"Whatever for? Are you about to suggest he had some dodgy connection with Professor Krotkin? I hope I can assume the Krotkin I met wasn't an actor too."

"No, your Krotkin was real enough. However, your association with him has provided both sides with an unexpected bonus. The Russians haven't divulged their end of the network, but Krotkin and the real Homilly were indeed into a smuggling racket. You were their unwitting courier. I have to say the Russians are extremely grateful for your assistance over that, Peter."

"Oh, I bet they are. And were there other bonuses? I assume your actor friend didn't mention violin playing in Siberia without some good reason," Peter said sarcastically.

"Well, we were concerned about your relationship with Kuznetsova. She was under pressure from her husband to extract the maximum amount of cash from every foreigner she met. We didn't want you to become a victim, so used our Doctor Homilly to warn you off. What we didn't realize at the time was that the German she'd been squeezing had given you a similar warning. So you got a double hit on that one."

The image of Lydia floated across the room. Peter thought she had come out of all this confusion rather well: an overbearing husband lost and a passage to England gained. And what of Anna? God forbid she was involved in this web of intrigue. He hardly dared ask about her role.

"So what did you and your fellow plotters get Anna Lebedeva from Intourist to do?"

Derek looked blank. "Anna Lebedeva? Never heard of her. Friend of yours, is she?"

Peter nodded his head, enjoying a moment's relief. But there was still too much for him to absorb all at once. There were large areas where he had no idea what was fact and what was fiction. He wasn't even sure he knew who Derek was anymore. "Were you the mastermind of this little wheeze, Derek? Are you really a spook yourself, masquerading as a company director?"

"It's pointless speculating on such matters. I am and have only ever been a businessman. When requested, I like to assist different government departments. The firm gets a lot of credit from my cooperation."

"In that case I'm entitled to know what benefit has been derived from my unwitting participation in this game of deception."

"Peter, I'm pleased you asked, because the whole operation has been a great success," Derek said eagerly. "The Russians are delighted. They identified you correctly, allocated the right resources to monitor your activities and secured the evidence. A real feather in their cap."

"And this little scheme included my scheduled arrest and interrogation in that jailhouse?"

"They did overreach themselves with that episode, I have to admit. It's a shame our people couldn't have acted faster to prevent it. But no harm done."

"I'm so glad you think so! I was taken there in hand-cuffs, treated like a criminal. And because I couldn't be let into your little secret, I had to endure the worst hours of my life in that stinking place. I expected to be there for days with rye bread to eat and a bucket to pee in. They could have stuffed me on a goods train to Siberia for all I knew. So, no harm done? I beg to differ."

"Apologies. I meant only in retrospect."

Derek's inadequate response only increased Peter's anger. He slammed his fists on the table and swore openly.

"So because it was just a stupid exercise, is that why they've fabricated this story about a case of misidentification? Who's going to believe that? Certainly not all their security personnel who must have spent months watching and trailing me."

"There will be a satisfactory explanation for all those involved on the Russian side. They will understand that things are not always how they appear. On the British side... well, calling it a misidentification will be a good way out. After all, apart from you and I, who else knows of your arrest? John Metcalfe is the only one, other than the Ambassador and Head of Chancery. So none of us will be mentioning this little incident, will we?"

Peter shook his head. "There's another side to you I never knew existed. Your duplicity is astounding."

"I've only got your interests at heart, Peter. We need to draw a line under this operation. In any case your time here is limited."

"Really? According to whose diary?"

"It's your promotion, your next job I'm talking about. That's the main reason I came to see you. The final decision was only taken on Saturday."

"So you didn't know the Russians planned to lift me on Sunday evening. I thought you were all cosy with them?"

"Don't forget this test was being controlled at the highest level. Your arrest and questioning was a local initiative. I was only informed about it early this morning. That's when the decision was made to call an end to the exercise. All objectives had been achieved."

Despite Derek's explanation, Peter remained defiant. The more he heard, the more he despised the whole business. "This has been quite a revelation," he said. "Really opened my eyes it has."

"So, would you like to hear about your new job now?" Derek asked, drawing Peter's file in front of him and flicking through the pages.

"I may as well, since you've come all this way to tell me."

"It's very exciting," Derek said, becoming quite excited himself. "The job title, as I intimated before, is Senior Consultant Eastern Europe. You'll start in April, earlier than we thought I know, but we are keen to get it up and running as soon as we can. Good news, isn't it?"

Peter looked at his director, refusing to share his euphoria. "So, where's the new office going to be located?"

"Sorry, didn't I say? It's going to be Budapest."

"That's a shame," Peter said tersely.

"Aren't you pleased? You might show a bit of enthusiasm," Derek said testily. "I worked damn hard to get you this promotion and appointment. It wasn't easy, I can tell you."

"No, I'm sure it wasn't. I'm not ungrateful, it's just that I'd rather remain in Russia."

"No can do. The decision's been made. The office is going ahead in Budapest."

"So you said."

"Come on man. This is the chance of a lifetime. Stop being so damn negative about it."

"I'm not. I'm sure it's going to be a great opportunity and a huge success."

"That's better. You'll love it there once you're settled."

"Derek, I don't think you're hearing me. Thanks for the offer, but I'm not going to move. I'm staying here."

Derek's face tightened. "You can't do that. You can't go against instructions."

"I'm afraid I can. I'm resigning from the firm."

Derek stood up, but thinking better of it, sat down. "That is the most extraordinary thing I've ever heard in the whole of my professional life," he said. "Have you gone mad?"

"No, not at all. I intend to work freelance in Russia. I have my visa. I've also got to know and love this country.

It's where I want to be."

"You wait till the other directors hear about this. There'll be a big explosion I can tell you." Derek paused and, collecting himself, continued in a more conciliatory tone. "Look Peter, I know you had a rough time of it last night. Your arrest wasn't supposed to happen like that. Don't hold a grudge and sacrifice your career for the sake of it. There will be compensation of course and also a tax free sum for your cooperation in the whole exercise. Put it behind you. Forget about it."

"I cannot forget nor do I wish to. And it's not just about last night. From the beginning, you deceived me, Derek. You lied to me. Without my knowledge or agreement you involved me in some dirty, underhand scheme to try to enhance your own standing with certain senior government figures. There is no way I could ever trust you again. I have no wish to continue to work for you personally nor for any organisation with which you are associated."

Derek winced at the vehemence of Peter's attack. Nevertheless he was not prepared to let this discourteous and contemptuous young man have the final word. "I'm sorry you feel that way. When you grow up a bit, you'll realise that there are a lot of things that have to be done which are none too ethical. It's not always possible to remain virgin white if you want to achieve certain goals." Derek paused to tidy the papers in front of him, then spoke without raising his eyes. "In this particular case, it was a worthwhile conspiracy. I consider I did the decent thing in misleading you."

Peter looked at Derek in disgust. "I wish to go now," he said. "Would you unlock the door, please?"

At about the time Peter Standridge left the British Embassy, in another part of town Yuri Poliakov was standing alone outside the office of his Deputy Director in the Interior Ministry. Standridge was on his mind, in fact he had been thinking about him almost constantly since returning from Pavlozavodsk. He felt a great sense of achievement after all the months of painstaking work which had brought him to this point. He was hoping Deputy Director Popov would be equally pleased.

The secretary ushered Yuri into the large office, pointing to the chair he should occupy. She sat down beside the Deputy Director, her notepad at the ready. Popov took his time to finish what he was reading. Eventually he put the file to one side and looked at Yuri.

"Poliakov, good afternoon. For once it gives me pleasure to see you. I'm delighted you were kept busy on your trip to Pavlozavodsk. It turned out to be rather a good suggestion to go there in pursuit of Pumpkin. I recall it was my idea, was it not?"

"Yes sir," Yuri replied, not wishing to contradict his Deputy Director, nor fail to give him credit for something he hadn't done.

"No doubt you are also wondering why I'm seeing you without your immediate boss being present. Most unusual I have to say, even unprecedented, and as you know, quite contrary to our procedures."

"Yes sir. I was surprised to be summoned without Section Head Zagarin."

"In fact, it will not be indiscreet of me to tell you I discussed certain matters with Zagarin earlier today. He tried, how shall I put it, to influence my superior judgement about the Pumpkin affair. He was convinced we were wasting our time and deplored the use of valuable resources for this operation. He wanted them, in his words, *allocated to more advantageous projects*. It was then that I showed him the photographs from Pavlozavodsk. Satisfying for me, humiliating for him."

Yuri felt it was not his place to comment on the behaviour and opinions of his Section Head. He chose a neutral response. "I agree the photographs were exceptionally good. They provide the kind of evidence we normally only dream about."

"Quite so, quite so. All the members of Meat-Hook are to be congratulated, but I think the work Kalashnikova did on the train was exceptional." Popov became misty-eyed. "I'm sure you know Poliakov, from your intimate contact, that she is a very talented woman in many different areas. I need to harness her experience and draw on her knowledge by working even more closely with her. I have been so impressed that I have created a new position, just for her. She is to become my personal security advisor with an office next to mine. She deserves that, don't you think?"

"Yes sir, I agree. She has earned it, most definitely earned it." The temptation to dwell on the illustrious Tania was there for Yuri too, but he closed the shutters in his mind to her bewitching image. Since she was going to be around the building, he would bump into her soon enough. And when he did, he would treat her as just another colleague, another official. Whatever had passed between them was finished and filed away. He was never going to allow anyone to entice him from his Olga again.

Yuri glanced at Popov and, as his daydreaming also seemed to be coming to an end, he returned his attention to the matter at hand.

"Sir, I spent all this morning going over the photography. If I may suggest, I believe we should get the Cryptographic Department to decipher Pumpkin's notes. They're going to provide additional evidence for when he's brought to trial."

"I'm sure they are – but I think you're jumping the gun, Collator Poliakov." Yuri felt firmly put in his place by Popov's change of tone. However well he had done, he was still only the most junior of all officials. "I'm sorry to speak out of turn, sir," he said meekly, but Popov waved his hand dismissively.

"What you must now understand, Poliakov, is that there

exists a surprising amount of interest in this case at a very high level in the Ministry. In a sense I have been relieved of decision making as far as Pumpkin is concerned. Orders are now coming from the very top."

Yuri was amazed. What had happened to make this minor matter of such interest to the most senior figures in the Ministry that now they wanted to control it? Didn't they have more important things to do?

"But, sir, with respect, this was only ever a very low level operation. What Pumpkin was doing, although illegal, was hardly going to undermine the State."

"Indeed that is so, Poliakov, based on the evidence that we have. But I suspect the involvement at the top level is because there is more, which, you, in your very junior position and even I, in my much more senior position, cannot know about."

Yuri felt he was getting out of his depth. He was losing confidence in his belief that, out of everyone in the Ministry, it was he who knew Standridge best. Something was going on which he could not grasp, but it was obviously big and probably very sensitive. Perhaps he should feel flattered if this were so, since it was he who had first identified Standridge as a foreign agent. If there was more, then in a sense, all credit to him.

"Might this high level interest be as a result of Pumpkin's relationships with Russian citizens?" Yuri volunteered, anxious to see if he could extract more information from Popov. "Despite our success in Pavlozavodsk, we were disappointed he didn't meet any contacts either there or on the train journeys."

"It is possible. But we know from his dealings with Krotkin and Kuznetsova that these contacts were criminal rather than espionage related."

"Although Pumpkin himself seems to have been an innocent victim each time."

"We think that is right. In Kuznetsova's case, she too

appeared to be manipulated by her husband and has narrowly avoided being charged for extortion along with him. I understand she is abandoning him and going to play her violin in England for a change."

"I'm disappointed by this. I was so sure there was an espionage ring involving Pumpkin, Gooseberry and Kuznetsova. It seems I was wrong."

"Even so, everyone is very pleased with your work. If you had not focused attention on this trio, the *Militsia* would never have had enough evidence to arrest and charge Mr Kuznetsov."

Yuri felt smug, sensing that even the things he got wrong had somehow turned out right. Was there more he could learn? "And Professor Krotkin? Do we have any news on how that investigation is progressing?"

"As you know, at first he would not say anything, and then, when he did, it was all denial. How can someone arrested with an envelope in his hands containing hundreds of dollars in large denomination notes deny he had them?" Popov said. "Even intelligent men can be fools."

"But couldn't the money be payment for the painting we now know Pumpkin took to London for him? As far as we can tell, it wasn't a priceless work of art and it did have a genuine export certificate "

"The British have been so helpful. They have taken the icon apart. Very fine holes had been drilled through the wood and filled with a powder. Their initial analysis shows it to be a substance not dissimilar to red mercury."

Yuri feigned astonishment: he had heard rumours about red mercury, but like many other officials, doubted its existence. Was this another case of disinformation? "That's extraordinary. How had Krotkin become involved in such a business?" he asked.

"He's being very helpful now. His British contact is partly to blame it seems. He had a good system for selling, but lacked the raw material. Krotkin had continued his contact with Stroynov after they met in Siberia. Stroynov apparently had his large fingers in many pies and was able to source quite a quantity of the stuff. Curiously they used to produce it in Stambov, but there's no link here with that other criminal Kuznetsov."

"Very devious and very skilful."

"There were also indications they were jeopardising the security of the State. As you appreciate, this substance they were smuggling has very serious military implications. You won't be seeing either Krotkin or Stroynov again for a very long time, if ever."

In Popov's presence, Yuri had to subdue his feeling of triumph and be content with the lesser sense of satisfaction. He had no sympathy for either man. Krotkin would never know it was his rejection of Yuri's application to the Institute for Foreign Languages which would bring him down. Nor could Fat Alex have guessed that, through his constant flirtation and attempted seduction of Olga, Yuri would be his destroyer. Revenge may not be sweet, but it still tasted good.

"What will happen to Pumpkin?" he was bold enough to ask.

"It's difficult to say, now there is this controlling interest from up there," Popov replied, raising his eyes to the ceiling. "Pumpkin has been released, whilst further investigations and enquiries are carried out. That's the official line."

"I would have thought he'd be kept under arrest until these had been completed. I mean, he could disappear."

"He's not allowed to leave Russia for the time being. As for disappearing, you will know that only happens officially in our country."

"But justice must be seen to be done," Yuri protested. "He was deliberately collecting information around the country and, as at Pavlozavodsk, he was often steered towards particular targets by his controllers. There's got to be a price to pay for doing that."

"There may be or there may not be. You mentioned his controllers... well, who are his controllers, Poliakov? Perhaps they're not the people you think they are." Yuri suspected Blossom, of course, though had no proof of her involvement nor of any others. But when he saw Popov looking at him in a certain way, an unmentionable possibility slowly entered his mind. "You don't mean he's..." Yuri whispered as Popov raised a finger to his lips.

"Not everything is always obvious from the start. You are capable of drawing your own conclusions. Naturally nothing will be confirmed and nothing denied."

Yuri smiled to himself. It did seem to fall into place and make sense, now he thought about it. He would never know for certain, but there did not appear to be any other explanation for many things which had puzzled him over the last few months. Of course, this Mr Peter Arthur Standridge, alias Pumpkin, had been working for his side, the Russian side, all along. How very, very clever to manage such a double act single-handed. What a convincing performer he was. Yuri nodded his head, full of admiration. "That's incredible, sir. Quite, quite incredible."

"Aren't you proud to belong to such a fine organisation, Poliakov? We must all continuously work towards perfection. Our leaders, amongst whom I naturally count myself, are clearly showing the way forward."

"Of course, sir. Leadership of such quality is rare and an example to us all."

Popov did not often smile, but he did now. "To change the subject slightly, would you like to hear about your promotion?"

Yuri gulped. "Promotion? What promotion?"

"Poliakov, you've gone up in my estimation in the last weeks. You're to be congratulated on your work... and as a reward you're to be promoted to Head of Internal Section with immediate effect. Zagarin has taken early retirement to grow cabbages at his *dacha*."

"Thank you very much, sir. It's a real privilege to work here. I'm greatly indebted to you."

"And another thing. There's a summer course in English at the Foreign Languages Institute. Now that Professor Krotkin's no longer there, I've managed to get you a place."

"Thank you again, sir. I shall really look forward to that."

"Now push off home and tell your pretty wife how generous I've been."

Yuri left the Deputy Director's office utterly elated. He could never have foreseen such an excellent outcome to his little scheme. Not only had he received recognition for uncovering both criminal and subversive activity, he had also advanced his career with this coveted promotion. He smiled broadly as he walked towards the metro station.

As the train snaked through the tunnel, Yuri continued to think about what had happened in Popov's office. The thing which really astounded him was the ambiguity surrounding Mr Standridge. He accepted he could be wrong, but he felt confident he had interpreted Popov's meaning correctly. It did disappoint him that he would never know for sure, since gaining definite proof was naturally out of the question. He also understood he was now on treacherous ground even surmising about Standridge's role. But the whole matter was quite staggering.

How had they managed to turn a very typical Englishman into an agent for themselves? Had someone as a result of his, Yuri's, detailed reports approached Standridge and persuaded him to work for them as well? Perhaps the persuasion was more a threat of exposure if he was foolish enough to decline the invitation.

Yet in whatever way he was recruited, it was a stroke of brilliance. Who would suspect such an unexciting and innocent looking man of being a double agent? Even

346

Yuri, despite being so involved with him and the closest observer of his activities, had missed the connection. He had to admit admiring the way Mr Peter Standridge had hoodwinked him by his behaviour. He lived in interesting, but confusing times.

Olga was waiting for him when he reached home. She seemed even more delighted with his promotion than he was. She too had some excellent news.

"I've got us a new apartment," she said, breathless from kissing him. "It's in a block about a kilometre from here, near the Taganskaya Station. Yuri, the apartment's high up on the ninth floor, its got a view of the river and the Novospassky Monastery. It's so beautiful."

Yuri didn't bother to ask how his darling wife had managed to accomplish such a feat. No words were necessary as they waltzed dizzily into the bedroom.

Outside a light snow began to fall.

CHAPTER 22

Spring lifted the white sheet of winter, exposing Moscow in all its beauty and all its ugliness. The buildings revealed their true shape and form, displaying colourful roof-lines and sculptured windows. Parks and spaces rediscovered their hidden green and trees tentatively sprouted buds and unbound leaves. Amorphous mounds lost their disguise, once-sparkling white hummocks turning dirty grey as heaps of stone, broken timber and autumn refuse protruded from the melting snow. The city flexed and reasserted itself, shrugging off the long embrace of ice and cold.

Yet even in mid-April, retreating winter was not done for. It counterattacked with sudden blizzards and sharp showers of cascading snowflakes. The wet, whirling crystals settled, colonising the freed rooftops, parks and pavements, but failed to hold their ground. Such assaults enjoyed brief success, then faltered before the warm front of advancing spring.

Peter Standridge took pleasure in the changing season as he made his way along the street. He walked steadily, relishing the smells and sights now the thaw was under-way. But for all its attractions, he remained wary of the hazards. Slush soaked boots and shoes were normal, but mini avalanches from uncleared roofs could still tumble without warning and falling icicles sharp as arrows pierce unprotected heads. Like other passers-by, he was alert to wild, speeding drivers, who would splash the pavements in icy, muddy water. Yet none of this could detract from his feeling of contentment.

Such optimism was not misplaced for things were going well for him. Almost three months had passed since his resignation, though the firm had tried its best to change his mind. Another director had even flown out to Moscow, tempting him with a package and prospects which sounded too good to refuse. But he had resisted and felt the stronger for it. Still they did not give up on him, confirming that if he ever wished to rejoin Duggan Meade, they would consider his request most favourably.

In return Peter completed a number of outstanding projects before they parted company. He had already received a couple of commissions for his freelance work and was in discussion with a Ministry official about going into business together. A number of fledgling companies were emerging under the liberalisation and some kind of joint venture appeared the way forward. Peter was in no doubt he had made the right decision for both economic and moral reasons.

There was not much contact with the Embassy any more. Some news filtered through from other business-men he knew. Chris and Jean Burroughs had departed unexpectedly at the end of January and gone to South America. Ruth Rumbelow had left in March for the Paris Embassy. Peter secretly hoped she would find the lover she so ardently desired in that romantic city.

The exception occurred only the previous week when Peter encountered Jocelyn Misterton near the Bolshoy and bought him a coffee.

"Thought you might like to know Lydia Kuznetsova has been a huge success in London," Jocelyn said. "I've not had the chance to thank you for keeping her sweet for Queen and Country. An enjoyable duty no doubt. She's such a lovely and talented lady."

Although Peter had not seen her since the Embassy concert, it was nevertheless nice to receive acknowledge-ment for his contribution.

"She's staying on for a while," Jocelyn added. "Lots of engagements. I've got her address by the way. You should look her up when you're next over. Your German friend already has."

"I'm not sure I'll be going back for a while," Peter said evasively. "I'm rather tied up here at the moment. But thanks all the same." Even so, he was quietly impressed old Rudolf Metzinger had sniffed Lydia out in England. Not one to give up easily was Rudi, despite his earlier disillusionment.

Peter had moved out of the Hotel Leskov with all its memories once the firm ceased to pay his expenses. He had settled in with Anna in her tiny apartment, entering her space like a welcome intruder. He was considerate of her territory, but was reprimanded whenever sensitivity deserted him. Inevitably in their new proximity, they discovered a deepening pleasure in each other.

Anna continued to beguile him as she gradually spread her affections to his things. He liked the way she handled his few books, admired his prints of Sussex countryside, kissed his photographs of family, all scant reminders of a man displaced from home. She would wear his pullovers, caressing the wool with delicate strokes, and he would enjoy the lingering scent of her long after. She would run her hands over his tailored suits, finger his cotton shirts and bury her face in the items he wore closest to him. It was as if she was searching out his very soul through the clothing of his body.

Peter found his love for her more sensual through her foreignness. She looked and smelled exotic, not fully European, not fully Asiatic but that exhilarating fusion of Russian. She surprised him with her passion, her pleasure, her sorrow. He revelled in her flashes of mood, her quick anger, her soft returning smile. He admired her resilience, her inner strength, her spirit and her faith.

He too explored her through the intimacy of her apartment, her music, her poetry, her art, her icon in the corner. He too loved her clothes but found her incompa-

350

rably beautiful without them. He adored the smoothness of her skin, the perfection of her face, the shape of her body. He was enthralled by the way she moved, how she performed the simplest task. He was captivated like a slave who sought no freedom.

He had opened himself to Anna, but retained his English composure. She teased him for it, but loved the natural reserve, the calmness of him. He sensed he provided a safe anchorage for her in a turbulent sea of change. But he kept his inner secrets close. She could never know of his arrest and imprisonment, of his involuntary participation in cloak-and-dagger games. He felt a duty to shield her from the inquisitiveness of the State, to protect her from the scheming minds of others.

Peter did his best to put all that behind him. He did, though, occasionally think of Krotkin, wondering what had happened to him and whether they would ever meet again. A man of surprises he certainly was, but perhaps he tried one surprise too many with his profiteering.

It was Anna who alerted him to a report on the trial. There was even a photograph of him standing beside his co-defendant, one Alexander Stroynov. Krotkin looked a broken man, hunched and hollow faced. Peter could not understand how he had become involved in such a business. Anna assured him he would be returning to Siberia for another spell, if they decided not to shoot him.

For some reason she was intrigued by the case, reading in *Komsomolskaya Pravda* that, in contrast to Krotkin's reasonably unblemished past, his accomplice was nefarious with a history of prosecutions. But, curiously, few of these were successful. Judging from the photograph, Peter jokingly suggested that the rotund Stroynov had the air of a man confident he would get off even these current charges, serious though they were. Anna merely shrugged, admitting it might happen. Peter, with his British innocence, failed to see how such an outcome could be possible.

Smiling as he always did when he thought of Anna, Peter skirted round a large puddle of meltwater and fractured ice. He could see the tall building ahead of him where, he was told, he should turn left. His map seemed to fit the layout of the roads, although there was confusion wherever a street name had been changed. He was in no hurry and could afford to take his time.

It was Anna, too, who was responsible for sending him to this unfamiliar part of the city. She had tackled him one evening.

"Peter, I love you, but your Russian is lousy. If you're going to live here, you've got to do something about it, you've got to make it better."

"Well, you teach me."

"Don't make funny jokes. Either I would be too gentle with you and you'd be an idle student, or more likely I would get very angry with you for your bad mistakes and you'd go all stupid like a sheep. It simply would not work. I shall find you a teacher. It won't cost too many *roubles*, especially if you do some English conversation in return. And when you're better, we can talk in Russian. It's a very beautiful language you know," she said, wrapping her arms around him, "and particularly sexy when spoken by an Englishman."

Peter turned the corner and spotted the apartment block he needed. The lift took him to the top floor where he found Apartment 94. He remembered how Anna had said she would reward him for his progress. He could not want for more incentive and quickly rang the bell.

After a minute, a man about his age answered the door and looked at Peter enquiringly.

"I'm Mr Standridge, Peter Standridge," Peter said to him slowly. "I have come for my Russian lesson with Mr Poliakov."

"I am Poliakov," replied the young man. "Yuri Poliakov. Please come in my home."

Peter walked in, removing his coat. They shook hands and Yuri led the way across the main room. A small table had been set neatly with dictionaries and textbooks and a chair either side. Two glasses and a bottle of mineral water had thoughtfully been provided.

"My wife, she does all this," Yuri said pointing to the table. "Also she is person who makes these lessons for us. So now, please sit."

As Peter made himself comfortable, he glanced out of the main window with its view over the river and the city. "That is most spectacular. You are very lucky to have such a view," he said, thinking of the outlook from Anna's window over their dismal courtyard.

"My wife, she likes this very much. In old apartment in different block, we have only wall to see. No good for my wife."

"No, of course, this has to be much better," Peter said, a little enviously.

Yuri tapped his pencil on the table. "So no more looking from window. Now we must make work. Please, you must say to me why you want lessons in Russian language."

"I'm going to be living and working in Russia more permanently now. It's important for me to be able to speak the language better than I do. I know it will be difficult, but I must be successful. It's also helpful for me that you speak some English."

Yuri shook his head. "My wife, she says I speak English too bad. She says I talk like old camel. So you must make my English better or my wife no more give me food, no more love me."

"We'll have to work very hard then, won't we?" Peter said laughing. "Do you also need English for your business?"

"My business?" Yuri asked, before realising what Peter meant. "Ah, now I understand your question. I have no business. I work in Interior Ministry. My director says

English will be good for me in Ministry. He has made summer course for me at Language Institute in Nizhny Novgorod."

The thought crossed Peter's mind that his presence in Yuri Poliakov's apartment was a remarkable occurrence. Would it not have been the Interior Ministry which was involved with Derek Carbonnel's little training exercise? Was it not strange, too, that this pleasant young man was going to Krotkin's old Language Institute?

"How interesting," Peter said. "I met the Institute Director, Professor Krotkin, a couple of times."

"Now there is new Director," Yuri replied. He liked Mr Standridge's manner. For a man who must obviously know so much about, well, almost everything, he was behaving in a very understated way. Yuri wondered, too, whether Mr Standridge's controllers had had a hand in organising these language lessons. Perhaps he had been planted to keep an eye on Yuri by the big men in the Ministry. He remained in awe of this enigmatic Englishman.

"Yes, I had heard some reports that he'd left the Institute," Peter said. "But whoever is in charge, it's important your English is good enough for the start of the course."

"I hope also, as I have not good opportunities to speak much."

"So it will be useful to do Russian and English each time we meet. Perhaps we could do one hour of Russian, then one hour of English," Peter suggested. "So first you are the teacher and I am the student and then we change round."

"Like hunter who becomes the hunted," Yuri replied.

They smiled at one another, appreciating in their separate ways the irony of this apt remark.

NICHOLAS KING has spent much of his life living and working abroad, notably in North America, the Far East, Russia and Eastern Europe. Except for a two year break, he has lived in Bristol with his artist wife Helen since 1986. He now devotes himself to writing and had a mini-saga published in the Arvon Foundation collection for 2001. *A Decent Deceit* is his first published novel.